11/12

BROKEN SOULS

BROKEN SOULS

SECRET SINS | SACRED SINS

CD REISS

FLIP CITY

Broken Souls
By
CD Reiss

This book is a work of fiction.
No one's this crazy except the people in my head.

Previously released as THE SINS DUET

SECRET SINS

ONE

HOTEL ROOM - 1982

"How old are you anyway?"

The guy asking had long strawberry-red hair and wore only shorts and a single sock. He'd tattooed a treble clef on his Adam's apple that started a symphony of notes all over his chest and abs. His name was Strat, and whenever his shirtless torso showed up in *Rock Beat*, Lynn went crazy trying to play the song he'd had drawn on his body. It sounded like crap.

"Eighteen, asshole," I snarled, letting loose a yard-long cone of cigarette smoke. I stamped out what was left of my cigarette. "You going to call or what?"

He and Indy snickered. I saw them look at each other over their cards. They thought they had my bra off next. They were wrong. Only two hands beat a full house, and if one of them had a straight flush or four of a kind, I was tits to the rail.

"I'll raise you." Strat tossed a ten in the center of the table.

We'd been going for four hours already. Indy had met me on the beach and, after a short chat, invited me to play poker. Yoni and Lynn were already in the hotel room for the possibility of a threesome, which was how I'd ended up on the beach alone. But poker? I could do poker.

My friends hadn't lasted long. Yoni and Lynn had passed out when they ran out of cash. Keeping up with a couple of cash-rich rockers who didn't know what to do with their first chunk of advance money was hard.

Indy/Indiana McCaffrey played guitar for Bullets and Blood. I'd met him on the beach first. I'd stayed cool even though he was completely gorgeous and charming, but when Strat came into the hotel suite, I almost had a coronary. I was a huge fan. I'd played their debut album, *Kentucky Killer*, for two weeks straight until Dad took my cassette. Took the Walkman too. I bought another of each but hid them.

"Call," I said, tossing in my ten.

Indy threw down his cards. "Y'all are too rich for me."

Indy had sun-kissed brown hair and a ginger beard. He was down to his skivs and a bandana around his neck, toned and tan from head to toe. I'd taken all of his money, and Strat and I had been pretty equally matched. Now I was going to break him.

"Too rich and too young," Strat said, popping a peanut.

Lynn coughed on the couch. Stretched.

God, please don't let her puke.

"I told you. I'm eighteen."

I don't know if I mentioned this. I wasn't eighteen. I won't say if I was younger or older. You can go figure it out.

Strat laughed. "Flygirl..."

Flygirl was a pretty common way to address a girl in the eighties, crossing race and geography, but I still felt as if it made me attractive to him. Strat chewed his peanut as if it had the mass of a pack of gum, chin up, looking at me in my bra. I felt naked.

I *was* naked, but I hadn't felt like it until his eyes swung around the curves of my body. I wanted to tell him to go fuck himself, but he finished before I could get a mental jacket on.

"You got a mouth like an old lady," Strat said.

His stare froze me in place. The backs of my thighs got sticky on the pleather.

"Never heard a girl talk like you."

Green was the rarest eye color, and his looked like precious Chinese jade.

He was so hot.

A hot rock star.

I put my cards down, snapping each one in the fan as I laid them out. "Aces full of sevens. You got anything in your hand besides your dick?"

Indy whooped. "She's got you, Stratty-boy. The pot and… what do you have left? Pants and a sock, bro. Go for the sock."

Indy was an amateur. He was beautiful and brilliant, but he didn't act twenty. He acted like the guys my own age.

Or whatever.

Strat hadn't taken his eyes off me. Hadn't even glanced at my full house. Didn't even look down when he laid his cards on the table. I couldn't move for too many seconds. His look wasn't a look. It was a black hole. All gravity.

I tore myself from his gaze and looked at his cards.

Four deuces.

Fuck.

Losing to deuces was insulting.

Strat leaned back, the coils of his song all over his ripped body. The pot was his, but he didn't reach for it. He just worked me over with his eyes, arm over the back of his chair, knees apart, daring me to search for the bulge in his shorts. I breathed deeply but couldn't get enough air. My lungs had shrunk.

Indy looked at me under the table. "No socks, man. Shit. You're down to not too much."

I was in over my head. Way fucking over. Yet I liked it. More than liked it, I was comfortable when I was out of my depth. All the moving pieces, the inconsistency of the cards, the mess I was making excited and soothed me, a contradiction that translated into *belonging*.

I could fix it. I fixed it every time. My grades were amazing. I was the liaison for the Suffragette Society. I ran the school stage crew like a military operation. It was too easy. If you wanted an omelet, you had to break some eggs.

I'm not saying I chased musicians around after the sun went down because I sat on the edge of my bed and decided to make a mess of my life in order to fix it back up. Insight like that is no more than Monday morning quarterbacking.

I stood and put my hands behind my back, reaching between shoulder blades.

Strat licked his lips, taking his eyes from my crotch and leveling them on mine. I looked right at the motherfucker and pinched my bra hook. He was going to see my tits. The nipples were already hard from his attention. I had pretty good odds on a little damp spot where my panties had been on the pleather.

"Why don't you stop for a minute there?" he said.

I stopped. I didn't have to. Rules were rules. The bra came off. But he was effectively changing them.

Also, I didn't want to take my bra off.

Strat leaned forward a little. A blade of copper hair slid off his shoulder and swung in front of his cheek.

"What?" I asked. "Scared of a little tit?"

"Who are you?" he asked.

"Cinnamon." I flicked my head a little, and my own red hair got out of my eyes. "But you can call me Cin."

"Yeah. No. You got backstage last week from the admin office. I know you didn't fuck Herve Lundren to get there either. Then you and your friend show up places you shouldn't be. The loading dock behind the Wiltern. The thousand-dollar-a-plate dinner at Vilma. And Indiana here fucking stupids right into you."

"Stupid's not a verb, asshole," Indy said.

Strat didn't get distracted. Indy could have broken into the "Star-Spangled Banner" and it wouldn't have snapped the drum of energy between Strat and me.

"Cinnamon's not even a name," Strat added.

"Your mother name you Strat?"

"*Rolling Stone* revealed my name three months ago."

"Stratford Gilliam," I whispered.

He leaned back again, but he didn't spread out. He crossed an ankle over a knee. "Something's up. You have cash. Enough to play with us. No eighteen-year-old has a wad of twenties inside hundreds."

"I'm a fan. I like your music."

"What's your name?"

"You deaf? Cinnamon."

"I can call you Cin."

I touched my nose.

"Tell me your name," he said, "and you can keep the bra on."

He'd read me like a street sign. I didn't want to take that bra off. I wasn't ready for what that would lead to.

Yet I'd wanted to see if I could get out of it.

Dad asked me once why I loved trouble. Why I seemed to enjoy it so much. Why I made my own if I couldn't find it in the wild. I had no answer. Still didn't.

I didn't want it to get out that I was in a hotel suite with Bullets and Blood. If I told this guy my name, I could get into trouble, and not the enjoyable kind.

"Your name." The word *name* was silent on his lips.

My hesitation didn't seem to bother him. He played me at the right tempo, continuing when I thought I'd break and just snap my bra open.

"I've seen enough tits in my time," he said. "But you. Maybe you're a fan, but it's something else. You're different."

Show him your tits.

My fingers twitched on my sides. I was throbbing everywhere. My body wanted him, and my mind was running a four-minute mile in the other direction. I'd lost control of the situation, and as much as I dabbled in trouble, I never lost control of it.

Lock it down. Don't even think your name. Don't even think it. Don't even.

"What's your name?" he asked again.

I swallowed and decided to take off my bra. He'd try to fuck me, and we'd see where that went. I'd fought off men before. My hands crawled to my lower back.

He blinked, and in that split second his jade eyes were hidden from me, I changed course.

"Margaret Drazen," I said, putting my hands on my hips and leaning hard on one foot. "You can call me Margie."

"Nice to meet you, Margie." He lazily picked up the deck of cards.

"Your deal."

TWO

FIVE THINGS ABOUT BEING ME

1. I come from a long line of money. I've got more money in my trust than most people see in a lifetime. I've never worried about having it or getting it. I don't have to work, but I like to. Really like to.
2. I'm connected. If I don't know who I need to know, my father does. I've never had much cause to call in favors or know the right people, except to get into concerts and parties when I was younger. But I can. And knowing that makes all the difference.
3. I grew up quickly. I was born mature. Strat had it right when he said I talked like an old lady. He said that before I was fed shit on sterling silver spoon, then the talk got real and I saw life for what it was. So the politics and backstabbing in law school were child's play. Intra-office bickering is white noise. I win. End.
4. Bullshit makes me really impatient, and drama is bullshit. Drama's never about right and wrong. It's about *feelings*.
5. Feelings are for children. See #3.

THREE

LOS ANGELES - 1994

LAW OFFICES ARE SNAKE DENS. I LEARNED THAT AT STANFORD WHEN I butted up against the old boy network for an internship at Whalen + Mardigian. But I didn't bitch about the partners inviting the guys to a strip club and pulling interns from the group there, because I had the luxury of my own privilege. I felt bad for the women who didn't have my smorgasbord of options, but see... that was a feeling. See Chap. 2 - No.5

So I made clerk at Thoze & Jensen, a multinational firm with twelve offices in the States and an impressive presence overseas. Tokyo. Frankfurt. Dublin. Johannesburg. Hong Kong. But the firm was still as backward as a third-world country. An impenetrable fortress for anyone outside the Harvard / Princeton / Yale Testosterone Mafia, meaning—women. All women, with or without Ivy League degree. We could clerk and we could be associates, but we'd never partner.

We'd see about that.

They hired me as an associate right out of law school but had to clerk me until I passed the bar. Until then, I got a six-figure salary even though I didn't need it.

How?

Easy. I brought them a client.

You thought it was going to be some scandal.

It could have been, but when choosing between sugar and vinegar, it's best to remember vinegar works best as a preservative.

I was a clerk until I passed my bar, and despite what you may think, I couldn't buy that. Nor did I want to. I rented a house in Culver City and covered it in sticky notes. From the table where I kept my keys, (*Strickland v. Washington. Defines inadequate defense as it relates to result*) to the bathroom mirror (*Ford v. Wainwright. No death penalty for mentally deficient*). Even my car had a note stuck to the windshield (*TORTS – Tarasoff v. Regents. Responsibility of psychiatrist to warn potential victims of harm. Responsibility can be litigated with commensurate award for damages.*)

I didn't have time for men or friends. No one understood me anyway. No one but my family, which was more than enough. I had six sisters and a brother. I was the oldest, and I'm still not telling you my age, or you'll start doing math in your head instead of paying attention.

I WAS HEADING for a meeting with the senior partner on a copyright case I'd just been put on, rushing through the waiting room, which was a shortcut to the conference room, with an armload of depositions and pleadings, rattling hearsay exceptions in my head. There were ten categories, and I always forgot one. I walked across past the white leather couches with my folder, feet silent on the grey carpet.

Excited utterances.

Dying declarations.

Declarations against interest.

Present sense impression.

Present state of mind.

Doing good. Almost there…

Prior inconsistencies.

Public records.

Business records exception.

Ancient documents.

And….

And I beat my brain for the last one.

The man pushed himself off a couch as I was looking in my head for the tenth exception instead of out of my eyes for tall guys in suits.

I was midair, shouting, "Family records!" as if getting backed into reminded me that families couldn't be trusted to keep a story straight. The folder I was delivering to the conference room went flying. A shoe fell off. I landed on my butt bone with my legs spread as far as the pencil skirt allowed.

"Oh, shit, I'm so sorry!"

I put my knees together and got back up on my elbows to get a look at the clod who had knocked into me.

He was a god. The kind of guy who could model but didn't because it was too boring. Clean-shaven with brown hair pushed to one side. A bottom lip that had the same fullness as the top. Blue eyes. I had a metaphor for the color tooling around somewhere in the torts and procedures, but it all went blank when he put his hand down to help me up, and I saw a tattoo creep from under his cuff.

I looked at him again.

He looked at me.

"Cinnamon," he said.

"You can call me Cin." The words came automatically, as if coded in my myelin.

I took his hand, and he helped me up. My response might have sounded smooth and mature, as though I wasn't thrown off at all, but it was the opposite. I'd memorized that answer sober, drunk, and dancing. I even said it in my head when someone mentioned the spice. Back when I was a stupid, reckless, wicked girl, it was a calling card.

I got up, not making eye contact with the stares coming from the entire waiting room.

"I'm fine," I said, acting meek. When all the clients returned to staring at their magazines, I turned to the man who had knocked me down. "You going to stand there and let them trample my case file, Indiana McCaffrey?"

I smiled a little, and he smiled back. Wow. Had I been so unconscious when I met him that I'd thought he was only okay-looking? A close second to Stratford Gilliam? Seriously? How had he matured from twenty into this perfectly-chiseled version of a man?

I bent down to get my papers, and he put his hand on my shoulder.

"Let me be the first to get on my knees," he said, crouching before I could respond.

I couldn't believe he remembered me out of the thousands of girls who had thrown themselves at him. I knelt next to him and scooped up papers.

"I go by Drew now," he whispered. "My middle name."

"I go by Margie. My real name."

"I remember."

"I didn't expect you to," I said quietly.

He tilted his head just enough to see me, then he went back to picking up the files. I could see the tiny holes in his ears where he'd let his piercings close up.

"Who could forget you?" he said.

"Oh, please. Flattery only soils the intentions of the flatterer."

"Where's that from?" He tapped the stack on the carpet in an attempt to straighten them.

"My head."

He handed me his stack, and I jammed it into the folder.

"You haven't changed a bit."

I swallowed hard. I didn't have a problem with most of my misspent youth. I'd had fun and finished the job before I completely ruined my life. But I worked in an uptight law firm with a brand made of sedate blues and sharp angles. Former-rock-and-roll-groupie heiress wouldn't look good on them.

"Miss Drazen?"

It was Ernest Thoze standing by the reception desk, senior partner and my boss ten times over. I could have bought and sold him, but that wasn't the transaction I had in mind. I wanted to earn his respect.

I glanced at Drew then back at Thoze. Shit.

Thoze the Doze + Drew the Screw = I-Had-No-Rhyme-For-How-Much-I-Didn't-Want-That.

Thoze tapped his watch.

"Six minutes," I said. "I got it."

Thoze nodded and paced off. I was always ten minutes early, and fucktard over here had just given me seven minutes of reorganizing to do.

Fucktard smiled like a rock star. I remembered why I couldn't keep my eyes off of him or Strat.

"I knew you were meant for big things," he said.

I turned to face him, getting close enough to hiss. "It's been real fun reminiscing, but let's cut it short. I have a meeting. I'm sorry about Strat. That was fucked up. I wish I could have been there for you, but I didn't know until it was too late."

I didn't wait for a response, because seeing him made me *feel* things. Physical things. Emotions. Perceptions. He made me wonder if my hair looked all right or if my skirt showed enough/too much leg.

I paced off to my meeting, listing all the ways people could tell lies of perception.

Excited utterances.

Dying declarations.

Present sense impression.

He must be a client.

Present state of mind.

Prior inconsistencies.

Gotta be a hundred copyright claims after Strat split.

Declarations against interest.

Business record exception.

Just keep cool and don't give anything away.

Public records.

Ancient documents.

And motherfucking family records.

Boom. I pushed open the glass door to the conference room with finality.

I reorganized all the packets and laid one at each of the six seats with thirty seconds to spare. I opened the blinds that covered the windows looking out into the hall, letting everyone know the room was ready.

Life wasn't like books, not that I had time to read. But in books, there were fake coincidences and chances that changed fake lives. In real life, things happened because you made them that way. I'd never expected to see Indy again because I wasn't looking for him, and when I did see him, I assumed he was a client.

When he walked in ahead of Thoze and four other lawyers, plopped his briefcase down on the visiting lawyer side of the table and smiled at me. My heart sank.

Not a client.

FOUR

1982 – BEFORE THE NIGHT OF THE QUAALUDE

IT WAS THE ERA OF THE DELOREAN WITH A CAR PHONE THE SIZE OF A LOAF of bread. The era of payphones and beepers. Reagan, *E.T.*, *Rocky III*, poisoned Tylenol, and Love Canal.

I lived all of it and none of it. I looked at the world through a peephole in the front door, outside to inside. Everything was tiny, far away, and in full focus.

My friend Lynn was the lens. She was a card-carrying groupie. She'd gone to Carlton Prep, same as me, and she was, unfortunately, dumb as a box of rocks. The product of two beautiful, stupid people who made a ton of money for being beautiful despite their stupidity.

She was entertaining as hell though. Connected. Older. Fully-sexed. I didn't want to be her, but I knew I had to go through her stage in life. And she needed me because she had a habit of getting her ass in trouble, and I had a habit of creating ways to get her out of it.

The Breakwater Club used to be stuffy and traditional but had changed to a venue for hip Hollywood parties on weekends. They let you smoke anywhere outdoors, but not inside. Which was annoying, especially on March nights when it could get down to fifty degrees by the beach.

Lynn struck a wooden match, hands shaking. She leaned on a

concrete planter and cupped her hands over the flame. The corner of her cigarette lit. She sucked hard to pull the cherry. Behind her, the ocean crashed and the sand darkened close to the waterline.

"So fucking annoying," she said. "Like second-hand smoke ever killed anyone."

The guy smoking next to her checked her out with a smart smile. She wore a tube top and a skirt so short that her underwear showed when the wind blew.

I took the lit cigarette from her and pressed the tip to my own, filling my lungs with delicious nicotine. Yoni and Fred were inside.

"Are they both in there?" I asked.

"Yeah. The two of them. The hot ones."

That would be Strat and Indiana. Vocals and guitar, respectively.

And hot, for sure. Lynn and Yoni had been chasing them around for a week. Lynn had taught me so much about how to get through doors. How to ask person A for a favor because they knew person B.

I took it all back. She wasn't dumb as a box of rocks. She was dumb as a box of fox.

"I think tonight's the night," she said softly, leaning into me. She held up three fingers and twisted them around in a bastardization of "fingers crossed." Code for a threesome, which the two boys were famous for and what she had been trying to get herself involved in for a week.

"It's, like, fifty percent more romantic," I said.

She blinked. Didn't get it. I sighed.

"Yoni's in for girl-on-girl," she said. "I'd ask you but—"

"No thanks. Not tonight."

Not yet. I wasn't ready for that kind of thing. I'd done some low-level groping, but nothing close to the intensity of what Lynn chased after.

Yoni poked her head out. Her furry blond bob was held up with a big lace bow, and she wore fingerless, elbow-length gloves with dozens of silver bracelets at the wrist.

"Lynn," she said sotto.

Half the people on the smoking deck turned at the sound, then back to what they were doing.

"What?" Lynn asked.

We stepped to the door, and Yoni came out.

"They have a suite upstairs. Talking about a poker game. You got cash?"

"Yeah," Lynn answered.

"I'm in," I said.

Yoni's gaze sizzled over me, and I realized my error. I was going to be a buzzkilling interloper.

I stamped my cigarette out under my short boot. "Never mind. I'm going to take a walk. See you guys later."

I didn't wait for a response. If Lynn wanted to screw one or both of those guys, I could get a cab home. I didn't go to the street though. I went down the wooden steps to the beach. My feet felt the cold of the sand even through my boots. It had rained earlier in the day, and my steps made half moons of darker sand visible in the floodlights. I walked to the waterline out of reach of the light, not looking back, and sat with my knees to my chest, hugging myself against the cold.

The light disappeared and the night took over a few feet from the line where the sand got flat and wet, streaked with the movement of the tide and punctuated with intestinal piles of seaweed.

I didn't have any feelings one way or the other about the orgy. I wasn't interested. But I liked poker.

I dug my heels in the sand. Fuck this. I didn't know what to do with my body, with my place in the world, with my family. I was trapped in all of it. The water broke, foaming and hissing, a few feet from me. I didn't know if the tide was rising or receding. Didn't matter.

I didn't know what I believed in.

Desperation defined the lives of my friends. They were desperate to fit in, to make their families happy, or to decide who they were immediately. I didn't understand the hunger for approval or validation. The backstabbing and garment-rending over people with dicks made me uncomfortable. Men motivated tears and anguish that seemed unjustifiable. Weird. Out of character. I had friends who were normal one minute then started to have a freaking embolism when their bodies changed.

I felt it too. But we all took the same courses in school. We'd all known it was coming. Why act as if it was a shock?

I'd backed away slowly until I didn't have friends who couldn't cope. No one knew what to do with me. I didn't even know what to do with me. I knew I didn't fit in, and I didn't care. Maybe it was my version of rich girl ennui. Maybe I was just too smart, too good at too many things. Or too acerbic to make those warm girly relationships. I depended on no one. Didn't feel useful.

I felt as though I had more going on in my head than most people, then I thought I was out of my mind for believing that. So I reached out, trying to make more friends. Then I realized how empty relationships were. I realized I really did have more going on in my head than most people, and I started the cycle over.

Lynn had disappeared into the club, on her way to the suite to have a threesome or foursome, and I was left on the beach. I could have made it a fivesome, and why not? What would be the difference either way?

Screwing one or ten people didn't need to be an earth-shatteringly meaningful experience, but I should know why I wanted to besides boredom.

"It's not ennui then," I said to myself.

My face squeezed tight, reacting to having sand thrown in it before my brain fully registered that two shirtless men had run past me, kicking up sand. They dove into the freezing surf.

God damn. Los Angeles was pretty warm in March, all things being equal, but the water was fucking cold.

They swam to the place where the waves rose cleanly and treaded water, looking toward the horizon. When a big one rolled in, curling at the top at just the right moment, they flattened their bodies and rode it in. They got lost in the white froth, then they came up sitting. They high fived. The wave they had ridden continued past them, past the boundary of wet sand, to the dry line six inches from my boots.

Tide was coming in.

One of the men came toward me, pants heavy with water, hair dripping, short beard glistening in the lights of the boardwalk. "Got a towel?"

"No."

"Fucking cold."

"Shoulda thought of that before you went in."

Behind me, the other guy snapped a white hotel towel off the sand and gave it a shake before putting it around his shoulders. He had music tattooed all over his chest. That would be Stratford Gilliam. Unbelievable in person. Even in the dark.

"She's got a point," he said and darted back to the club.

The guy with the ginger beard was Indiana McCaffrey, and he was supposed to be fucking Lynn and Yoni. Instead, he was standing over me, shivering.

"I have fire," I said, handing him my cigarettes and lighter.

He took them and sat next to me. "Thanks." He pulled out two cigarettes, handed me one, and lit both with trembling hands.

"You should probably get inside."

"I like being cold."

"Sure. That's why people move here."

He blew out a stream of smoke. It took a hairpin turn two inches from his lips when the sea breeze sent it behind him.

"You from here?" he asked.

"Los Angeles born and raised. Fermented in Pacific brine and air-dried in the California sun." I flipped my hair so the wind blew it out of my face. He was more beautiful in person than in any magazine. I didn't know how I got to be sitting on the beach with Indiana McCaffrey, but once the cigarette was done, he was probably going to split. Every second counted. "Your Southern accent's mostly gone. You could be a newscaster."

He nodded, or he could have been shivering. "My father didn't like me sounding like a hick, so he beat the accent out of me."

"What else did he beat out of you?"

He glanced at me. "Besides the shit?"

His pupils were dilated eight-balls with blue rings. He was on some sensory-enhancing drug. Quaaludes maybe. Supposedly the blue capsules made you horny and happy enough to melt the awkwardness out of the threesomes. That's what Lynn said. She got blued whenever she could. I kept away from blues. I didn't need to be any hornier or happier.

The top layer of his hair had dried, and it fluttered in the wind as he looked down, rolling the tip of his cigarette against the edge of the sand.

"Shit's the first thing to go," I said.

He smiled, looking up at me with a cutting appreciation. As if I'd touched him in a way I hadn't even tried. Asked him something real. I'd just been fucking around, but I'd hit a nerve, so I didn't shrug it off and ask something different or dismiss the question.

"Came a day," he said, putting the filter to his lips. "Came a day I stopped feeling anything good or bad. He'd beaten that out of me good. I like or don't like things. But everything else?" He flattened his hand and cut the air straight across our eyeline.

"I get it," I said. "I have the same thing. No beatings though."

"Everything's better with a beating."

I laughed, and he laughed with me. For a guy who had no feelings, I kind of liked him.

"I saw you play the KitKat Lounge the other night," I said. "And the party after."

He twisted his body to face me and looked me in the eye. "I knew I'd seen you somewhere."

"I didn't want you to think I was pretending to not know who you were."

"Fair enough."

"But you don't have to stay here to be polite. It's cold."

He shrugged. The shivering had slowed, and his skin had dried. "My friend's upstairs with a couple of girls, and I'm not in the mood tonight."

"I think those girls might be friends of mine."

He turned back to the ocean, mimicking my posture: knees bent, elbows wrapped around the peaks of his legs, shoulders hunched. "You want to go up there, it's room 432."

"I was on the beach to avoid that scene."

"Why's that?"

"Wanted to see if you two idiots would get hypothermia."

He turned to me again, chin at his bicep, hair bending over one dilated blue eye. "How old are you?"

"Eighteen. Why?"

"We're getting a poker game together at midnight. You in?"

I had nowhere to be until morning. And because I didn't give away my hand with my voice or body, I was very good at poker.

"I'm in."

FIVE

1994

THE COPYRIGHT CASE WAS PRETTY SIMPLE. BANGERS, A UK-BASED PSEUDO-pop-rap band, had used a few bars of Haydn in their breakout song. Haydn wasn't protected under US copyright, obviously, but Martin Wright was, and he claimed Bangers had used his recording of Opus 33 repeatedly in the song.

Bangers countersued for libel, denying the claims and producing proof that they'd hired a string quartet to play the piece. Martin Wright couldn't prove it was his recording since he claimed they changed the speed so that they wouldn't sync up.

"By way of introduction, everyone, this is Drew McCaffrey," Thoze said.

Drew nodded at everyone, and I thought he lingered on me, but maybe I was mistaken. Maybe I lingered on him.

"Mister McCaffrey is here from the New York office, where he represents the interests of... god, how many musicians?"

"All of them, if I could."

Ellen giggled, sighed, caught herself. She was newly divorced, in her mid-thirties, and suddenly giggling. She was tall and attractive. Well put-together in her daily chignon and Halston suit. Closer to

Drew's age and expertise. I had the sudden desire to lick him so I could call him mine.

Thoze continued. "Martin Wright, the cellist, was LA-based at the time of recording, and he's trying to bring this through a favorable court system. Thank you for bringing this to us, Mister McCaffrey, but no one has a case." Thoze closed his folder. "I say we send Mister Wright on his way."

"They stole it," Drew interjected.

"You can't prove it," Peter Donahugh said, brushing his fingers over his tie to make sure his double-Windsor knot was still where it ought to be. "No one can. The cost to the client would outweigh the award."

Drew put his pen on the table, taking a second of silence to make his case. I'd known a musician puffy from drugs and alcohol. The guy across from me, taking three seconds to get his thoughts together, had the same blue eyes, but he also had a law degree. He still had guitar string calluses on his fingers and a tattoo that crept out from under his left cuff.

The *Rolling Stone* piece I'd read hadn't gone past Indy's devastation over Strat's death. I never heard about Indiana again. Didn't know his career choice post-mortem.

God damn. This suited him.

He pressed his beautiful lips together, leaned forward, and turned his head toward Thoze the Doze. I could see the tendons in his neck and the shadow the acute angle of his jaw cast against it.

I remembered how that neck smelled when I pressed my face against it.

"It was the most popular recording of Opus 33 when the song was mixed." Drew laid his fingertips on the table like a tent. "These guys, Bangers, didn't have a peanut butter jar to piss in. Moxie Zee charged an arm and a leg to produce, but he's a lazy snake. He billed the band for hiring a quartet that never existed, and I know him. He isn't searching out the least-used version of Haydn's Opus."

"A case is only as good as what you can prove," Peter said.

Drew kept his eyes on Thoze when he answered. "He's produced a bunch of paper. Not one actual cellist."

"We're not in the business of proving what isn't there." Thoze wove his hands together in front of him. "Absent something that proves malfeasance, we have nothing."

"What am I supposed to tell Martin? We don't care?"

"Tell him we're looking for something we can act on."

Thoze stood. His assistant stood. Peter and Ellen stood. I took the cue and gathered papers. I looked up at Drew to see if he was going to react at all, and he was reacting.

He was looking at me as if I had an answer. I couldn't move. Ellen tried to linger in the conference room, but in our shared stare and shared history there sat a thousand years, and Ellen didn't have that kind of time.

She cleared her throat. "Margie, can you grab me a coffee from the lounge on the third floor?"

"There's coffee right there," I answered from a few hundred miles away.

"It's better on three."

"I'm going for breakfast," Drew said, not moving. "I'll grab some coffee. Donuts too."

"Send the clerk. That's what they're for."

Was Ellen still talking?

"She can come."

Ellen paused then slinked out.

As soon as the glass door clicked, Drew spoke. "What are you thinking?"

"I'm thinking I had no idea you had a brain in your head."

It really was amazing how his lips were so even, top and bottom. How had I not seen that? Or the way his eyes were darker at the edges than the center?

"Things changed a lot since then."

I was feeling things, and now with his voice sounding like a cracked sidewalk, I knew he was too. That wouldn't do. It made me uncomfortable, as if my skin was the wrong size.

"I'm sorry. About Strat. I know you guys were close."

I'd broken the spell.

Drew pulled his gaze away and put his briefcase on the table, snapping it open when he answered. "Thank you."

"Was it bad?" I had no business asking that, but I had to because I should have been there. I should have done the impossible, leapt time and space, presumed a friendship I might have made up, and been there for them.

"It was bad."

He plopped his briefs in the case. I was supposed to get up and straighten the room out, but I couldn't stop watching him, remembering what he'd been to me for a short time and how those few weeks had changed me.

"What studio did Bangers record in?" I asked.

"Audio City." He slid his case off the table and went for the door.

Just as he touched the handle, I spoke. "Have you done a Request for Production?"

He didn't open the door but turned slightly in my direction, curious and cautious. "I don't see what that would prove."

I stood. "I'm only a clerk."

"I'm sure that's temporary."

I pushed the chairs in, straightening up as I was meant to. I didn't want him to feel pressured to take advice from someone who hadn't even passed her bar yet. Someone who had been no better than a smart-mouthed groupie all those years ago. But I wanted to be heard.

"You want to scare the hell out of them, you call in some favors at Audio City," I said. "Take Teddy out for some drinks. Be seen. And you file a Request for Production to aid discovery. Teddy hands over the masters."

"They'll be mixed down. They're useless."

"There's more to a tape than the music. There's pops and scratches. Match them to Wright's master. It's like a fingerprint."

"That's not true."

"It's true if you believe it is. You're not trying to prove anything. You're trying to get Moxie Zee to crack."

He took his hand off the door handle. I noticed then looked away.

"What you want," I continued, trying to sound casual, "is for your client to be paid for his work, right? I mean, cellists make a living but not that much."

"Not Drazen money."

I ignored the jab. One, he smiled through it. Two, though I tried to be as anonymous as possible in the office, it was nice to be known.

"No." I pushed the chair he'd sat in under the table. "Not Drazen money. If Moxie Zee is caught lying, most of his artists won't care. Some will think it's cool. But he works for Overland Studios as a music supervisor under his real name. Overland's risk averse. They're not keeping a guy who might have already exposed them to a lawsuit."

"And you think Moxie will pay off Martin under the table over a fingerprinting technique that doesn't exist?"

"People are pretty predictable."

He nodded, bit the left side of his lower lip, tapped the door handle three times, then looked me up and down as if he wanted to eat me with a dick-shaped spoon.

"You're still crazy," he said softly, as if those three words were meant to seduce me.

They did. He was half a room away, and every surface between my legs was on fire. I would have swallowed, but I didn't even have the spit to do it.

"How old are you?" he asked.

"Eighteen."

He walked out, letting the door slowly swing shut behind him, and I watched him stride down the hall in his perfect suit.

Men loved tits, legs, ass, pussy. Men loved long hair and necks. They loved clear skin and full lips. But some men, the right men—men like Drew and Strat—loved cutting themselves on sharp women, and I hadn't been loved for the right reasons in a long, long time.

SIX

1982 – BEFORE THE NIGHT OF THE QUAALUDE

BULLETS AND BLOOD WAS ON THE VERGE. *KENTUCKY KILLER* HAD CAUGHT fire and made the small label enough money to keep the lights on. But then the Big Boys went after Bullets and Blood, sending hip-looking A and R guys around with pockets full of promises. They introduced them to music legends like Hawk Bromberg, with his little flavor-saver and sideburns, who talked up his label and everything they'd done for him.

This was background noise in the weeks following, but the morning after I cleaned them both out at poker, I knew nothing. I'd kept my bra on, put my shirt back on, and stretched on the couch for a few hours. Woke up with a headache and a throat that felt like a bag of dry beans.

I had to get to school.

Lynn was gone. So was Yoni. The hotel room looked over the beach and, in the yellow of the rising sun, seemed expensive and luxurious in a different way than the night before.

"Morning," Strat said from the balcony. He leaned on the doorway in a shirt and stonewashed jeans.

Behind him, Hawk smoked a stubby brown cigarette as thick as a middle finger, looking at me as if he was eight and I was a piece of birthday cake. He was a legend, but I wasn't flattered. I was disgusted.

"Where's Indy?" I asked.

"Out for a swim."

Had Strat even slept? He still looked perfect, but maybe my standards were skewed. He looked as though he partied all the time, and that was what I found attractive about him.

"I gotta go."

"You should come around later."

Hawk nodded, picking the slick brown butt out of his teeth. He sang about heaven and earth with a voice like a fist, but I wasn't loving his real presence.

"Sure." I didn't have time to chitchat. My father was coming back from a business thing in Omaha, and I had to be home.

"Do you have my beeper number?"

"No."

I didn't have time to scrabble around for a pencil and a piece of cleanish paper so I could set off the little black box on Strat's belt. He wouldn't even answer it. He was a rock star.

"Eyebrow," he said. "Six-oh-six E-Y-E-B-R-O-W."

"Six-oh-six? Kentucky? I thought you guys were from Nashville."

"The beeper's from Kentucky."

I didn't move. Just waited for the long version.

"My dad moved to Kentucky. He's a doctor. He upgrades every six months."

Mister Big Rock Star was either too frugal or too busy to get his own damned beeper. Or too much of a kid. Or too attached to his parents.

No matter what angle I looked at that from, no matter how the light hit it, I found it charming.

I HAD no intention of using that number for anything, though I'd never forget it. My driver was off. So I got a car at the hotel's front desk and sat back for the short ride from Santa Monica to Malibu. It was six thirty in the morning. I had ten minutes to get back.

Nadia, Theresa's nanny, would be up because she didn't sleep. Hector, the groundskeeper, was probably already working. Maria, Graciella, and Gloria. Definitely rousing Carrie, Sheila, and Fiona for school. Dressing them. Making sure homework was done. Deirdre, Leanne, and Theresa would be causing havoc. If I got right in the shower, there was a pretty good chance no one would notice I had even been out.

Except Mom. She was a wild card. She usually slept until eight, but if she drank the night before, she actually woke up earlier. And if she caught me out, she was unpredictable. She'd been pregnant six times since I was born, so she always seemed to be in a constant state of flux. Big. Little. Tired. Energized. Horizontal. Running. One person. Two. She was as likely to lock me out and act as if everything was normal as tell my father, which would be bad. Very bad. All bad. He did not like losing control. He seemed to have two emotions: cold calculation and satisfaction.

I loved him. I loved both of them. But I never knew what to make of them. In the end, I realized they didn't go on and on about how they felt but concerned themselves with actions. I respected that. It was what I thought it meant to be an adult.

I knew I'd pushed it. Playing strip poker with two guys in a semi-famous rock band in a semi-luxurious hotel room? And telling them my name?

My God. I didn't know what my parents would do to me, but everything about it was trouble. Dad cared about what people thought. He cared about appearances and chastity. Even if he wasn't in town, he had the nannies dress us all up and take us to church on Sunday. He made sure we had ashes on our forehead and palm crosses in our hands. He never mentioned God at all, but the Catholic Church always loomed as the ultimate authority.

I'd asked him why, and he said something odd.

He said, "Invisible gods are ineffective."

I had to hope that Strat and Drew had no reason to find out who the Drazens were. How old their money was. They wouldn't. I wasn't anyone to them. I made myself invisible in my mind when the cab got to my house. I gave the cabbie one of Drew's hundreds, ran into the side door, and made it into the bathroom without being seen.

I washed the night away with scalding water.

Six-oh-six eyebrow.

Go over pre-calc in the car.

History

Comp

Stupid's not a verb, asshole.

Forty minutes to memorize a hundred Latin conjugations

Tennis

Photography

Eat something

What's your name?

Catholic Women's Club

Chess Strategy Club

Then?

Then?

Then…

SEVEN

1994

"I KNOW EVERYTHING COMES PRETTY EASILY TO ME COMPARED," I
whispered to Drew/Indiana in the hall before swiveling into my
cubicle. I had to pick up my things before doing Ellen's donut run.
"But I put some work into being here. I'd appreciate it if you didn't
mention we knew each other eleven plus years ago."

"Am I so embarrassing?" He smirked as if he had me over a barrel.

Typical man, thinking it was all about hard work now/today/this
week. If word of our history got out, I'd be a slut and he'd be a hero.
I'd be fending off advances in the copy room, getting censured for shit
I did a decade ago, wondering why I never got the good cases, and
he'd fly back to New York and get promoted.

"It's not shame and never was."

"That's my Cinnamon."

"It's Margie now." I spun to face him, my back to my desk and
spoke quietly. Terry, the other clerk, was a foot away through the grey
half-wall. "Full-time. This is my life. Like I said. I have plenty of
privilege but no dick."

"It's 1994."

He said it as if we had entered the modern era and his dick didn't make a damned bit of difference in the workplace. Only a man could think something so utterly incorrect.

He must have seen me boil, because he put a hand up before I could explode. "I'm just giving you a hard time. I never intended to say a word about anything, but I'm in town for the week."

I opened the bottom drawer of my desk and got my purse out. "Fine." I slapped the drawer shut.

"Fine?"

"I have no feelings about it one way or the other."

"Good to see you haven't changed." He winked and slipped out.

EIGHT

1982 – BEFORE THE NIGHT OF THE QUAALUDE

I DIDN'T HAVE TO REMEMBER E-Y-E-B-R-O-W OR SIX-OH-SIX, WHICH I happened to know was a Kentucky number from a friend at Carlton Prep. I got a beep in the middle of chess strategy with a Nashville call back number. An hour later, I was in the passenger seat of a Monte Carlo driving into Pacific Palisades. Strat was behind the wheel, and Indiana was in the back with Lynn and Yoni.

I had no idea why I was there. I wasn't the prettiest girl who hung around them. I hadn't screwed either one of them, though apparently Yoni and Lynn had had a fine time with Strat before the poker game had gotten under way. I didn't understand why I was there because I didn't understand men.

Yet.

It came to me many years later, while reading *Rolling Stone*. During the interview, Indy was sitting in front of a mixing board they'd installed in the Palihood House (He was "producing" because that was always the story arc. Small-town beginnings>cohesion of the group>artistic satisfaction>commercial success>drug use>break up>The Bottom>redemption>rebuilding/branding). His hair was scraggly but intentionally so. His shirt was clean. He'd lost the puff around the eyes, and he was talking about Strat.

"He was like a brother to me, but more. A partner. And when he died, man, it was like someone ripped me open."

In the passenger seat of the Monte Carlo, with the two of them still poker-playing strangers, I didn't know they were like brothers. Years later, reading the *Rolling Stone* article, that Monte Carlo ride came back to me.

I'd been so clueless about how close they were and how lonely they were.

I always assumed I was brought into this world fully formed. Maybe I wasn't. Maybe I didn't understand people the way I thought I did. I chewed on that then forgot it, because it only turned up the heat on a cauldron of stew that had everything and nothing to do with the Bullets and Blood boys.

Indy leaned forward and pointed at a locked gate closing off a road into the foothills of the Palisades. "Up here. Code's fifty-one-fifty." He turned to me, and I could feel his breath on my cheek. "Wait until you see this place."

"It's nice up here," Lynn said before cracking her gum. She was in a black lace corset and tiered skirt. Red, red lips and black, black eyeliner.

"This is the ass-end though," Yoni chimed in. "It's the Palihood."

"Yeah, anything east of the park."

"South."

"East."

I rolled my eyes.

Strat ignored them. "He can't afford it."

"We just got a quarter-million dollar contract." Indy leaned back and kicked Strat's seat.

Strat shook his head. "Have you read it?"

"You don't read Greek either."

Driving up the hill under the clear spring sky, the fact that he'd read the contract and understood it made me look at Strat's arms, his music tattoos, the muscles of his legs, and respect him with a sexual heat.

We pulled up to a house made of glass and overhung with trees and surrounded by tall bushes. When we got out of the car, the shade was a welcome respite from the blasting sun, and the birds cut through the white noise of the freeway.

"It's nice," I said.

"And I can afford it." Indy pointed at Strat as he headed for the front door.

"Fuck you can," Strat muttered.

Yoni and Lynn had no interest. They'd started bantering about the coyotes in the hills, bouncing with excitement, as we went up the cracked steps onto the pocked flagstones.

"Ye of little faith." Indy opened the door. "I have the down payment next week. Made escrow already."

The black linoleum floors shined, and the sightline went through the house, over the west side, and to the ocean. Yoni and Lynn were already checking out the bean-shaped pool in the back.

You'd think a musician on the cusp of fame wouldn't want to be tied down to a house. He'd want to ride the tour bus and fuck a few hundred girls. That was the norm. But Indy stood in the empty space between the front door and the horizon and lit two cigarettes before handing me one.

"I can move in next week."

"Dude," Strat said.

"Dude," Indy snapped.

Strat turned to me, hands out, pleading. On the whole ride up, I'd wondered why they brought me, and I feared at that moment that they'd gone to the library or talked to their lawyers and found out who I was. Now they were going to ask me for money, and I couldn't give it to them. There was no other reason to put me in that car.

I liked them, but that house had to cost two hundred grand.

Would they threaten to tell Daddy things? The poker? The bra? The smoking? Would they tell him I drank and I kissed? Or that I was a cocktease?

When I brought the cigarette to my lips, my hand was shaking. I didn't know which scenario terrified me most. I inhaled the nicotine and blew out rings as if I had control of this. Whatever this was. It was my first cigarette of the day, and it made my palms tingle.

"Why the fuck am I here?" I asked.

Strat stepped forward, finger pointing at me then Drew. "Keep me from killing him."

"Fuck you," Indy retorted.

I didn't have anything much more intelligent to offer. "It's a nice house. Needs work. Get an accountant to tell him if he can afford it."

"Let me give you the short version." Strat's comment was directed at me but meant for Indy. "Two fifty minus fifteen percent to WDE. Two twelve and a half. Eighty-three grand. Minus three points to our producer. Two-oh-five. And by the way, we, you and me and Gary—the *band*—we have to recoup *their* points."

"We will. I'm telling you."

"Two-oh-five divided by three? Sixty-eight thousand dollars for a three-year contract. And you haven't even paid your taxes yet."

I rolled my eyes and looked at the ceiling. If Strat and / or Indy noticed me acting my age, they didn't say anything.

"There's income, fucktard." Indy patted his pockets and found a thick marker best suited to sniffing and writing graff. "I need a napkin. Fucking find me a napkin. An envelope. I gotta write on the back of it."

"Fifty grand for the studio we gotta pay back," said Strat the Sensible. "Recoupable. Producer. Recoupable. Equipment rental. Re—"

"Stop it!" I shouted.

I'd had it with the two of them. I didn't know much of anything. I didn't know how to run a business or how to make money, but I knew how to think like a rich person. Maybe that was why they'd brought me.

"You guys. You're so cute with your middle-class shitsense. You act as if it's money to spend. It's not. It's money to make more money. You." I pointed at Strat. "You move in here with Indy. You take your sixty grand, and you set up a studio in the garage or the living room. I don't care where. You." I pointed at Indy. "Get a commercial loan. You lay down the next record here and collect the fifty grand instead of paying it in recoupable expenses. You rent it out to your other musician friends and let them pay your mortgage, and you pay down that fucker because at eighteen percent interest, you're getting killed."

I took a pull on my cigarette. It was so close to the filter that my fingers got hot. Jesus, figuring that out felt good. Whether they did what I said or not, putting it together had been damn near orgasmic. "I need a fucking beer."

NINE

1994

THE SAN FERNANDO VALLEY, VAN NUYS IN PARTICULAR, WAS A HELL OF parking lots and freeway-width avenues. Everything looked new yet coated over in beige dust. Drew and I had split right after the meeting, slipping down the back elevator. It was like the old days when I had a ten o'clock curfew I ignored.

We pulled into the back of Audio City, where the entrance was. Drew put the car into park and leaned back.

"You gonna open the door?" I asked.

"I haven't seen these guys in a long time. Give me a minute to think."

"Get back into your rocker head?"

He smiled, and something about that made me feel really good. "Yeah."

I switched my position so I was kneeling on the seat, facing him. I yanked on his lapel. "Take this off. You look like a fucking lawyer."

"Right. Okay." He wrestled out of his jacket and tossed it in the back. His shirt had light blue stripes and a white collar, and his tie was just skinny enough to be stylish without crossing the line into new wave.

I grabbed it and let it go so it flopped. "Come on, take this off."

He undid it. "I forgot how bossy you are."

"I still can't believe you even remember me."

"You're not forgettable."

"Please," I said. "There were hundreds of girls."

He yanked at the tie, slipping it through the knot. "I was obsessed with you the second you opened your mouth. You scared the fuck out of Strat. He thought he was going to lose me to you."

He leaned his head back on the seat, raising his hand languidly and touching my chin. My eyes fluttered closed, because I'd been too busy to let a man touch me in years, and this man knew how to touch. He ran his finger along the edge of my jaw, down my neck, and I grabbed it before it could move lower.

"We're working."

"What happened to you?" he asked in a whisper.

"I went to law school."

"Before that. You split. We couldn't find you. Strat hung out outside your house. We went to all the clubs. Your friends didn't know where you were."

He didn't know what he was asking. He thought he was going to get some reasonable, sane answer, but there wasn't one.

"It had nothing to do with you," I lied. It had everything to do with him. Every single thing.

"What did it have to do with, Cin?" His voice dripped sex and music, and I wondered if that was just his way of getting back into character.

I reached for his collar and ran my finger under it, revealing the stand of tiny white buttons. "The collar comes off."

"You need to tell me where you went."

"I took a trip."

"We waited, and you never showed up."

He moved his fingertip down my shirt. My breath got short, and I couldn't take my eyes off of his lips.

"Sorry. I flaked. You guys were too intense for me." I didn't know why I had to make it obvious that it was more than that. I could have kept my voice flat and subtext-free, but my inflection got away from me. If he couldn't tell I was hiding something, he was an idiot.

And he wasn't an idiot. That was shit-sure.

"You're not going to tell me, are you?" he said.

"No."

He took his hand away. Relief and disappointment fought for dominance inside me as he flipped his stiff collar up and unbuttoned it.

"We had a good time," he said. "Good coupla months."

"Seven weeks."

"I wasn't even thinking about how long it was going to last. But I was so fucking stupid anyway. Strat was smart. He played at being a reckless musician, but man, he was sharp and fifty years older in his mind. He told me to chill out. He told me the thing we were doing was temporary, and I argued with him like a moron." He shook his head at his stupidity and got the last button undone, snapping the collar away from his neck.

"Looks better," I said, smoothing down the Mandarin.

He took my wrist and sucked me in with the tractor beam of his gaze. "I thought I'd be the one to lose my shit when it ended. But it was him."

I pulled my hand away. I couldn't pretend I didn't care for another second. "What happened?"

"I could ask you the same thing."

"You could."

But he didn't, and I opened the door to end the conversation.

TEN

1982 – AFTER THE NIGHT OF THE QUAALUDE

RICH FAMILY. PIG RICH. SIX NANNIES, TWO COOKS, AND A CLEANING STAFF rich. Multiple estates. We were our own economy. My dad wouldn't experiment with losing a chunk of it for another twenty-plus years.

My father had two brothers, and my mother had a sister she barely spoke to. She'd never said why. She never said much that was worth listening to. She hadn't seemed young to me until the autumn of Bullets and Blood.

This realization happened at a party. We had two hundred people in the house for my parents' anniversary. String quartet. Black tie staff. Open doors to our swimming pool with lotus blossoms and candles floating in it. Attendance was mandatory, so I had to tell Indy and Strat to get their laughs elsewhere.

All the family and business partners were there, all the wives clustered around the couches and most of the men hovering around the bar. Except Aunt Maureen. She never hung around the women. She was my "cool aunt" who ran a business and told the guy she'd been with for the past ten years that she saw no point in getting married. She was talking to my dad and a few guys in suits I knew by sight but not name. I was close by, hanging on every word, when I heard her say something about negotiations with a blue chip company. It was a

bunch of numbers and percentages I understood because I
remembered everything the adults in my family said about business.
But at the end, she laughed.

The sound had a clear, tinkling quality her voice usually lacked.
She sounded so young.

Wait. She *was* young.

She was eighteen years older than me. A little less, give or take.
And that made my mother fifteen and change when she'd had me.

Over the ice sculpture and through the floral arrangement in the
center of the ballroom, I looked at my father and did more math.

I almost laughed at the symmetry of it.

But it wasn't funny. It took me too long to realize what had gone
on, but I told myself I wasn't going to be like my mother. I didn't hate
her, but I didn't respect her either. She was from a good family. She
was beautiful and smart. But she was nothing. She did nothing. Her
life was a vacuum that purpose had fallen into, never to be seen again.

I wasn't going to be that, but I was already on the way.

Me in my blue dress and little gold hoop earrings, dressed like a
prim little miss. A chiffon-and-silk lie I let them believe. I felt sick.

I was thrown off balance by the impact of a small child. Fiona was
five, and she had her arms wrapped around my legs. The others
followed. Deirdre and Leanne hugged my legs too. Carrie and Sheila,
at nine and eleven, stayed close, looking excited. I was only missing
Theresa, who was a year old and had started walking two weeks ago.
They looked up at me with eyes in varying shades of blue and green,
hair from strawberry-blond to dark brown red. That was what
happened when a redhead married a redhead, and my insides curdled
like milk on the stove.

"Who's watching you guys?" I was talking about everyone but
directed the question at Carrie, the oldest of them and most likely to
put together a coherent sentence.

"Everyone's outside. Are you having cake or not?"

How long had I been staring into the middle distance?

Long enough for everyone to move to the garden, leaving a few
clustered stragglers by the French doors. I let my little sisters lead me
outside, where sibling hierarchy was determined by proximity to the

cake. I'd lost any will of my own and hung behind all of them. I didn't really want cake. I'd been sick to my stomach for days, fighting a headache, feeling tender everywhere, but I had a compulsion to act as if dessert mattered.

My mother and father stood behind the cake, smiling for the professional photographer. He wore an *LA Times* press pass. The camera was nowhere near me, but I felt exposed. They'd want a picture with me, and I couldn't. I just couldn't. I could stay relatively anonymous in the world, but people read the pages of news about the Reagan presidency, Beirut, Studio 54 closing, and Hollywood celebrities. After those, but before the stock ticker, came the society page. Weddings. Anniversaries. Deaths of monied men.

My father tapped his glass with a spoon. He was over six feet tall and looked every bit the oligarch he was, with a full head of dark-red hair. My mother was more strawberry, and she held her head high when he was nearby. On that night in particular, she beamed a little brighter.

The guests quieted, and even the photographer put his camera down when Daddy raised his whiskey.

"Ladies and gentlemen," he said, projecting to the back of the room, "thank you for coming. I hope you're all having a good time celebrating this, my anniversary with my beautiful bride."

A chorus of tinkling rose as more spoons met glasses.

A great sound, I thought. *They should try it in the studio.*

My sinuses filled up, and I almost started crying, but my father kissed my mother quickly and went back to his speech.

"We have an announcement!"

Let's hear it, Declan!

Hear! Hear!

"Eileen is about to make me a father for the eighth time!"

"Get off her, for Chrissakes!"

The shout from the back ended in uproarious laughter and cheers from everyone but the children, who didn't understand it.

Except me. But I wasn't a child. Never was, and never would be.

The photographer started snapping again. Dad and Mom indicated we should come behind the table so we could all smile in dot matrix patterns for tomorrow's paper, and I couldn't.

I'd hit my limit. I was going a hundred miles an hour, and the brick wall had appeared inches in front of me, without warning.

I'd taken a pregnancy test that morning. I'd put it away without looking at it and decided I wasn't going to think about it. Not until after the party. Pretending bad things weren't happening wasn't like me, but then again, nothing bad had ever happened to me.

I'd bought it as almost a joke because my period wasn't that regular. But it wasn't funny.

The compulsion to look at the results weighed like a rock in my chest, exploding in slow motion. I had to hide before the shrapnel shredded me from the inside.

My room was a good three-minute expedition across the house, and I took it at a run, slipping on the marble and righting myself. I was crying hard by the time I reached my hallway. Somewhere in the journey, I'd let it go. Everything.

Oh god oh god oh god

I was a sensible person. I knew I had options, and the first step to exploring them was to know what was happening. The nausea and headaches. The tender breasts and belly. The feeling at the root of my hips that something was *happening*. I had to scratch pregnancy off the list so I could move to the next possibility, but I knew I wasn't scratching shit off any list. I just knew.

And when they'd announced Mom was pregnant (again), I couldn't wait another second.

When I got to my room, breathless in my pale blue dress, I slapped open the medicine cabinet where I'd left the little plastic jar. If the liquid was one color, I could forget the whole thing. If there was a brown ring at the bottom—

"Are you all right?"

I spun at the voice in the doorway, leaving my back to the open cabinet. My father stood in the doorway, still thrust forward from his run up the stairs.

"I'm fine," I said.

"Your mother thought you'd take it hard. I told her you were made of steel." His smile was one hundred percent pride.

"I just ate something that didn't agree with me."

I spun and snapped the medicine cabinet door closed, but it bounced back, leaving an inch of the inside exposed. I turned back to my dad, hoping I wasn't disrupting the liquid. Taking the test with eyedroppers and test tubes, I'd felt as if I were in lab class. I didn't want to do it all again. And I didn't want Dad to see it. And I didn't want to be pregnant. And I wanted to rewind the whole thing, so I didn't stupid my way through life.

"You've been so busy with your extracurriculars, your mother is worried." His eyes left mine and went to the medicine cabinet. He wasn't looking in the mirror. They traced the edge, moving up and down.

"I'm a little tired. Can I skip the cake?"

"Be back down in half an hour for pictures."

His sharp expression meant that was an order. I could be green around the gills, and I'd be expected to smile for the camera.

"Okay." I wanted him to go away.

He looked from behind me to my face, scanning it. I felt made of thin blown glass, hollow and transparent. Too fine. Too delicate. Worth too much to be broken without everyone I cared about getting upset over the loss.

I tilted my head down and went around him, to the doorway, where the promised comfort of my bed waited. He'd have to follow me out and leave me alone for thirty minutes. I could do a lot of calming down in half an hour.

I'd just stepped onto the carpet in my room. It was mauve and grey. And by the second step, the colors became a woolen blur as I was pulled back and spun around.

Dad's face was beet red. He held a clear plastic vial in his left hand as he gripped my arm with his right. "What is this?"

"You're hurting me." I tried to squirm away, but he only gripped me tighter.

"What have you done?"

I was so scared I could barely think. My father had never raised a hand to me, but I'd always known there was an ocean of violent potential under his smooth veneer. A cold, deep sea that remained placid but was ever-threatening.

"It's negative!" I shouted, not knowing if that was true. I hadn't gotten a look into the vial before he stepped in.

"This?" He turned the vial toward me, open top to my face.

The yellow liquid had been slipped down. At the bottom, a brown ring of thicker membrane slid down, going elliptical before drooping into a line of accusation.

I didn't have an answer. Not an excuse or reason. Nothing but an explanation of what I'd been doing with my free time, which I was sure he didn't want to hear.

"Who is he?" Dad growled.

Wasn't that the question of the year.

"Let go!"

"Were you raped?"

"What?"

"I'll kill whoever did it."

"Dad! No!" I was crying now. I hadn't had enough time to process what I'd done to myself. I felt the spit and tears as if they were someone else's. Dad's face was lost in a wet, grey cloud, and my breath came in hard sobs. I choked out what I thought was a bit of reassurance. "It wasn't rape."

He twisted me around until I was facedown over my white footboard, the thin wood painful on my abdomen. While I was trying to navigate around that and the tears that flowed with the force of a storm, I felt a sharp pain on my bottom.

A strange clarity cut through my sobs, and my crying stopped as if I'd skidded to a stop at the edge of a cliff while the tears dropped to the bottom.

Dad spanked me again, and the impact turned breaths into grunts. I tried to turn, but he held me and whacked me again. I was confused, pinned. I looked around at him. His hand was raised with fingers flat, and elbow bent to strike me again, and he was looking at his hand as if it had done something he didn't understand.

Then in that split second, he looked down at me, and we made eye contact. He saw me but didn't. I didn't know what he saw. I didn't know what math he was doing in his head. The violent sea within him didn't calm. It didn't drain into a huge funnel and gurgle away, but the tide changed and moved like a lumbering beast, receding over the horizon to a place I couldn't see.

He let me go. I slumped over the footrail. I took two deep breaths, and only the first one was an incomplete hitch.

I had neither choices nor time. My family, for all their money, was very Catholic, very rigid, very traditional. I had tons of privilege but no rights. So if I was going to abort this baby, it was now or never. Let them disown me.

I had to run away.

ELEVEN

1994

BUSINESS HAD BEEN ROUGH FOR A FEW YEARS, BUT AUDIO CITY WAS STILL the best music studio in Los Angeles. It had a certain something. Reputation-plus-talent-plus-acoustics-times-equipment-equals-hotter-than-hot. Before my parents' anniversary party, information like that had mattered to me. But sitting with the head engineer in a soundproof room that smelled of stale sweat and cigarettes, all that mattered was the plan—a ruse to get a settlement—and the client, a cellist who might have been ripped off by a wealthy producer.

"You were the only band in our history who canceled studio dates," Teddy said.

I vaguely remembered him. Back then, before Bullets and Blood, I'd slinked in with Rowdy Boys. Teddy'd had a full head of hair and a smile full of straight white teeth. When I sat in the booth with him and Drew (née Indy), Teddy was made of comb-over and nicotine stains.

"We got our own place," Drew answered.

"Still running from what I hear."

"Yup. Switching over to digital."

Teddy shook his head and snapped a pack of cigarettes off the mixing board. "Fucking digital." He pushed open the pack with his thumb and offered me one.

I took it. Then Drew surprised me by taking out his own pack and lighter.

"It's the future," Drew said, shaking out a smoke.

"Fuck the future." Teddy lit mine then his own.

I pulled on it, tasting the dry heat of tar and letting the nicotine run through my blood. I hadn't smoked in umpteen years, and I'd forgotten how much I liked it.

Teddy picked a little piece of tobacco off the tip of his tongue. "Digital wouldn't help you with your cello problem." He flicked the speck of a leaf away. "It's those pops and hums that make magnetic tape sound warm. It's what got you here. If we recorded on digital, it wouldn't mean shit."

"Yeah," Drew said.

"Digital's gonna kill music."

"Sure."

"But you don't care no more." He flicked his hand at Drew, from his fancy shoes to his conservative haircut. "Lawyer."

"Douche."

Teddy surprised me by laughing. "Yeah. Know thyself, right? I got it. Give me that production request or whatever you call it, and I'll show it to our lawyer. He'll get back to you." He held out his hand to shake Drew's.

Here was the problem. The request for production wasn't worth shit because the fingerprinting thing was made up. Even a shyster lawyer would figure that out.

"How about a deal?" I said.

Teddy's hand froze midway up, and he looked at me. Drew looked both surprised and curious.

I swallowed hard. "Let us down into the master archives for a Bullets and Blood record. The debut was recorded here, right?"

"Right."

"We'll just peek at the Opus 33 masters. See if it's worthwhile so you don't have to blow two hundred an hour on a lawyer. In return, Indy here will show you how they're going digital. Show you the right equipment. So you can decide for yourself if you can switch."

Teddy stubbed his cigarette into a half-full ashtray. I glanced at

Drew. His head was tilted down and toward me, thumb to forehead to hide his expression. His cigarette burned hot to the filter as he smiled.

"Yeah," Drew said, looking up. "We'll do a consult. Above board. You can probably go digital without switching completely. I know you get people and lose people because you're analog. Let's see if you can't do both."

Teddy considered, looking away, then back at us. Shifting his box of smokes, shaking his foot, then nodding to himself.

"Yeah, why the fuck not?" He stuck his hand out again, and Drew grabbed it. "Why the fuck not?"

TWELVE

1982 – BEFORE THE NIGHT OF THE QUAALUDE

THEY STARTED GETTING THAT STUDIO TOGETHER ALMOST IMMEDIATELY. They had recording and tour dates to keep. So during the day, the house was filled with workmen, artists, and sound engineers in leather Members Only jackets.

I was confused about Strat and Indy. For the next week or so, I was with them all the freaking time. Like a piece of furniture for the new house. Sometimes they beeped me, and sometimes I E-Y-E-B-R-O-Wed them. I met them wherever they were, and we proceeded to act as though we were all in some kind of relationship.

But they didn't make a move. Strat had eyes like fingers—they had a way of getting between my skin and my clothes. But he never did anything about it. Not in the week after I told them how to have their house and live in it too.

Once, when we were at a party in Malibu, Indy put his hand on my shoulder and said something in my ear. I don't even remember what it was, but the music was loud, so he had to talk in my ear if he wanted me to hear him.

Strat came up right after that, like a hawk, and put his finger in Indy's face, lips tense. Indy shrugged. It was the first time I saw them act like anything but best brothers.

Indy put up his right hand. "Pledge, asshole."

"Fuck you." But Strat put up his right hand. I could see the matching snake tattoos inside their forearms. "Pledge open."

"Nothing," Indy spat. "Nothing, okay?"

"Closed, dude. I'm sorry."

They put their hands down and hugged, back-slapping as if they'd had a whole conversation.

"What was that about?" I asked when Strat drifted off.

Indy shrugged, and someone came to talk to him. Male-musician-slash-producer-slash-A and R guy. Thirties. Black plastic sunglasses with red lenses hiding his blued-out dilated pupils. Cartoonishly hip. Guys like that were always talking to Strat and Indy, and they had a way of making sure I was treated like a life support system for a pussy. It would take three minutes for him to angle his body so that he was between Indy and me, then he'd turn his back to me.

Like clockwork, I was looking at the back of his jacket.

Fuck this. I didn't understand any of it. I went inside, picking my way through couplings and conversations on my way to the front door. I'd opened it, letting the cool West Side breeze in when Strat caught up.

"Where you going?" he asked, nipples hard from the night air.

I let my hand slip from the doorknob. "To buy you a shirt."

He gave me that look. The one that made me warm and tingly. The room was full of women wearing strings and little triangles, yet he was looking at me as if he wanted to devour me skin to bone.

Yes, it turned me on, but it also annoyed me.

"What was that about back there? With Indy?" I asked.

"What was what?"

"Fuck this."

I opened the door, but I didn't get far. He leaned over and pressed it closed.

"You don't know?" he asked. "You can't tell?"

"Since the first day you brought me to this house, you've treated me like a little sister—"

I had more to say. Much more. A speech worthy of Ronald Reagan, but he laughed. I just ate those words, chewed and swallowed them, because I'd seriously misread something. He opened the door, still smiling like a fuckhead.

"Beep us," was all he got to say before I left.

I had an orange button on my beeper. I pressed it, and my driver pulled up. Like magic. His job was to take me to and from whatever activity I had going on. His job wasn't to tell me where to go or tell my family where I was. I barely made it half a block back toward home before I knew I'd beep six-oh-six E-Y-E-B-R-O-W. Or Indy. It didn't matter. I was addicted to them the way Lynn was addicted to blues. The excitement of their company was the best drug in the world.

THIRTEEN

A COMPREHENSIVE LIST OF WHAT IT MEANS TO BE MATURE FOR YOUR AGE.

1. You see people through their lens, not yours. So there's less getting offended. Less reactive bullshit.
2. You have perspective but not experience. You know it all shakes out in the end. So small problems are small, and big problems are small.
3. You get cocky because you're mature and you know it. Stupid mistakes are other people's problems.
4. Your body is still a slave to your brain, and if your brain is thinking about grown-up shit, like sex, your body is going to be a hotbed. And if your body matures early… well, follow the yellow brick road. The Emerald City has its legs spread for you.

FOURTEEN

1982 – BEFORE THE NIGHT OF THE QUAALUDE

THE HOUSE IN THE PALIHOOD HAD A THOUSAND SQUARE FEET OF unpermitted add-ons. Some even made sense. Most didn't. One bedroom was five feet wide and had outdoor wood siding on one wall. One add-on was only accessible via five treacherous two-foot-high steps to an attic the shape of an inverted V, and another bedroom was only accessible from the outside patio and through a closet.

I arrived one afternoon after a respectable activity I could never recall in black pumps and a Chanel jacket. The house was dead except for the open door and obscure punk playing from the sound system the boys had installed over the lead-painted walls and chipped molding.

I didn't announce myself. I never did. I was a piece of furniture, more or less. I heard voices from one of the spare rooms. I passed through the third bathroom, into the closet, and almost opened the louvered door to reveal the sound when I stopped. A cry had come from the other side of the door.

The louvers gave me a choppy view, but I saw enough skin to make me take a step back. I heard panting. Groaning. A man's voice. Strat. I took a second step back. Stopped. The doors had a space between them, and I leaned forward and looked.

I recognized the girl from her silky brown hair. When she moved, it swayed over her shoulders. She was on her hands and knees. Strat was behind her, fucking her so hard my face flushed and my body's heat level went deep in the red. I could smell them. Their sweat and something funkier. The scent between my legs plus a man. I touched the wall. I needed it to hold me up.

Leave. Turn around.

"Take it, baby," Strat muttered, hands gripping her ass. His skin was satin with sweat.

I wanted him. I wished I was the girl with the brown hair, taking it. I shifted a little so I could see the place where their bodies met. His cock sliding in and out of her.

God god god I want it.

I was blocking the way, but I didn't want to go back and I couldn't go forward. All I could was hope that no one wanted to go into the spare bedroom right then. I shifted, nervous someone else was near me.

The second woman had curly blond hair and generous naked hips. I wished I was her, naked with them. Laughing about some whispered words.

You're nuts. This is so past what you're ready for.

"You want to eat her out, baby?"

"Yes," said Straight Brown Hair. She turned to Luscious Hips, still getting fucked, and her eyes lingered on the louvers for a moment.

She saw.

"Let me kiss your pussy."

No. She didn't.

Luscious Hips sat right in front of Brown Hair and spread her legs. I didn't think my clit could have been more engorged or my pussy wetter. I was glued to the scene as she laid her face between her friend's legs. I couldn't see what she was doing, but Strat, that voice…

"Eat her hard. Suck on it. *Mmf.* Yes. Make her come."

"I'm so wet. So wet," Luscious Hips shouted.

Strat put his hand between mouth and cunt. I didn't know what he was doing, but the intersection of those three things aroused me so much. I did the unthinkable. I stuck my hand under my skirt and tore my panty hose open to get under my cotton briefs.

I nearly collapsed at my own touch.

"Get it wet," Strat commanded as the girl on her hands and knees sucked his finger. "It's going in your ass."

Did he say that?

I think I'm going to die.

The girl who was getting fucked had her face in Luscious's pussy as Strat stuck one finger in Fucked Girl's ass.

"Yes!" she looked up long enough to affirm.

Strat put in two fingers. She shouted, face planted in pussy. Luscious had Fucked by the back of the head, pushing her mouth into her cunt, pumping her hips across Fucked's face while Strat pumped away and got three fingers into her ass.

Oh god, I want that I want that.

But I didn't want to come. I pinched my clit to shut it up. I had more to see.

Luscious came, crying, "Eat my pussy eat me god yes baby yes eat me." She groaned and threw her head back in relief.

God, that was hot. I wanted someone to eat me out.

Strat held out his hand and said something to Luscious. She reached into the night table and pulled out a bottle of baby oil.

What are you doing, Stratford?

He poured it on Fucked. Down her back and in the crack of her ass. Then he massaged it inside.

"You ready?" he said, handing the bottle back to Luscious.

"Fuck me in the ass."

I swore the backs of my thighs tingled, and every nerve ending between my legs nearly exploded.

He pulled his dick out of her and moved it up between her ass cheeks.

He's going to do it.

Fucked's face tightened and she grimaced, eyes shut, teeth grinding, as Strat slowly but purposefully put his dick in her ass.

"How you doing, baby?" he asked.

"All the way," she said. "Take my ass."

I watched his dick disappear in her asshole, and I squeaked.

They didn't hear me.

I thought they didn't.

Luscious put her hand between Fucked's legs.

I didn't see the rest. I heard the squeaking bed, the shouts and moans, Strat barking when he came in her ass. My eyes were closed as I stroked myself to the most explosive climax of my young life.

As soon as it was done and the three of them were laughing and panting, I pulled my hand out of my panty hose. A line of pussy juice stretched between my second and third finger. I curled them into a fist and backed out of the closet.

Strat was right. I couldn't handle him.

FIFTEEN

1994

"Aa-*choo*." I was on my fourth or fifth sneeze.

Audio City kept a rust-painted trailer-slash-shipping container in the north corner of the back parking lot. Teddy had given us the padlock key, and when we opened the back doors, we found a wall of banker boxes stacked to the ceiling. They were ordered by date, with the older shit deeper in the back, except when they weren't. We had to look at every box and hope that the label was correct. We found Martin Wright's Opus 33 sampler master box pretty quickly, about a third of the way through. It was labeled with his name and the year. Drew put it on a low pile and wiggled off the top. The box had become misshapen from dampness. The smell of mildew got sharper with every pile we unearthed.

Contracts. Invoices. Master tapes. A pencil case.

"That's weird," I said.

Drew handed it over. Shiny orange vinyl marked with pen. I pulled the zipper open. It was empty inside but dusted with fine white powder. I held it open for Drew.

When he looked, he laughed. "Of course. We could probably open up all these boxes and sell coke out of the back of this container."

I zipped it closed and tossed it back in the box. "He's a cellist. I can't even imagine what the rest of these have in them. We taking the whole thing?"

"More likely than not." He jiggled the top back on.

We'd found what we came for, but we were both hesitating. He looked toward the back, where another ten feet of solid banker box stood. A thick wall of musical history.

"You're thinking what I'm thinking," I said flatly. The container was hot and oppressive, yet I didn't want to leave it. "We did come for the *Kentucky Killer* masters."

"You have to get back to the office."

"More likely than not."

"You can't stay here with me. Already you've been with the visiting attorney too long."

"And a law clerk can't call in sick for the rest of the day or anything."

"You'd have to make it up over the weekend." He put his hands on a high box and slid it down, then he put it in my outstretched arms. It said "Neil Young – 1990."

"Yeah. I hate working weekends." I put the box with the rest of the early nineties. "Maybe five minutes. Then I'll grab a taxi back to the office."

"You should run into the office and call. I don't want you to get in trouble on my account."

He had dust on the shoulders of his shirt, and he'd rolled up his sleeves, exposing the tattoos on his inner arms. I'd done a good job stripping the lawyer costume.

"Five minutes." I held out my arms for another box. "Ten. Honestly, I already told Dozer traffic might keep me here. And I have a family dinner tonight. So they don't expect me until tomorrow."

"Saturday."

"Come on, you know the drill. Six days a week, et cetera."

He slid another box off the top. I'd never heard of the artist. He put it gently in my arms, still holding it. "I'm glad you got your shit together."

"You too." I whispered it because I wasn't just returning a nicety. I was speaking a deep truth.

Seeing him again wasn't just a happy coincidence. He scared the shit out of me. I didn't do feelings. They didn't rule me. I did what I wanted, when I wanted, how I wanted. But I was scared, and fear made me uncomfortable.

I decided discomfort was all right though. I wanted to be around him.

His fingers grasped my elbows while he held the weight of the box. "I'm not together. I just have a law degree."

He wanted to tell me something, and I wanted to tell him something. We couldn't. We were different. We didn't know each other and we never had, but the pull was there. I wanted him to know me. I wanted to tell him my secrets. Not because of who we'd been, but because something about his puzzle pieces fit my puzzle pieces. I felt a clicking, like the snap of one piece into another.

I stepped back with the box, and his fingers brushed my arm as I pulled away.

That felt nice.

I turned away and put the box on the pile. Fear was uncomfortable, but the rainstorm between my legs wasn't much better.

SIXTEEN

1982 – BEFORE THE NIGHT OF THE QUAALUDE

I HAPPENED TO KNOW THAT MOST STARS, REAL STARS, DIDN'T GET mortgages. They paid cash or had their corporations loan them the money, so they paid interest to themselves. But Drew and Strat, and Gary to a lesser degree, were normal guys on the brink of becoming real rock celebrities.

We lived on chips and pretzel rods because we were young and skinny. Indy lounged on the blue velvet couch, plucking on his guitar, and Strat scratched his head over the papers laid out over the coffee table. I had my legs slung over the arm of a matching blue velvet chair.

"Can you start booking the studio in August?" I asked.

Indy strummed his twelve-string. Even without an amp, the sound was thicker than a six-string, and he got his fingers into the narrow spaces between them as if he'd been playing since he was seven.

"Yup," Strat said.

He didn't have a shirt on, and I tried not to look at him. Strat was so beautiful it hurt. The promise of sex had diminished since poker night. Part of me said to hell with them, and the other part just wanted to know why.

Indy, Gary, and Strat were tight. Real tight. They'd grown up together in Nashville. Only sons in their families. Graduated from their local suburban high school. Like cupcakes dropping out of the same pan. Different, but all from the same batter.

An empty pack of Marlboro Reds landed in my lap.

"We're out," Strat said.

"There's a carton in the fridge," I said.

His knees bounced, and the swirls of musical staffs buckled where his body folded. A snake coiled around his firearm, biting inside his wrist. Gary and Indy had the same snake tattoo. Gary had married young and fathered up quick, so he wasn't around unless there was music to be made.

"Tell me what that snake's about," I said. I wanted to get him a box of smokes, but I didn't want to do it because he'd told me to. He was a bossy jerk. Sexy and powerful, but jerky.

"It's about you getting a fresh pack."

I didn't move. Indy ran his pick over his twelve strings. I didn't think he was paying attention.

"You all got matching tattoos so you could be a fucking asshole? Shit, I can get one too."

"Why? When you're a bitch already?" Strat's words and tone didn't match. The words were cruel and divisive. The tone was warm and friendly. His face invited me to kiss it, as if he was the only one who would tolerate Margie-the-bitch instead of Cinnamon-the-groupie.

It took me a split second to put together a snappy retort, but Indy cut it off by putting down his guitar and standing. He shot Strat a dirty look and paced out of the room. Strat watched him.

Something was going on, and Strat was too cool a customer to tell me.

I bounced off the chair and followed the guitarist. The house was barely furnished or painted. The guys didn't have the money or time to do the fancy stuff. They had parties, but everyone sat on the floor and in folding chairs. I crossed to the south side of the house where I could see the pool. They'd had that cleaned and finished because to have a party, you needed a pool.

The kitchen had nothing of use in it. Paper plates and plastic forks. The gas was hooked up but was used to light cigarettes and heat spoons of white powder. The fridge had beer, vodka, cigarettes, and a china tea saucer with blue pills arranged around the center circle.

Indy stood in front of the fridge, pulling out a carton. He flipped his wrist, and the box spun midair, dropping on the island counter with a *slap*. Red-and-white packs swirled out. I grabbed one before it fell off.

"It's not your job to do what he tells you," I said.

"Can I ask you a question?" He took a pack for himself and cracked the plastic, letting it flutter to the floor without a second look. Both of them were fucking slobs.

"Sure."

"What do you want?"

"Life, liberty, and the pursuit of happiness?"

He didn't respond, verbally or otherwise. He just wedged out two cigarettes and held the pack to me. I took one.

"Stop the bullshit. You're past that." He took a zippo from his pocket and clacked it open. *"We're* past that."

He lit me. I blew out a stream as he tilted his head to light his own, cupping it as if we were in a hurricane instead of a kitchen. He was unselfconscious in that second, and I admired his face and shoulders.

"Be more specific then," I said.

He clattered a glass ashtray between us. "You don't wonder what's going on here?" He pointed his finger down and made a circle.

Here. I knew exactly what he was talking about, yet he was so vague I could have kept the game going on long enough for Strat to stroll in for his smokes. But I couldn't. I was as tired of this shit as he was. Both. Neither. All. None. The space between them was getting uncomfortably tight.

"You mean that you guys are always beeping me, and you keep me around but no one's fucking me?" I ask.

"There you go."

"Yeah. I wonder that."

I wondered it at night, when I was home alone with my hands under the sheets. When I felt inside myself, the edge of the unbroken membrane tight on my finger. When I imagined some composite of the two of them was on top of me. Or one or the other. Or they fought over me, and both won. I didn't know what or who I wanted, but my body got wet for both Sexy Strat and Sincere Indy. Not that I knew what to do about it. I was old for my age, but there was nothing like actual experience.

"Little Stratford and I, we don't fight over women."

"Okay."

"That's the deal."

"You're implying you're fighting over me," I said.

"Yeah."

"You know what that does for a girl's ego, right?"

I didn't actually believe him. That was the problem. I was cute as hell, but come on.

"When I needed Strat, he was there for me. My father was a drunk fuck." Indy rolled the ashes off the tip onto the amber glass of the ashtray. "Still is. I needed this house for a reason. The guest house in the back? It's for my mother. To get her out of there. So when I finally talk her into leaving him, she has somewhere to go where she feels safe. If I'm hotel to hotel on a bus, that's great, but it's like leaving her to rot. And the guy in there"—Indy jerked his thumb toward the living room, where his best friend was probably still looking over paperwork —"he gets it. I can't do any of this business shit without him. My head's not in it. He's giving up a chunk of his advance to make this house and studio happen."

"I'm glad, Indiana. Really. He's a great friend." I stamped out my cigarette. "What do you want out of me?"

His frustration was bigger than anything we said. His fingers curled, and his teeth gritted. He stepped forward and put his hands just under my chin, an inch from touching them, as if it was as close as he could get. As if his palms and my jaw were the north sides of two magnets.

"I'm fucking nuts about you," he growled, then leaned down, so his face was level with mine. He smelled like tobacco and cologne, with a hint of music and risk. How many times had I watched his fingers on a guitar and wished they were on me? "You have to make a move," he said more softly but with urgency. "You have to choose."

"You're not supposed to have feelings." I said it as if "supposed to" mattered at all.

Strat's voice came from the patio. "Dude." He took the length of the kitchen in three steps, snapped up a pack of cigarettes, then pointed at Indy with the same hand. "Watch it."

"Is he telling the truth?" I asked. "You have a deal about me?"

"A deal?" Strat asked, ripping the plastic off his pack. "I wouldn't call it a deal."

"What do you call it?" Indy asked. "A pledge?"

"Call it a fucking truce."

"You guys are both…"

Insane.

Annoying.

Beautiful.

Looking from one to the other, knowing I could have either, I couldn't pick an adjective, much less a man.

I'd never liked feelings, even before I consciously pushed them away. They made me feel like seven people living in the same skin. Now I had these two guys looking at me as if I was supposed to say something.

What did they want out of me?

One or the other?

What was normal about this? I hadn't kissed either one of them.

Or anyone.

I threw my hands up. "Fuck you both."

I walked out. I didn't want the car to get me. I wanted to walk this off. This bullshit. This pressure. I couldn't admit I was in over my head. I'd never admit a situation existed that I couldn't handle, especially not something as basic as two guys wanting me to choose between them.

I was warmed by the setting sun, but the air chilled my skin. Good. I wanted sensory distraction. Anything to make this shit run in the straight line.

What did you expect?

Nothing. I hadn't expected anything.

No, I'd expected them to choose. I'd suspected that one of them liked me, and the other one kept me around as a courtesy to the other, and I expected that the one who liked me was Indy. And that brought about the bigger question.

Which one did I want?

Both. Neither. Either. Some fourth choice.

"Hold up!"

I thought about not turning around. Just walking to the nearest cross street and calling the driver. I got three steps while deciding what to do. I heard the footsteps quicken behind me, and I turned to see Strat. He was wearing the jacket he kept by the door.

"You got dressed. Nice going."

"Hold up," he repeated, grabbing my elbow.

I yanked away. "You guys need to work it out and get back to me."

"No, baby. You need to wake up. That guy back there? You're not going to find anyone better in your life. You turn your back on him, and you're an idiot."

I was surprised. Here he was, the god of them all, lean and sharp with a voice like a fallen angel, advocating for his friend.

"Why do I feel like a pawn in some game you guys got going?" I asked.

"It's not a game."

"What if I want you?" I didn't mean to say I wanted him, even though I did. I didn't mean to imply I'd made a choice because I hadn't even known there was a choice to be made.

"Sorry," he said, narrowing one eye and shaking his head slightly. "I'm not that kinda guy." He started to walk away.

"I saw you," I called, and he stopped. "With two girls. Couple of days ago."

"Yeah?" He tilted his chin up as if I could swing at it if I wanted, he didn't care.

"It was hot."

"That shit's not for you, Cin. That's a couple of blues and boredom. Not your scene."

"How do you know?"

"You're too good for that shit. He's too good. This is fucked up, the whole thing. I don't know who you are or what planet you're from, but it's not mine. It's his." Without another word, he walked back up the hill, long hair flipping as he stepped into the wind.

I watched him turn into the gate, then I hit the little orange button on my beeper. If I went right home to change, I could make it to the Suffragette Society planning committee. I needed to get away from this weird fucking scene.

SEVENTEEN

1994

I'D STOPPED SNEEZING. EITHER WE HAD GOTTEN SO DEEP INTO THE TRAILER we hit ancient allergens I didn't react to, or my body just gave up.

Drew's arms and shirt front were covered with dust, and he had a war-paint-shaped grey streak across his jaw. It was getting late and his cheeks were getting a dark shadow. I felt as if we were no closer to the box for Bullets and Blood, and I was close to giving up. But every time I thought to mention it, I stopped myself. I enjoyed Drew. His connection to my life before. The pain we shared. Even the shared pain he didn't know about.

"I kept the business going, even after the band broke up," he said. "Gary wanted to find another lead, but I was done. I just wanted that house." He picked up a box. Looked at the label. The handwriting had changed an hour earlier. Someone must have gotten another job.

"Did your mom ever move in?"

"Yeah. After my dad died of liver failure."

I took the box from him. *Rick Springfield*. "Fuck him then."

Drew laughed. "Yeah. Fuck him."

I laid Rick's box on top of the others. We'd developed a quick system so we could get all the boxes back in place, but it would still be a big job. We were deep into the woods.

I went back in to meet him. I was going to say something like, "Hey, I think we gotta ditch this," but he stood over an open box, looking at the contents with silent reverence, and I knew. I stood next to him. It was late, and the trailer's fluorescents flickered blue.

"Is this it?" I said, standing next to him, staring at the box's contents.

Master tape boxes. Ampex. Four of them. A folder. An envelope. He put his hand on a box marked *Kentucky Killer*. They'd recorded it for Untitled Records at Audio City before I came into the picture.

"Nothing happened," he said, more to himself than me. "When we did this, we could have been anyone. But nothing happened."

"You're not the first."

"Remember his voice? The way he grumbled then sounded clear in one breath? He developed that here. Before that, he sounded like a girl all the time. See, he could imitate any voice perfectly. Any accent. He could repeat Russian back to a Russian perfectly and not understand a word of it. But he didn't want to sound like anyone else. So he was trying to create this new sound during that first session, and he sucked. So bad. All over the place. And we were so fucking high. Really high. Everything sounded like shit. The studio smelled like pot and donuts."

He took a break to smile into nothing. He was beautiful. Radiant.

"What changed?" I asked.

His eyes moved toward me, and the answer was in his intensity.

"After you left?"

"His voice. What changed his voice?"

"We were laughing at Gary. He was doing an imitation of his kid. She was two and said pickups instead of hiccups and fillops instead of flip flops. And…"

A smile spread across his face. He pinched the top of his nose between his thumb and first knuckle.

"Strat couldn't breathe. We thought he was still laughing but he was choking on a fucking donut." He took his hands away and looked at the ceiling. "Oh my God, what happened? I remember. I gave him the Heimlich. He spit up this wad of donut that looked like an oyster. We're laughing. I nearly broke his ribs and we were laughing. But his voice…his esophagus must have gotten shredded or something. Or his throat felt different and knew how to do it. He had a way of hearing that went right to his lungs. He did it once and never forgot it. Fucking gift."

He tilted his head back to the box and slid out a set of reels.

"You miss him. I'm sorry."

"I wish I could have stopped him."

I didn't expect him to put his arm around me, but he slid it over my back, up my spine, and over my shoulder, then he pulled me to him. I watched as he took the top off the smaller box. Inside was a clear plastic reel with brown magnetic tape. It didn't look magical, but to him it was, and we stood in silence for a minute as if praying to it. Then he put the top back on as if shutting out a thought.

His arm tightened around me until I had to loop my arm around his waist. From there, the rest was a dance. He turned. I turned with him. He bent down. I leaned up.

He smelled different. He was cologne and tweed. Sharp and clean.

I turned my head before our lips met, and though that movement came with the knowledge that I didn't know this man, I considered telling him what had happened to me.

EIGHTEEN

1982 – AFTER THE NIGHT OF THE QUAALUDE

I DIDN'T KNOW WHAT TO PACK, BUT I KNEW I HAD TO GO. I YANKED MY smallest Louis Vuitton suitcase from the back of my closet and slapped it open. I didn't know what to put in it, so it was first-grabbed-first-served.

Outside, the anniversary party was breaking up. Long black cars headed down the drive, just moving dots of white and red lights. I didn't have much time.

I had to get out of there.

Out of that house and to an abortion clinic. I'd come to terms with being disowned. I wasn't having this baby. Not now. Not scared in my room with a party going on downstairs. Not with my mother getting a hundred congratulations for being just as pregnant as I was. Not with the spanking I'd just gotten still stinging my ass.

He'd never done that before. Would he do it again?

I picked up the phone to beep... who? Lynn or Indy or even Strat, who was the last guy I'd beep unless I was desperate.

Which I was.

Desperate.

Time was slipping away, and the consequences of my stupidity were going to land like an anvil in a cartoon. I'd be flat. I didn't know what my parents were going to do, didn't know if my father had even had a chance to tell Mom anything. But I couldn't get the last half hour back. I'd spent it staring out the window, trying to sort my head out. Identifying feelings for what they were. Useless.

This is fear.

Ignore it.

This is shame.

Pat it on the head and send it away.

This is regret.

Kick it.

I tapped the headset on my upper lip. Lynn's family knew my family. All my friends were from the same circle. I'd be sent right back home.

E-Y-E-B-R-O-W

I dialed so fast my fingers slipped on the buttons, and I had to start over. *Ring. Ring.* Three beeps.

I put in my number. They wouldn't know it. I'd always called from the car phone or a phone booth. Never from home. They didn't know where I lived. Smartest thing I ever did on one hand, because it protected them. On the other hand, when the beep came through, he wouldn't know who it was from.

So I waited.

When the phone rang, I picked it up in a rush. "Strat?"

He was outdoors. I heard traffic whoosh and the sound of music far away. A party? A show?

"Cin? What's up?"

His voice was rock candy, sweet and rough, making a beeline to the part of my brain that didn't do any of the good thinking. He must have caught the remnants of panic in my voice, because he didn't sound like his usual casual self. And what was up? What could I tell him over the phone from my own house?

"I need you to meet me at Santa Monica and Vine at midnight. At the gas station."

"What's wrong, baby?"

"Don't call me that." As I was finishing my sentence, the doorknob to my room turned.

"What—?"

I hung up before I heard the rest of the question.

NINETEEN

1982 - THE NIGHT OF THE QUAALUDE

PALIHOOD WASN'T EVEN A WORD BEFORE MY FRIENDS GOT SNOBBY ABOUT the wrong side of Pacific Palisades. But it took Palihood House a week and a half to get a reputation, which Strat shrewdly made work in their favor.

Sound Brothers Studios. They trademarked it on a Tuesday and filed corporation papers by Friday. The sound boards weren't even set up yet, and they were already stealing business from Audio City.

Their parties were riddled with musicians. Some were at the height of their careers. They expected blowjobs. Hawk Bromberg could scream over classical guitar, which qualified him to get his dick wet within minutes of arrival. It was an entitlement, and that night, he got a look at me in my cutoff shorts and Marlboro miasma and decided he was entitled to me.

I clapped the heel of my denim wedge against the shag carpet and listened to him talk to me as if I wanted to fuck him. I didn't want to fuck him. I wanted Indy and Strat. I had the keen and unpleasant sense I'd lost them both by not choosing.

Hawk was telling me something about how record execs are all assholes and sellouts. Those cats weren't artists. They didn't understand the process (man) and those dudes are about money and not the music (man). Did I dig?

I did dig. His eyes were wet and his lips were dry, and I could dig it. I was as relaxed and happy as I ever got. Tiptoeing through fucking tulips.

"They got a bathroom in this place?" he asked.

"Yeah, sure. I'll show you."

I was like the lady of the house, even though I wasn't screwing either of the men who lived there. I was polite, I kept my pants on, and I kept my blood alcohol level low. I got to be in love with both of them without having to choose between them.

I wove through the crowd, Hawk behind me with his hand on my back, which I thought nothing of. He just didn't want to get separated. Indy saw me through the crowd, out of the corner of his eye while talking to Willie Sharp. Lynn winked at me when I passed her. We had to stop a few times to say hi to this one or that, but I was mindful of Hawk's needs and pulled away quickly to reach the quiet part of the house. Strat was in the kitchen, sitting on the counter with his feet on the island while two girls giggled at his side. One had her hand on his leg.

I told myself I wasn't jealous because jealous was a feeling—and I didn't have those. Also, Stratford Gilliam wasn't mine to get jealous over. That had been established.

The line for the bathroom was down the hall. I would have told him to just go pee in the bushes like all the other guys, but he'd said bathroom, not bushes. Maybe he had to do a sit-down session. Maybe he had a phobia.

"I'll take you to the bedroom suite," I said.

You're rolling your eyes.

I'm rolling my eyes too.

There are some mistakes you only make once because the stakes are so high, you don't know how to make them a second time. This was one of those mistakes.

I took him through the closet to the louvered doors. The bedroom had a futon and a night table from a thrift store. White blinds over the windows covered the view to the overgrown side driveway.

I pointed at the half-open door to the bathroom. It was done in pink marbelite and floral wallpaper. The house hadn't been redone since the 1960s, and the new owners were soon-to-be rock stars blowing their wad on converting half the building to a studio. No one had time for swanky bathrooms.

Hawk smiled at me and flipped his sunglasses to the top of his head. His eyes were red-rimmed and older than his years.

"It's over there." I pointed again and turned to walk back into the hall. I wanted to see what Strat was doing. It was a compulsion I didn't understand, but if he was going to fuck someone, I wanted to see it. See her. Or them. Just to make sure I'd completely lost him.

Hawk didn't go to the bathroom, and I was so lost in my own thoughts and intentions—again, you could see this coming a mile away—that when he grabbed my arm, I was annoyed, not scared.

"What?" I was still being polite, so I cut the sharpness out of my voice.

"You're really cute," he said, lightening his grip a tiny bit.

"Thanks."

"Sexy. Got a really smart mouth. I like that."

"You can let me go now."

He did. I was relieved about that for half a second because he closed the patio door.

I crossed my arms and leaned heavily on one foot. "Dude, I'm not watching you pee. Not my thing, all right?"

"What's your thing?" He stepped closer to me, tongue flicking his bottom lip the way it did when he played guitar. The girls loved that. They went nuts. But he wasn't my thing.

"My thing is getting a beer."

Oh, Jesus, that was what he was after? My thing. Indiana was my thing. Strat was my thing. Those two assholes made me feel so damn good and they barely even touched me.

"How do you like it?" His hand reached for me, and I curved away.

"I like it on Wednesdays. Today's Saturday. Sorry. My legs are closed for business."

I tried to get around him, but his hand shot out and gripped my jaw. He pressed his fingers together, and my mouth opened. I bent my knees trying to get away, but he held me up.

"Your mouth's open like a dick-shaped hole."

Did I mention he was a brilliant lyricist?

I grunted and pushed him away, and he slammed me between the wall and his body, his erection pressed against me. The first hard-on I'd ever felt. I squeaked.

He held two little blue capsules in front of my eyes. I tried to focus, but my entire face hurt from his grip.

"You're going to love this." He popped one capsule in his mouth and jammed the other one to the back of my throat. "Swallow."

I shook my head, trying to scream and failing. He pressed my jaw closed. I tried to breathe, letting the weight go from my legs, but he wrestled himself down with me. I slapped his face, and he took it with a snarl.

"You like it rough. I knew it. I could tell."

I couldn't move. We were crouched in a corner, his knees and the hand on my mouth leveraged against the wall. His face was slick with sweat, and his tongue kept licking a dry spot on his lips.

I *hmphed* against his hand. If I spit enough, maybe it would slide off of my face. Maybe someone in the party would hear me scream over the music. But the extra spit dissolved the gelatin capsule, and my mouth was flooded in bitter juice.

"Good girl," he said.

If I'm so good, why are you still holding me down?

I couldn't say that with his hand over my mouth. If I could move before the Quaaludes took effect, I could get to Strat or Indy and they'd protect me. But once they were in my blood, I'd be high and horny. I wouldn't be myself. I'd probably open my legs like it was Wednesday.

He could fuck any girl he wanted. That party was full of pussy for guys like him. Why me? I wanted to ask, but he still had his hand over my mouth. The other hand pulled my knees apart.

"You're such a pretty little thing. Think you're so tough. Everybody wants you. Did you know? We talk about it. How we want you and you don't give it up. Well, now we can talk about how I got you to give it up."

I breathed hard through my nose, my hands curled into his jacket. I didn't know how to get away as he kept saying things meant to flatter and arouse me.

"I see those nipples under your shirt. So tight. Baby, you're so sexy. You're gonna want it so bad in a few minutes. You're gonna beg for it. Don't fight it." He pushed his hand up the inside of my thigh, fingers reaching into my shorts, touching my skin. My actual pussy.

I kicked, and one of my denim wedges came off.

"See?" he said. "Not dipped in gold."

I squealed and squirmed anew, and he got the crotch of my shorts in his fist and pulled. I slid onto the carpet, and my shorts came down to mid-thigh. I opened my mouth to scream, but he shoved four fingers in it, blocking the sound.

There was a slap from somewhere, and I thought he'd hit me, but I was wrong. I could smell and hear the party, and suddenly Hawk was off me. I gulped for air. I pushed him away but only swung in the air. I was just completing an action I couldn't a second before.

"Hey, man!" Hawk shouted, but it was too late.

He bounced off the closet door, and Strat punched him in the face. The two girls from the kitchen were in the doorway. The one with a lipstick-smeared face ran away, and the other stood in shock and horror as Strat pulled his fist back again. The muscles of his back tensed and stretched, moving the musical staffs like undulating waves.

It landed with a crunch. The girl screamed and looked at me, which was when I realized my shorts and underwear were right above my knees.

"Tell him you wanted it!" the girl screeched from the doorway.

"What?"

"He's gonna kill him!" she shouted.

As if in answer, I heard a crack and the closet doors rattling. I tried to get up, and my hand landed on one of my denim wedges. I landed on my elbow.

I didn't feel anything. That was my normal state of being, but this particular numbness covered confusion and hurt. I got to my knees as Strat hit Hawk again.

The girl who had been in the doorway was pretty brave. She got between the two and tried to push Strat away. She definitely made it harder for him to get a clear shot, and the time she bought was enough to get Indy in the room.

It all happened so fast, with such complexity, that my shorts were still down. That's what stopped Indy in his tracks. Not the blood smeared across the Grammy-winner's face. Not his partner's pulled back fist. But me. My naked body.

Shit.

I pulled up the shorts.

Indy turned to Strat and put his hand on his shoulder and pushed, wedging himself between Strat and his punching bag.

"What's happening?" Indy said it so gently, it was a harmony of a hundred thousand heavenly tones.

"Fuck him." Strat spun to me, and Indy followed.

I was on my knees, butt-to-heels, arms crossed over my chest. "I'm fine."

"You are not fine." Strat's words were clipped.

With his eyes, Indy took me in, then his friend, then turned to Hawk, who was just getting his feet under him with the help of the girl with the smeared lipstick.

"Get out," Indy said, swinging his arm wide. "All of you. Out." Indy helped me up. He looked me in the eye. "What did he give you?"

"Lude."

He shook his head. "I wish Strat killed him."

Oh fuck. Was I going to cry?

For the love of fuck.

Stop it.

He put his hand on the back of my neck. The next thing he said was so gentle and strong, and his voice sounded like a layer of gravel floating on the deep blue sea.

"You're safe now."

The sea rose, moved forward, curved to bubbling white at the top, and dropped on me. I couldn't stop the stream of emotions any more than I could have used matchsticks to hold up a tidal wave.

———

FEELINGS. Joy. Lust, fear, gratitude surprise
arousalhatedisgustangerlovelovelove.

Lubricated with Quaalude and a narrowly avoided rape, they
crushed me into sentence fragments. I couldn't get anything out that
made sense. I was crying a flood of shit I'd held on to for months.
Maybe years. Maybe forever.

The room was empty except for Indy and me. Strat had taken
Hawk out by the collar. Indy had shouted *out* and closed the door
behind all the gawkers.

Indy took me by the chin and looked in my eyes. It was getting
dark, and I was covered in tears, but he saw enough to let my face go.
"They're dilating already."

I'm fine. I thought it but couldn't speak.

He picked me up from the shoulders and under the knees. My
other wedge fell off as he carried me

where are you taking me

to the futon, where he tried to set me down

I don't think so

but I held onto his neck and pulled him down until his face filled
my vision

see? I'm not crying anymore

and he put me down but stayed close. He looked reluctant, but his
pupils were like bowling balls. He was with me on whatever plane I
was on. The pupils didn't lie. He'd popped whatever I'd been fed, or
some other inhibition-reducing drug.

is it now? Make it now

He smelled like a man. My brain wasn't making sentences but

musk and sweat and chlorine from the pool

the scent alone drove a spike of desire between my legs so hard it
was almost painful. I arched my back from it, and my eyes fluttered
and my lips parted and

"It's the lude, Cin."

everything felt good while the potential for more good feeling
seemed like a limitless void I could fill right now, right there. I put my
hand between my legs and rubbed myself over my shorts because

oh God so good so good

all the void was inside me, and I had to fill it up. He had to fill it up. He had to. He was beautiful, and I loved him. The little voice inside my head that said that was the drugs talking. I knew that voice was on to something, but I didn't care.

I took Indy's hand and put it between my legs. I was so hot he sucked air between his teeth when his fingers landed there.

"I want you," I whispered, suddenly aware enough to put together three words.

"No, you don't. It's the—"

"The lude. I know. I can say what I feel."

I spread my legs and

are you really doing this?

moved his hand under the crotch, and his fingers pushed the rest of the way through, until he felt how wet I was.

"Holy—"

"Oh my—"

"—shit."

"—God!"

He ran his fingers along my seam, and the second time over my clit, I exploded, mouth open, silent, muscles tightening, knees bent.

It was the most powerful, yet unsatisfying orgasm I'd ever had. I needed more. I was empty. Full of emotions. Full of joy and lust and a swirling ambition, and in the vortex of those was a centripetal void shaped like his body.

He thought for a second / million years and put his lips on mine, opening his mouth, giving me his tongue.

This is it.

I trusted him. The weight of his body, the thrust of his hips pushing the shape of his dick to me. I grinded against him as if it was my job. I was going to come all over again, clawing at his shirt, pulling it over his head. The arousal was so deep I couldn't see past it.

"How old are you, Margie?"

"Eighteen." I pulled off my tank top. "Give or take." I wasn't in the habit of wearing a bra, and I didn't even have the shirt all the way off before I felt his teeth on my nipples.

"I'm twenty," he said.

"Nice to meet you."

He pulled my shorts and underpants off in one move and kneeled between my open legs. His bare chest had a dusting of brown hair and a tattoo of a treble clef with a bird over his heart. I reached for his waistband, but my arms weren't long enough.

He grabbed my wrists and put them over my head, pressing them to the wall, and kissed me. "I've wanted you for a long time."

"I know."

"I shouldn't," he said. "You're not straight."

"Neither are you."

"True, true."

He rolled off me and lay on his back. He hooked his thumbs in his shorts, picked up his butt, and pushed them off.

His dick.

My heart dropped to below my waist. I wanted that beautiful thing. Maybe I did have a dick-shaped hole because it went on fire at the sight of it. I straddled him as soon as the shorts were off.

It was the lude. I couldn't even think. He pushed me down, the length of him on the length of my seam, rubbing where I was wet. I slid up and down, a tease of the act itself.

"Ludes make you come so many times," he said. "So do it. Come now."

The words. I didn't know what words could do. The permission cast a shadow with the light of inhibition. I ran myself against him, clit to cock, and came again, fingers digging into his shoulders. I took a breath to wonder if I was doing it right. I looked to him for cues and knew I must be all right because he was biting his lower lip, pushing against me.

Sex was so good, and I was still a virgin.

"Yes," I said. "Let's go."

"You're so hot. So hot." He took his dick by the base and shifted it to me.

I positioned myself over him then

this is it, Margaret

pushed down. His face knotted with concern when

now or later but now is better

we hit resistance but

"Wait," he said.

I pushed down hard, and something ripped. Something hurt. I froze for a second with him buried inside me, surprised at the stretching pain at my opening and the snug fit inside.

"You didn't tell me." He breathed it, gritting his teeth not in anger but a need to keep his head on straight against the knowledge that his head wasn't his own.

I needed him. I couldn't pretend I was experienced or even competent. I'd seen what I'd seen and knew what I knew, but it wasn't enough. The Quaalude made me eager and optimistic, flooded with the feeling that nothing could go wrong.

"Show me what to do now," I said.

He took me by the back of the neck and pulled me over him until I was an inch from his 33rpm eyes and I could taste the whiskey on his breath.

"I don't want to hurt you."

"I'll already remember you forever. You gonna make it count or what?"

He stroked my cheek with his thumb. His words were hard, but his tone was a caress. "Are you sure you don't have a set of balls somewhere?"

"You should be the last one to ask that."

"You're really special, Margie. You don't need me. You don't need anyone. That's what I was afraid of all this time, that I'd end up inside you and I'd never see you again."

How many minutes had passed since Hawk made me swallow? Fifteen minutes? Twenty? The room had gone from deeply angled sun to a wash of blue, yet time was nothing.

I didn't understand any of what I was feeling. The unmotivated elation caused by the drug I'd been force-fed was a bucking stallion behind a wood fence. With every kick, the lock bent. Soon the fence was going to crash down in a splintered heap and I was going to promise him an eternity together for another and another and another orgasm.

"Do I move like this?" I shifted my hips in a circle and drove down until I felt a pressured pain deep inside and my clit rubbed against him.

He groaned. That was good. He took my hips and shifted me up then down again.

"Like that," he said, hands running up my waist to my tits. He pinched them, and a new shot of pleasure ran down my spine.

I moved up then down until he was deep in me.

"Push against me here." He took a hand off my tit to press the front of me against him, so my nub rubbed against his body.

I gasped.

"When you come up, angle yourself so you get it the whole way. Go."

I did what he said, letting my clit feel the length of him. "Oh, God. That's. Fuck."

We moved slowly, up and down, pressing deep, the friction and pressure bringing me close to a third orgasm.

"If I make you come on your first time—"

"Gold star. Fuck. God. Gold star it's so good."

"You have to come soon. Please come soon I'm so-close-no-I'm-there." His eyes closed, and his jaw got tight.

I thought the drug had made me feel good already. I thought it had aroused me more than normal, but I wasn't even halfway there. The bucking stallion of emotion broke through the gate, and I was blindsided by a rush of joy. I cried out from the chest-bursting, brain-exploding emotional high. My world washed bright yellow, and as I dropped down on his dick, deep and hard, my orgasm flooded orange, deep red, explosive, centered on cunt and mind, mixing at the heart of something so vivid I couldn't see who I was past it.

I dropped on top of him, barely breathing. His chest heaved under me.

"Gold star," I gasped. "I'll remember you forever."

He laughed. "You haven't even started to remember me."

TWENTY

1983

Strat died about six months after the last time I saw him, and I found out about it six months after that. I was in the library, catching up on schoolwork with a newfound ambition.

The library magazine rack was in front of my Debate Team materials, and I stopped when I saw Strat's music-strewn bare chest on it. I bit my lower lip. I'd been home a month and hadn't called him or Indy. I didn't want to explain about the baby or whose it was (or wasn't). I didn't want to revisit any of it. I was a new woman.

But he was majestic, and the photo was dark in a way that made it mysterious. I was curious.

TWENTY-ONE

1982 – THE MORNING AFTER THE NIGHT OF THE QUAALUDE

THE MORNING AFTER I'D HAD A QUAALUDE SHOVED DOWN MY THROAT, I woke up on the couch with a headache. Indy was already in the kitchen, slogging down a glass of water.

"Where'd you go last night?" he asked.

"Good morning to you too." The light tasted too yellow. The air hurt. The floor and sky were too loud.

"Here." He shook three aspirin out of the bottle into my palm. The circles were too perfect and too white, the big B etched into them too capitalized.

He filled a glass of water for me. I washed the pills down and drank the entire glass.

"Thank you," I said, handing the cup back.

He took it then took my wrist and pulled me toward him. Bone creaked on bone, but it didn't hurt. I let myself lean on him.

"I have to tell you something." He spoke into my ear and stroked my back. That didn't hurt either.

"Mmm."

"I want to take another crack at last night, but without the ludes."

"Mm-hmm."

"Or Strat."

I swallowed.

Jesus.

Last night.

I hadn't forgotten as much as I'd woken up feeling like I had Dengue fever or something. But, yeah. Last night had happened.

I leaned back until I could see his eyes. "I think I just need to sleep today."

"Are you okay to stay?"

I shook my brain. Yes. I was supposedly on a camping trip. I hated camping, but I'd had to lie.

Right? I had to wrap my life in lies.

"Indy, I have to tell you something. After I tell it to you, you're never going to want to see me again."

He did something that took my breath away. He leaned over and swept my feet from under me, getting his arm under my knees. "Never tell me. Never say it."

His lips tightened a little, and without saying a word, I was sure he knew.

"Are you sure?"

"Yes."

I help up my hand. "Open pledge."

He laughed, and though it was loud, it didn't hurt my head. "My hands are occupied. Assume it's up."

"Swear you don't want to know. Swear you're already okay with whatever I was going to say."

"I do. Close pledge."

I slung my arm around his neck, rested my head on his shoulder, and let him carry me to his room.

I had a life in the weeks that followed, but not much outside Drew. I helped with the studio, hammering and painting, getting boxes and running cables. I could have done that forever, lost the world and gained my soul.

But there wasn't a soul to be had.

TWENTY-TWO

1994

"Evidentiary privileges," Drew said, sliding a box up high.

I gave him the next one. It was after dark, but we were almost done. I'd spent the entire process watching the veins on his forearms, the way his biceps strained his shirt, the movement of his lips when he spoke.

"I just did that one," I complained.

"You don't get to stop until you can bill two-fifty an hour. Evidentiary privileges."

I picked up another box and brought it to him. They weren't heavy. "Attorney-client. Doctor-patient. Spousal. Priest-penitent."

He pushed the box to the topmost position in the pile, and I gave him the last one.

"Done." I slapped my hands together.

"Contracts, quick—"

"You can't go from evidence to contracts like—"

"Construction. Give me rescission remedies."

I put my hands on my hips. He was making it hard, and I loved it. "Builder in breach. No remedy. Owner in breach. Builder gets market value of work done."

He stepped toward me. "Land sale," he said in a velvety, non-demanding tone.

"Payments less land value."

He touched my elbows, pulling them toward him, so they weren't impatient angles on my hips. "Sale of goods."

I let my arms go around his waist. I wanted him right there, on a stack of boxes, breathing mildew and old air. I'd been with a few guys since Ireland, but I'd never felt so comfortable. Had he only been back in my life a day? Had it been just that morning when he knocked into me in the waiting room? I felt as though we'd picked up where we left off.

"Are we still in rescission?" I purred.

"You're really cute when you're buying time."

"The contract is canceled and either party can sue for breach."

I tilted my head up, breathing in his Drew / Indiana-ness. I could practically taste him.

"Not quite." He spoke in breaths, his lips grazing my face. "Non-conforming goods need to be established before cancellation and injunctive relief."

Our lips were going to touch on "injunctive." I was on my toes, leaning up, my hands feeling the tightness at his waist.

But when thunder ripped through the air and rain suddenly pattered on the windows, I jumped too far back for him to reach.

"Crap," I said.

Without a word, we scrambled to the two boxes we'd put outside. He put them into the trunk of his Audi rental, and we scrambled inside.

"Where are you staying?" I asked. "I mean... just..."

"They have me in a condo in Century City."

The firm had apartments for visiting clients. They must use them for visiting attorneys as well.

"That's across town from the office," I stated the obvious. For clients, Century City made sense. For an employee, it was stupid.

"I get the real Los Angeles experience, traffic and all." He started the car. "Where are you headed?"

"I live in Culver, but my car is downtown, and I have a family thing tonight in Malibu."

"That's a mess," he said.

"I can get a cab Downtown."

At rush hour, then I had to head west. I'd get to dinner with everyone after ten, and I wouldn't see my brother. He was having trouble at school, and though it wasn't my job to correct it, I was the only one he listened to.

Mostly, I didn't want to get a cab downtown. I wasn't done with Drew.

I spoke before I thought it out. "Are the partners taking you to dinner tonight?"

"That was last night."

"Come to dinner at my family's place then. You can ogle the size of it. We have a great cook, and I have seven siblings to play with. If you like kids, that is."

"I love kids."

Of course he did.

TWENTY-THREE

1982 – FIVE WEEKS AFTER THE NIGHT OF THE
QUAALUDE

THE PREGNANCY TEST WAS IN MY BAG, A BIG SQUARE LUMP ON A HEAVIER
lug of books. I didn't usually carry all my things. We usually bought a
separate set of textbooks for home, so all I had to carry were my
notebooks. But I had to hide that stupid test. The nannies and
housekeepers had started looking suspicious of my comings and
goings, and I never knew when one of them was going to innocently
(or not so innocently) slip or snoop.

The band had gone to Nashville to meet with a producer. Two
weeks. Perfect. I was supposed to get my period in that time.

But I didn't.

On the day the boys were set to return from Nashville, I got a beep
from the Palihood house number. I went up there with my backpack
and without a plan. I didn't know what to tell them. I couldn't even
take the test until the next morning, so what did I expect? What did I
want? Should I even tell them I was all of nine days late for my period?
I mean, so what? I'd been late before. My schedule was all screwed up.
What was the point of worrying them into thinking I was going to ask
them for anything besides the number of an abortion clinic?

The side door was unlocked, and I walked in unannounced as

always. I thought of putting my bag by the door, but the elephant in the room had been zipped into it, so I kept it slung over my shoulder.

I was about to walk into the kitchen because the beer and cigarettes were there, but I felt a vibration in the floor. Standing still, I listened. Birds. The freeway. The ticking of the clock. Men talking behind walls. And music.

I went to the side of the house I'd only seen down to the studs.

The studio was sheetrocked and painted. Floors down. Gold record and band photos hanging in the hall. The window to the isolation booth sealed and egg-carton-shaped soundproofing on the walls.

Strat stood in front of the mic, copper-gold hair tied at the base of his neck, unleashing a note I couldn't hear. The door to the adjacent engineering room was ajar. I peered inside. Indy sat at the control panel while a goateed guy I'd seen around untangled some wires.

"Dude," Indy said into the mic, looking at Strat through the window.

"Dude," Strat said into his own mic. "Really?"

"Warm as the girl in the middle," Indy replied joyfully.

My heart twisted once, sharply. I reprimanded myself. It was a metaphor, for Chrissakes. I told myself I didn't care. I had no feelings on the matter one way or the other. I liked Indy and he was fun, but only until he wasn't.

I didn't need to be special to him.

How much longer are you going to tell yourself that?

I opened the door before I could answer myself.

Indy turned. Then the engineer. The man whose baby I could have been carrying jutted his chin toward me in greeting then turned back to the egg-carton-lined room.

"Give me the next verse, Stratty." He jotted something in a notebook, not even looking at me when he said, "Close the door, Cin."

I closed it quietly and gently placed my bag on the couch behind the board as if a sleeping monster were inside it.

Strat wore a white T-shirt and black jeans with a chain that made a U from his front belt loop to his back pocket. It swayed with him as he sang. His voice was magic. It had been too long since I'd heard him.

"I need to talk to you guys," I said.

"I think we need to kill the preamp," Goatee said.

Indy moved a lever so slightly it could have been nothing at all. A low-level version of Strat's voice filled the room as he hummed to himself near the mic.

"No," Indy said, not even looking at me. "Make it work. We're not cheaping out on vocals."

"Sure, but..." a pentameter of technical terms I didn't understand followed.

Indy parried with another jumble of engineering nonsense, and Goatee thrust with his own as he counted a bunch of bills he'd pulled from his front pocket. My request for an audience had been denied apparently.

In the booth, Strat jotted notes, tapped his foot, and hummed verses.

I'd never felt like an outsider with them before, but I'd never seen them working either. It was a bad time. I'd come back after I did the test. Or not. But either way, I was doing what I had to with or without their permission.

I picked up my bag. When the handles got taut from the weight, I had to exert a little more energy to pull the whole thing up, and I wished I could lean on someone. I wished I hadn't always been so far removed, so cold, so non-demonstrative. I wished I was used to emotions because I was having them and I couldn't define them. They were moving through me so quickly I couldn't define them, much less cope with them.

I slung the bag over my shoulder and saw myself in the glass's reflection. I was translucent. Overlaid onto Strat's indifference.

I hated this. Needy. Childish. Whining. Grasping. Desperate. I saw myself from the outside. Out of control. Floundering. Hungry for validation. A few synonyms for "it's going to be all right" wouldn't cure me of the problem. Not even a little. So why did I want them so badly?

When I opened the door, Indy spun in his chair. "Didn't you want something?"

"It can wait."

I left, saving myself from myself. I could handle emptiness. I could handle solitude and isolation. This rush of neediness was going to kill me. If either one of them had started patting my head and saying he was going to help me/be there for me/whatever you want, baby, I would have told him to fuck off.

So when I heard Indy's voice behind me, I was tempted to just keep walking down the hall. But the needy part won. I turned to at least tell him, "No worries. I'm good." His posture, half in and half out of the engineering room, told me that would have been a welcome dismissal.

But I couldn't. That hot bubbling mess inside me wouldn't be silenced.

"You all right?" he asked.

I think I'm pregnant.

I'm sick in the morning.

"I'm fine. Welcome back."

"Thanks." He leaned back into the engineering room, and I took the opportunity to walk a few more steps down the hall, rescued and abandoned at the same time. "You coming back tonight?"

"Why?" I didn't turn around, keeping him at my back.

"Why?"

I didn't know how to answer. Didn't know how to move or think. I only knew how to blurt out my problems.

Something inside me feels like turned soil.

And I'm late.

And I knew how to shut myself up. I barely knew how to breathe without feeling the tension between breath and words.

"Yeah," I said. "Why?"

"Because we're back, and people are coming over. What's the problem, Cin?"

He wanted an honest fucking answer. He knew my fucking name, but he wouldn't even fucking use it.

Cin.

Cin, my ass. My fucking left tit. Taking my stupid stunt of a fake name and throwing it at me like a bucket of ice.

"You're working. We'll talk later."

If I'd been able to just walk away, things might have been different, but we were young. I had to offer him one chance to give me what I needed. But no, that wasn't to be. Indiana Andrew McCaffrey had to stake out his territory.

"Maybe." He waved at me dismissively, and with that, the potential to have my needs met went down the shitter.

"What do you mean maybe?"

"People come over, and it gets hard to talk. So it's cool."

I threw myself down the hall toward him, the weight of my bag pushing me forward, finger extended. "It's cool?"

He shrugged and looked back into the engineering room as if he was dying to get back in there. I'd never felt so alone in my entire life.

"Yeah."

"Don't you dare tell me you won't make the time to talk to me. I've never asked you for a goddamn thing, you—"

"That's fucking right." His tone was a cinderblock wall, and I shriveled inside even as I kept my own wall high and hard. "Look, if you're gonna turn crazy, you won't be the fucking first."

"What?"

"I'd be surprised. You didn't seem like the type. But before we 'talk,' I'm going to pull out what we said the night we met. Feelings aren't real, so we don't bother. Right? You're not getting crazy. Right?"

Crazy. The world and everyone in it was crazy. Because I had feelings. I didn't know what they were or who they were even for. Maybe I had feelings for a way of life that was about to end.

"Look," he said, rubbing his lower lip with his thumb. A little swipe of discomfort. "We're really busy right now. There's no time for this."

Whatever my feelings were, Indy wasn't going to help me sort them out, and fuck him. I didn't need him or his help. He didn't even know what to do with his own damned feelings.

"Better get back to work," I sneered.

I took my crazy and went down the hall without looking back.

Fuck him seven ways to Sunday.

Fuck both of them.

TWENTY-FOUR

1994

THE AUDI CUT THROUGH THE RAIN LIKE A MACHETE, AND DREW DROVE AS if he lived in a place where it rained more than two months out of the year. I felt safe. Again.

"I saw you in *Rolling Stone*," I said as if I was just trying to make conversation. I flipped through a black wallet of CDs. Doubtless a small fraction of what he had at home.

"That was such a joke."

"Too redemptive?"

"I did half the drugs they said I did."

"That's still a lot."

He smiled. "Yeah. There was plenty. It was the eighties. What can I tell you? I was a wreck. *Sound Brothers* was making a ton of money, and I was wrecked over Strat."

I slid a disc from the sleeve. *Kentucky Killer*. The album that turned me into a groupie and got them the deal that financed the studio. The one with the masters in the trunk of the car.

"I'm sorry about that," I said.

He shrugged and looked in the rearview before changing lanes as if he needed something to do with his hands and mind. "Yeah, thanks. I just... I didn't know. After you were gone, we started fighting. Bad shit. Fistfights. I don't know what was wrong with him. Or me. Maybe it was me. I think about it a lot. Was it all really my fault? I mean, he blamed me for letting you go. He said he wouldn't have. So I shut down. I didn't even want to look at him. I got very involved with the studio. He had the business head, and I kept just wanting to do shit my way."

"You made the studio a real success."

"I never felt like that without him. Feels like I'm treading water most days. He said the studio should be passive. It should run itself while we made music, and I just kept getting more and more involved in the day-to-day. I could barely show up to our own sessions, and Gary had a kid, so he was checked out. Strat just lost it. Went back to Nashville."

"It wasn't your fault."

"It wasn't. He had a bad heart. Congenital aortic valve something. If he knew, he might have decided to take too much heroin instead of amphetamines."

"Was that supposed to be funny?"

"Yeah."

"It was."

I'd mourned Strat's death. He'd died from only a slight overdose of uppers. His heart couldn't take it. I'd thought about that too deeply, reading too much into a heart that couldn't stand the exertion. I sought out details about his demise to avoid the sadness. I told myself he was a jerk, that he didn't matter, that he was in my distant past. But it did matter. A haze followed me, because he was indeed my past. I'd owned that life, that past, those stories that built me, and it all went and died while I wasn't looking.

"He cared about you," Drew said, glancing at me before he put his eyes back on the freeway. "We went to meet you on Santa Monica and Vine. And that neighborhood…" He shook his head. "Of all the corners to pick. We didn't know if you'd been dragged into an alley and murdered."

I shot out a laugh at how close to the truth he was. "I'm sorry I flaked."

"You didn't flake. We went to your house—"

I sat ramrod straight, eyes wide, adrenaline flooding my veins. "You did not."

"Did. We got a lawyer to find out where you lived, and we got ten different kinds of runaround. Then a guy with a gun and a badge opened the door. He flashed an order of protection and made threats. We stopped coming around."

"They never told me."

Of course they hadn't told me. I was indisposed and powerless.

"I'm sorry," I said, looking at my open hands as if I was trying to set the past free. "I just couldn't take it anymore. I..."

Deep breath.

This is important.

"I just needed to start over."

"I was an asshole to you," he said.

"You were fine. It was me. I was in over my head."

"We figured you weren't dead, so we just... well, we didn't forget. I let it go, but I didn't forget. Figured it was the way I'd talked to you the last time I saw you. Strat was pissed off. He was the one you called, and he insisted you sounded upset. I told him Cin didn't get upset. Cin is together. She never lets her feelings get the better of her. But he swore up and down. He paid a detective to watch the house until the day he died."

"Eight months after I flaked."

"You didn't flake."

"How do you know?"

"I know you. If you needed to get away from us, I get it. That's not flaking."

I made a breath of a laugh. He knew me. Sure. I always did what I said. If I said "meet me at Santa Monica and Vine," then I was going to get off the bus at Santa Monica and Vine with my smallest Louis Vuitton suitcase.

The rain pounded the windows, marbleizing them to opacity. The windshield wipers did nothing to break the stream. I gripped the edge of the leather seat because the red lights ahead of us got too big too fast.

Drew snapped the right blinker on to get off the freeway. It was miles too soon, but it was the only safe option.

He would have been a good father.

I covered my face with my hands. Did I steal that from him?

Note to self: "Not feeling" stuff doesn't mean you're not feeling it. Being unemotional and cold doesn't mean you don't have a pot full of emotions waiting to boil over. It means the heat hasn't been turned up enough, and the pot just hasn't been there long enough. It means the pot hasn't reached capacity.

But it will.

And your heart will beat so fast and hard you'll want to die. Your eyes will flush with tears, and your throat will close like a valve's been turned. Regret will fill you on a cellular level until the very tips of your fingers tingle with self-loathing.

"I'm sorry," I said.

He parked the car and shut it off. "You didn't make the rain. Just give it ten minutes."

"No. I'm sorry I didn't flake. I'm sorry I didn't tell you what happened. I'm sorry I left you there. I'm just sorry for everything."

"Margie? What's happening?"

He put his arms around me, but I pushed him away violently. Once I told him, he would be sorry he'd ever touched me.

"I was pregnant."

I could see the entire diameter of his blue eyes as he looked at me in surprise, jaw slack, expression otherwise empty. Was it surprise? Was I wrong in thinking he already knew? Or was that wishful thinking?

I swallowed putty, looked into the pouring rain, and ground my teeth until I could breathe enough to speak. "I was going to meet Strat and get an abortion because I didn't want you to talk me out of it, and I was so damn mad at you. After I called, I tried to get to you. I climbed out of my bedroom window, but my parents caught me in the driveway and sent me away."

He shook his head, eyes narrowed as if I'd just dropped a bomb in his brain and he had to make sense of the pieces.

"Do not pass Go," I continued. "Right to LAX. A fucking convent in

Ireland. I'm sorry. I'm so sorry. I should have called when I got back. But I was fucked in the head, and I couldn't deal."

He got a white handkerchief out of his pocket, and I snapped it away to wipe my eyes. It didn't even begin to do the job.

"Where's the baby?" he asked, pointing at the elephant in the room.

"Adopted."

"Where?"

"Jesus, Indiana! How the fuck should I know?"

He looked out his side window, probably so he wouldn't have to look at me.

"My parents came to Ireland during my last trimester to set up the adoption, so the baby's probably there."

Funny how I still thought of it as a baby. He or she had to be Jonathan's age already.

Drew looked back at me, all the surprise and distance gone.

"My mom was really pregnant too, which was just great because she hated me for getting knocked up at the same time. She had her baby in the hospital, then I had mine in the convent, and Dad just took it. I didn't even hear it cry. A week later, they took me home. Mom had post-partum. Dad acted like the whole thing had been a fun trip and the bad shit never happened. Which, you know, I'll admit that worked for me."

The shadows of the rain fell on the curves of his beautiful face in an overlay of wrinkles and age. Yet he looked twenty again, an overwhelmed artist on the verge of a life of riches and fame. A kid with nothing but mistakes to make. He'd seen a lot. He'd lost his best friend. Faced the death of his father and the surrender of his mother. He'd been strong for his family even when all the perks and goodies of a life in the spotlight tempted him away.

And I hadn't given him a thought.

I'd been so wrapped up in my own problems for eleven years that I hadn't thought about him or what he needed. Wasn't he as much a part of this as I was? Didn't he have the right to know? To claim what was his?

Well, there was that.

"It never occurred to me to find you. I was thinking about what was easy for me. And even when I saw you in the office… I was still thinking about myself. I'm sorry."

I didn't want him to speak, but that was the problem, wasn't it? I'd never wanted him to speak. I'd wanted him to go away. In the front seat of his rented Audi, with the rain pounding the glass, that changed. I wanted to know what he thought. I'd suffer the slings and arrows he threw at me if he'd just say what was on his mind.

He opened his mouth to speak, and I'd admit I flinched a little.

I wanted him to like me, to want me, to love Cin again and learn to love Margie. I should have felt like a little whiney bitch for that, but I didn't. I didn't have the energy to berate myself for wanting to be wanted.

"And…" he started, and I braced myself, "who were you thinking about when you invited me to a family dinner?"

It was crazy to laugh, but I did. I wasn't used to having this fucked up soup in my guts. I was off balance from the pendulum of emotion. Walking on a lubed-up balance beam. Of course I fell, but at least I fell on the side of laughter. If I cried another tear, I was going to have to wring out his hankie.

"Me!" I said. "I wanted to spend time with you again, and I was totally thinking of myself. But you look different. And we can call you Drew and never even talk about what happened. They won't know."

"But I'll know."

I stopped in the middle of a lateral mood swing. Just froze.

He wasn't talking about the baby and whatever right he had or didn't think he had to it. No. His face wasn't hurt or victimized. It was rigid with rage.

"Don't pretend it's about me," I said.

"Why not?"

"Just don't." I was almost screaming. I sounded crazy. Drunk on *feelings.*

"It's about you."

"No, it's—"

"Did anyone stand up for you? All this time? Has anyone—"

I couldn't hear another word. I yanked the door handle. It slipped with a deep clack. I grunted and pulled it again, even as Drew reached over to close the door.

Neither the downpour nor the unknown neighborhood slowed me down. I didn't care about my work shoes or the cold rain that soaked my white shirt. I was sodden before I got three steps away from the car.

I didn't expect him to pull away and leave me there. I figured I'd grab a cab or find a payphone while he stayed in the car and followed me. Because who would run out into this shitstorm? What normal person would leave the car running, the headlights on, and jump into a fucking monsoon to grab my arm?

"Let me—"

"Shut up!" he shouted, already soaked, hair flat on his scalp, eyelashes webbed with water. His shirt stuck to him, translucent enough to reveal the treble clef over his heart. "For once, shut that mouth and listen. I never forgot you. Never. Not a day went by in that studio without me thinking about you. How you think. How you talk. How you felt when I was inside you."

"You shut up! You forgot me, and you should have."

"I didn't."

"I was nothing." I jabbed my finger at him. "I was a short-term habit."

He continued as if I hadn't even spoken, water dripping from the angles of his face, along his cheekbones and jaw, meeting at his chin and falling in a constant silver line. "When Strat died, I couldn't save him. I wanted you there. I needed you. As soon as you called him that night, I should have had the balls to go right to your house and get you. Now that I know what happened, I know it was the biggest mistake of my life. I'll always regret it."

"Then you're a fool."

"I am."

In the urban dark of the street, with only the headlights of the Audi illuminating the diagonal sketch marks of rain, I didn't see him move, but I tasted rain warmed by the heat of his mouth. He was too fast and was kissing me before I knew what was happening.

He kissed my breath away.

He kissed my defenses to dust.

His lips dared me to feel nothing.

He turned me from solid to liquid.

One hand cupped my chin, and the other pulled me close from the back of my neck, and fuck him fuck him fuck him because I put my hands on his chest again, to his shoulders, his neck, the back of his head. My fingers dug into his wet hair. I felt close to him again, as I had all the years before, when I held his heart in my hands and someone else threw it away.

"I'm not abandoning you again," he said between kisses, running his face over my cheek like the water that spilled over it.

"Don't be stupid."

"Please. Let me earn this."

I pushed him away. His right eye was crystalline in the headlamps, bathed in light and rain.

"You've lost it, Indiana."

"I have. Slowly. Since I saw you this morning."

My teeth chattered as I looked him up and down. I didn't know what to make of him. I didn't know what to feel.

"I used you," I said, speaking the truth to myself as well as him. "I was looking for bad things to do, and you were there. I used you to fuck myself up."

"I know." His treble clef heaved under the wet fabric, a scar from a dream he'd once had. The footprint of a thing he'd loved and lost.

"I can see right through your shirt," I said. "It's indecent."

He pulled me to him, and we ran back to the car. He opened the door for me, and I leaned over inside and popped open the driver's door. It had barely closed behind him when he stretched across the seat and kissed me again. I put my hand on his wet chest, and he put his up my skirt. I let him, wrangling my body around his, opening my legs for his touch.

"That's not the rain," he said, sliding a finger inside me.

"God, no," I groaned. "It's you."

He drew his knuckles over my clit. "Look at me. Open your eyes and look at me."

His beard was soaked to dark brown, and droplets of water clung to his lashes. His hair stuck to his forehead.

"You're beautiful," I whispered. Then as he rubbed me again, I groaned, driving my hips forward. "Take me."

I reached between his legs and felt him. He sucked a breath through his teeth.

"We're not done." He yanked his belt open. "I'm going to fuck you right here, right now. But it's not the last time. Do you hear me?"

"Yes."

I would have promised him beachfront property in Nevada, especially after he took his dick out.

I wiggled out of my underwear while he reached into his wallet for a condom. Good man. No need to make the same mistake twice. I swung my leg over him, positioning him under me.

He pressed the head of his cock at my entrance with one hand, and with the other, he took my jaw. "This is not the last time. Say you understand."

"I do. I get it. I swear."

Was I lying? Maybe. But he was pressed against me, and every nerve ending between my legs vibrated for it.

"Say it."

"This is not the last time."

He pushed me down, entering me slowly.

"Look at me," he whispered again.

"You feel so good. It's hard to keep my eyes open."

"Feel it, Margie. Feel it."

He pushed me onto him, driving down to the root, every inch a reminder of what we'd had and what we were—a reimagined beginning with a past that ended us.

TWENTY-FIVE

1983 - AFTER IRELAND

EIGHTEEN, GIVE OR TAKE. MOSTLY TAKE. I COULD GET AWAY WITH A LOT
because I looked and sounded like an adult, and in a lot of ways, I was.
I didn't take shit, and I knew my own worth. That went a long way,
but I was still as greedy as a child. I craved experiences. New things.
Broken. Unraveled. Unwound. I could test the world. See what I could
make anew.

I would have been a sociopath if I hadn't learned to give a shit
when I got back from the cold stone convent in the old country. I'd
eaten the shit sandwich I'd been fed, shed my rock groupie skin, and I
acted like the oldest of eight.

The first time my mother put Jonathan into my arms, she looked
nervous. She hadn't wanted me to touch him for the first week.
Anyone else could, but not Margie. Maybe because he was the
precious only boy of her eight children, but she handed him over as if
I'd drop him or something. Or my irresponsible behavior would rub
off on him. I didn't take it personally.

Post-partum wasn't properly diagnosed back then, so she was
treated like a hysterical female, and I wasn't treated at all. I felt as if my
guts had been ripped out and replaced with sawdust. I didn't eat. I

didn't talk much. We were both in deep pain and acting as if nothing had ever gone awry.

Eventually I took Jonathan from the nurse while Mom napped. He was everything. He had a little tuft of red hair and crystal-blue eyes that would eventually turn green. I'd held just about all of my siblings, but there was something about Jonathan. And the smell. Baby smell wasn't new, but his was different. It was the scent of heaven and earth. He held my finger with his tiny hand, and it didn't feel as though he did it out of newborn reflex. His grip felt like a plea. A connection. A deal rubbed with the salt of the earth.

I was going to make it my business to be there for him. To make myself useful if not to my own child, then to the brother born at the same time. I pledged it to him.

I straightened out so quickly, my family got whiplash. I never spoke to Lynn or Yoni again. I didn't make friends, but I made a few appropriate acquaintances.

It wasn't even hard.

"Did you breastfeed any of us?" I asked as Mom popped the bottle from Jonathan's mouth.

He was three months old, and I was still acclimating to my new life. Or my old life, depending on how you looked at it. It was the life a normal person my age should be living, not the life of someone who'd been whisked away to a foreign country to be tutored by stiff Irish nuns so she could secretly give birth to a baby she would never hold.

"Heavens, no. Why would I do that?" Mom handed the baby to the nanny to burp.

Her name was Phyllis, and she held her arms out but looked at me. She and I had set a pattern. Mom left before the baby kicked up his milk, and as soon as she was gone, Phyllis handed him to me. I slung him over my shoulder and patted his back, pressing my cheek to him so I could get a whiff of his baby smell. Best in the world.

I knew I was making Jonathan a replacement for the baby they gave away, but I couldn't help it. He smelled so good.

"I'll protect you, little brother," I whispered then put his little hand up against my own as if swearing on a stack of Bibles. "I pledge it."

I studied and behaved. I was a model of good and right behavior. I won my parents' trust back by staying in, helping my sisters with their homework, and finding a deep well of ambition.

You might think I was somehow browbeaten into good behavior. That I resented it. That I lost a wild part of myself to meet the expectations of others.

But it didn't feel like that. I felt wonderful. I helped Carrie and Sheila with their homework while Dad was off doing business and Mom was in her room. I wiped chocolate off Fiona's hands when she found the baker's cocoa in the back of the cabinet and ate the whole box.

I did everything but feed Jonathan. Mom insisted on feeding Jonathan until he started walking, then she abdicated, like with everything else. She was a figurehead, and oddly, I was okay with that. I loved her arm's-length parenting because she gave me room to fill my days with something meaningful to me.

Daddy was not an affectionate person, but after he spanked me for getting knocked up, he was never closer than half a room away. Even when I struggled in the back of the limo on the way to my flight to Ireland, he left the manhandling to an Italian bodyguard. He watched from the seats across with his jacket in his lap.

"One day," he'd said as Franco held me down, "one day you'll see this is for your own good."

I stuck my middle finger out at him.

"Who's the father?" he asked. "Who did this to you?"

I got my hand from under Franco's arm and stuck up my other middle finger.

"I'm going to find out."

All he'd have to do was dig around the groupie scene and he'd know, but he was so far removed from it, and I'd kept it so far away from my regular life, that I had hope he'd leave Strat and Indiana alone.

He sat next to me during the whole flight over. Just him, and he scared me. He checked me into the convent and left. They sent letters Sister Maureen made me answer. I said nice things, but I was shut down until he and Mom showed up three months before the baby was due.

"You look good," Mom had said. She was farther along than I was.

I felt gross being next to her like that. "So do you. How do you feel?"

"Better than ever." She smiled and rested her hand on her belly. She loved being pregnant. I didn't know how she felt about raising children, but she loved carrying them. "We found a family for your baby. They live here. It's a good home."

"Thank you."

I hadn't fought that part of it. I didn't want to be a mother at that point, and I had no choice anyway. I was sure they'd done all the diligence in the world.

"Your friends miss you. They come by to let us know."

"Who came?"

She rattled off a few girls I knew from the Suffragette Society and Jenn from the Chess Strategy Club, then she looked at Dad.

He sat in the corner with an ankle crossed over his knee, staring at me. The movement of his head was barely perceptible, but he gave her a definite no to whatever she was asking. Mom was a lion when it came to everything except Dad. So she acted as though no one else had come, smiling as if our family dynamic was as normal as peas and carrots.

I went into labor three days early.

Dad was there when I gave birth, not Mom. I hadn't expected him to be in the room. I tried to ignore him, and once the pain got really bad, I could pretend he wasn't there. The midwife handed him the baby still slimy with goop.

"Is it a boy or a girl?" I'd asked, trying to catch my breath.

He didn't answer. No one answered. Sister Maura just shushed me, and Dad took it away. By the time I delivered the placenta, I knew they'd never tell me a thing.

I'd flown home alone. My sisters had greeted me like a long-lost child. Even my mother had been overcome with happiness when I walked in the door.

Dad seemed cautious. He treated me as if I were a museum artifact behind a velvet rope.

When I got into Wellesley, he congratulated me with a handshake and a genuine smile, but he never touched me again.

I had to hang up a lot of my family duties when I went to Stanford Law, but I was always there. I called teachers when Fiona didn't understand her homework, chewed out Father Alfonso when he fire-and-brimstoned Deirdre, and tried to keep Jonathan inside the lines as he proved, time after time, that he could push every boundary with a cocky smile.

By the time I was studying for my bar, I felt as if the eighties were behind me. My parents had done their best, and I had a good life ahead. Sometimes I even felt gratitude.

TWENTY-SIX

1982 – THE NIGHT OF THE QUAALUDE

I BECAME ENAMORED WITH THE TASTE AND FEEL OF HIS NIPPLES. THE ODD red hairs on his chest next to the brown ones. Quaaludes made you horny and happy, and we laughed a lot. I was getting ready to let him fuck me again. It hurt in a different way when he touched me. I was sore. But the internal pain had left.

I laid back and bent my knees, swinging them, smoking a cigarette. The cheap quilt under me felt good. Soft. Warm. Made for my skin.

And him. He was good. Very good. Kissing between my tits and down my belly. He was going to do to me the thing the girls had done with Strat. He was going to taste me. I tucked the cigarette between my teeth and put my fingers in his hair, spreading my legs for him.

When the door opened, I looked to see who came in but didn't move otherwise. I didn't jump or act ashamed, and neither did Indy.

"Dude," Strat said.

"Dude." Indy propped himself up on his elbows. "You get rid of Hawk?"

"Yeah. Party's over." Strat leaned down, plucked the cigarette from my lips, and put it between his own. He had no shirt, and the musical notations across his body curved around his nipples in a way I wanted to taste. "Said he gave you a blue lude. Looks about right."

"Yeah. Blue."

He blew out smoke.

I looked down at Indy, and he looked back up at me with a wicked smile.

"Naughty," I purred, reading his mind. I turned back to Strat and stretched, elongating my body, luxuriating in my nudity. I knew it was the drugs, and I didn't care. "You gonna give that back?"

He put the cigarette back in my mouth, peering down at me, through me, making some kind of calculation. I inhaled the delicious nicotine without touching the cigarette. Just sucking. Then I jutted my jaw at Strat. He took the butt from me and stamped it out in the ashtray on the floor.

"You're both luded," Strat said.

"Yup," Indy said then turned back to my belly.

I patted the mattress, staring at Strat. His long copper-red hair fell on each side of his face, and his jaw was rough with a day and a half of growth.

"Don't be a stranger," I said.

Strat glanced at Indy, who looked back at him intently and said, "You heard the woman."

The singer hesitated, looking from Indy to me. I'd never seen him hesitate before.

"I know you want to," Indy said. "One less thing to fight over."

In the seconds that passed, those two men who had grown up together and sacrificed for one another had a conversation without words. There had been a pledge, I knew that. But what was happening now?

I waited for what felt like hours but was probably breaths, and put one hand in Indy's hair while holding out the other to Strat. "Come on. It'll be fun."

I didn't think about the role reversal until years later, when I read about his death in *Rolling Stone*. Even then I smiled. I could practically taste him.

"Do what you want," Indy said. "But I'm eating this pussy right now."

And he did.

He opened my folds, exposing my clit. Even that felt good, but when he laid his tongue on it, my neck arched.

"Oh, *God!*"

As if called by my prayer, Strat leaned next to the bed and kissed me. Not just kissed. He put his tongue in my mouth and claimed me. Indy brought me to orgasm with his mouth while I cried out into Strat's, a conduit from man to man. I lay there gasping, wanting more.

"Yes," Indy said, kneeling.

Strat was over me, pants down, cock out. So fucking hard and straight, I had to reach for it.

"You sure, Cinny?"

"Yes." I stroked him. I didn't know what I was doing, but it couldn't have been that bad.

"I want your ass. I'll try to make it good for you."

"I know."

Indy pulled me up to my knees, and I kissed him.

"Say you're sure to me," he whispered. "It's a lot for your first time."

"I want it now."

Behind me, Strat kneeled on the mattress and stroked my body. I felt his erection on my lower back.

"What about you?" I asked Indy.

"Yeah. But, Cin. Margie. I'm crazy about you. This doesn't change that. I want to know you."

I didn't tell him I wasn't knowable because the ludes made me feel elated and open, with years ahead of me that were going to start with these two men, on this mattress—now.

"Okay."

He smiled then got me under the arms and threw me on my back. "This is gonna be fun."

I laughed, and the next minutes were spent in some kind of heaven. The two of them covered me with their mouths and hands. Strat put his fingers in my mouth and I sucked them, groaning for him while Indy sucked my nipples to exquisite pain.

"Wet, Cin. Make them wet."

I did, licking between his second and third finger.

Strat pulled them out. "Good. You ready?"

"Yes."

I didn't actually know what I was supposed to be ready for until he bent my knees so deeply, Indy had to get off my tits and my hips lifted off the mattress. I was completely exposed, and they looked at me. Both of them. Indy played with my cunt, and Strat rubbed my ass with his wet finger. They watched my face.

The finger pressed forward, and my asshole yielded. I felt it everywhere. My entire body reacted with a shudder, tightening around him at the same time as my clit engorged. Indy slid two fingers into my pussy and leaned down to kiss me. I took the kiss, ate it, moaned into it, even when Strat got two fingers in me, burying them inside.

"Going for three," Strat said a million miles away. "Relax."

I'd never been so relaxed in my life, but that third finger broke through the high with a shot of pain. I tightened.

Indy took his mouth off me and turned to Strat. "Lube, asshole."

Strat flicked his hand at the night table. The same one the girl with the luscious hips had opened. Indy opened the drawer and found the same bottle of baby oil. He handed it over.

Strat popped it open. "Open up."

I lifted my knees, and Indy leaned over me and spread me wide. Cold, dripping oil fell on me, and the two of them spread it around, inside, outside. Making sure I was slick and ready, talking like two lawyers making sure every t was crossed and i was dotted.

I felt like the center of the known universe, swirling a galaxy of pleasure between my legs.

"Guys," I groaned. "That's so nice. Please."

"She's ready," Strat said to his childhood friend. He scooted back until he was sitting against the wall, cock out like a flagpole.

Indy helped me up. "Okay, face me on your knees."

He maneuvered me until Strat was behind me and could get his hands on my waist.

"Open," Strat said. "Pull it open."

My ass cheeks were slick with oil, but I dug in and opened them as Strat put pressure on my hips to lower me.

"Slow," Indy said.

"Slow, baby," Strat said.

Indy kneeled in front of me, eyes still dilated black, biting his lower lip as I went down until I felt Strat's dick against my ass. It seemed no different than the last barrier I'd broken that night, so I pushed down.

"Slow." Indy demanded when he saw my face. "We have all night." It was different.

"Relax." Strat reached around and gently rubbed my clit.

Between the baby oil and my body's arousal, I was so wet that I didn't feel the least bit sore, and the pleasure relaxed me. My ass opened a little, and I bore down until the head was in. I stopped. Gasped.

"Can you take it?" Indy asked.

"Yes."

I got myself to a crouching position and lowered myself completely. Strat's cock went in all the way, and I continued down, down, stretching, taking every inch inside me. A sharp breath shot out of me with a crack of pain, but I didn't stop until he was rooted in my ass. Then I smiled, because I was stretched and full.

"So hot," Indy muttered, stroking his own cock.

I raised myself, feeling the sensation against the walls of muscle, then I went down again.

"That's it, baby," Strat said from behind me. "Take it. Take it hard."

"Indy?"

He took a deep breath and leaned forward. We shifted, realigned, and got my pussy right to take him. One hand on the wall behind us, one on my shoulder, he got his dick in.

It was a feeling I would never forget and one I never could repeat. All I had to do was stay still as they fucked me like two musicians with the same beat. One in, one out. Then both in at the same time.

Complete fullness. Stretched to my limit. Desired. Loved. Fucked endlessly everywhere. Both goddess and vessel.

"Touch yourself," Strat said. Neither of them had a free hand in the balancing act.

I jammed my fingers between Indy and me. I let out a long groan when I was close, but it was taking longer than I thought. It was too much. The pleasure wouldn't center where it needed to.

Indy put his nose astride mine and grunted into my cheek, exploding inside me.

I didn't think it was physically possible to feel any more pleasure or another slice of sensation, but I did, gathering vibrations between my fingers.

"Come, baby," Strat growled. "I want to feel it."

Indy pulled out and leaned back. His dick was slick with me and still stiff. "I got it."

He leaned down and flicked my clit with his tongue, then he sucked it hard as Strat pinched my nipples.

That was it.

As I screamed in pleasure, Strat pulled me down until he was deep inside me, and I came, ass pulsing around his cock.

"Ah, that's it," he groaned. "Fuck yes."

My orgasm was barely over when he pulled me up then slammed me down. Three, four, five times, then he came into me.

I leaned forward into Indy's arms, and we fell together, resting for fifteen minutes before we fell asleep in a heat of slick, euphoric flesh.

TWENTY-SEVEN

1994

"I THOUGHT YOU WERE GOING TO BE THE EASY ONE," I SAID. THE RAIN HAD lightened to dime-sized splats and rushing veins on the windshield. The inside of the car smelled of salt water and sticky tar.

"What's that supposed to mean?" Drew asked, brushing his fingers through his hair as he drove. It had loosened from its stiff lawyer-do and fell in his face the way it used to.

I'd settled into a mellow trust with him. The same zone as I'd fallen into eleven years earlier. "Strat was like an animal in a jungle. You were comfortable. Accessible."

"Accessible? That sounds a little demeaning."

"Just a little? Shit. When that flew out of my mouth, my subconscious was going in for the kill."

He smirked, elbow on the edge of the door, rubbing his thumb on his bottom lip. Had he done that before? At the Palihood house? I didn't remember. He seemed pensive and maybe a little hurt. I felt protective of him, even if I was the one I was protecting him from.

"If it's any comfort, you were the one who hurt me most." I put my hand on his knee. He put his hand over mine and squeezed my fingers together. "After that night, when it was just us, I really started to like you."

"That's no comfort whatsoever."

"Didn't think so."

The rain stopped as if God had flipped a switch. If it were daytime, the sun would have come out.

"I wasn't out to hurt you," he said. "I was out to not get hurt."

"Get off here." I pointed at the exit, holding my next thought until I knew he wasn't going to drift on the slick road. "You know you don't have a case. Your cellist."

"Yeah. I know."

"Make a left here. And you knew I was working in the LA office."

"Read it in the company newsletter. Fine print on the last page. New hires."

"Martin Wright? Does he really think he was ripped off?"

"Every couple of weeks. Especially when he doesn't take his meds."

I closed my eyes and took a deep breath. If I was being honest with myself, I'd known it all along. The case was built out of ice cubes and set on a frying pan. He didn't have to come to Los Angeles for it either. He could have managed the whole thing with faxes. So why? I'd gotten easier to find. There were a few hundred TV channels and libraries had computers now.

Fuck it. He was a goddamn lawyer. He could have found me anytime.

"What do you want?" I asked.

His Adam's apple bobbed down and back up with a deep swallow. He squeezed my fingers again. "Something came across my desk. I don't do international cases, but I was helping an associate, and I saw your name."

"House at the end of the block with the hedge and the gate. Where did you see my name?"

"It wasn't yours. Your family's." He pulled up to the gate and stopped. The gate was closed, and outside his window sat a wet keypad waiting for my code. He put the car in park and shifted to face me. "I didn't think it had anything to do with you. I came to LA to see if you'd thought of me at all. Strat had all the girls. I did all right, but…"

"But? What came across your desk?"

"You were different. Cin—sorry. Margie. I never stopped thinking about you. When I saw your name twice in a month, I had to do something. I should have sent an interoffice or something, but I didn't want to freak you out."

"This has been so much more successful."

"Did you think about me? All that time? The baby—"

"No."

He looked stricken. Or maybe confused. Then he tilted his head a little as if he didn't believe me. Fuck him. But gently and sweetly. Again.

"Between having the baby and crashing into you in the hall, I didn't think about you once."

"Not once?"

"When I read about Strat dying, of course. Sometimes 'Blue Valley' comes on the radio. But otherwise, no. Not really. You haven't even existed to me."

Behind him, a tiny light in the corner of the keypad went from orange to green. The camera was on. There was a disembodied *bleep* a second later.

"Enter my code, or security's going to be out here with an agenda." He rolled down the window.

"Sorry," I said. "I'm just telling it like it is."

"It's fine." He stuck his hand out the window. If his posture and tone were any indication, it wasn't fine. Not at all. "What's the code?"

"*My* code. We each have our own."

"Okay. What is it?" He looked at me expectantly, fingers poised an inch from the keypad.

I choked back a sob that nearly broke the speed barrier rushing up my throat. "Fifty-one-fifty."

I pressed my lips together to hold it all back and squeezed my eyes shut until little bursts of light exploded in the darkness.

"Just press it," I said, running my words together. "Just do it. I didn't forget you. I thought you didn't want me, and I was okay with that. I just took my lumps, but I think about you every day. Every time there's music anywhere. Jingles in commercials. Muzak in the elevator.

You're there, and sometimes you're mocking me and sometimes you're holding me, but you're there. I didn't want you to know that. Ever."

He squeezed my hand, flipped it on his knee, and put our palms together. I didn't open my eyes, just felt him there. Heard the clicks and beeps of the buttons. When I opened my eyes, the windshield was clear, but my vision was fogged.

Drew leaned over and ran his thumb under my eyes. I pushed him away and flipped out his hankie. He smiled. I sniffed as I wiped my face.

"It's okay," he said. "It was a crazy time. We were both kids. And you had a lot on your plate. I should have been there for you."

The gate creaked open. God, the last thing I wanted to deal with was my family.

"I don't know how I feel."

"But you feel something." He rolled up his window.

"Yeah." I sniffed as he pulled forward.

"That was all I wanted to hear. Because I'd hate to think fucking in the front seat of a rental was our last time together."

DREW PULLED around the circular drive and planted the Audi close to the front door. The stones were wet and glistening in the front lights. The fountain tinkled, and the spring flowers leaned against the direction of the wind. Cars lined up on each side of the drive, and the valet staff hung out under the eaves.

Harvey, our butler, ran out with a black umbrella and opened my door. "Good evening, Ms. Drazen. I'm afraid they started dinner without you."

"Thanks. It's fine."

"Watch your step."

"It's not raining anymore." I indicated the umbrella.

"There's mist."

I'd grown up with this type of attention and found it was always best to let people do their jobs the best way they knew how.

Drew stood by the trunk of the car, trying to not look off-put by the butler and the huge span of the umbrella. But I knew better. Whenever a regular person saw the Malibu house and the staff, they had to hide their reaction.

I was about to tell Harvey that the fountain sounded louder than usual when Drew looked down. Water was pouring from the trunk.

"Crap," I said, keeping it clean for Harvey. "Aren't these things waterproof?"

Drew didn't know how sensitive the butler was, so he cursed up a storm as he opened the trunk. Three inches of water sat at the bottom, soaking the bottoms of the banker's boxes.

"We'd better bring them in," I said then turned to Harvey. "Can you find us some dry boxes?"

"Indeed."

I took his umbrella, and he dashed inside.

"Well, now your case against Moxie Zee is really dead," I said.

"And to think I was betting my career on this fingerprinting technique."

He picked up a box from the bottom. I held my arms out, and he placed it on them.

"Let's go in the side door. Avoid everyone. This way."

Drew took the second box and closed the trunk. "I was looking forward to meeting your family."

"No, you weren't. Trust me."

I took him to the side of the house, through the five-car garage I rarely saw because we had a valet to move cars around, to the part of the house the eight of us hid out in. The real kitchen. Not the ones the caterers heated up stuff in, the one everyone could see. But the kitchen the cook and his staff used. We curled up in the pantries and cooled off in the walk-in fridge. Sheila had made herself an apprentice and actually learned to cook there.

"Margie!" Orry shouted with a thick French accent, a clump of his grey comb-over flying up as he jogged to me. It looked like a parking barrier going up and down. He'd been our family chef for as long as I could remember.

The kitchen was alive with shouts, flames, *chopchopchop* for the night's dinner.

"Hey." I turned my cheek to him so he could kiss it. "This is Drew. He…" I caught myself. I didn't want to send the staff buzzing. "He works with me."

"Nice to meet you. You're not putting those on my butcher's block."

"I thought your bed would—"

"I'll laugh in advance. You can go in the wine cellar. Shoo. Before Grady forgets the blue in black and blue. *Grady!*" Orry was off, shouting to his grill chef about the temperature of the sea bass. Dad was picky about his blacks and blues.

"You running a restaurant?" Drew asked, juggling the box to keep stuff from falling out the bottom.

"It's Good Friday. Day of fasting and woe followed by gorging on fish. Come on." I jerked my head toward a narrow, half-open door and headed for it. He followed.

The lights were already on, which was good because I didn't have a free hand. We walked carefully down the creaky wood stairs to the cold, dry cellar, into the tasting room. It had only a few racks of seasonal wines that the sommelier decided should be consumed sooner rather than later, clean glasses, a refrigerator for cheese, and a metal table with stools. I put my box on the table, and Drew put his next to mine.

"Feel like a drink?" I said.

"Actually, yes."

I picked up two glasses and a bottle at random while he unloaded a box, laying the masters out in a line. The labels had fallen off.

"Are they ruined?" I asked, popping the cork.

"Yes, but no one cares about Opus 33." He found a file and opened it. Half-wet contracts. Runny-inked documentation. A package of bowstrings. "They must put away anything left in the studio. I had no idea they even cleaned the place. Ever."

He slid the top off the second box. Deep breath. His history was soaked inside.

"Here." I handed him his wine and held mine up for a toast. "To… I don't know what."

"To Stratford Gilliam. May he rest in fucking peace."

We clinked glasses. I looked at him over the rim as I sipped the red nectar. It went right to my head.

Stratford Gilliam.

May he rest in peace.

TWENTY-EIGHT

1982 – THE NIGHT OF THE QUAALUDE

Six hours before I crawled out from under Indy, I'd been a drug-free virgin. But in the early morning hours after Hawk got kicked out of the house and I fulfilled a fantasy I didn't know I had, I had a sore asshole and a sour feeling in my bones. I'd seen Lynn's grouchy ass after she was luded, and I empathized for the first time.

The Palihood house was dead quiet and lit only by the moon through the windows. I padded to the kitchen naked, bold in my crankiness. I wasn't doing that blue shit again. Feeling scrambled and rancid afterward wasn't worth the happy hornies. I could get horny on my own, thank you. And happy was pure bullshit anyway.

At least that was done. I didn't have a single virgin part of my body anymore.

I filled a glass with water and slogged it. Refilled. Drank. Refilled. Drank more slowly.

The pool lights were on under the perfectly flat bean shape. Maybe a swim would cheer me up. It wasn't until I got to the screen door that I saw the orange pin of a lit cigarette making an arc from Strat's mouth to the side of the couch.

"I hear you, Cin."

"How did you know it wasn't Indy?" I asked from behind the screen.

He arched his back and neck until he could see me. "He walks like a fucking elephant." He lay flat again. "You're naked."

I opened the door. "Yeah. My ass hurts."

"Bad?" He looked over the pool and dragged on his cigarette.

I took his pack off the table. "No. Just irritated." I sat and lit one.

"That can't happen again."

"Did I blow your mind?" I dropped his lighter on the table with a *clickclack*.

"That guy's like my brother. He cares about you. Really cares about you."

He had a towel over his waist, but the rest of him was bare. The musical staffs on his chest rippled. I hadn't tasted them. I hadn't done much of anything but received him. I felt cheated.

"And what about you?" I said.

"He and I have a deal."

"Oh yeah?"

"You're his."

"You flip a coin or something?" I said it without breathing, half joking, half too far on the wrong side of a lude to be anything but negative. I emptied my lungs, letting the nicotine rush make my hands tingle.

"Played a few hands."

"You serious?"

"He pulled a straight."

I leaned back on the couch. "You could have asked me."

He stretched his arm out to the ashtray. The muscles were given definition by the tattoo. What a gorgeous thing he was.

"Nah." He stamped his butt out with a flutter of orange embers. "We didn't want to fight."

"How do you explain your dick in my ass then?"

He shrugged. "One night."

I leaned on the arm of the outdoor couch and stuck my cigarette in my teeth. Fuck them. I wasn't a baseball card to be traded around. "Fuck you guys."

"You did." He got up and stood over me. The towel was gone, and his cock stood straight and hard between us.

"One night," I said. "Did you agree ahead of time?"

"If the situation came up, yeah. That was part of the agreement."

"Fuck you twice." My voice dripped with honey. I hadn't intended it, but the sore feeling in my ass had abated, and the poor judgment of my cunt went live.

We regarded each other, above and below, half-drugged and young, looking for stupid excuses to do stupid things.

"You might get your chance. It's still night."

"For a few hours. Then, yeah, I'm his."

He touched the inside of my knee. No pressure, just a touch. "Open your legs, Cin."

I pulled my knees apart slowly. He kneeled on the couch and spread them, tilting forward to kiss me. He kissed like a man. As if he was marking territory with his tongue. I wrapped my arms around him.

Just once, I told myself. Just the once, I could trade them the way they'd traded me.

I let Strat take me. There was no other way to describe the way he held me down, pushed on my clit until I was close, then slowed down to keep me on the edge, kissing me tenderly right before I came and he exploded inside me.

Only then was I satisfied.

TWENTY-NINE

1994

THE WINE WAS GOING TO MY HEAD. IT SEEMED AS IF DREW PULLED THE Bullets and Blood masters out with special reverence. I'd laid a towel out to soak up the water, and he placed the boxes on them gently.

I was going to have to tell him that the baby that had split us apart might not have been his. We'd been careless with our bodies then.

But when I saw him pull an envelope out of the box and I felt the bond that he'd had with his friend, I felt a real pull to tell him and a stronger pull to just bury it forever. Why bring it up? To what end would I risk hurting him with his friend's betrayal? I didn't fool myself into thinking I meant so much to him that my betrayal was equal to Strat's. The only thing I risked by telling the truth was damaging his memory of his best friend. I didn't want to turn that bond into a lie.

I was a coward. I owed him the truth.

"Drew. Indy… I—"

A young man's voice came from the top of the stairs, yelling in French. Orry shouted back. The door slammed. Feet scuffled along the wood, and a boy barreled into the room, shirt half untucked, ginger hair askew.

"What the—?"

"Jonathan," I said, noticing his frozen, terrified features.

"Margie. When did you get here?"

"This is Drew. He works with me."

They nodded at each other, practically grunting like apes. Little Jon was a man already, too tough for his own good.

"What's wrong?" I said. "You look like you just saw a ghost."

He swallowed. The kids came to the wine cellar when they needed to get away from the bullshit of the huge house. Sometimes to hide. Sometimes to sulk. I knew where to find Fiona during report cards' week, Leanne every twenty-eight days, Carrie whenever Dad was home.

"I'm all right." He started back upstairs.

Drew thumbed through an envelope.

"Wait," I said to Jonathan. "Try this."

I handed him my glass of wine. He was in fifth grade, but he was allowed to sip, and I wasn't ready to let him go back up to whatever was bothering him. He took the glass. Treating him like a grown-up worked, and he seemed calmer when he handed it back.

"It tastes fine," he said.

"Come in the storage room with me for a sec. I want to talk to you. Drew, do you mind?"

"It's fine." He looked up from a wet, runny note for a second and locked eyes on Jonathan.

I thought nothing of it. Not Indy's slack jaw or the way his eyes went a millimeter wider. I just pulled my brother into the inner chamber and sat him on a case of ancient vintage.

"What's wrong?" I whispered.

"Nothing."

"Jon."

"What?"

"Let's be efficient with our time. You're going to tell me. Might as well get it over with."

He pursed his lips, crossed his arms, jutted his jaw. I leaned on a low shelf and waited.

"You can't tell," he said.

"You know I won't."

"You need to really swear."

Jesus. To be in grade school again. To make the big little and the little big. To think you had control when you didn't and adulthood was just childhood layered over with manners and privilege. When lies seemed like easy answers to uncomfortable truths.

"All right," I said. "Let's do this. Let's take a pledge. We hold our hands up and swear anything we say is secret. When we put our hands down, we lock it closed and go back to normal."

He thought about it for a second, then with a short nod he said, "Okay."

"But there's another thing. We cannot lie. Not when the pledge is open."

"Fine."

I held my hand up, and he mirrored me.

"Pledge open," I said. "What happened?"

He took a deep breath and looked at the corner of the room. "Kerry and I were outside when it started raining, and we got stuck in the pool house."

Kerry was the daughter of one of Dad's associates. She was a year older than Jonathan and pretty smart.

"Go on."

"We started doing stuff."

Jesus Christ, use a condom.

He's not ready.

He glanced at me, tearing his attention from the corner for half a second, then planting it back. I didn't answer the glance or egg him on. I knew what was coming, more or less. Mom and Dad weren't very forthcoming about sex with the kids, thinking my early knowledge led to my early downfall.

He spit out the next line. "I think she broke it."

"Broke what?" I knew the answer, but my mouth ran before my brain caught up.

He wouldn't say but pointed at his crotch with both hands.

Do. Not. Laugh. Do. Not. Laugh.

"What makes you think it's broken?"

"She touched it. It got… it got weird then…" He looked at the ceiling.

I had to finish for him. Putting him on the spot wasn't working. He was in fifth grade, and though he'd started getting big, he was still a child.

"It got hard then felt tickly then white stuff came out?"

His eyes went wide. "Yes."

"It's not broken."

"How do you know?"

"Aren't you and your friends talking about this amongst yourselves? Girls? Sex?"

"I didn't have sex with her!"

I waved it away. "I know. Okay. I'm just going to assure you, it's not broken. You're fine. But tomorrow, let me take you to lunch and I can tell you why. All right?"

He took a deep breath of reprieve. "Yes."

"Until then, keep away from Kerry O'Neill."

"All right."

"Tuck your shirt in."

He did it, jamming the shirttails into his waistband as if Daddy was in the other room. He took a step toward the doorway.

"Jon. Stop."

"What?"

I put my hand up then down. "Close pledge."

"Close pledge."

We went back into the tasting room. Drew leaned on one of the benches, hair flopped over his face like a rock star, shirt dry like a lawyer, with a manila envelope in one hand and a white rectangle in the other. He looked at it then Jonathan.

"What?" I said.

Drew just shook his head as Jonathan bolted up the stairs with barely a wave.

"Strat mailed stuff to Audio City. I don't know why." He put down the manila envelope. Old stamps. Crap handwriting. He laid out the contents. "A note for me, and pictures of when we were kids. He was... he was so hurt. He couldn't show it because you were mine. But..." His voice drifted to silence.

"Drew?"

"When you left, he acted like it was nothing." He pushed the runny letter toward me.

I couldn't see much but my name, my real one, and phrases... *she was yours but... never wanted this... like a brother to me...*

"I knew about you and Strat. He told me in pledge," Drew said.

"In Nashville."

"Yes, but I—"

"That's why you were such a dick when you got back."

"I regret that."

"I deserved it."

He looked at the picture, shook it, pressed his lips together, and gave it to me as if it was the hardest thing he'd had to do in his life. I took it but kept my eyes on his. I had no idea what he could look so distressed about.

"What is it?" I asked.

"Just tell me what you see."

I looked at the picture.

Two boys about twelve years old, arms over shoulders, a suburban sidewalk stretching behind them. I recognized young Drew McCaffrey by the flop of his hair and the shape of his eyes.

And the other boy? I recognized him. I knew who he was. He was Stratford Gilliam, a kid with only a few more years to live, but that wasn't the kid I recognized. He looked like the three-dimensional kid had been transported from my house onto a two-dimensional surface.

I swallowed. None of this computed.

"It's a coincidence," I whispered.

Not unless Stratford Gilliam fucked your mother.

I couldn't do the math in my head.

Twelve-year-old Strat was a clone of my brother, Jonathan.

No. The other way around. Jonathan looked exactly like Strat.

I looked up from the picture. Drew stood above me, confident and together as if he knew something I didn't.

"Your family name came up in the Dublin office. Your baby's adoptive family is suing your father for breach of contract."

"I don't understand."

Don't you?

"They never had your real name. I presume it was to protect you. It took that long to find him."

"There would be two babies."

"We checked the public records. Your mother's eighth child was stillborn."

I took a step back, covering my mouth so I wouldn't scream. The calculus suddenly made sense. A sick fucking sense.

"I didn't know what I'd find here," Drew said. "But I didn't think this. I thought it was simpler. Not until I saw—"

I didn't hear anything else. Just my little brother's—

son's

—voice in my head as he spoke French with a perfect ear for tone. As I saw the lines of his body superimposed on Strat's—

his father's

—and the face which was unmistakably from the same gene pool.

I did the math with my senses. Heard the voice and saw the face. Smelled the new baby smell that seemed of my own body and knew, just knew, he was mine.

"I can't." My breathing got choppy. I was shaking.

Drew grabbed my wrists. "Margie."

"I can't tell him."

"You don't—"

"Oh, God."

"*Shh.* It's going to be all right."

He tried to gather me in his arms, but I pushed him away and I ran. I flung myself up the narrow stairs into the chaos of the kitchen. How many people were in the ballroom? Fifty? A hundred?

"Margie?" Orry asked, a piece of raw fish in his thick hands.

Everyone in the kitchen was looking at me, sauté pans frozen mid-agitation, break knives up, colanders dripping starch-thickened water into drains.

I heard Drew clop a couple of elephantine steps up from the cellar.

Cornered.

Your brother is your son.

I didn't even know what I was running from. I was a spider in a tub. I couldn't get up the sides. Couldn't get away, even on eight legs, from the glass bowl coming down.

"Margie?" Drew called.

A second had passed, and in that second, every feeling I was supposed to have in the past few decades dropped on me. I felt my shell break under the pressure as my insides got bigger than my outside, slowly giving way to hairline fractures. I couldn't do this here. I couldn't break with the kitchen staff staring and Drew climbing the stairs.

I ran out of the kitchen, following the map of my childhood.

Through the morning room, the library, the kids' playroom, and the breakfast room to the back deck. I threw myself down the wooden stairs to the beach where I almost collapsed on the cold sand. I got my feet under me and ran toward the wall of sound and water. The horizon. The darkness on the outskirts of the lights of civilization, where the water flattened the land.

I fell with my knees in the water and the rush of the tide in my ears. I stayed there and wept. I wept for what I'd done to sweet Drew. For acting as though Strat had no feelings. For my son who I was never, ever going to hurt by telling. For my misguided parents who had lost a baby and taken mine into their hearts.

The lip of the next wave reached me, soaking my calves and the top of my head. I wasn't mature enough for any of this. No one was. But I didn't cry for myself. I cried for everyone I'd hurt.

The water got louder than I thought possible, blowing at my ears so much that my lungs felt the pain, and the earth went out from under me. I spun in space, clawed the wet sand, tasted rough salt and foam. The sea wrapped around me like a vise, yanking me against it, pulling me to the air, where Drew had me in his arms.

He put me on the sand, and his voice became the sense inside the ocean's chaos. "Margie?"

He was cloudy and grey. My eyes couldn't focus. My chest couldn't hold my lungs, and I coughed. Sucked in a breath. Was I drowning or crying so hard I couldn't breathe?

His hands on my cheeks.

"Talk to me," he said.

"I don't know what to do."

"I know."

"I want to claw my heart out of my chest."

I realized I was gripping the front of my shirt as if I meant to literally claw through skin and bone.

He took my hands, leaning over. "It's all right. Margie. Can you hear me?"

"Yes. I'm sorry. I was young. I put you in a terrible position."

"No. Don't you dare. Don't you ever blame yourself. Ever. I was the one to blame. I should have known better."

"I never admitted I loved you."

"Neither did I."

"I was scared."

"I don't want you to be scared. Not ever again."

I reached for him, and he held me on the beach. I was cold, but I wasn't. I was hurt, but I was healed. I was alone, but no, I wasn't. Not at all. I pressed my face to his neck and let him encircle me so tightly I thought he'd break me.

"I'm so sorry," he said.

I couldn't see his face in the embrace, but mine was scrunched with the push of sobs.

"I didn't tell you what I knew the minute I came to LA. I didn't know what I was walking into. I was afraid you'd shut down. I was afraid I'd still have feelings for you. And I do, Margie. I do."

I nodded.

"I know you just got blindsided tonight."

I choked out a laugh. We loosened our hold on each other until we were face to face. I brushed the sand from his cheek.

"Blindsided," I said. "Good word."

"I had no idea. I want you to know. I had pieces but didn't know the puzzle."

I nodded. "No one would believe the truth."

"What should we do?"

I knew he'd asked a broad question. He was talking about us, the world, the firm, my family, our past, our future. But I couldn't think past the tide of feelings. They may have gone back out to sea for the moment, but they'd be back. If I knew anything about emotions (and I didn't know a damn thing but this), they'd be back.

"Let's slip around the side and go to my place," I said.

"You've got a crappy track record of sneaking out of here."

"This time I have you with me."

He smiled and shifted a strand of hair from my face. "You do. You have me."

He kissed me with the passion of a promise. We stood and walked off the beach together.

THIRTY

1995

Kentucky.
More than halfway to New York.

I DIDN'T DIG GRAVEYARD SCENES OR TALKING TO GUYS WHO WEREN'T
really there. I didn't understand putting flowers down for a dead guy
who hadn't seemed to like them when he was alive. The young
groupie hated downer shit, and the jaded law clerk—no, lawyer—
didn't have the time.

And there was still the whole issue of feelings.

I told Drew when he opened the car door for me, "Doing
something for the express purpose of making yourself feel sad is fake.
The thing is fake, and the feeling is fake."

"The lawyer doth protest too much."

He held his hand out for me, and I took it, letting him pull me out
of the car. I didn't need help, but he liked helping. Didn't take me long
to figure that out, and who was I to refuse him his pleasure?

He'd given me too much in the past six months. He'd stood by my
decision to let Jonathan stay my brother, to let my parents think I knew
nothing about their loss. Though my father had masterminded the

entire fairytale, his scheme to keep his grandson in the family was meant to protect my mother.

I couldn't refuse my father that, but mostly, I remained silent to protect my son, Jonathan. I'd die with that secret. I'd sew my own mouth shut before letting it pass my lips.

The only other person who knew was the man holding the flowers in the parking lot of a Kentucky cemetery.

———

THE LITTLE NOTES all over my house were long gone.

"I'll end you," I whispered to Drew one night, wrapped in sheets and darkness, my voice shredded from crying his name too many times.

He kissed me. I could taste my pussy on his face.

"You always threaten me before you fall asleep."

That was when the worry swept in. The worry that my family would be upended. That my brother would lose his mind. That my mother would go off the deep end. And my father, ever unpredictable, would hurt the messenger if the messenger wasn't me.

"You're the only one who knows." I touched his face in the dark. "I trust you. But I will end you."

He pinned my hands over my head. "I'll end you too."

We'd had this discussion a hundred times. In bed, over dinner, in earnestness and in jest. "I'll end you" wasn't a threat. Not really. It was a way of telling him how deeply I trusted him.

"Not if I end you first," I said, pushing my hips against him.

"How are you going to do that, Cinny-sin-sin?"

"Test me."

He let my hands go and wrapped himself around me. "Never."

"Smart guy."

He didn't move and barely paused. "Come back to New York with me. I can't live without you. The city feels like a tomb."

I sighed. We'd been long distance for too many months. "Speaking of testing... I'm sitting for the bar in August."

He got up on his elbows, eyes wide and blue, shocked and delighted. I'd waited to tell him so I could drink in that expression.

"The New York State Bar?" he asked.

"No, asshole, the old man's bar on Seventh and B. Of course the New York State Bar."

He was off me like a shot, sitting straight, suddenly awake. "You have to study. Have you been studying? We have to get on it."

"Relax. It's easy."

He scooped up my entire body and covered it in happy kisses.

I hadn't forgotten what had brought us together, but it was all drowned out by a feeling of safety and joy. I had to admit, as feelings went, those were pretty good.

———

THE PARKING LOT of the Kentucky cemetery was empty but for a few beat-up trucks. Our shiny black Audi was the brightest object for miles. Drew had parked it in the middle of the lot, away from the wooden poles poking out from the earth at odd angles. The rusted chains between them were shaped like kudzu-wrapped smiles, one after the other on the edge of the rectangle—smile, smile, smile. The sky was the color of the asphalt, and the freight train clacking at the river's edge lumbered slowly, as if showing off its eternal length like a peacock showing off his blues.

I'd passed the New York bar six months after passing the California bar. I threatened to rack up forty-eight more states for fun, and Drew threatened to tie me to the bed.

That had worked out well.

Everything had worked out well. I was leaving. Maybe for a few years, maybe for good, but I was going. I never imagined I'd leave Los Angeles, but the thought of such freedom made me feel silly and lighthearted.

Me. Margaret Drazen.

I got goofy in the weeks before we finally left. Daddy hadn't been happy when we told him, and he eyed Drew as if maybe he remembered him from twelve years before, when a young man had shown up at the door asking for his oldest daughter.

But, you know, tough shit.

When Drew insisted we take 70 (apparently, I wasn't supposed to say *the* 70. Just 70 without the article), I didn't think anything of it. But he swung off the interstate and went south into Kentucky.

"Six-oh-six E-Y-E-B-R-O-W," I said from the passenger seat.

He glanced over. "I need to."

"I know."

We stopped at a light and he put his hand over mine. "I went to the funeral, but I didn't visit the... you know. The thing." He looked away.

"There's a florist up ahead. You don't want to show up empty-handed."

He'd bought a bunch of yellow flowers because they looked fresher than any of the others. Stillness shrouded us on the way to the cemetery. I pressed my hand on his, rubbing the rough patch on his fingertip where guitar strings had calloused the skin.

I took his hand again in the parking lot, and we walked down the gravel path, counting lanes and ways against our printed map.

We found the grave exactly where it was supposed to be. Just another stitch in the houndstooth pattern of grey stones on the grassy hill. It said what it was supposed to say. His name. The relevant dates. Where the others had their defining roles—Father, Wife, Mother, Son, Baby—Stratford Gilliam had a clef like the one on his neck, short five-line staff and a quarter note tucked between the two lowest lines.

"I feel stupid," he said. "It's just a rock and dirt."

"Yeah. It's stupid."

That was why we were together. We shared a cold, calculating cynicism. We were immune to sentiment.

"I like the musical note," I said. "It's cute."

"I picked it. I drew it for his dad and faxed it over."

"Really?"

"Yeah. It's..." He swallowed hard. "It's F. The note." He blinked. Smiled with his lips tight in a thin line. "It's so dumb." His voice cracked.

"I bet."

He looked away from the grave and shut his eyes. "I picked F
for…" He shook his head, shot a little laugh that was sticky with
sadness. "Friend. I needed it to be F for friend. Like I was in
kindergarten."

I put my hand on his cheek, thumb under his eye, ready to catch
the tears that I knew were coming. "I'm embarrassed for you."

He opened his eyes. So blue. Bluer than the cloud-masked sky that
day. He wasn't the man I'd met so long ago. The musician on the edge
of fame. So close to the dream. So close he could save the world with it.

But he was. That man was still in him. Sometimes I forgot about
that twenty-year-old with the potential he had a lifetime to fulfill.

He laid the flowers down. I rubbed his guitar callouses as we
walked back to the car.

"You should play music again," I said.

"No."

"You're not doing him any favors."

"It's not about Strat."

That was a lie, but I couldn't prove it.

"You're right. The world is better off without you making music."

He laughed a little and wrapped his arm around my neck, pulling
me close and kissing the top of my head.

"I mean it," I said. "You're sexy with a guitar. Chicks dig it."

"You sure you could stand the competition?"

"Have you met me? I don't have competition." I walked backward
in front of him, each of my hands in his. "You don't have to be a rock
star. Just write some songs. See how it sounds. You might like it." I bit
my lower lip. "I might like it. I could be your groupie all over again. I'll
let you fuck me if you play."

He pulled me to him. "You're going to let me fuck you whether I
play or not."

"I hear South Dakota has the easiest bar exam in the country."

"I'm not moving to South Dakota."

"Then you better get that guitar out, Indiana McCaffrey."

"You're threatening me," he growled with a smile. "You know what
that does to me."

"What?" I reached between his legs, and we laughed.

I ran back to the car, and he chased me, pinning me to the driver's side door with his kiss. I pushed my fingers through his hair, pulling him closer. I wanted to crawl inside him and live there forever.

He ripped his face away from mine long enough to speak. "I love you, Cinnamon. You're too precocious. Too smart. Too much of a pain in the ass, and I love you."

"Even in South Dakota?"

"I'll play again!" He laughed. "I'll play if you love me."

"You bet your ass I love you."

"Case closed." He kissed me again, pushing me hard against the car with the force of his erection pressed against me.

I groaned into his mouth.

"There was a hotel behind that florist." He spoke in gasps. "Wanna go make the bed squeak?"

"Yes."

We kissed again with an urgency that defied logic, as it should.

The freight train finally lumbered away, the bell on the last car dinging in victory. On the other side of the tracks, the rolling hills dissolved into infinity, and we drove right into it.

———

SACRED SINS

ONE

"MERRY CHRISTMAS."

I should have been startled when he spoke. The law office was dead quiet. But I'd known he was there before his voice was even in range. I had a way of knowing when he was near me.

"Not for a few days." I dropped my pen as if it had always been hot and I was finally sick of the temperature. "Don't rush me."

Drew leaned over me and kissed my forehead. I reached around his neck and pulled him down to me. I was entitled to a good, long Christmas kiss. No deposition in the world was going to deprive me of his lips.

"Beer," I said before kissing him again, tasting his tongue.

"I just had a few."

"You had two. I'm getting something artisanal past the Heineken."

He gave me his entire mouth, daring me to get every last flicker of flavor. I had it just as he yanked away.

"I'm going to take you right on the table if you don't stop."

"I was locating the bar you went to."

He smirked and dropped into one of the mesh ergonomic chairs. His cuffs were rolled up to the elbows, showing his tattoos and forearms rippled with muscle from weekends and late nights playing guitar. He worked three blocks to the west at a small, quiet firm that had three big, needy clients.

"I went to Madigan's." He flicked away a few pages of a deposition and rested his elbow on a clean rhombus of conference table. When I stayed late in the office, I kept the light low and directed at my work. It helped me concentrate.

"I know." I slipped my right foot out of my shoe and put it on his lap. He caressed it. "And you were with Jaewoo, who made you try what he ordered…" I scrunched my face, trying to pinpoint the sharp, seasonal flavor at the back of his mouth. Sweet honey and cinnamon. "Glögg? Are they doing Glögg?"

"Of course they are."

I slid down my chair so my heel could press the hardening flesh between his legs. "Jaewoo's such an effete little Bohemian."

Jaewoo, one of two of Drew's bandmates, was in his twenties and treated his parents like ATMs. The only way a musician could do experimental instrumental soundscapes in dark clubs and tiny venues was if they had generous parents, a trust fund, or a career in law.

"He wants us to tour this spring." Drew didn't look at me when he said it. He considered the slopes of my foot as if he wanted to sculpt them. He was a fool if he thought that would distract me.

"When are you leaving?"

"Come on."

"You want me to come? That's sweet."

He finally looked at me, blue eyes dark in the night. The windows rattled against the winter wind. I wasn't going anywhere, and unfortunately, he wasn't either.

"I want you to come, and you will." He pulled my foot aside, spreading my legs and sliding me to the edge of the chair. "Right in this office."

In the wet heat of the moment, it seemed like a perfectly fine idea.

"No," I gasped. "Home."

"Losing your nerve? There's no one here."

I gripped the arm rests and pulled my butt to the back of the chair.

"It's not my nerves I'm worried about. I don't want to lose another job."

He leaned back, letting me stand and organize my stacks. He knew I could afford to lose another ten jobs, but he respected my need to work. I loved practicing law. Loved fixing problems, putting pieces together, arguing, breaking a story down to get to the root of it. But the fact that I didn't need to work meant I didn't do well with authority. My mouth had gotten me in trouble more than once. I couldn't stand bullshit and didn't suffer fools easily. I could have started my own firm, but not in New York. My connections were in Los Angeles, and my love had made it clear we were not moving back to LA.

Drew got behind me, pressing his erection to my lower back and his lips to the back of my neck.

"You should tour," I said, trying to concentrate on putting my work away while he pushed against me. "You're a great lawyer but—"

"I'm an adequate lawyer."

"You were meant to play music."

"I am playing music."

"You're holding yourself back." I put the last of my files in my briefcase. His hands found my breasts and made it hard to decide if I had everything I needed to take home.

"I am. From fucking you. Right here. Now."

Drew was a deft subject-changer, and he usually did it after he'd aroused me into bad decisions or when I was doing ten things at once.

He reached around me, laid his hands on the lid of my briefcase, and closed it. His breath was warm on my neck. His lips traced a line from my jaw to my jacket.

"Don't keep me up all night," I said. "We have to get up in the morning."

"Early," he whispered. "Before your mother calls and turns our tickets to Greece into a guilt trip."

"Dead early. With the birds."

"With Santa."

"Speaking of..." I said, opening my briefcase and plucking out a credit-card-sized black box. When I turned, he kissed me, pressing the box between us. "You're going to mess up my bow." I tapped the corner on his chin. "Merry Christmas."

He took it. "I thought we were waiting until we got there."

"This is time sensitive."

He pulled the red bow apart and draped the ribbon over my shoulder before wiggling off the top.

"Oh, honey!" He tipped the box so I could see what I knew was there. A packet of birth control pills. "It's what I've always wanted!"

"They'll make you cranky the third week."

"I'm well aware." He put the box on the desk and his arms around my waist. "Why do I want these again?"

"I was wondering if you'd hang on to them since I'd like to not take them."

"You'd…" He drifted off as if his attention to my expression made sentences obsolete.

"Let's do the thing."

"Really?" Suppressed joy made his mouth twitch with a smile and his fingers curl and straighten at my back.

"Jonathan's sixteen. He's a man. What's done is done."

"Really?" He repeated as if he couldn't believe it.

"Yeah. Really. I need to move on and make a kid I can raise."

"Before we're married? Man, your parents are going to have a collective coronary and I'm going to love it."

I laughed, because I could. I'd cleared my desk, gotten my ducks in a row, put out the fires. Name the cliché, I had nothing on my docket but Christmas in Mykonos.

TWO THINGS consistently improved over the years: wine and compound interest. Everything else had a way of dying off, souring, or inspiring complacency. A state of gratitude was exhausting to maintain. Yesterday's blessings were today's entitlements.

I knew Drew and I would get there some day. But not yet.

Not yet.

We huddled together under the covers, smelling of sex and

satiation. His breathing got shallower and slower. The wind on the thin windows was high-pitched.

We rented a two-bedroom on 82nd Street and Second Avenue.

I liked being away from my family, and he loved the thrum of the city as much as he loved me. We'd talked about getting married, then never got around to it. Late at night, after a few beers, he'd tell me that he didn't want to see my father walking me down the aisle. His mother had passed, and he didn't know how he'd dance with my mother without slipping the secret.

We had everything we needed, and soon we'd have a non-toxic family of our own. A family that wasn't radioactive to him.

We were packed and ready for the flight. Our first Christmas away from the Drazens. Just him and me on a Grecian island. His guitar leaned against our bags. He'd play on the beach, making up songs as he went. Some would be silly. Some would be serious. All of them would get me flat on my back.

I couldn't sleep. I was waiting for the call that would preempt the trip. Family or work. One would keep me home, one wouldn't.

Sleep was the luxury only an unoccupied mind could afford. Mine couldn't run in twenty directions and empty out at the same time. It was like shampoo and conditioner. The two could pretend to coexist in the same bottle, but in the end, one canceled out the other.

The alarm screeched at 5:20. Drew flicked on the light, bathing us in warm yellow light. His body was still toned and gorgeous. He kept his ink fresh, and the casual playing he did kept his arms roped and strong. He put his eyes on me, grazing over my body from knees to throat as if he wanted to dress me in desire.

"God…" He shook his head.

"Why are you taking the Lord's name in vain this time?"

"You're so beautiful."

"Flattery's not getting you laid." I tapped my wrist.

He laughed, looking out the window into the winter sky. "You get more beautiful every day, and I just get older."

He wasn't much older than I was, but the march of years was hitting him hard.

"You could be a rock star and meet a bunch of groupie girls."

"Been there. Met a great one in Malibu this one time.."

"You could travel across the country." I straddled him. "A lone guitar-string cowboy."

He held out his hands and I took them, leveraging myself against him. "More like twelve guys farting on a bus."

"You'll be happy and realize you don't need me."

I was joking. There wasn't a pretty young girl in the world who made me feel insecure or threatened. Drew was mine. I was his. Neither time nor distance could change that. But his expression changed, and I knew he didn't take it as a joke.

"That won't happen," he said, serious as a death in the family.

"I know. I was joking. You need me." I got up and gathered my clothes.

He propped himself on his elbows, watching me.

"Come on, lazy-ass." I put my foot in a pant leg. "Get up."

"You know how it'll go? If I give up law?"

Gloriously naked, he stood and kissed me as if he knew I'd never leave him, because I wouldn't. I loved him more than my own life. I loved his insecurity and his power. Loved his past and future. His fluid mind and hard body.

"You'll take me on tour so I can look at all your contracts and suck your dick before you go onstage?"

Mentioning a blow job had a predictable effect on his body, and my knees got too weak to hold me. I got on them.

He tapped his wrist. "We have a flight."

I ran my cheek over his hardening cock. "I frontloaded fifteen minutes into the schedule for unexpected events."

The house phone rang.

"Oh, you're joking," he groaned.

"Leave it." I ran my tongue along his shaft, and he gripped a fistful of my hair. I licked off the taste of the previous night.

The ringing wouldn't stop. Then my cell phone buzzed on the night table.

"It's five thirty," he said before making an *ahh* as I took him down my throat. "It's two thirty on the west coast."

"Are you saying that means it can't be my family?" I took him again.

"I don't know what I'm saying."

The ringing was incessant. Demanding. Non-stop. When his phone sprang to life, we gave up and answered.

It was the beginning of the end.

TWO

LOS ANGELES

"I GOT US ANOTHER FLIGHT OUT TO GREECE ON MONDAY," I SAID TO Drew while holding the phone to my ear. We were outside LAX, waiting for the limo, standing next to a cart of bags stuffed with bathing suits and flip-flops.

He nodded. I'd offered him an out, but he'd been resigned to changing our plans from what we wanted to what he dreaded.

"Thank you for coming," Mom said through the phone.

"Only a couple of days, Mom."

"Fiona will die in a mental institution," she continued. "They can lock her up for years. She needs a big sister."

Fiona had three big sisters, but Carrie was away and Sheila was working with the family lawyers.

"No problem," I lied. "We're checking into a hotel then I'll be there. Give me a few hours."

I hung up with my mother as Drew spotted the family's driver.

"Any news on what happened?" he asked as the limo pulled up to us.

"Fiona stabbed her boyfriend, lost her shit, wound up in a mental ward."

"Nothing good comes from having that much money."

Did I resent Fiona for getting herself into trouble hours before Drew and I were going to start our first holiday away from my family? Take our first crack at starting our own brood?

I had every reason to resent being rerouted, but I didn't. Helping was my duty, not an obligation. When I got calls from Los Angeles, I was filled with a sense of purpose. Yes, it was self-defeating and strange. I hid the feeling from Drew, but I couldn't hide it from myself.

The driver got out before the car was in park, as if he needed to save milliseconds of my inconvenience.

"Who's representing her?" Drew asked as we crouched into the back seat.

"My father has Smithson & Klein."

"Corporate sharks."

"I know. Heartless predators representing my crazy, drugged, promiscuous, and sensitive sister."

"You're going to have to step in." He took my hand in resignation. He knew the reality, but he didn't like it. I squeezed his hand, apologizing for the vacation I was about to ruin.

DREW and I began surrounded by sound. The rhythmic pounding of waves on the shore, the grind of guitar strings, the laughter of early adulthood.

Five years later, with enough history between us to fill a century of almanacs, what I treasured most about our time together was silence. Inside it was acceptance. If he didn't like what I needed to do or how I was treating myself, he'd say so. I trusted him that much. He'd never let me do wrong to myself.

He held my hand across the back seat of the limo as the car moved ever so slowly onto the 10. Every hour was rush hour. Cars lined up on the freeway like pearls on a six-strand choker.

"I'm sorry," I said.

He leaned into me slowly, planting a tender kiss on my cheek. "It's all right."

"I know we weren't supposed to spend Christmas with my family."

"Extenuating circumstances."

"They're really overwhelming."

He shrugged. "You didn't come from nowhere."

Six sisters. A brother who was really my son. A father whose moral code I could never figure out. A family tree dotted with criminal acts and questionably acquired wealth.

I loved them. Down to my crazy sister Fiona and my mother, whose emotions were so all over the place she was twenty women in a one-woman suit.

"And I didn't leave for nothing. The drama's nonstop."

I loved them and they loved Drew. He'd let Fiona teach him how to tack a horse. Spent a Thanksgiving helping Sheila study for the bar. He'd been the one to drive Jonathan to the airport for his first national baseball championship, then called me from the plane to tell me he was going with him. He'd done everything and more to get close to us, but he was never fully comfortable with the drama.

We were staying at a hotel in Beverly Hills. It was central, but far enough from my family to give us some privacy, and the security was good.

The drama in question revolved around my sister Fiona. She was a camera magnet who loved being rich more than she loved money. She craved attention, living as if her only pleasure in life was pleasure. A pure bacchanalian.

"What did your mother say?" Drew asked.

"She has three days to prove she's sane or they're putting her away, which might be a good thing, because the tabloids are loving it. Rich girl goes crazy and stabs boyfriend. They're ready to put her head on a platter."

He waited a second to ask the obvious question. "Did she do it?"

I did corporate law, defending clients from accusations and arguing in courtrooms. Questions of guilt or innocence weren't my job. Drew did copyright law, which was handled in boardrooms. His question of Fiona's guilt was a consideration as a human, not a lawyer.

"Probably."

"How's Jonathan taking it?" he asked, knowing he was always my primary concern.

"Apparently, he and his girlfriend, Rachel, got drunk at Sheila's Christmas party. He woke up on the lawn and she drove her car over Blufftop Cliff. He's upset. I didn't even know her. I would have known her if I was here. I can't..." I said with no intention of finishing the sentence. I didn't know what I couldn't do. Anything. Walk. Breathe. Think. Exist.

"Jesus," Drew muttered, looking out the window.

"It's a mess. He's playing it tough apparently."

We fell back into a warm silence where he was my companion. Never my judge.

"They're going to try to draw you back in," he said once we were off the 10. He twisted around to face me, putting his leg on the seat and his arm around me.

"I'm a big girl."

"You're a cupcake when it comes to them."

"What was the song? About the cake melting in the rain?"

"You stayed in New York for a reason," he snapped. "Every time we go back and you have to look at that kid, your heart breaks."

I opened my mouth to object, sitting straighter and stiffer as if I was going to spring, but he leaned on my shoulders and pressed his fingers to my lips. I wanted to bite them off. His words stopped me.

"Last Christmas, you spent the entire trip asking Jonathan how he was. Like you were trying to stuff fifteen years of motherhood into Christmas break. Then you gut-cried for two weeks." He brushed his fingers along my cheek.

He'd stayed by me when I called in sick because I was so overwrought, grieving for a child who was always and never mine. I couldn't allow myself to have another. I felt locked up, as if I'd poured concrete inside myself to prevent it. Another child would be a betrayal of the one I couldn't claim. Jonathan didn't know he was mine, and I'd never tell him, but when I imagined having another baby, my insides recoiled at my treacherous desires. It felt like infidelity. Disloyalty. I was supposed to wait for something. I didn't know what, but something. It didn't make sense, but the wall of grief I stood against wouldn't budge.

What if Jonathan needed me and I'd moved on? Or I stopped loving him?

That worry didn't make any more sense than the deep, dark concern that he'd find out and hate me. None of it made sense.

I walked this road without a map and dragged him along behind me. It wasn't fair.

So I'd decided to put the pills in a box and live my life as if it were my own, but here we were, in Los Angeles again.

"I'm sorry," I said, referring to all the crazy, nonsensical shit I couldn't say.

"I love you, Cinnamon."

"I love you, Indy."

"I can't stand seeing you hurt."

"I'm fine."

"Yeah, I know. You're just peachy."

I kissed him, because kissing him made me believe I was, indeed, just peachy fine.

WE DROVE BACK from Westonwood Acres— a mental institution for the wealthiest children in the country—in silence. Fiona was a mess. The media was all over it. Dad was calculating an escape route from shame. I was trying to figure out what he'd do before he did it.

Mom, graying hair pulled back, adjusted the pictures on the piano. No one in the family played, but appearances mattered. Any cultured house required a black grand piano. The more susceptible it was to the greasy ovals of little fingers, the more exquisite the cleanliness.

Outside, Drew stretched on a patio chair, enjoying the cold December sun. I wished I was with him, watching the pool man skim the water's surface in a wooly 49ers beanie and letting the white noise from the gardener's gas blower drown out the tense niceties between the family.

Despite the bedecked Christmas tree, the mood in the house was not festive. Daddy had disappeared to read the fine print in the *Wall Street Journal* as if he had an investment to move.

A man making 550K in interest per day only moved money to engage in fiscal masturbation.

Done adjusting, Mom went to the kitchen to wipe the sterile counter as if it was her job, which it wasn't. Her lack of facility at it was illustrated by the way she wiped around the glass vase of flowers without lifting it.

Theresa watched Mom as if she wanted to bore a hole in her head. At eighteen and change, she was the "good girl," the one we could always count on to do the right thing. Her red hair was tied in a low ponytail, and her pearls made a perfect line against the neckline of her sweater.

Needless to say, it was tense.

"Where's Jonathan?" I asked, getting juice out of the fridge. I thought the query only meant something to me, the mother-not-mother who was worried-not-worried about his absence.

Apparently, I was wrong.

"He's fine," Mom said thickly.

"That's not what she *asked*, Mom," Theresa snapped.

"He's at a friend's," Mom relented.

"Hey there," I said to Theresa. "What's your problem?"

"I don't know. Mom, what's my problem?"

Mom shook her head as she folded the paper towel in halves and threw it away. "Nothing that's your business."

Theresa pounded the marble countertop of the kitchen island. "It is. She's my friend and no one can find her!"

"Wait, hang on." I held up my hands for peace. "She's your sister."

I'd thought she was talking about Fiona. It occurred to me too late that her friend was Rachel, Jonathan's girlfriend who had driven over Blufftop cliff to her death two nights before.

"It's not—" Mom started, but I couldn't hear the rest over Theresa, who turned all her unexplained rage toward me.

"No one cares because Fiona's got all the attention. Rachel is my friend, and Jon's as upset as I am. But all you can talk about is Fiona the fuckup."

"Wait—" I was about to ask her to explain, but she was too wound up.

"You don't get to live three thousand miles away and come here on Christmas—when we call you with something serious—so you can waltz in and take over stuff and not know what's going on. You don't get to tell me who I'm talking about. You get to *ask*."

"Okay, who—"

"No one!" Mom shouted.

"Don't say that!"

"Theresa." Dad appeared in the doorway, paper folded in one hand. His voice cut coldly through emotion and objection with a single command for one girl to be quiet.

Theresa obeyed because that was what she did. But when Drew opened the sliding glass door to the patio, letting in the air and the blower noise, he opened the tension a crack.

"Hey," he said, making eye contact with me, where I spoke volumes.

Shit's hitting the fan.

You don't have to be here.

As a matter of fact, go back outside.

Theresa wedged her anger through the crack in the tension. It was enough for action, not words.

She picked up the vase of flowers and smashed it against the counter. It broke with a *pop*.

"Theresa!" Mom burst into tears.

"I hate all of you!" She ran out.

I started after her, but Daddy said, "Leave her," so I did.

It's worth mentioning that Drew was the one to pick the glass up from the floor.

"How did this happen?" Mom was in full blubber, eyes dripping like a broken vase of flowers.

I put my arms around her. "It's okay, Mom."

Drew put the largest pieces on the counter and crouched for more. Daddy shook his head, looking at his daughter's boyfriend on his knee like a servant.

You might wonder how I knew what he was thinking.

Trust me. I knew the guy.

"She and Jonathan. They were my sweetest babies."

Drew made eye contact with me as he dropped a handful of glass shards on the wet counter.

I know it hurts you to hear that, he said.

It hurts so bad, I agreed. *But keep quiet.*

I won't watch you hurt quietly much longer

Mom separated from me and reached for a paper towel.

"Maria can do that," Daddy said, pushing the towels out of her reach.

"The staff is off today." With nothing to do with her hands, Mom sobbed again. I snapped off a length of towel and handed it to her.

Daddy left the kitchen, shaking his head. By the time we'd squeezed out the last towel, Drew had slipped away too. It was just as well the men had left. I couldn't talk around them.

Mom stood next to me at the sink, letting the hot water run over her hands.

"What's going on?" I asked.

"Nothing."

"Tell her," Theresa said from behind us.

"Leave it be," Mom said.

"She's one of us. Just tell her."

"Leave it *be!*"

"Can we dispense with the drama?" I shut off the water.

"Daddy was cheating on Mom with my friend."

Mom and I spun around, me in shock, and Mom in something like rage but more like angry resignation.

"Which friend?"

"It's complicated," Mom said.

"Which friend?" I repeated, knowing the answer. When they didn't reply, I spoke it aloud. "The same one Jonathan is dating?"

Yes. The answer was yes. The word wasn't spoken and didn't need to be. While I'd been shacking up with my lover in New York, building a career and a life, my family had been twisting in on itself. Eating its tail. Collapsing in slow motion.

We had secrets we didn't even speak of under pledge. Secrets about Daddy and the way he looked at young girls. Mom was fifteen years older than her oldest child. So we watched. Declan Drazen's seven daughters had promised to speak up if they were touched. Pledge was solidified among us for that purpose, but we'd never once used it for that.

Some days, I thought the fact that he'd never touched his daughters made my father a saint. Most days I thought my standards were too low.

I should have been shocked and horrified by what I learned in the kitchen that Christmas. I wasn't. I was just glad he hadn't touched Theresa.

"If you're not leaving," I asked my mother, "what are you going to do about it?"

"I moved into Carrie's bedroom." She laid her hands flat on the counter. One on top of the other. The tops were scalded from the water. "And I had… a procedure."

My eyes met Theresa's. Whatever it was, it was news to my sister too.

Mom held her chin high, but the effort to do so was evident. The procedure hadn't had a mole removal or a face lift. No. Something else. Something that stank of revenge.

"Mom?" I said. "Was this an obstetrical procedure?"

"Might have been." She ran her hand over the marble as if she missed the busywork of the paper towels. "If he'd let me get my tubes tied years ago, I wouldn't have been in that position in the first place."

"You had an abor—?!"

"You're forty-six!" Theresa snapped with a touch of disgust.

"And Catholic," I added, as if that mattered. When push came to shove, those who could choose inevitably did, one way or the other. The church could rail against it for the rest of eternity. The government could send it to back alleys. Abortion was always a choice. Always.

"If either of you are so devout you have a problem with it, you can pack up and go any time," Mom said, straightening her spine. "But I'm not bringing another child into this family. No more. And as far as my age goes"—she pointed her chin at Theresa—"the doctor said perimenopausal fertility is common. We weren't trying, but things happen. God willed me another baby and God can send me to hell if He wants to."

"You could just leave him," I said.

She spat out a laugh. "And go where?" She reached for a high cabinet, revealing a row of tall bottles. "God, do we not have any… here." She pulled down a blue bottle of gin and set it on the counter, resting her hands on it.

I took down three glasses, and Theresa pulled out the ice tray. When Mom didn't move, I took the bottle from under her while my sister filled the glasses with cubes.

"I know you don't respect me," she said.

"Not true," Theresa said.

"I have eight children. Most of you are settled. But not Jonathan. He's strong but not strong enough. Not now. If I split this family now, what would happen to him?"

How many years had I asked myself the same thing? My mother had shouldered the same duty with a seriousness I'd never given her credit for.

"He'll be fine." Theresa, who wasn't old enough to drink, picked up her glass as soon as I'd filled it. "Trust me. He'll be okay."

Mom and I took our glasses. She looked at me, and an understanding passed between us. I'd never told her Jonathan was mine. Maybe she knew. Maybe I was imagining it. Maybe it didn't matter. In whatever way she could, Eileen Drazen was watching over him.

Why had I felt so alone? Why had I held off having my own life to do what others were already doing? I wanted to run to Mykonos and let Drew fuck me pregnant. So god damn pregnant.

I let the flavor of the cold gin flower on my tongue and swallowed. "Can you bear it if you stay?"

Theresa put down her glass without drinking. "She shouldn't."

"I have to," Mom said. "This family is all I've ever had."

She was protecting Jonathan, but she was also protecting herself. I couldn't deny her that. I had to trust her with the son we secretly shared.

"To us then." I raised my glass. "To all of us."

Mom touched her glass to mine, and with Theresa reluctantly joining us, we drank to our family.

"Ugh!" Theresa cried. "This is gross."

I laughed and watched her take the rest like medicine.

"What's gross?" Sheila stood in the doorway, carrying a briefcase. She wore a matching pantsuit that had to cost two grand, but the line of her fly didn't match the line of her blouse, and her right lapel was half folded under her shoulder bag. Twenty-six years of twisting rage was taking its toll on her posture. She put down her case and bag. "None for me?"

I poured her a glass. "How's Fiona?"

After finishing her law degree, Sheila had gone right into a white-shoe law firm Daddy had retained for decades. I'd refused the same kind of job in favor of making my own way.

"She's nuts." She slammed back the drink and waved me for another. "Our lawyers are saying Westonwood might be the best thing for her."

"Sheila Drazen," Mom lectured, "don't you say that."

Mom didn't like broad insults of her sweetest babies.

"Ma," I said.

She looked at me, eyes a little wide. I met her gaze and let her read me. Without a word, I told her I'd handle it.

I went out to the back patio. Sheila followed as I knew she would. She'd always been ambitious. The faster I walked, the harder she'd chase.

"Hey," she said, sliding the door shut behind her, "wait up."

I didn't. She caught me in the rose garden.

"You don't think she's crazy?" she asked.

"Yes, I do." I let her walk next to me. "But it's not relevant. Your job is to get her out. You think you're working for a law firm. You're not. You're working for the Drazens.."

"Well, no, Margie, it's not like that."

"Yes. Yes, Sheila, it is like that. Have you done any background on your bosses at Smithson & Klein? Sixty percent of the firm's income isn't from billable hours. Do you want to know the source of the other forty percent?"

"What's the difference?"

"Your boss is on the board of Harmony Health, which owns

Westonwood. Keeping Fiona Drazen locked up does wonders for their brand."

She didn't know. She spent too long thinking about her answer.

Too much had happened already. I couldn't untangle it all.

With nothing else to say to my sister, I walked away to find Drew.

"I won't be undermined," Sheila called out. "In five years, I'll be running this show. It could have been you, but you took off to New York. So it's me."

"Take it, Sheila. But do the job."

"You can't just stroll back in here and start breaking shit," she said.

"I can break shit from New York too."

She stormed off to the house, trying to look as if she was together, but I'd stepped on her toes and bruised her ego. She was too emotional for this job.

I WENT TO FIND DREW. I needed to share space with him. Feel his presence near me. I could deal with the tangled insanity of my family if he was close. My father had been in a relationship with a girl one third his age. My mother had had an abortion to either spite him or shield the family. I didn't know who or what to protect. My normal life? My son? My brother? The sisters who were bound to be affected?

I was falling down a rabbit hole and only Drew could catch me. He was the North Star. The skies spun, but he was still and steady. The point of connection between myself and the rest of the world.

He wasn't by the pool or watching television. I was on the way up to our room when the heavy wooden door to my father's study slid open.

Drew came out. My father was leaning against the edge of his desk.

"Hey," I said. "I was look—"

I couldn't finish. Not with Drew's eyes wide with terror, dry with a drain of emotion.

In the study, Declan Drazen didn't move to follow or greet me.

"What happened?" I whispered.

"Nothing, sweetheart," Drew said.

He needed to be attended. If I let him simmer, he'd say things he shouldn't. I put my hand on his arm and tried to look him in the eye, but he turned away.

I looked at my father. "Daddy?"

"We can't talk man to man, Margaret?"

"He wants me to make an honest woman out of you," Drew lied. "I told him you're too honest as it is."

Daddy laughed and stood away from the desk. "Indeed you are." He shifted some things across it. "Indeed you are. I'd like to talk to you for a minute. About your sister."

Go, Drew said without saying a word. Permission was in his expression and posture. *I love you. I'm fine.* He kissed my cheek and went down the hall.

"He's quite the character," my father said.

"Don't underestimate him. It's a mistake."

"Easy one to make."

I followed Daddy into his office. He closed the wooden pocket doors. The back wall was solid glass overlooking the garden, and the bookcases were filled with expensive first edition novels we'd learned nothing from.

"I appreciate your help with your sister," he said just as the gardener shut off the gas blower.

I wakened to how loud it had been in contrast to the quiet I was about to get used to. "My pleasure."

I waited for the *but.*

"But I have people on it."

"I'm cheaper and I give a shit."

He smirked and flicked a speck of broken glass off his sleeve. "You never had to work."

"I like working."

"You should work for us."

"Us?"

"This family. On the business side."

Move back to LA and work with my family. Might as well leave Drew right away. Save the trouble of a protracted breakup. "I'll think about it."

"Something else you should think about." He leaned on his desk. I wondered if he did it to make himself shorter. At six-four, he was intimidating when he stood straight.

I sat down to show him I wasn't intimidated, even if I was. "Okay?"

"That man. With the tattoos?"

"The one you were just talking to?"

"He concerns me."

"Why?"

He gave a little huff and crossed his arms.

"Dad. I want the truth."

"The truth."

"Why he worries you."

He shook his head as if I were an errant child. "Last Christmas, he took me aside. He was drunk, or at least halfway there."

I made an effort to keep my limbs and face relaxed, but there was nothing I could do to keep the nerves at the surface of my skin from tingling.

"I assumed he was asking for your hand, but alas, he'll never do that."

"What did he say?" I asked tersely.

"Why don't you ask him?"

"I will. But I have the feeling I'll need corroboration."

"He said, 'You need to be aware that your daughter and I know.'"

The tingling went up my neck. "Know what?"

"I asked him the same question, and he repeated, 'We know.'"

My cheeks got hot.

"Do you have any idea what he's talking about, Margaret?"

I lied without even thinking. "He found out how Grandpa O'Drassen made his money and how you've built on it."

"Should I worry?"

This was a rhetorical question. Daddy didn't worry. He took care of business.

"Probably not. He chased money behind a client who wasn't paid royalties. The licensee had transactions through DRN Consulting.

Which is yours. It passed through a real estate deal and came out clean on the other side."

I'd described a standard money laundering operation and Daddy didn't even blink. He certainly didn't deny it, but he didn't admit it either. His stoicism could grate on a girl's nerves. Hard work and good decisions my ass. The kind of money we had came from decades of duplicitous dealing.

"Turns out," I said, "Grandpa had the same kind of business with the Carloni crime family."

"They never proved it."

"That doesn't make him innocent."

"In America, it does." He pushed away from the desk, standing to his full height. "Keep his curiosity to a low roar. I don't want to have to fix him."

"What—?"

Daddy left the room before I could ask what he'd meant by that.

THE HOUSE WAS huge enough to lose eight children in the dozens of corners a kid could hide in. A grown man who'd had a conversation with seven layers of meaning could hide just as easily.

I found Theresa before I found Drew. She was in the side drive with a Prada knapsack and fresh eyeliner.

"Theresa!"

She ignored me.

I'd spent ten minutes skulking around, looking for my boyfriend, and I was in no mood to be ignored. I caught up to her as she set her hand on the door of her Audi, and I grabbed her arm. As if she'd known I was there the whole time, she spun around, shaking me off.

"Theresa."

"Leave me alone!"

"No. I need to know if you're all right."

"I'm fine. I hate him and I hate Mom and I hate Jonathan."

Ice ran through my veins. "Don't you ever say that."

"It's true." She set her jaw and blinked away tears, showing more control than I'd seen in some adults.

"Let me give you a piece of advice."

"I don't need a Dear Margie session." She tried to open the door, but I leaned on it and held up my right hand.

"Open pledge."

"Really?"

"Really," I said.

"I refuse."

"You're not allowed to refuse. That's the rule."

She held up her right hand, but the rest of her body challenged the submission. Leaning on one hip, eyes rolling, jaw misaligned, she was a cartoon of adolescent resistance.

"Pledge open," she said through her teeth.

We put our hands down and she crossed her arms.

"That little outburst?" I said. "In the kitchen?"

"It was a stupid vase."

"Fuck the vase, Tee. I'm talking about the tantrum."

"Is there a question coming?"

"I'm not going to ask you what you were trying to achieve. I know the answer."

"You're not supposed to open pledge to lecture me."

I stepped closer. I wasn't above threatening her if that was what it took to get through. She averted her gaze, going from defiant to petulant.

"Never, ever act weak in front of Daddy. He'll eat you alive." She started to object, but silenced herself when I held up my hand. "You acted weak. Acting weak is a tactic to get the opposition to underestimate you. That's the only excuse to use it, and it wasn't yours. For as long as you live in this house, you keep your pearls on a string and the clasp in the back. Do you understand me?"

She moved her gaze back to me, but not in defiance. She tried to see through the wall I'd built around myself. I didn't know how to let her see that I was sane. She'd have to find the cracks herself.

"Is that what you do?"

It wasn't what I did, but it was what she needed. "Stand straight. Keep your chin up. Act like you're above it."

"Never let them see you sweat?"

"Unless you want to have your choices made for you."

"I have to get out of here," she said. "My own career. My own life. Like you."

She thought I had my own life? I'd done a good song and dance. Wait until they all saw what Margie Drazen having her own life really meant.

"You will have your own life," I said. "But only if you keep your shit straight."

"Okay, Margie. Okay. I'll keep it together. I promise." She held up her hand.

I mirrored her. "Pledge closed."

"Closed." She grabbed the door handle. "I'd hug you, but I'm still mad at you."

I stepped back. "Way to hold a grudge, sister."

NORMALIZATION IS the most profound and useful of human survival instincts. We become numb to pain and pleasure at the same rate. Repeat something unique and it becomes ordinary. Pain turns to irritation turns to tedium through the magic of normalization.

Maybe normal was what we were. Maybe normal was Drew and me living in the same apartment, being in love, fucking on the regular. Maybe normal was having meals together, kissing each other before we went work, watching TV on the couch.

Normal was me that Christmas, looking for Drew. Finding him in the Drazen wine cellar, where—years before— we'd realized Jonathan was mine. Taking the bottle out of his hands was my normal—the long-suffering mate of a man too attached to his drink.

In a Beverly Hills hotel, I walked him to the suite door. I didn't know if he was trying to follow the swerves and swirls in the carpet pattern, or if he was in a constant battle with the rotation of the earth. Right, left, right, left, crossing one leg over the other in a dance that would've been impressive if it didn't make me wonder if he'd fall on his face.

He took his key out of his pocket and tried to slip it in the door. He missed once, he missed twice. Before a frustrating and embarrassing third attempt, I snapped the card out of his hand, slid it into the slot, and got us into our suite.

When he wanted to fuck, things really stopped being normal.

"Stay still," I said as I pulled his shirt over his head.

He tried to get at mine, but I slapped his hands away. That simple movement made him lose his balance, and he tipped to the left, crossed his right foot over, put his hand on the dresser, and managed to keep himself relatively upright.

I went for his pants. He slapped my hand away. I was sober, so it wasn't such a big deal for me. It was almost normal.

"Do you want me to help you get undressed or not?"

He unbuttoned his fly. "You don't need to treat me like a child."

I folded my arms. "Stop drinking like a frat boy."

He continued as if I hadn't said anything, getting his own damn pants off. "Not like… your fucking family. I can't watch them do this to themselves… no more holidays here. Not another fucking holiday with your fucking family."

He had no idea how irritating his family was. His aunts, uncles, and cousins were so *nice*. I wanted to punch each and every one of them in the face. If any of them ever had an edge, it had been smoothed over by sweet, genteel Scandinavian manners. The only relief had been his brother-in-law who belonged to a motorcycle club. He could at least carry on a conversation about something besides the weather or the best route between the house and church.

What kind of person complained about that? What kind of person complained about a family being normal?

Drew stepped out of his pants and left them on the floor. He had a bone to pick, and I knew this guy. Drunk or sober, he was gonna pick that shit clean.

"None of you can say a fucking thing to each other without meaning twenty other things, and you expect me to decipher which of those twenty things I'm supposed actually respond to?"

"You confuse inference and implication."

"I may have had one too many, but don't throw your high horse bullshit around right now."

"Maybe you should go to bed."

"And that kid, that sharp little brat, being raised in that fucking family. Your fucking father…"

"Stay away from him and you'll be fine."

"Your father knows, and he thinks you don't know. And he looks at me like I'm a fucking pushover. Like I gave you away. Like I pawned you off, or worse, that I couldn't control you."

"That was sixteen years ago!"

"It was yesterday. It was yesterday I fucked a girl so young that her parents could send her away."

He didn't usually get to the point so quickly, and that was always the point. His guilt for loving me when I was so young. I kept telling them it was all right. I kept telling him he'd more than made up for it. But it's that nice person guilt. He was raised by nice people, to be a nice guy and not do things that aren't nice, like fuck young girls.

He rubbed the heels of his hands into his eyes like a little boy, and I wondered if I was the one who'd fucked somebody too young for me.

I took him by the wrists and pulled him down. "Drew, you need to go to sleep. Tomorrow you can tell me what you and my father were talking about."

"I hate your family."

"I know. But don't you ever, ever hate Jonathan." I made my voice so saccharine sweet, I could've been presenting him with a birthday cake. "Because I'll leave you so fast your dick will snap off."

He didn't sober up as much as get a little clarity. It didn't last.

"I don't hate Jonathan." He almost said it without slurring.

"Good." I cupped his face. "Because I love you."

He patted my shoulder, brushing by me to make his way to the bedroom. I hadn't wanted to fuck when we came in and I still didn't want to. But I was left in the hotel room feeling as if we had unfinished business. Something that was supposed to happen before he went into the bathroom and closed the door.

When I heard the click of the door and the shower running, I knew what was missing, but it was too late to ask for it, and I'd never had to before.

He hadn't said he loved me back.

That was not normal.

The situation called for an hour on low simmer, covered. Remove cover at bedtime, stir. Raise heat. Bring to boil. Salt to taste. Serve.

Instead, my phone rang. It was Sheila. She was exhausting, but I picked up the phone anyway.

"Everything's fine," I said without offering a greeting. I didn't want to fight with her. She could drive the entire Drazen operation in the ground or become queen. I didn't care.

The shower sputtered out. I wanted a chance to catch Drew before he boiled over.

"You heard?"

"Heard what? I'm here."

"Where?"

We'd crossed signals and if I told her "where," the crossed lines would turn into a knot of misunderstanding.

"Nowhere. What did you call to tell me?"

"If you know already, I'm not repeating it."

Releasing a cloud of steam, Drew opened the door with a towel around his waist and old tattoos covering his chest. The towel was low enough to expose the V still at his hips, and the tattoos were vivid enough to remind me of the sexy fucker with the guitar-string callouses on his fingers.

"I'm sorry," he said, "I was…"

I pointed at the phone and mouthed "Sheila" with rolled eyes. He'd react poorly to my being on the phone with my family minutes after we'd fought about them.

Because they took over. They encroached. They expected me to jump at the drop of a hat and I filled expectations like a force of nature filling a vacuum.

"Margie?" Sheila was getting impatient. "Are you there?"

"I'm here."

"Never mind," Drew said, whipping off his towel. "Forget I said anything."

"No... I..." Between my sister with her gossip and my man about to put clothes on, I had only one choice.

"I have to go," I said to Sheila.

"I'll see you there."

"Don't get off," he said. "I mean, for what? So another one of them can call you in fifteen minutes?"

"Wait..." I held my hand up to him. "See me where?"

"Or this." Drew got his pants on. "So you can meet—"

"The hospital," she said.

"With another one of them to *not* say anything—"

"The hospital?"

As soon as I said that, Drew shut up as if I'd dropped an anvil on his head.

"You didn't know?" Sheila said.

For the love of Jesus Christ on a unicycle, I wanted to punch her in the face. Drew stepped into his pants without resentment or unspoken accusation.

"Obviously not," I said, meeting his eyes across the room. The bitterness between us was utterly gone, but the exhaustion remained.

"Jonathan," Sheila said. "He tried to commit suicide."

THREE

1999

I BLAMED MYSELF.

Would Jonathan have tried to kill himself if I'd been acting like his mother? If he knew his real father? Would he have wished so hard for death if I hadn't kept my secret from him?

Wasn't it his secret too? Had I denied him the desire to live? Did he know, in his gut, that everything was wrong?

Drew and I packed up our shit to take to the Malibu house. There was no rhyme or reason as to why we left the hotel as a base. We didn't discuss why we'd want to consolidate our presence. We just did it in a silence broken by only the most mundane matters.

Did you get everything?

Can I pack the toothbrushes?

Will the bellman pick up the bags?

Should I call a car?

The hotel room didn't mean anything to me, but when the door closed for the last time, it clanged a little, and it sounded like something hollow had broken.

The present became the past.

"Margie?"

The reality I'd built was the hollow thing, and that closing door had shattered it.

My heart was encased in a steel fist. It pounded against the crushing pressure, expanding as the fist tightened, pushing against my lungs.

"Margie!"

I couldn't breathe. My heart was engorged with blood. No space for air. My chest hurt. There was too much in there for a rib cage that couldn't grow.

I was on my knees and he was in front of me. My biceps hurt where he gripped them. The pain kept me from falling over completely. I could see every hair on his face. Every web in the blue of his eyes.

"Cin," he said as if he wasn't talking to me but to some shared past where I was stronger. "Breathe. It's okay. It'll be okay. Breathe with me."

He took an exaggerated breath, inhaling through his mouth and exhaling a second later. Nodding, he did it again, and I followed. One after the other.

"Good," he said before continuing. Breathing. I'd been doing it since the day I was born, but forgot how. "Okay. Good. Can you stand?"

"It hurts too much."

"You can."

"Can't. It's my fault."

"Hush. Don't start saying that to yourself or you'll believe it. It's not your fault. None of this mess is your fault."

"I ran away." The fist tightened, letting me know it could come back any time I called it.

"No." He caressed my face, moving my hair off my cheeks.

"Yes."

"You didn't."

"Yes, Drew, yes, I did. I went across the country so I didn't have to deal with my son and now look what's happened. He tried to kill himself." I yanked his hands off me. "His life is so fucked up he took a handful of pills so he'd die."

"Can you imagine if you'd stayed?"

"What's that supposed to mean?"

"What if you'd told him, when he was eleven, that you were his mother? How was that going to be not fucked up?"

I stood, straightened my clothes, took a deep but unsatisfying breath that filled only the corners of my lungs. "At least I would have been there."

Drew got up, one foot at a time, as if he wanted to extend the task. "He has sisters already."

"None of them could save him."

"And you wouldn't have either. Come on. Let's be there now."

Every core belief I tried not to think about was tied up in his statement. I couldn't have saved Jonathan. I would have been as fragile as the rest of my sisters. Whatever power I believed I had was because I'd run. I'd saved myself. I'd abandoned him. I'd left him behind to forget him. To gather strength for myself.

I'd had the choice to be weak or immoral. There had never been a third option.

Drew didn't mean any of those things, nor did I believe them.

That didn't make them any less true.

Drew took my hand. "What I'm saying is—"

"Don't abandon him again," I interrupted. "I have to be there because I can."

"Be there now."

"Right." I rubbed my face with my free hand. "Why do you put up with me?"

"Because I love you, and I know what you need."

"You. I need you." I could breathe again. "Sometimes, I forget him. But sometimes, I wish he was mine so hard I feel like it's true."

"Me too," Drew said. "Me too. Sometimes I wish we were all one unit. But this is what it is, and he's going to be okay." He crouched slightly so he could see my face, as if to make sure he didn't need to repeat it over and over until it became a fact.

I took a deep breath and decided to believe him.

DREW WAS THE STABLE ONE. He was the steadiness of my breath. The ground under me. He didn't need me as much as I needed him. Did I assume this because he was all I ever had? Or because it suited me?

As Jonathan's suicide attempt soaked into the fabric of my family like a dark stain, I closed myself off. I wasn't allowed to think of him as anything but my youngest brother whose life wasn't affected by my choices. I had to lock away the guilt where my mother and sisters couldn't see it. My relief at his survival was deeper and more self-serving than I could let on, and my powerlessness in arranging his emotional recovery was more painful.

At Jungco's, a restaurant in Beverly Hills, Drew had dinner with us but stayed outside the circle of concern. He didn't seem resentful, but thoughtful and quiet, as if he was observing a change and making a decision.

Taking his hand, I whispered, "Hey."

He sipped his club soda. "Hey. You doing all right?"

"Yeah. I'm fine."

"It's Monday," he said.

I cringed and looked at my watch. Our flight to Greece was long gone. "I'm sorry."

He shrugged. "This was more important."

Clasping his fingers tightly, I shut out the chatter of my siblings and the clink of dishes. "Thank you."

He kissed me gently, with a longing I thought I understood. I thought he yearned for time and attention, and maybe he did. But in the weeks that followed, I figured out the ache behind his kiss was for a family he was giving up on building.

Right then though, in the back room of Jungco's, with my parents and three sisters surrounding me, I didn't see it.

I should have known him better.

I should have known myself better.

When the kiss ended and I opened my eyes, Drew was looking over my shoulder with hard concern. I followed his gaze to my father, who was talking to the waiter.

"What?" I asked Drew. "Did he say something?"

"He doesn't have to."

We all went back to the house. Drew didn't speak of it again. We made love under the sheets with the curtains drawn as if we could ever make a space that was fully ours.

MY PARENTS and I left early the next morning to move Jonathan to Westonwood for psychiatric evaluation. Fiona was already there. Jonathan was being admitted. Twenty-five percent of us were institutionalized.

Jonathan wasn't on speaking terms with anyone. He was going to be fine. Physically, he was in good enough shape to fail at suicide. Emotionally, we couldn't tell if he was planning to succeed at another try.

The admitting room was done in raw teak and dusty blue, which contrasted against his red hair. He slouched in his chair as if he were melting in the heat of insolence. By living through a bottle of pills he'd been given a reprieve, and so had I.

Our parents and Frances, the administrator, had left with some paperwork, and I was alone with him.

"They must be negotiating a bulk discount," Jonathan said, breaking his silence.

"You'll have someone here to watch out for you."

"Fiona?" He shook his head. "She's the one who needs watching."

I sat across from him, leaning as close as I dared. "Jon. What happened?"

"Fuck this. That's what happened. Fuck all of it. Do you know what he did? Our father?"

"This is about that girl. Rachel?"

He tapped the wooden arm of the chair, alternating his right thumb and pinkie. He didn't look like a careless teenager. He looked like an adolescent lion bursting into fierce adulthood. "You keep thinking that. Sure. It was over a girl. If that's the story everyone's going to believe, then fine."

"It's normal to be upset when someone you love dies."

"I know that. And thanks. Yeah, I'm upset. But when I thought about *him*." He stopped tapping long enough to jerk his thumb toward the door and the people behind it. "I loved her. But he set me up with her to make a man out of me. Or keep me close. Or keep her close. Or I was Humbert's cover."

I smiled and looked at my hands when he quoted Nabokov. Funny how we all parsed our father's tactics but never actually understood them.

"I snapped," he continued, regaining his fingers' rhythm. "I feel stupid. Now I'm going to have to explain it a hundred times." He bent his neck until he was looking at the ceiling. "And right now? In that other room? He's setting it up so no one believes me. One day, Margie. One day I'm going to get him back for this."

"Jon."

"Don't. Please, Jesus, Margie. Just don't."

"I'm not going to try to talk you out of revenge, or retaliation, or whatever you're thinking."

He sat up straight. I was jarred when Strat's green eyes looked right into mine. He was intense, this boy. He was a mighty force who had turned his power back on himself. Given the wrong set of circumstances at too young an age, he'd do it again.

"What then?" His question was a challenge.

"Your time will come. I want you to live for it. Survive for it."

"You're going to help me?"

The question knocked the sister out cold so the mother could speak without thinking. "Yes."

"I'm not living with him."

"Yes, you are. When you get out of here, you're going to be good. And you're going to wait."

He shoved his body against the back of the chair as if he wanted to straighten it out. "How long?"

"I don't know."

The ball of energy wouldn't be contained. He stood. Paced to the bookcases and back. He'd become a man while I wasn't looking, with wiry muscles around a taut male frame. He was bigger across the shoulders than Strat. His torso was longer. And unlike his biological father, he was prone to despair.

"You're the only one I trust," he said. "You're the only one who can stand up to him. You're the only one."

I was.

I knew it.

My mother was too weak. Our sisters too distracted. I was the only one who loved Jon enough to self-destruct, even if he didn't know why.

———

DREW and I were in the attached guest house beside the rose garden. Two stories with two bedrooms were fully furnished to accommodate any taste. The kitchen had new china and silverware. The sheets were changed even if no one was there. It was a glut of space that would make a New Yorker cringe.

I found Drew in the bedroom. He hung up the phone when he saw me.

"How is he?" he asked.

"Intense. Pissed at himself. Pissed at Dad. He's pissed and intense."

"Reasonably."

"It's reasonable as long as he doesn't take it out on himself again."

Drew tossed his guitar case on the bed and unlatched it. "And how are you?"

He pulled the acoustic out of the case. He took it everywhere. When he didn't drink to escape, he noodled on the guitar. Some of my fondest memories took place in our apartment as I worked on briefs with him strumming in the background.

"I'm okay." I sat in the window seat with my back to the garden. I wanted him to play, but he sat with his instrument on his knee.

"You're okay," he repeated, turning the tuning knobs. "Why don't I believe you?"

"Because you're normal."

He laughed with a strum. I was glad he had a guitar in his lap and music at his fingers. Maybe he'd be amenable to what I was about to suggest.

"Can you play the thing you played when I had the flu?" I asked.

"Sure." He twisted some knobs, and after a few test strums, he played a melody without words. I'd never seen him write it down, but he plucked out the tune from memory. I was blanketed in the sanctuary of his love.

"Thank you." I put my feet on the seat. " Jonathan hates Daddy."

"All boys hate their father at that age."

His comment was true but rote. It applied to normal people in average circumstances.

"I promised him something," I said.

"What was it?"

"That—when he's ready—I'll help him go up against my father."

The rhythm of the music slowed as if Drew was distracted, then picked up again. "That's dangerous."

"It's fine. I think I can soften it if I'm here to watch them."

I braced for a reaction, but he kept his eyes on the strings. Neither denials nor rejections were forthcoming. Naively, I took that as consideration of my suggestion that we stay in Los Angeles. Wisely, I changed the subject.

"What did he say?" I asked. "Yesterday. When you were in my father's office?"

"I think you need to ask what I said."

"What did you say?"

He tapped the body of the guitar and looked at me. "I'm sorry."

"You said you were sorry? For what?"

"I'm apologizing to you." A minor chord rang from the strings. He'd shown me the difference between major and minor chords, and it was one of the only things he'd ever taught me about music that I could hear.

"Why?"

"You told me not to be emotional with him. You warned me. It really did give him the upper hand."

I busied myself with the curtains, opening them to the back patio.

The sun shot through the glass. The ocean slammed into the shore below.

"I told him," Drew whispered in a space between sounds.

"Told him what?"

"That I know."

I knew exactly what he was talking about. There was a finality to it, yet I couldn't accept it with just three words. "Know what?"

"That he stole your child."

Another minor chord hit loudly.

I put my hand over my mouth, speaking through it. "What did he say?"

"He asked if it was mine."

"And you said?"

"It wasn't. But that I would have raised him as mine. And I would have loved him and you just the same."

The song changed. It was no longer a comfort when I was sick or hurting. He'd changed it into something threatening.

My hand shook against my chin. "You shouldn't have done that."

"Yeah. Probably. You warned me, but I couldn't take it. Watching you get hurt over and over. I figured if he knew, it would pull the rug from under him, but it was like nothing. It was like I gave him ammunition. I've dealt with some of the most powerful guys in the music industry and their shark lawyers. I've never felt so in over my head."

"What did he say?"

"He neither confirmed nor denied. Like the CI-fucking-A. He did say that of the two of us, he was glad Strat was... how did he put it? Out of the picture."

That sunk in. My father didn't give out information like that without a purpose. "Oh, my God."

"He said he was very particular about who his daughters were with and you'd gotten away from him earlier than he'd expected. He said you taught him a lesson about when to intervene. He'd been too late with you apparently. And that was why extraordinary action had to be taken. Those were his words. Extraordinary action."

He plucked his strings in the rhythm of the words "extraordinary action."

"You have to go back to New York," I said.

"Yes, we do."

I kneeled in front of him. "No. Just you for now. I have to clear this up."

"I'm not going without you."

"Indy."

"Cin." He called me by the name I'd claimed when we met. "I'm not abandoning you here."

"I'll meet you back home."

He didn't answer, just moved his fingers over the strings. I hadn't forgotten that I wanted to stay. On the contrary, the knowledge that I had to pushed against my ability to hear him.

"Home," he said, gently slapping the body of the guitar. "Have you thought maybe this is your home? And it will be until you cut yourself off from these people?"

"You're my home."

He cupped my face like he had when I'd fallen apart in the hotel hallway. "Cinnamon, you're the love of my life. I can't imagine being without you. But he said Strat had no business touching a girl your age and he got what he deserved."

"He's one to talk."

"He's right. I've been watching this whole thing from the outside, knowing how long I've loved you. Sometimes I look at you here and I see that girl and I think how fucked up it all was."

"It was the eighties," I said. "And you aren't that much older."

He ran his thumb along my cheek without laughing it off.

If I couldn't comfort him with stock answers, I'd comfort him with confidence. "I won't let him hurt you. I'll kill him."

"What about you? What about your hurt?"

"I'm fine."

"I can't live thinking I stole your life."

I held his hand against my face. "I gave it to you. With both hands and a bow on top."

"I know."

That was it? *I know*? I dropped my hands away and leaned back, still kneeling. "What's the point of this conversation, Drew?"

"Ah, she's back." Quick strum. "Welcome. I don't know the point. I'm laying my cards out. Pair of deuces. Every penny in the middle of the table. Down to my underpants. It's time for extraordinary action."

"Define extraordinary." I stood.

"Will you go to New York with me today and never come back?"

"I told you. I'll meet you there."

He stood, holding his guitar at his side. "Then extraordinary is defined as unexpected and self-defeating." He put the guitar in the case and snapped it closed. "Also manipulative. Come home now, or I'm not going to be there when you get back."

"I won't be blackmailed."

"You're used to it." He waved his hand with that palm up, indicating the entirety of my family. "Maybe it's the only way to get through to you."

"Don't you ask me to leave Jonathan."

"You can't help him. I've removed your power to do so. Now either I remove myself so you can try to protect him without me or I remove you to protect you. We can't have both. And Cin? Just to be perfectly clear, we're not living within driving distance of this house. Ever."

He meant it. This was a line in the sand. No tide would wash it away.

A fist pounding on the door stopped us.

"Margie!" It was Theresa.

"What?"

"Daddy wants you to go with him to the lawyers."

It was a strategy meeting about Fiona and Jonathan. The press. The spin.

"In a minute," I called without moving.

"He said the car is here."

"I said in a minute!"

"Whatever." Her footsteps scurried away into nothing.

Drew nodded. "You'd better go."

"Wait for me," I said, looking out the window. A cab waited. A long black car was beside it in the driveway, my father at the door.

"Is that your cab?" I asked.

"It's ours."

"Just wait."

"One day," he said, picking up the case, "you'll see I'm doing you a favor."

"I need you. You can't."

"Choose. You need your family or me. You can't have both. Don't you see? The best thing I can do for you is save you from them or let you do things his way. Us being together isn't possible. He'll never let it happen with me knowing about Jonathan."

He was right. I hated him for it, but not as much as I loved him.

"Fight for me, Drew."

"I am fighting for you. Maybe one day you'll see it. I'm fighting harder than I've ever fought for anything."

"I can't choose."

He dropped his hands from my face. "You already have."

DREW WAITED at the open door of the cab as the driver put his bags in the trunk. I was at the point of a triangle, equidistant from the cab and the black car.

Drew was really going to make me choose.

After all our years together, he couldn't wait a few days. But I knew as well as he did that we weren't talking about days or a week. We were talking about how we chose to live our lives.

Reality be damned, I was still mad.

"Margaret," my father said from inside the limo.

The man I called the love of my life didn't make a move one way or the other to convince me I should go with him. He was leaving it up to me.

I didn't ask myself what I wanted. I didn't have to. Spite and anger could push buttons rational thought wouldn't touch. My choice was made out of love, but it felt more like bitterness.

Because… how dare he? Knowing what he knew. Being who he was. How dare he ask me to leave Jonathan?

The cab driver slammed the trunk shut. Drew didn't move.

"Goodbye, Indy," I whispered. He didn't hear me. He'd need to see my actions, not hear my words.

I got into the car, next to my father. The door was shut behind me.

"Where is he going?" Dad asked, referring to Drew.

"Home."

He nodded. Wordless approval. Fuck him.

"I'm going back to New York tonight," I said, testing the waters. Maybe if I said it, I'd do it.

"Jonathan just needs a good talking to. He needs something to do with his time besides get moony over a crazy, deluded girl."

"Who you were sleeping with too apparently?"

Daddy swallowed and looked in a corner for half a second. I'd taken him by surprise. I had the upper hand for a single moment. I didn't care about his infidelity with a seventeen-year-old. It was old news. I had something older to use in that rare moment.

"I talked to Drew," I said. "He told me everything."

Dad smirked, and like that, my moment was over. "I doubt that."

"I want you to understand, we know what you did to me. What you did to Mom. And especially Jonathan. Especially him."

"What I did? I gave your mother the son she always wanted and I gave my son a life."

Was he admitting it? I was taken aback by the idea that he'd cop to the truth, but he didn't stop there.

"You weren't keeping him," Daddy continued. "He had a stable family instead of a fifteen-year-old single mother who didn't know who the father was."

"Fuck you." My growl had sixteen years of hurt and rage behind it.

From his face, my father thought it was cute. "I don't expect you to thank me. But I did everyone a favor. You. Your mother. Jonathan."

"They don't know. It's not a favor if they're ignorant."

He leaned into me and spoke with a conversational tone that made a lie of the seriousness of his words. "That *is* the favor. And if you tell them, you'll do more harm than good. You know it's true. And if I ever believe your boyfriend—or whatever you call him—gets it in his head to contravene the kindness I've done, I'll do whatever I have to do to stop him."

A threat uttered in a solemn tone can be dismissed as posturing. Daddy wasn't posturing. He sounded as if he was talking about the weather.

"If you touch him..." I wasn't as good at making light of a threat. "If anything happens to him, you're going to be very, very sorry."

I should have had the upper hand again, but he met my stare with his own unwavering gaze as if I were reciting the lines of a closing argument he'd already prepared for. He was on the offense. Instead of denying the worst or backing out of his threat, he doubled down on how much he could hurt me.

"Stratford was a drug addict. What's Andrew's poison? Drink? You're going to blame me if anything happens to him, too?"

"Test me, Daddy. Just try to test me."

He sat back, looked out the window. No one I'd ever threatened had ever seemed less defensive. Whatever I expected, he did the opposite. I could learn from him. I could learn a lot.

So could Jonathan. Given the right grooming, my son could turn into my father.

That would be my fault too.

"You're under stress." His play at compassion proved my point. Whenever I expected him to turn left, he veered right. "It's been a hard trip, and we're putting a lot on you."

"Don't placate me."

He fixed his collar and flicked a spot of dust off his cuff.

I could still go back. Never see any of them again. Start a family from scratch. Just Drew and me. Weren't my promises to him at least as important as my promises to Jonathan?

They weren't.

If I was going to do what I'd said, then I was doing it one hundred percent.

The car pulled up behind the lawyers' building on Wilshire. Valets scurried across the red brick drive to open the doors.

I *was* under stress. And they *were* putting a lot on me. All true. But I got out of the car determined not to be soothed or manipulated. I got out with a plan.

The doorman held open the glass door, but I didn't go through.

When my father met me on the other side of the car, I spoke quietly but firmly, standing my ground until I was done. "Here's the deal. I stay, but on my terms."

Dad folded his hands in front of him. "Out with it."

"Your children are getting older and you're losing control. Stuff's going to start slipping. I know where our money comes from, and Carrie's starting to find out from that man you made her marry. Sheila's incurious, but she's not stupid. You're five years from going to prison or losing everything. I'm going to keep that from happening."

"How?"

"You're going to carefully lose it all."

He tilted his head as if my moving to a lateral subject had gotten his attention. "Carefully? How does one carefully lose everything?"

"One makes shitty bets and uses the losses to hide assets."

He nodded in appreciation. "You learned a lot in New York."

"From now on," I continued, "I know every pie we've got our fingers in. I manage the money, and I keep the secrets. You leave Drew alone, and you stop trying to make Jonathan the fucking scion."

"You want the keys to the kingdom?"

"I demand them."

The doorman let go of the handle, swinging our reflection into the rectangle of glass.

"You've turned from a worthless whore into a formidable woman," he said as if it was high praise. "I guess I have Andrew to thank for that."

"No. This is all on you."

I walked to the doors so he wouldn't see me shaking. I wasn't sure if I'd avoided being manipulated or if I'd walked into a trap.

DREW WAS GONE.

I gave him long enough to fly, land, and walk in the door. I called our co-op. I got his voice on the machine.

You've reached the McDrazens. We're either out or ignoring you. Leave a message after the tone. If this is a legal emergency, beep us and we'll call you back.

"Drew," I said. "Indy. If you're there, pick up. We have to talk." I waited. He didn't pick up. "Indiana Andrew McCaffrey. I am not fucking with you. This is it. If you can't coexist with the people who raised me, then maybe this is over. But you should be man enough to pick up the phone." Nothing. "Fine. It's for the best."

I put the receiver down and stared at it. Got ready for bed. Tried to read a book.

What had I done?

Made a deal with the devil. Taken on a criminal empire to protect my son. Given my life with both hands, convinced it was my decision.

It was never my decision. I had been built to lie and manipulate. It was in my genes. I'd avoided it by force of will, but when Jonathan tried to take his own life, my will was broken and the real me spilled out.

At one in the morning, I called again.

The message was new.

You've reached Margaret Drazen. Leave her a message after the tone. To reach Andrew McCaffrey, please call Franklin, Devon, and Milch during business hours.

I hung up without leaving a message. He was there. Right there. Probably listening with a bottle of something amber in his hand.

I opened the patio doors and let the salt air and crashing waves give me advice. The wind told me to ignore him and let him call me when he was ready. The waves advised an immediate one-way plane ticket. Neither had a middle way.

At eight eastern, I called his office at Franklin, Devon, and Milch to find that he'd taken the week off. They said he was coming back. I knew better.

I called our place again. Listened to his voice. The tone. The seconds of silence.

"Drew," I said into the tape, going onto the patio where the wind flipped my hair and the tide beat a rhythm against the shore. "You have to be back by now. If you're packing, you need to stop and pick up the phone. Please. I'm begging you. I don't beg. You know I've never begged in my life." I bent myself in two as if I were on a crashing plane. "Please. Let's figure it out. You can live here with me. You can make music like you should be. We can be together and I can protect Jonathan. Please. Talk to me. I'm lost here. I don't know what I'll become if you go. Please don't leave me."

I waited, but he didn't pick up. So I begged again, breathed, waited. The machine ran out of tape and cut me off.

That was the end.

FOUR

LOS ANGELES - 2013

SOME THINGS GET BETTER WITH TIME. OLD WOUNDS AND CHEESE, FOR instance. Trees. Coral reefs. Coal turned to diamonds and dinosaur shit turned to oil.

Time fermented value into the worthless and transformed the ordinary into the extraordinary.

Time also broke down memory into component parts. I could remember Drew's singing but not his speaking voice. I remembered his scent, his smile, and sometimes his taste. I remembered more from our first months together than anything that happened after we moved in together.

Mostly, Jonathan reminded me of Palihood and the two men I couldn't choose between. For a while, he was the connective tissue between who I became and what I'd lost. He was passionate about everything. Curious about history and business, fanatical about art. He loved music and painting deeply, but decided he was a patron, not a participant.

I watched him but never told him what he was to me. As long as he was all right, I wasn't even tempted. He graduated from Stanford, went to Wharton for his MBA, played baseball, had girlfriends, and when he discovered the Drazen Group was broke—a lie my father and

I had created to put the family under the radar—he pitched a way to get us back into the black.

He seemed okay, so I was okay. The status quo was a magical place where time cracked memory into a few fleeting thoughts, wearing down their edges until they were frictionless ball bearings in the wheels of life.

There were always problems. Love was never easy for any of us. The Drazens were trouble, but nothing I couldn't manage. Until Jonathan grew up and took over some of our real estate holdings, there wasn't much on paper, so we weren't an appealing target for investigation or media coverage.

One Christmas Eve, soused and relaxed, Jonathan sat with me on the deck of Sheila's house, overlooking the wine-dark winter sea. It was late. Everyone was in bed or lounging in their own corner. I had a blanket wrapped around me, and we had a bottle of scotch on the table between us. His sock feet leaned on the railing.

"I think I see Santa," I said, pointing at a plane streaking across the sky.

"If I have kids," he said, "I'm not doing the Santa bullshit. It's all lies."

He was almost thirty-one and had a reputation as a guy who went on a sex binge after his divorce as if he wanted to fuck the memory of his wife off his dick.

"You're having kids?"

"Of course I'm having kids. What did you think?"

"I don't know. Guess I thought you'd find a woman to do that with."

The standard jabs usually ended in the standard excuses about time and how there was plenty of it.

This time, he twisted in his chair to face me and held up his hand. "Open pledge."

Thinking he was going to tell me a secret about a special someone, I put up my hand without question. "Pledge open."

"Why aren't you married?"

I nearly choked on my own spit. "Jonathan. Are you serious?"

"There's nothing wrong with you." He indicated the body under the blanket, landing on my face. "You're nice looking. Smart. If you were gay, that would be fine, but you're not. So what's the deal?"

My arms stretched tighter around me, making the blanket taut. We were in pledge. Only the absolute truth would do. Had I known he was going to broach this particular subject, I would have avoided putting up my hand. "I date sometimes. But I'm not easy. I'm not..." Dateable? Marry-able? Emotionally attractive? "I don't defer and I don't like small talk. I like getting to the point."

"Fuck or don't?"

"Sometimes. And that hasn't turned up anyone worth my time. Also, I don't really care if I get married or even date. It's not a priority and men can sense that."

"What about that guy?" He spun his hand in a circle as if he could draw a specific memory from the air like cotton candy.

"Which guy?"

"The one from when I was a kid."

As warm as it was under the blanket, my guts went cold. I barely thought about Drew anymore, but when I did, his presence came from my own head—not someone else's mouth. "He couldn't handle it."

"Handle what? You?"

"You're being a real pain in the ass."

"I know." He didn't take it back or clarify. He untwisted himself and put his feet back on the railing.

"Us," I said. "He couldn't handle us. The family. Dad had him on eggshells half the time, and the other half he drank himself into a state of inconsequence."

"Did you love him?"

"Jesus Christ, Jon, really?"

"I take that as a yes?"

"Why are you so curious?"

He shrugged and picked his scotch off the table. "I'm self-involved. I want to know if I'll ever forget Jessica. That's all."

"You will." Talking about his problems made me realize how tense I'd been when I was the topic of conversation. "Can we close pledge?"

He looked at the bottom of his drink. "Do you know what happened to him?"

"Damnit, Jon."

"You don't have to tell me. Pledge closed." He put up his hand then reached for the bottle. "I didn't know the subject was painful."

It wasn't. Not usually. Not even on Christmas, looking out over the blackness of the horizon. It wasn't pain. It wasn't regret. It was a dull, humming grief that was as ambient as ocean waves.

"He was a musician," I said. "He could be anywhere."

"He taught me how to smoke."

"He did not."

"Totally did. Disgusting habit. We both choked. But if I ever wanted to know about something I couldn't ask Dad, he was my man."

Wiggling out of the blanket, I picked up my glass and held it out. "Can you pour me, please?"

He poured two fingers and waited with the bottle up while I drank it, burning away the ice in my guts, then he poured me more before putting the bottle down and gazing over the sea.

"Fuck him," I said. "He left us all."

He nodded, looking into his drink. His profile was a roadmap of his ancestry. Strat's nose and the sharply-cut Drazen jawline.

"You'll forget her, Jon," I said. "And you won't be like me. You'll find someone else."

"I don't want to." He held up his glass for a toast. "Here's to me being like you."

"I'll toast to you being you." I completed the toast and drank before he could object.

It would be close to a year before he collapsed into his girlfriend's arms at an art show. A year of the status quo wearing memories into harmless spheres with no jagged edges. Until one ball bearing hit another and they broke into heart-shredding shards. Jonathan's heart was bad and no one had told him his father had died of an overdose but might have lived if it wasn't for a heart that didn't work quite right.

Almost a year later, everything flipped. I was in the hospital, thinking of Jon as the son I'd lost, not the brother I'd had.

FIVE

2015

FOR YEARS AT A TIME, I REFERRED TO MYSELF AS A CHILDLESS SINGLE woman, even when looking in the mirror. I observed my flat stomach and thought, "Well that's because you've never had any children."

Funny how the mind works.

And when I ran into Will Santon, my head of investigations, and his four-year-old in the line for coffee, I thought, "I don't have one of those."

I guess I hadn't had one of those. I'd had a brother.

Right. Maybe my mind's tricks were somersaults into truth.

I hired Will to do the things I wasn't supposed to do. Unsanctioned information gathering. Tough interviews. Covert recordings. Spy shit. He had a good touch and was so smart I sometimes called him just to talk out a problem.

"Miss Margie!" she cried.

"Hannah," Will said, "it's Ms. Drazen."

Will was in his late thirties, looked late twenties, and had the mind of a man who had seen eighty years' worth of suffering.

"It's nice to see you, Hannah," I said.

Her eyes were the same gray as her dad's, and her skin was the rich brown of a mixed-race girl. She hugged her father's leg, twisting her head until her face was smushed.

"Have I ever told you how much I like your name?"

"It was her mother's mother's name," her dad said. The US Army had made him a widower when Hannah was just a baby. He was handsome and strong. We'd had a few tumbles in bed. It was fine. Great, even. But I didn't do emotions and he didn't do commitments, so we stopped fucking before either became necessary.

"I like it."

"She's going to hate it someday," he said, picking her up.

"Why?"

We moved up in the line.

"Evergreen name. That's what Wanda called it."

"Evergreen?" I said. "That's code for what?"

"Old lady." When he smiled, his face got less rugged, less angular and hard.

"As the proud owner of an evergreen name, I assure you, it never stopped me from being young."

An unmarried, childless woman in her late forties is the constant recipient of a certain look. Not pity. Not understanding. Sometimes curiosity. Often bitterness tinged with accusation. Maybe a lick of condescension. I constantly fell into the twist of a conversation, in the dark corners around what's unsaid. Saying I was young once opened me up to that look, and under normal circumstances, I would have regretted saying it.

But not with Will. He never made me feel like a spinster. He looked me in the eyes when he said, "I bet it didn't."

I leaned close to Hannah and said softly, pretending Will didn't hear everything, "Have you ever tried the snowman cookies?"

She shook her head.

"Would you like to?"

She looked at her father, who raised an eyebrow and said, "Not before lunch."

"I didn't ask you, Delta."

He kept his eyes on mine for a half a second. They flicked over my body, then back to my face. His jaw worked into a smile that never found his lips, a readjustment at the joint, a relaxing of the chin. Even past the short, dark beard, I could see every muscle. I wondered what his neck tasted like.

"We aren't in the office," he said. "You're not the boss."

"Of course I am."

"You're lucky Hannah's with me."

"I felt pretty lucky when I got up this morning." My smile took on a life of its own. Resisting it was making my entire face twitch.

"Next guest please!" The call dripped with cheerful impatience.

"Three snowman cookies," I said. "Two large coffees."

"Three?" Will asked.

"So she doesn't have to share."

That was the benefit of being a childless, unmarried, middle-aged woman. I got to write my own fucking rules.

"She didn't eat her vegetables last night," Will scolded.

"Nanette gave no treat!" Hannah complained about her au pair. "Daddy was out with Brian's mommy and there was no treat."

"Daddy was out with Brian's mommy?" I raised my eyebrow at Hannah.

"From my school. She's really pretty. Her name means angel."

Will shrugged.

I smiled. "You can have my cookie, Hannah." My phone rang. I would have ignored it, but it was passed through a cloaked number I used for emergencies. "Hello?"

I handed Hannah the bag with the treats, and Will took his coffee.

"What do you say?" Will asked his daughter.

"Is this Margaret Drazen?" asked the woman on the phone.

"Thank you," Hannah said, spilling crumbs on her father's jacket.

"Yes," I said, then mouthed the girl a, "You're welcome."

"This is Sequoia Hospital."

The color must have drained from my face, because Will let Hannah slide to her feet and watched me as if he thought he would have to catch me.

"What is it?" I snapped as if I were impatient for bad news.

The woman answered. "Are you the emergency contact for Jonathan Drazen?"

SIX

THE LAST TIME I'D BEEN AT SEQUOIA FOR JONATHAN, HE'D ALMOST DIED.
It took me seconds to decide this wasn't as serious. He was thirty-two.
Divorced already, with an ex dying to get her hands on his money. A
grown man with an empire of his own and a girlfriend he had actual
feelings for. He'd collapsed in front of her at an art show. It was
probably exhaustion or a virus. Dehydration. Whatever. Healthy men
in their early thirties rarely collapse from something that'll kill them,
but they don't collapse over nothing.

Trust me on that.

I'd convinced myself, before I even put the car in park, that it
wasn't suicide again. For a malcontent, Jon seemed pretty happy. He
was going to win this latest battle with his ex. His business was finally
separated from our father's. The girlfriend seemed devoted enough,
and because I'd had to fix this latest mess with his ex-wife, I'd learned
she shared his unusual sexual proclivities. He trusted me that much.

I was told he wasn't in the ER anymore. They'd moved him
upstairs to the ICU.

Still convinced it was nothing, I made my way upstairs.

As I watched the elevator lights blink, my eyes fell on the red button at the bottom of the panel. It was a circle with the word ALARM next to it, and braille raised underneath. The paint was scraped off the first A and the RM, leaving LA.

Leaving LA.

Drew rode this elevator with me in 1999. The city had been less crowded and the night had been darker. Jonathan had been no more than an elephant in the room.

I'd been so fierce then.

And now?

The doors opened on my floor before I defined what fierceness had turned into.

THE GIRLFRIEND WAS ALREADY SITTING on a mauve chair in a beige waiting room. Monica. She was five-ten, brown eyes, long dark hair falling out of an up-do. She was still in heels and a party dress.

"I think he was poisoned." Her voice usually had a throaty tone, but exhaustion and tears had made it worse. She twisted one of Jonathan's linen handkerchiefs.

She was distraught enough for both of us, which worked because I wasn't upset at all. Between a serious illness and foul play, I'd give about even odds. Throw in the possibility of indigestion or exhaustion and the odds of the other two shrank to mathematical irrelevance.

"Poisoned," I repeated so she could see how silly it sounded. "By whom?"

"Jessica. Maybe?"

"His ex-wife isn't that bright."

Her eyes darted around the corners and settled in her lap. Monica wasn't a shy woman, but she was holding something back, and her discretion could be easily confused for bashfulness.

"Your father was there. At the museum." A quick glance. A hardened jaw. "But he's not here."

"He went to get our mother."

She leveled her gaze on me. "Jonathan doesn't trust him."

The sentence had a weight that implied layers of meaning under Jonathan's well-earned distrust.

"Jonathan wasn't poisoned," I said. "This is probably nothing, and if you say what I think you're going to say, it will put me in an awkward position. I'm too old for awkward positions."

She blinked. "You're right. I'm a little stressed."

I put my hand on hers. "Trust me. You guys are going to be doing... whatever it is you do in no time."

It helped, in those moments, to think of Jonathan as my brother. These days, I rarely thought of him as anything else.

My phone beeped with a text. It was Will Santon.

—IS EVERYTHING ALL RIGHT?—
—Ducky—

*—I HAVE PEOPLE ON THERESA. **Does she need to know what happened?**—*

Right. Theresa was her own problem. She'd taken off with a mobster, trying to erase a lifetime of goody-two-shoes behavior. It was my job to hover in the background to make sure she didn't get into trouble.

—NOT YET. Don't think it's a big deal—

After verifying that my brother wasn't in a life-or-death situation, Will called on the secure line. He'd only call if he had something he didn't want to text. I excused myself and went into the hallway to pick up.

"How much time do you have?" he asked.

"Five minutes. Give me the bullet points." I approached the coffee vending machine and got out a card.

"Do you know a South African named Deacon Bruce?"

I hadn't heard that name in years, but I'd never forget it.

"Define 'know.'"

I made my beverage choice. Hot and black. My hands were cold.

"If he was extradited back here to face criminal charges, would he have anything to say about you?"

Deacon was my sister Fiona's ex-something. I'd had one interaction with him, and it involved tying her rapist to a tree. My first fix. Soon after I'd turned my back on Drew.

"What kind of charges?"

"I have no idea." He sighed as if he needed a moment to consider what he was going to tell me. "I overheard a phone conversation last night."

The machine rumbled. A paper cup dropped into the slot.

"You were on a date last night."

"Yeah. My brothers are paranoid. They found out my date is a federal agent who's on the Drazens."

There was always someone on the Drazens. They had a dossier on us the size of an unabridged dictionary.

"Way to pick 'em," I said.

"Can you answer the question?"

Hot black liquid flowed into the cup with a gurgle and a hiss. I remembered that year. It was ages ago, but in California, there was no statute of limitations on attempted murder. The coffee was a solid line. It looked still, but it flowed on and on.

"They'll never extradite him unless he wants to be extradited. Are you sure you don't know what they're looking for?"

"I don't. Do you?"

Had I been sloppy? Did I know something now that I hadn't known then?

Two men had loved Fiona. I'd used both of them, Jonathan, and others to avenge her rape by Warren Chilton. Deacon had wanted to kill him. I'd talked him out of it.

Maybe the entire thing had been too complicated to cover.

"Yes. I know." The spigot squeezed closed and the plastic door unlocked. Wincing from the heat, I took my coffee. "Before we met. 1999. You're clear."

"I'm not worried about me."

Pressing my hands against the hot sides of the cup, I wove back to where I'd started. "That's noble. But I am. You have a daughter."

"I won't let you get put away."

"Dear Lord," I prayed out loud, stopping in the middle of a wide, empty hallway that echoed, "I enjoy working with Will. Don't let him trust me too much."

"Your prayers are answered, sweetheart. I'll trust you until I can't."

No one else would have dared call me sweetheart. Will could get away with a lot. He was the only friend I had.

I backtracked down another hall and turned at a Monet print I recognized. "Good, because I can't replace you, but neither can Hannah."

I wound up back in the waiting room. Monica was standing with her hands folded in front of her, talking to two men in lab coats. Doctors.

"I won't argue with that," Will said.

"Your three hundred seconds are up." I softened my voice. Something in my brother's girlfriend's demeanor rubbed my hard edges smooth. "Really, I have to go."

I hung up and stood next to Monica. "What's going on?"

She pointed at the doctors, her face twisted into something crushingly sad. "I know him."

She was going to break into tears. He must be an old boyfriend or some shit. Nothing she should be getting her knickers in a twist about.

I took her by the biceps. "Keep it together."

She sucked her lips in her teeth and clamped her eyes shut. Took a big, gunky swallow. "He's a cardiologist."

The doctors, tired of waiting, came to us. Monica tried to keep her shit in a sock, but it didn't work. She sniffed hard. Real messy crier. Maybe this wasn't an ex-boyfriend. Maybe an ex-husband. Maybe a long-lost lover. Jesus, I'd cry too.

"Monica," the blond one said.

"Hi, Brad."

No love. No sexual tension.

"I'm sorry to meet under these circumstances. This is Dr.—"

He was talking. Telling the other doctor how he knew Monica. Neighbors. They were neighbors.

I fell into a hairline crack of time.

He's a cardiologist.

She was upset because he was a cardiologist.

Why would a cardiologist be coming into the waiting room to talk about my brother's indigestion/exhaustion?

Strat had a heart problem.

"I'm sorry," I said. "What did you say?"

Brad held out his hand. "I'm sorry, you're the patient's...?" He paused to let me fill in the blank.

"I'm his..." *Mother.*

"Sister," Monica interjected when the word fell back down my throat.

I was his mother, and my son's father had had a genetic heart defect that killed him when he overdosed. I was his failed mother who'd never fought for him because reasons. Because fear. Because I was just a kid.

Brad was talking far, far away.

Why would a 31 year-old man have a heart attack?

There must be ancillary problems. A genetic defect, maybe.

I was a smart person.

I was not emotional or hysterical.

He was saying something about staying calm. About the best cardiac unit in the country, but I couldn't hear it because reasons. Because I couldn't. Because hearing it might hurt too much. Because I'd had rock music in my head and drugs in my blood.

Because I'd loved both of them and I had nothing left for my own child.

Who I loved.

Who I loved, and who was in serious trouble.

"Can I have some water?" I croaked. "I think I need to sit down."

Monica led me to a chair, and there, for a crack of time that was indefinable, I fell down an abyss I recognized. But this time, there was no Drew to tell me to breathe.

They needed to know. For his sake, they needed to know.

My mouth opened and the secret hovered in the back of my throat, crouched and afraid of the light.

My hand closed around a cold cup. Water would wash the secret down or lubricate its journey. I gulped. It chilled my insides, mouth to sternum.

"Are you all right?" Monica asked, eyes big with worry.

"Yeah." My head was more clear. "Where are the doctors?"

Monica pointed at the other side of the room where they sat across from Mom, speaking in hushed voices. She had her coat and bag. Her hair was a mess. She must have just arrived.

I couldn't hear them, and I thought for a second that if I used the same hushed voice, they wouldn't actually hear the secret.

I got up and stood next to my mother. She took my hand as if it were a lifeline. I'd never felt more isolated than when she reached out to me. If I had to tell, I wouldn't do it in front of her. Daddy could break it to her if she'd even speak to him long enough to hear it.

"We were just telling your mother what we told you," Dr. Thorensen said.

What had they told me? I'd lost it in guilt and confusion.

"Go on," I replied.

"It's unusual for a man his age to present with a heart attack, but it's not unheard of. We're checking for blockages, heart defects, and the like. Until then—"

"So if there's a defect, you'll see it?" I asked.

"Yes."

"What if it's genetic?" I asked. "Will that make a difference?"

Dr. Emerson answered, "Only for his children. He'll have to keep on top of them."

"His father's heart's perfect," Mom said. "And mine too."

"Doesn't matter," Thorensen said. "Defects can skip multiple generations. Bottom line, if he needs a bypass, he'll get it once he's stable. This cardiac unit is the best in California and one of the top five in the nation. He's going to get all the care he needs. Just leave it to us."

Leave it to them. As if we had a choice.

"All right," I said clearly now that the secret of Jonathan's parentage had slunk back in my throat.

"Yes," Mom concurred. "We'll leave it to you."

They stood, and I let them go back behind the swinging doors without uttering a thing I didn't have to. They were checking. Strat's heart didn't matter.

SEVEN

JONATHAN WAS BEING WHEELED AROUND BETWEEN DIAGNOSTIC UNITS. WE were put in an abhorrently expensive private waiting room so we didn't have to feel any middle-class discomforts. Sheila came with a crossword book and files for the few clients she kept. Fiona came with an entourage she left at the door. Leanne was en route, and Deirdre was in the chapel. Dad came but was still in exile from Mom over a decade after she'd found out he was sleeping with a not-quite-legal friend of his daughter's. Forgiveness was in short supply. It was 1999 all over again.

There was nothing I could do but wait and manage business from the phone.

That night, Sequoia was as quiet as hospitals ever get, and the beeping machines only had the bang and clatter of brooms and mopping *whuh whuh splash* to compete with. Walking down the hall, heels clopping on the linoleum, I heard it.

Someone's earbuds weren't in all the way, or the nurses had a little radio.

Maybe I was going insane, but I heard it as sure as I was breathing. I heard it and stopped walking.

I knew plenty about falling in love with musicians, but I didn't know shit about music except the difference between major and minor. And I knew what I heard—two notes plucked in sequence from an alternate tuning Strat had tried to explain to me one day in 1982. It was the most distinctive thing I'd ever heard in the Palihood or Sequoia Hospital.

I followed it to an open door. Under the light of a single lamp, a man in his twenties with a short fade and soulful brown eyes sat by an older woman's bed, noodling with the strings as she slept. Nothing exceptional or original. At least nothing that sounded like anything the boys had made in Palihood. How had I heard Bullets and Blood?

The young man noticed my intrusion.

"Sorry," I said, backing away. "Wrong room."

Stiff-kneed and lock-jawed, I went to Jonathan's room. I hadn't heard what I thought I'd heard. Obviously.

The curtain was drawn. I slid my hand between the edge of the fabric and the wall, pushing it aside. Monica was on a chair, bent over the bed, her head resting on his thigh. His hand lay in her hair, and even with white tubes coming out of the veins, it rested there in security and strength.

They were unable to give Jonathan the bypass until tomorrow. He'd been too weak to move and too unstable to cut. Yet he'd laid his hand on his love's head to comfort her.

I'd made him. He was a man who loved and who was loved. A man who spoke and created meaning. Who heard and was heard. A fully realized human.

Quietly, I stepped into the room. His beard was growing in redder than the brownish ginger of his hair. Strat's had been more strawberry. Indy's had been browner. I'd liked to fantasize that Jonathan was really Drew's and one day we'd live together in some nuclear family fever dream. But he wasn't Drew's. The straight nose was Strat. The green eyes as rare as precious Chinese jade. The body like a tensed spring and the shape of the hands cupped over a lover's head or the curve of a guitar were one hundred percent Stratford Gilliam.

And let's not forget the heart defect that killed the father could kill the son.

I stood over him, thinking he'd look less like Strat if I got closer, but his cheeks were rock-star hollow and the artery in this throat pulsed in a rhythm.

"You look just like your father." The words assumed Jonathan was asleep and escaped.

"But he's an asshole," he replied, eyes opening into slits.

I had to reroute my train of thought around a hairpin turn. Monica was deeply asleep, lips smushed on his thigh.

"There's that," I said. "Good-looking guy though."

"You come to offer me a modeling contract?"

"I couldn't sleep."

"Must be nice."

I sat on the edge of the spare chair. "I'm sorry."

"About?"

About too many things to list. "Have you ever played music? Ever tried?"

"Piano, like all of us."

Right. We'd all had to take two years of piano. Sheila and Deirdre had played without any delicacy or touch. Carrie still enjoyed playing the last time I saw her. The rest of us had dropped it the minute our obligations were met.

"Why did you stop?" I asked.

"No talent."

"I don't believe that." I must have been tired to tell such a dangerous truth with such conviction. Backpedaling beat explaining. "You're good at everything."

"Not good enough." He looked at Monica. "Not like her. I could hit the keys, but when she plays… it's music."

Not everyone could tell the difference. I couldn't always. Not without Indy and Strat explaining what was good, what sucked and why. Even then, the appreciation wasn't instinctual. Jonathan may have suppressed his father's talent, but not his taste.

"I'm glad she's here."

"Me too."

"I wanted to see you before the surgery."

"*Shush.* We don't speak of it." He jerked his chin at Monica as if to say he didn't want to talk about it in front of her.

"I'll be waiting. All of us."

"Even Carrie?"

Of course he dug deep for the sister least likely to show.

"You're such a pain in the ass."

"When I'm better, I'm going to find her and make her feel so guilty."

"Spoken like a true Catholic."

He smiled. "Learned from the best."

I stood and laid my hand on his cheek. He closed his eyes.

"I really like you, brother."

Eyes still shut, he patted my hand before I took it away. His eyes didn't open. The machines beeped calmly and room stayed quiet enough to let me hear the hiss of the vents. He was asleep.

I kissed his forehead, remembering the first time I'd done that. The smell of him had been thick, sweet babyness. Now he was a man, and despite everything, I truly liked who he'd become.

JONATHAN HAD BEEN PREPPED and wheeled into surgery. Most of the family waited in the hotel across the street. Dad had a separate hotel room but made a second home in the hospital cafeteria.

I couldn't be cooped up in a room any more than I could eat bad bagels and exchange barbs with Dad, so I ran the hospital halls like a rat in a maze, working my phone like a weapon of mass efficiency.

"I want to know where Theresa is," I said into the phone with a stride that suggested a destination but guaranteed none. My goody-two-shoes sister had gone missing with her boyfriend, a notorious mob boss. "And if you can't find her, I want to know where the mafia don is."

"He's not mafia," Will said. "He's camorra."

"Same shit, different food." I kept walking at the same pace, weaving through people, turning corners into new wings, new waiting areas, avoiding doorways that required an ID card or a medical degree.

"I have a lead who says there's a war starting."

"Is he hiding her?"

Same shit. Different day. The chaos of the Drazens always had the same shape. Only the colors changed.

"Don't know yet. How's Jonathan?"

I stopped when I saw him.

A man by the double doors, far away, flicking in and out of sight as people passed.

Brown hair. Scruff at the jaw. Evenly-sized top and bottom lips. Eyes as blue as jewels.

"Indy?" I said, frozen in place.

He turned to look at me as if answering my call.

"What?" Will asked.

I walked toward the man. Big steps. Not quite running. Never taking my eyes off him. He wore jeans and a black sweater that was stretched at the neck. Hands in pockets. The slouch of the confidently unassuming.

"Margie?" Will's voice came through the phone.

Indy.

Drew.

Crossing an intersection of hallways, I got knocked off balance by a woman in scrubs. Her clipboard jammed right into my ribs.

"I'm so sorry!" she said.

"It's fine."

"Margie?" Will got far away.

When I looked down the hall, the man in the black sweater was gone.

It was just me in a sea of moving people.

WHENEVER I WENT home for the holidays, Jonathan and Drew talked as if they were drawn to each other. I'd always assumed it was because in a house full of women and my father, they were the only two sane men. Drew wasn't much of an athlete, but they threw the ball around. Later, Drew helped Jonathan learn his signals, catching pitches.

He was fourteen when I saw them on the back lawn with their gloves to the side. He was picking at the grass and muttering while

Drew listened with a beer centering him. I kept glancing over from the table as Fiona gossiped endlessly about people I didn't care about and Theresa *ts*ked. Carrie was with a husband she hated, and Leanne was changing out of an outfit my mother found inappropriate.

Drew put his hand on Jon's shoulder and spoke as my brother looked at his hands.

"What were you talking about?" I asked later that night, when Drew and I were alone.

"Girl problems."

"He's too young for girl problems." I was on the bed in my underpants, waiting.

"Tell that to his body," Drew said, peeling off his shirt. "And his mind, which… I can't even tell you what's going on inside it."

"What?"

Fly. Zipper. His pants dropped to his feet. "Not your business."

I pressed the magazine closed. "I have a right to know."

He crawled onto the bed and kissed my nose. "I swore I wouldn't tell his mother."

"Fuck that, Andrew McCaffrey. Is he all right?"

"He's scared."

"Of what?"

"Himself." He kissed my neck and shoulder. "Of his thoughts. His desires. He's fine. He's a good kid."

"Honey?" I said as his mouth worked its way across my breasts.

"Mm-hm?"

"If he needs a guy to talk to—like a normal guy, not my father—can you be there for him?"

"I already am."

"WHERE'S MONICA?" I asked Deirdre, who was in her usual waiting room chair with a magazine in her lap. I was still disconcerted about what I hadn't seen and how hard a part of me had tried to see someone else.

"I haven't seen her."

"All morning?"

I didn't wait for an answer. I called Jonathan's girlfriend.

"Where are you?" I asked, not knowing what I wanted out of her.

"Santa Monica and Cañon."

"I'm sorry." I must have heard her wrong. That was far away, and not between where she lived and the hospital. "Did you guys discuss you not coming or something?"

"What's going on?"

"He's in surgery, and I thought you might want to be here when he got out. Unless something changed with you two."

"No!" A bell dinged from her side and the receiver rubbed up against something as Monica muttered, "Excuse me," to a person on her side.

"What was that?" I asked before I realized the answer. "Are you on the *bus*?"

"Lot parking is fifteen dollars, and it's permit parking on the street over there at this hour. I don't need to blow gas money when the bus is fine."

Relieved to have a purpose, I got Jonathan's driver to pick her up. Problem solved, but the problems also dried up and I needed them.

The fancy waiting room felt like a prison, and I couldn't shake the sense that my past was standing behind me, breathing by my ear but afraid to speak.

I took a car home. A few hours in my own house would settle my nerves. Without thinking too hard about it, I found myself tapping on my phone in the back seat, typing his name. There was nothing I hadn't seen before. Two unlikely recipients of the same name. Not him. Not his sons. Nothing.

The apparition at the end of the hall couldn't have been Indiana Andrew McCaffrey. Obviously. He'd be fifty-two now, and the guy in the stretched sweater wasn't a day over twenty-two.

Sixteen years since I'd seen him.

Sixteen years between the time we met and the time he left.

My brain must have been reacting to the symmetry of it and making connections where there were none. It was nonsense and worthy of being ignored.

I took a deep breath, catching a hint of cologne I'd known very well a long time ago.

"For the love of fuck." I gritted my teeth as if biting back insanity.

The scent was the pliable scratch of tweed and the sharp caress of old leather. A little sawdust, and at holidays with my family, too much beer and scotch. It was Drew.

Looking up from my phone, I scanned the car. No air fresheners. New leather. Windows open a crack as we zipped across the 10 freeway at forty miles per hour.

My brain was firing off a memory because of some lateral neural activity. Or maybe it was plain spite.

"Danny?" I said, leaning toward the front seat.

The driver looked at me in the rearview. "Yes, Ms. Drazen?"

"Change of plans. Take me downtown to Spring Street."

"Yes, ma'am."

Without complaint, he got off on the next exit. I leaned back and texted Will to warn him I was coming to his office.

I'd made a decision I might regret, but I didn't have a choice.

EIGHT

I GOT OUT OF THE ELEVATOR AND HEADED DOWN THE HALL, BLOWING BY the tall, handsome guy in a suit. He spun around and walked down the hall beside me.

"You went right past me," Will said.

"I'm a little preoccupied at the moment, if you don't mind."

"I don't. But I wanted to grab you before you came in."

"I'm grabbed."

"The agent I was telling you about?"

"The one you're dating?"

"She casually asked me who I worked with." We started back down the hall. "Cooper and Gareth think she's with me to get close to you."

Like me, Will came from a big family. It was almost a mirror image of mine. He had five brothers, four of whom were younger than him, and the youngest child, Lyric, was the only sister. All his youngers worked for him, which meant at some point, they'd worked for me.

"What do you think?"

"I think I like her enough to stay close. But not enough to sell you out."

"You taking one for the team is feminism at its best," I said. "But your brothers should give you some credit. She might be going out with you because she likes you."

He stopped in front of a door marked *Santon Information Assets,* a name that didn't appear in the lobby directory. He'd only been in this new space for a year. I saw it when he was renovating. At first blush, it was a small, two-room suite, but behind locked doors, he owned a few thousand square feet filled with files and computer servers. He believed discretion was impossible without modesty.

"I need to know how you feel about it," he said before opening the door.

"I don't have feelings about it. It's cut and dry. If she wants a date, she can call me. If she wants to ask questions, she can get a subpoena."

"You have a way with words."

He opened the door. Gareth and Cooper looked up from their desks. Gareth was in his thirties, clean-shaven most of the time, and wore suits unless he was on the tennis court. The thick black frames of his glasses were often used to hide his expression.

Cooper was a few years younger and dressed like a hipster on a rooftop photo shoot. His worn-out jeans and half-tucked shirt presented him as someone who wasn't serious. He slouched and shrugged and ran his fingers through his dark, shoulder-length hair as if he didn't care about a damn thing. That was the biggest lie he told. He was a details man. Everything mattered.

They stood as if a four-star general had entered the building.

"Ms. Drazen," Gareth said at the same time Cooper chimed, "Margie!"

"Please sit," I said, putting my bag on a free chair. "You're making me tired."

They sat back down, and Will leaned on a desk with his arms crossed.

"How's Jonathan?" Gareth asked.

"Prepping for surgery. Thanks for asking." I sat down, crossing my legs as if I was staying a while. Six eyes looked at me expectantly. "Pass me that notepad, would you?"

I flicked my finger at a spiral-bound book at Gareth's elbow. He gave it to me and added a pen before I had to ask.

"I need you to find someone for me." I clicked the pen and wrote a down a name. "I knew them in the nineties. This was their address. The name of their band, their record company, their law firm." I was talking faster than I could write. "Birthday. Law school. Place of birth. Parents' names and I think this was their address."

Taking a peek up as I wrote, I saw them exchange glances. Will twisted his pinkie ring.

"Problem, gentlemen?"

After a pause, Will answered. "You're not saying 'he.'"

"What?" I remembered a restaurant on Delancey that Drew used to frequent and wrote it down.

"You're saying '*their* address' instead of '*his* address,'" Gareth added.

I actually hadn't thought about it and had had no intention of doing so. I put the pen down and handed Gareth the notebook. "Maybe I'm testing you."

The three of them hovered over it.

"Bullets and fucking Blood?" Cooper exclaimed. "Are you serious?"

Will kicked his calf.

"She's always serious," Gareth said, swinging around to tap on his keyboard.

"They were gods." Cooper snapped up the book.

"You were pissing in diapers when they split up," Gareth said dryly, navigating to Reddit on one screen and a Tor browser on the other. Engrossed in his new inquiry, he continued as if I wasn't there. "Then it was music production. Heroin. Infighting. Singer died. Cut to commercial before the uplifting denouement."

"Geniuses. Three guys sounded like a dozen." Cooper turned to me. "How did you know them?"

"Carnally."

Gareth turned a subtle shade of red and Cooper pretended he hadn't heard me. It was adorable. Seeing this, Will blurted out a laugh, then I joined him. The brothers bent over their work as we snickered.

"Let's leave these Boy Scouts alone," Will said, waving me into his office.

"Fuck off, man." Cooper punched a code in one of the room's doors.

Will closed the office door behind me. He had an expensive maple desk and plants in every corner. Pictures of his wife and daughter. The space had a warmth I rarely saw in the man. I sat on the short couch by the window.

"Water?" he asked.

"Sure."

He reached into a refrigerator hidden in the bookcase and got two bottles. He sat across from me, putting them on the table between us.

"The walls are soundproofed," he said, cracking open his bottle.

"You have yet to surprise me."

"Sorry about my brothers." He drank then pointed the mouth of the bottle at the door. "They think you're an old spinster."

"Oh, thanks. I needed to know that."

"Just saying I know better."

"Are you trying to get in my pants, William?"

He smiled and put down his bottle. I had no idea what was on his mind, but I was glad for the distraction.

"You hired me to work on the mess with Carrie," he said.

"You were so young and so well-connected."

"Remember when Leanne was held in solitary confinement by the Chinese government?"

"Oh, my God, Delta," I said through a laugh.

"And her boyfriend came home without her?"

"And you nearly pushed him through a brick wall?"

"Or the time your father found out you were giving Deirdre a stipend?"

"And she was passing it right to a fund for orphans in Congo."

"And Fiona."

"Fucking Fiona. You weren't around for the worst of it."

He didn't add our lies about Rachel or Sheila's anger management. He didn't mention all the money we'd found hidden by my grandfather to evade prison, or how we'd rerouted it to right as many wrongs as we could. He didn't know everything, but he knew far more than anyone else.

"We've been through a lot," he said.

"I sense a point coming."

"All these years, and you never asked me to look for him."

I cleared my throat, unwinding my legs and recoiling them in the opposite direction, wishing for the distractions of thirty seconds ago. "So?"

"So. I could have found him ten years ago."

"I didn't want to find him ten years ago. I didn't want to find him yesterday. And unless you want to stop cashing my checks, that's my call." I thought I was done, but I wasn't. "I mean, are you implying I didn't think you had the chops to find him? It wasn't you or your agency. If I thought you were shit at your job, I wouldn't be sitting here. I'd be across town at Brockton Associates, getting my ring kissed at eight hundred an hour plus expenses."

His hands were between his legs, tented against each other, fingertips touching, then tapping. He was counting. The motherfucker was counting the seconds go by so I'd have enough time to say something I'd regret.

"If I didn't know any better," I said, despite my better judgment, "I'd think you were trying to dig into my personal *feelings*."

His fingertips only tapped twice before he answered. "Do you want to find McCaffrey now? One hundred percent?"

"For the sake of argument? Let's say yes."

He looked at his hands then sat back, leaning his temple on his forefinger. "Then I have to tell you something that will make things uncomfortable."

"Is this where you tell me you've always loved me?"

He laughed. "No. Yes, but no." He readjusted in his chair as if he couldn't find the right position.

"Yes, but no?" I crossed my arms.

"Not like that. We had a few great nights."

"I was there."

"We stopped at the right time, but we didn't stop before I started caring about you."

I hadn't walked in the door expecting this conversation, and I wasn't getting trapped in a dialogue about our shared emotional shortcomings.

On the other hand, I cared about him too.

"If you develop feelings for everyone you take to bed, you're going to need therapy."

"It's more of an 'I want Margie to be happy' feeling."

"Great. Same for me. Are we done?"

He kept on going as if I wasn't already halfway out of my seat. "I've been waiting a long time for you to ask me to find McCaffrey. And then a couple of years ago... I stopped waiting."

He stopped waiting? Meaning it wasn't on his mind anymore? Or meaning...

"You already know where he is?"

"Gareth has to get me visual confirmation before I say yes."

I sank deep into the cushions, looking at the texture of the carpet without really seeing it, listening to the whoosh of the air vents without really hearing it.

All I'd had to do was ask. All this time... years, apparently... Drew was a single degree of separation away. He existed in my world, and my world changed. "Where is he?"

"Lately, he's been working as a session man in Seattle. Calls himself Trevor Stone. When he went underground, he went deep. Avoided all the celebrity gossip. The entire internet went dark on him."

He was that committed to never seeing me again.

That wasn't supposed to hurt. Nothing was supposed to hurt, but when my tower was torn down, it was demolished. Well, fuck him. He was going to have to work harder than that.

"Married?" I asked, rolling the word around my mouth as if it didn't cut like steel wool and taste like shit.

"No wife, no kids. He moves around a lot."

Will was pretending to look away, but I caught him gauging my reaction.

"I'm fine," I said.

"Are you?"

"Spit it out."

"I went to meet him."

Well, wasn't that just a blender in the gut.

"Did you just say you *met* him?"

"I wanted to see what kind of man would leave you. That's all."

"That's all?"

"It's my job to be curious."

In pure frustration with his defensiveness and opacity, I growled and held up my fists before banging the table. "Speak! Will Santon, I command you to fucking tell me the whole of it without stopping. Do not wait for me to ask a question. Do not pause respectfully. Do not hesitate so you can soften a blow. Just. Speak."

"First I need you to understand it was out of friendship."

"I understand, and if you stall one more time, I'm going to strangle you out of friendship."

"Okay, okay. More water?" He was smiling, the rat fucker. I was his boss, but he wouldn't let me boss him around.

"No."

"Good. Well, it was last year. Seattle, like I said. He'd done a good job of disappearing, but once we found him, we kept on him."

"We? Your brothers were in on it?"

"You're not allowed to interrupt if you want me to keep talking."

"You're insufferable."

"I know. And yes. Gareth, Cooper, and sometimes Braden kept tabs on McCaffrey. I couldn't do it myself without you knowing. You're up my ass thirty hours a week."

It was more like fifty according to his billing statements, but I didn't press for accuracy.

"I just..." He shook his head and ran his fingers through his hair. "When your brother got divorced, it bothered you. I don't care why, so don't tell me. Actually, when anything happens with him, you have a disproportionate reaction."

"You're really stepping over a line here."

"Fire me then. Because you had us digging up shit on your sister-in-law to help your brother with his divorce. All I could think was there was a guy out there you should have married and this was why you were turning into a lunatic. I had to meet that guy."

My arms were crossed so tightly they ached. "Under what pretenses?"

"I told him I was a music blogger."

A laugh shot out my throat. "Did he believe you?"

"No. He said Indy McCaffrey was dead to the music world. He thought you sent me."

He thought I sent—?

What?

I navigated between warm satisfaction and cold shock. Drew had thought of me. Considered me. Knew I existed in the world. How had I assumed otherwise? Hadn't I thought of him, even when I forgot him?

"How did he seem?" I asked. "Is he all right?"

Before replying, Will fidgeted with his pinkie ring. "Not..." He looked down as if rearranging his words. "I don't know him. Maybe he always looks like that."

"Is he drinking?"

"Not in front of me. I'd say no. He didn't have that bloated look drinkers get. He looked..." He considered again. "Hungry."

"Like he didn't have enough to eat?" I could fix that. I could do it without him even knowing.

"No. Like he didn't have enough... I don't know. Something." He shook his head. "I should have sent Cooper." He rubbed his fingertips as if to bring that one indefinable thing into existence.

"Are you a PI or a two-bit psychic waiting for me to fill in the blanks for you? Give me something I can work with."

Nothing was forthcoming, but I knew what he meant by hungry. I had the same emptiness in my heart. It was a pinhole that slow-leaked the possibility of loving anyone else. The pressure sucked my skin tighter over my bones, squeezing my insides until there was no room for sustenance.

"We found him because he spent some time in prison. Eighteen months for negligent vehicular manslaughter."

He'd killed someone driving drunk? God damn him. I didn't think I had any softness for Drew left inside me, but I'd fooled myself for years. The places in my heart he owned would never fully calcify.

If we'd been together, he would have had a driver. It never would have happened. Not that any of the what-ifs mattered.

What-if and coulda-beens weren't facts. They were ways to tease out sadness for him and anger at myself. Anger and sadness were pointless, and I knew it. But my mind kept what-ifing and could-beening until I broke the chain with a question.

"What else?"

"He asked about you," Will said. "I denied I knew who he was talking about. He said, 'Tell her if she wants to see me, she should just say so.' I've never had my cover blown so quick."

Drew was always instinctive.

I didn't believe in fate or soul mates or any of that shit, but strings tied Drew and me together. Just that day, I'd heard his songs and seen him in the faces of other men. I'd blamed the connections on misfiring neurons and triggered memories, but maybe the strings between us were being plucked. Maybe when I thought of him, he smelled cinnamon or saw a girl with red hair at the end of the hall.

My brain didn't do this kind of thinking. There was reality. It had definable boundaries. Then there was hot fakery of the imagination. It tricked you into thinking it was reality. I could use other people's illusions to achieve my own ends, but only if I hewed to the real.

In the real world, there were no strings binding me to an old lover.

There were no fated loves.

None of it.

There was my brother—my son—getting out of surgery in an hour. I stood. "This was fun."

"Was it?" Will went to the door.

"Not really."

He put his hand on the doorknob and stopped himself. "I'm sorry. I overstepped."

"Your intentions were good. Can you write me up a report on your meeting with him? Bill me."

"On the house." He opened the door.

Gareth was gone. Cooper was glued to a computer screen, nodding with headphones. His phone was turned upward on the desk. I'd know the album cover anywhere.

Bullets and Blood. *Kentucky Killers.*

"Cooper," I said.

"Yeah?"

"You always listen to that old crap or did I remind you of it?"

"Both. It's good shit."

I leaned over his desk and scrolled through the album's songs. "You should listen to the later stuff. "Taste of Cinnamon" is my favorite."

I patted his shoulder and left.

NINE

JONATHAN WAS FINE.

Finer than fine. Awake and making eyes at his girlfriend.

Mom, Sheila, Deirdre, and Fiona went to visit him. I went to find Dad in the cafeteria where Mom had banished him. He was a man of great power who could chill the bones of anyone who crossed him. Only Mom could make him look like an excommunicated altar boy at a corner table.

I wondered how Dad would look if our little secret got out. Or if Will's information meant people with badges and a warrant were on their way.

Would Drew see the news of Jonathan's collapse? Would he find out? After Will's revelation, he'd gone from a distant memory to a degree of separation away. I didn't know whether to be happy about his mental proximity or ashamed at what he'd see from so close.

I stood across the table from my father. "He's fine. You dodged a bullet there."

He stood and buttoned his jacket. "I'm sure I don't know what you mean."

"If it had gone south over a genetic defect, it would have been on us."

We went to the elevator.

"Guilt is unnecessary," he said. "I'm protecting your mother."

"She's barely spoken to you in sixteen years."

"That doesn't make her any less mine. If she dies tomorrow, she's still mine. If she takes one lover or ten, she's mine. She's never understood that."

"She never took a lover. Even in all this time. You cheated on her repeatedly."

"I was still hers. I was a fool, but hers. Those years are nothing. It's a blip."

"That's ridiculous," I grumbled.

"You don't understand because you've never had what your mother and I have."

I almost argued with him. I almost laid out the map of my life with all its roads not taken, all its territories unexplored, all the well-worn doubts of middle age.

The ding of the elevator stopped me. It wasn't worth it. There was no upside to unfolding that map. He'd file the information and use it later.

We were crowded in the back of the elevator when the doors closed, and in the moment of silence, I folded up my map and went back to the present day's proceedings.

Drew had asked about me.

He'd looked hungry in a way Will couldn't describe, but I understood.

I'd chosen my family because I hadn't had a choice.

The woman in front of me had earbuds in, and I was disappointed that the music she was blasting wasn't Bullets and Blood, but some woman I'd passed on the radio, singing a song of empowerment. Not even rock. Cin would have had nothing but derision for it. The string between Drew and me was weak. Or maybe the disappointment in a stranger's musical taste was the string.

What if…

The doors opened, and Dad and I pushed our way through to the hall.

What if I could go back and choose differently?

Would I be free? Or trapped in another kind of regret?

Before I could sort through the implications, we made it to my family, where my relief over Jonathan was mirrored so brightly, it cast my regrets in shadow.

"He's okay," Mom said in my ear when she hugged me. She repeated it as if she needed to say it to believe it.

"He is," I said. "Better than ever."

MY HOUSE WAS EMPTY. The chardonnay was chilled. All was well. The worry fell out of me and left a vacuum of emotion.

Nature abhors a vacuum as much as I abhorred uncontrolled emotion. Nature won the battle for the empty space before I even knew a war was going on, opening the gate to things I'd put away while I dealt with practical matters.

What if…

…we'd stayed together?

…I'd chased him?

I coulda…

…found him.

…helped him.

I filled the blanks with guilt and regret until Will's text came in.

—GARETH LEFT you a file on the ftp server—

"Not a moment's peace," I said to the phone as I put it down. "Go to hell."

I drank my wine while standing in the open space between the kitchen and living room. After a day surrounded by people, I'd wanted to be alone, but a house as huge as mine held an oppressive amount of silence that was only more noticeable with all the sounds inside it. The clock over the stove made a constant low grind. The vents hissed. My throat swallowing was the loudest thing in the room. The house was in a coma even when I was in it.

Will saw Drew.

I sipped the chardonnay and side-eyed my laptop—closed and quiet on my kitchen counter. It had information, but not the answers I needed.

If I'd chosen Strat, would he have lived? Would he have claimed Jonathan and me?

You asked Will to find Drew.

Will had gone to him, and in a way that was his business until he made it mine. But even before that, I'd taken an action in asking him to find Drew. I'd had nothing to gain from that. I must have been delirious. Sick and hallucinating. A flu induced by excavated grief.

The wine bottle and the laptop were in the kitchen. The stairs to the bedroom were through the living room.

When I pulled my glass away from my lips, I hummed a note. Swallowed. Hummed the next one. It was off by an octave or a chord or whatever, but it was the tune Drew had played when I had the flu. He hadn't known what to do for me, so he'd written me a song.

I hummed it louder, correcting myself when I got it wrong. I'd been so sick. Freezer burned. Stuck in a thick soup of half-thoughts that was stirred so often, I couldn't stay still. My joints had hurt. My head hurt. My teeth throbbed at the roots. My eyes had felt as if they were too big for the sockets. When Drew asked me if I wanted anything, his voice banged on my eardrums like a hammer.

He'd tipped a cup of lukewarm water to my lips even if I protested, and in the dark room, he'd played music because it was all he had to offer. It had been enough.

And you let him suffer.

I finished my chardonnay, remembering that night.

"Strat?" I'd said in a delirious haze. "Where's Indy? Strat?"

"I'm right here."

"I love you."

Drew had assumed I was talking to him—not a hallucination of his best friend.

The fact was, I'd been talking to both of them.

Leaning, stepping, choosing without consciously deciding, I went into the kitchen, opened the computer, and poured more wine as the monitor came to life.

As promised, Gareth's file was on the ftp site. Inside it was a file from two years before, when Will had gone to see him behind my back.

I hadn't been waiting for Drew to return, but what had I been waiting for?

Had the holding pattern just been a pattern?

"Shit or get off the pot, Margaret."

I clicked it.

The ink was barely dry on the PI report, but Gareth's work was clear. Drew a.k.a. Trevor Stone's apartment had been recently vacated. He hadn't shown up for a session. His agent said he'd turn up at some point. He always did.

So he was gone again.

If I asked, they'd find him again.

We could do this dance another sixteen years.

I opened the file from Will's visit as a music blogger. Without thinking, I clicked a photograph. Expectations were for gamblers and feelings were for children, so I didn't know what I expected to see or feel.

But when I saw the picture, I felt so many things, my expectations were irrelevant.

The color picture had been taken with the long lens the Santons used whenever they were far from the subject. Even in digital, it yielded thick grains and blown-out color. A solid haze of impressionistic blobs that would be inadmissible in a court of law.

Short hair. White button-front shirt. Talking to a man in front of a nondescript brick wall. A pickup truck parked at the curb. Sleeves rolled up. Sunny day. Hard shadows hiding his eyes. Lips closed as if listening. Those lips.

It was him. Everything about it was him.

I gasped, putting my hand over my mouth to keep from uttering his name. It didn't work. "Indy."

I said his old name, the name that had left my teenage lips so many times and was only said later when I wanted him to listen to that girl because he wasn't listening to the woman.

Enlarging the image made him into an offensive pile of blobs. Putting my face an inch from the surface didn't help. He only looked like himself when seen in context. He was in his posture and shape. The tilt of his head and the curve of his arms. His expression was in the width of his mouth and under his shaded brow.

If I'd thought about opening that photo before I clicked, I would have thought better of it. It was unnecessary and might dredge up tiresome feelings. But because of the wine or the hour or the relief that Jonathan would be all right... I'd acted without thinking and slid down a greased chute of obsession.

The photos were in one subfolder. I selected the entire list and bulk opened them. They flashed as they opened, only to be covered by the next one.

Back. Side. Three quarter turn. Mouth open to speak. Turned in a smile. Brow furrowed, cast in shadow, lit in the oblique angle of the afternoon sun. Walking toward the camera. Walking away. Going through a black iron door. Disappearing.

That took three seconds and was more than I'd seen of him in sixteen years, and those photos couldn't have been anyone else.

If he walked up to me on a dark street during a snowstorm, I'd recognize him by his face and expression. I'd recognize the hunger Will saw—not because he'd had it when he was with me, but because I saw in those grainy photos a mirror of my exhaustion.

His hunger was loneliness. It was a place I'd filled with family to the point of suffocation.

My glass was empty. I couldn't face the size or emptiness of my house. I wanted something more but didn't know what it was. Maybe I just had to leave.

"SO WHAT DID YOU WANT?" Sheila asked from across the dinner table. We'd just given the waiter our orders.

"Company," I said.

"Really?" She sipped her wine, observing me over the rim of the glass.

"Really. Tell me about the kids."

She blinked, pausing as if she didn't trust the question.

"I want to talk about something besides a problem."

"Kids are problems."

"Is Evan still in that special math program?"

Her face lit up, and she told me an anecdote about her ten-year-old son's advanced classes. How she couldn't keep up with his homework. Calculus. But he was such a genius, he ate it up. How Jenny, who we all called Jellybean, had sprained her ankle in gymnastics and made everyone crazy.

"I envy you," I said.

She laughed. "Me? Most days I swear if I hear 'Mommy' one more time, I'm going to get in the car and keep driving."

"But you have them."

"I'd rather be you."

"You still want my job? It sucks, Sheila."

"But you're free."

I was about to explain how trapped I was. If I couldn't extricate myself, at least I could give her peace of mind that she hadn't gotten the raw end of the deal.

But before I could, she focused on a space over my shoulder and waved. "That's the guy who works with you, right?"

I twisted around to see the host leading Will and a woman in her thirties to a table. She had blond hair cut just under her ears and inoffensive features a four-year-old might describe as "really pretty."

"Hey," Sheila said, standing.

Will and the woman stopped. He seemed pleased to see us, and she was perfectly relaxed until I stood and she looked right at me.

"Will, you know my sister, Sheila."

He nodded. "Nice to see you. Angela, this is Sheila and Margie. Friends of mine from work."

"Do you want to join us?" I said, hoping to both expand the night two more people away from loneliness, and get a chance to intuit something from the federal agent asking about an incident in 1999.

"I think our table's ready," Angela said.

"Next time then."

"Next time."

They went to their seats with polite goodbyes. Sheila and I ate dinner and talked about nothing but the kids. It was a perfectly pleasurable evening except for Angela, who made it a point not to look at me, except when she did.

It was as if she wasn't happy Will knew me.

TEN

I'D SLEPT LIKE A BABY. I DIDN'T HAVE A WORRY IN THE WORLD. JONATHAN was going to live and I'd managed to not blow the secret of his parentage.

It was six in the morning on a bright, shiny fucking day.

There's nothing like Catholic guilt though. It creeps up on you when you're least unhappy. The knowledge that Jon was mine and Strat's ate at me. My silence chewed me from the inside out. He could have died, and it would have been my fault. Nothing could fix that.

Monica had been hanging around Sequoia Hospital as if she worked there. Which she didn't. She was a waitress who lived hand-to-mouth and she was missing shifts.

That, I could fix.

"What are you doing?" Daddy asked when he saw me in his office, digging around the wall safe before his staff even had breakfast out.

"Taking five grand."

"For what?"

I counted it out in twenties. "For none of your business."

"If it's none of my business, you can take your own money."

"This is handy. And it's not your business, but it's your concern. So smile about it."

"Is it for that waitress my son is keeping around?"

I pushed the five aside and tossed the rest of the cash into the safe then slapped it closed. *His* son. He always claimed Jonathan without any irony.

"He's in love with her. Desperately." I spun the combination dial. "If you could get out of the way of that, everyone would appreciate it."

"Envelopes in the sideboard," he said. "Bottom shelf."

I opened the cabinet and grabbed an envelope.

"Did you hear about the shooting?" Dad asked. "Paulie Patalano was shot in the head a few hours ago."

"Didn't you hire him for something?"

"No."

I slid the money in. "Was Franco there?"

Franco and my father had a mutually beneficial relationship.

"Theresa was."

I stopped. Theresa, the good girl, had taken to a capo named Antonio from a rival family. It was a mess I was trying to clear up.

"I'll take care of it." I put the envelope in my breast pocket.

"I realized something," he said when I was next to him. I stopped, and he looked at me. "I'm leaving the business in good hands."

"You have heart problems too?"

"Hardly."

"Good thing, because if anything had happened to Jonathan, I was ready to tell everyone he was mine."

I didn't mention this ultimate betrayal often because there was no point to it, but ever since Jonathan's collapse, I'd thought of little else. Secrets had a life of their own. When called, they grew and swelled, pushing the limits of their shell.

"And break your mother's heart?"

"I'd break yours if I thought you had one."

"Always so clever and so cruel."

"I don't come from nowhere."

"I do have a heart, Margaret. I gave it to your mother a long time ago." He cleared his throat softly and averted his gaze for a moment. "And seeing him like this…" He meant Jonathan, but didn't want to say the name in relation to his illness. "We, your mother and I—we've been in separate rooms too long. I don't want to spend another moment away from her. Life is too short to live without love, don't you think?"

"Yeah. I do."

I tried to leave, but his voice stopped me.

"That man. The one you have doing your security?"

"Will?"

"You should let him love you."

"Jesus, Daddy. Is there anything you don't meddle in?"

"Not when it comes to my children, no."

Our phones went off at the same time. I vibrated, and he chimed. There was only one reason we'd both be texted at the same time. Then my phone rang. I was the contact. I was the fixer. I was the hub point of the family, so I'd be the one to get the call.

Daddy and I looked at each other, frozen. Blood drained from my face. My fingers went so cold, I had to slide them across the glass three times to answer the call.

"Doctor Thorensen," I said. "How is he?"

"We have some bad news. Can you come to the hospital for a meeting?"

JONATHAN WAS HOOKED up to every beeping monitor ever invented. One of his heart valves had ripped open and he was bleeding into his chest. That was the short story. We were getting the unabridged version at the meeting.

They'd tell us there was a defect they'd missed. That it was genetic and I could have stopped it. That was the worst-case scenario and it was the only one I could come up with.

I had to see him first. I had to have his face and eyes clearly in my mind or I would say something in that meeting that hurt him.

"I'm not here to make you upset," I said, leaning over his bed so he could see me. He looked less like Strat and more like a wax figure.

I'd told him the truth. I wasn't there to make him upset. I'd come pre-armed with a piece of good news—I was taking care of business while he was laid up. He could relax.

"Oh, good. You're here to tap dance."

A smart-mouth through and through.

"I love that you have the energy to joke but not give a shit about your condition."

"I give a shit. Guy came and told me I'm in a world of trouble. There's just nothing I can do about it."

"They called us into a meeting." I wasn't supposed to be talking about this. I wasn't supposed to be stressing him out.

"Let them do their jobs. I can't..." He drifted off.

I put my hand on his shoulder, away from the wires and tubes. "I took care of something while you were down. It's going to create drama."

"Okay."

"Okay, you have no problem with it?"

"Okay, tell me what it is."

"Monica's broke. She hasn't been going to work because she's been hanging around Sequoia Hospital like she works here."

"Fuck."

Stress. I'd put the bad news before the good and caused stress. I was better than this. I said the right things at the right times. My brain was backward and my heart was inside out.

"I'm giving her money and saying it's from you," I said. "You're going to back me up."

"Yes."

"Good." I took my hand away. All I had to do was leave on an upbeat note.

"Margie?"

"What?"

"You're my new favorite. Thank you."

New favorite sister. One of seven chanted in a line from oldest to youngest with equal weight.

Not fair. None of it was fair. I was his mother and I'd been robbed. He'd been robbed.

I couldn't stay, but I couldn't go.

I was the fixer, and I'd stayed the fixer for him.

This mess was special. I couldn't fix it. I could only make it worse.

"I'm keeping tabs on every dime," I said, "because you're going to get better, you little fuck. I don't know how, but this isn't how it ends. Do you understand me? It's not ending like this."

———

YOU'D THINK my father would try to shut me out of the meeting for either my own sake or his. My threat must have fallen on fallow ground.

The windowless room had a long table and a big flat screen TV at the head. My parents sat across from each other. Mom was a grudge holder, but the fact that they were in the same room meant Jonathan's trouble had softened her.

I sat next to her and took her hand. "It's probably nothing."

"Have you seen him? He looks—"

Dr. Emerson came in. He was a white guy with silver hair and a tag over a polo shirt and light gray pants with grass stains at the cuffs. Must have called him in from the golf course. Great.

Dr. Thorensen, the head of the department, followed in all his Nordic glory. A few nurses and a secretary sat down. They all looked as serious as a heart attack, which was a bad analogy but the only one I had.

Mom squeezed my hand.

"Mrs. Drazen, Mr. Drazen." Thorensen nodded at both in turn. "Margaret." He pointed at a woman to his left, tapping a laptop. "This is Grace Harcourt, our assist on admin—"

"Cut the introductions," I said. "What's happening?"

He cleared his throat and nodded to Emerson, who slid the laptop closer and touched a button. White-on-black scan of the inside of a chest came up.

"During surgery, when we sutured Mr. Drazen's aortic valve here"—he pointed—"we found a malformation. It's an unusual genetic irregularity, but I'd seen it before so I knew how to work around it."

I held my breath. Was that Strat's irregularity? Had he gotten it from his father like he'd gotten his nose and his ear for music?

Mom tugged her hand away. I was crushing it.

"But," Emerson said as he switched the scan, "this morning we were alerted to a leakage here."

He pointed at a blob I couldn't make head or tail of. It all looked like a mess of gray and black. The whole room was actually turning into an unintelligible abstract of lead and ash.

"We did a full scan." Another slide. "And found damage to his aortic valve." His voice slowed. The vowels elongated.

He said I was in a world of trouble.

"This isn't something we can repair."

"What do you mean?" my mother cut in. "You can't sew it up?"

"The heart is a delicate organ. It's not—"

"Is this your fault?" Mom asked. "Is it from the suture?"

Emerson and Thorensen exchanged a glance before Thorensen said, "If we'd known about the condition before we started—"

"How were we supposed to know?" Mom squeaked from somewhere beyond the ringing in my ears.

My hands squeezed together in my lap, and I wished more than anything in the world that it was Drew's hand in mine. He knew.

...if we'd known...

He'd shared and kept the secret.

"What's next?" Dad said, trying to get control. He was taking my role because I was in a state of complete panic.

...about the condition...

Drew would have made me tell.

"Right now, our best option is a heart transplant."

...before we started...

"So there's an option?" Mom. Ever hopeful.

"I'm going to review how the transplant list works," Thorensen said, taking Emerson's place in front of the screen. "There's an emergency list specifically for cases like these..."

Thoren*sen*. Emer*son*. Sen. Son.

"The challenge is not the surgery itself..."

Sen *son sen son* the universe was taunting me with my son's doctors' names.

...if we'd known...

"But a donor. Jonathan has a rare blood type which..."

...about the condition...

"We can continue to drain his chest..."

...before we started...

"But his chances without a—"

"Stop!" I shot up straight. "Stop it! There's something you don't know."

"Margie," Dad said softly.

"Before you touch him again," I continued, "you need—"

"Margaret!" Dad stood. "You're confused."

"No, I'm not. He's not your son."

Mom gasped. "Margaret!"

"Mom," I said, looking at her.

She was white as a sheet, eyes wide, lower lip trembling. She thought I was accusing her of being unfaithful to Dad, but that was the least of it.

My father was already at our side of the table, hands on my mother's shoulders.

"Jonathan is..." I started the sentence but couldn't finish it. My son. Those were the two words I had to say. Two simple syllables. I ordered myself to speak, but the words wouldn't come.

Never, ever tell.

Jonathan was my son.

Say it.

The secret made it past my throat, but my tongue held the words as it had done for two decades. I didn't know how to say it. Didn't know how to break the box I'd put the secret in.

"I'm sorry, doctors," my father said, "but my daughter is suffering from a bit of a hysterical delusion. Eileen—"

"She's lying, Deck. I never, ever did such a thing."

"I know. Let's take a walk, darling."

Mom didn't push him away. My accusation covered her rage against my father like an old stain getting a new coat of paint.

Dad hustled her out, and when the door closed behind them, Mom wouldn't hear.

So be it.

So fucking be it.

Maybe I didn't have to smash the box. Maybe I could just describe it and let them figure it out.

"Doctors," I said, sitting, "I'm going to tell you a story about me and a guy named Stratford Gilliam."

"The musician?" Thorensen asked.

Emerson shifted the laptop back to the admin, who started tapping at it.

"No typing," I said, getting my voice back. "This isn't part of the permanent record, and to be honest, everyone has to leave but the doctors."

After an uncomfortable pause I sat through like a woman in total control, Thorensen dismissed the staff. Then it was just the three of us and the scan of Jonathan's heart.

I cleared my throat. "In 1982, I did a one-year study abroad in Ireland." I danced around the story, going from the easiest part to the hardest. "In a convent. I gave birth to a baby."

I looked in the direction of the doctors, but not at them. I was looking through them to those moments with my son. "A boy."

He smelled so good.

"He was taken from me and put up for adoption."

"1982?" Emerson asked, glancing at the laptop where Jonathan's stats were. His height, weight, birthday.

"I had him in '83."

And his eyes were blue…

"Are you all right?" Thorensen asked.

…before they turned green as rarest jade.

"My father came and took him. And when I got home, I had a baby brother."

"Ms. Drazen—" I didn't know which one said my name. They were smothered in a mass of gray and black. Only the memories were clear.

"Strat, his real father, had an undiagnosed heart condition."

"—you may need to rest—"

"He died from it. He overdosed and he would have lived, but his heart gave out."

"—this is—"

"I never told anyone. I had to protect my mother and Drew."

"—check her pulse—"

"He's mine." The words spilled out.

A voice in my head told me they didn't believe any of it, but I couldn't have stopped the four words if I'd wanted to. They left my lungs at speed, spinning my heart like a top, centrifugal force pounding the blood against the outer walls.

"He is my son."

ELEVEN

FAR AWAY VOICES. METAL SCRAPING. WHEELS SQUEAKING. PHONES ringing. Sounds at the end of a long, dark tunnel moved toward me until they were made in real time, real space, on the other side of my consciousness. I was lying down. Closed eyes were a choice now, my eyelids turning bright lights soft gray.

Did I tell them?

Regret.

Did they believe me?

Hope.

Was Jonathan still dying?

Fear.

Opening my eyes to the dropped ceiling above, I felt groggy and thick with an ache in my bicep. My eyes were too cloudy for the wall clock, but I could see the whiteboard with my name and (17mg diazepam). I looked at my wrist. There was a band around it. I moved it aside so I could see my watch.

Seventy minutes had passed.

Did I tell them?

Hope.

Did they believe me?

Fear.

Was Jonathan still dying?

Regret.

The fist with the watch clutched something with corners. I uncurled my fingers to find a yellow Post-it. I sat up on one elbow, fighting the Valium's demand that I sleep, and opened the square.

One handwritten word.

I blinked.

Rubbed my eyes.

Blinked again and made out the letters.

Palihood.

THE CAB DRIVER made eye contact in the mirror. "You all right, lady?"

"Yeah." My voice was thick and slow. I'd been fighting to keep my eyes open. I thought I was winning, but obviously the battle had been all too visible. I'd made the right choice. If I'd taken one of our cars, the driver wouldn't have asked questions, but I wouldn't mistake his silence for discretion.

"If you OD in my car and I don't take you to the hospital—"

"Picked me up a block from the hospital."

"I know, but I'm liable."

"Not OD. Administered by best."

I had to stop dropping pieces of sentences. That wouldn't look right.

Deep breaths. I took deep breaths and fell asleep on the 10 freeway. Two blocks from my destination, I snapped awake.

"There's a shortcut through this alley," I said, pointing down what looked like a driveway but wasn't.

He turned into it, car rocking on the cracked pavement like a ship at sea. Some things never changed no matter how much property values went up.

"Here." I leaned forward, pointing at a familiar house. It had a real estate's For Sale sign and a gate with a chain and a lock box holding it closed.

Drew had sold the studio to buy our place in New York and it had obviously changed hands a few times since then. It had been reroofed. Re-stuccoed. The front door was new and truly awful. Chain-link fencing surrounded the property.

I opened my wallet and took out a hundred dollar bill. "This is for the ride here." I laid it in his hand, then took out another. "This is for you waiting for an hour. If I don't come out, you can go. Got it?"

"If you don't come out, are you dead or something?"

"Maybe." I left the cab before he could ask more stupid questions.

Walking more or less straight, I checked the keybox. Locked. The padlock. Locked.

We'd forgotten the keys a few million times. Locks weren't a deterrent. I went down the neighbor's driveway, trying to look as if I belonged there, which I didn't. Not in 2015.

The chain link ended where the neighbor's fencing began. They'd built a gate in their fence between the properties—ostensibly as a fire egress, but really, they'd been fans. Decades later, it was still latched but lockless.

I snapped the gate closed behind me. The yard was paved over with patches of thorn bushes and volunteer tomato plants. I went up the cracked back steps. The door was ajar. I pushed it open, realizing that what I was doing was crazy and dangerous. That I didn't know who'd put the note in my hand. That the Valium was making me pay so much attention to basic functions that I was a slave to inertia.

The kitchen smelled of mildew and dust. It was dark except for stripes of sunlight through the blinds. I flipped a light switch. It clicked, but nothing happened. Electricity must be shut off. I put my bag on the counter of the kitchen island. It was probably filthy and I didn't care. I wanted my hands free.

"Drew?" I said into the darkness. "Indiana Andrew McCaffrey, stop fucking with me. I'm in no mood."

My eyes adjusted. I stepped farther in, letting my hand drift over the counter edge. They'd changed it to cheap flipper granite. The cabinets were presswood veneer. But still, I touched them as if they were original Douglas fir and my name was Cin.

"Margaret."

His voice didn't surprise me. I didn't jump ten feet or stiffen with shock when I saw his silhouette against the doorframe. Hearing him was a relief. The binds keeping my shit together weren't unknotted completely, but they loosened. I hadn't felt tense in a long time because I was so used to being in a state of taut readiness.

"Indy."

His stage name came from my lips without a thought.

"I'm glad you came."

Sixteen years, and he was glad I came. Fuck him.

"I didn't have your number." I tossed his Post-it on the counter. "Or I would have called and told you to shove this cryptic little note up your ass."

"Not for lack of trying." He stepped into the kitchen. The stripes of light caught the blue of one eye and curved along the lines of his face. I swallowed so hard it hurt. He'd aged, but hadn't we all? "You sent someone to look for me."

He was a shadow. Blue-black on gray-black. A ghost in a dark room. A phantom with a voice cobbled together from memories. When he raised his hand, I wasn't afraid, because he didn't exist, but when he touched me, he became form and substance.

I jerked away. "Don't."

"Sorry."

"You should be."

"I can't believe it's you."

"I'd clock you if I didn't think I'd fall over doing it."

"Let me explain."

"Fuck you."

"By the time I'm done, the Valium will be worn off. If you don't like the explanation, you'll be able to stay on your feet when you punch me. You might even get in two."

I wanted to hear him. I wanted to clock him, sure. But I was curious and I wanted to bathe in the sound of his voice for a while.

Then I would tell him to fuck off, with or without punching him.

"Are we having this conversation in the kitchen?"

"The guitar room's still there, more or less," he said.

"Lead the way."

I knew how to get to the guitar room, but I needed a moment to walk behind him. My thoughts weren't going to get gathered if he was next to me.

New fact. They weren't doing so well from behind either. Not with those jeans or the way his jacket hugged his shoulders.

The guitar room had been a private studio used for experimentation and noodling. With the blinds pulled, I saw that the counters were bare and the instrument hooks on the walls were empty, but the room hadn't otherwise changed. I sat on a linoleum counter and Drew stepped into the light.

His eyes shone from within as he looked at me, top to bottom. The harsh light shadowed the crow's feet at the corners and highlighted the years of concern on his cheeks. The scruff on his chin had gone gray at the edges of his mouth to match the gray at his temples.

"Hard years," I said.

"Not for you." He smiled. "Apparently."

"Flattery's beneath you."

He sat on the counter opposite me, where a mixing panel used to be. He opened a cabinet and reached for a case of bottled water.

"I brought provisions." Leaning forward, he put one bottle next to me.

"Always the Boy Scout."

He cracked his bottle open. "You need help with yours?"

The Valium's drowsiness was no match for the last few minutes, but it made gripping the bottle cap difficult.

"Jesus, McCaffrey." His insult to my competence gave me just enough strength to open my bottle.

"You look good," he said as I drank. "Not flattery. Fact."

"Yeah, I know. I own a mirror."

He let out a short laugh. "Same." He shook his head, looking down. "Same but better."

What was he after? He had me at a disadvantage. He knew who I was and where to find me. He was still a shadow with a voice and face I recognized, answering to the name of a man I'd once loved.

"Okay, look. You show up in the middle of a crisis, throwing around compliments like pretty beads. Tell me what you want. If it's to tell me how much you missed me, you can sleep well at night knowing I missed you too. But that's all irrelevant. I have to get back to the hospital. There's a lot going on."

"I know about Jonathan."

"You watch the news. Good for you. So you know this was a shitty time to stick notes in my hand."

"It is. And I'm sorry."

"Great." I slid off the counter and, wresting control from the drug in my veins, stood without swaying. "Can we reconvene?"

"Please sit down."

The command was unimpeachable. My mind told him to fuck off, but my body obeyed.

He'd never spoken to me like that.

He'd never spoken to anyone like that.

"Thank you," he said when I settled my ass back down.

"It's your pleasure."

"I guess there was no way to start out on the right foot."

"Two lefts don't make a right."

"But three do."

"Zing." The word was barely a whisper. I wasn't in the mood for snappy rejoinders, even if I'd started it.

He settled back, rubbed his nose. I'd forgotten that it was a little crooked from when his father broke it, or how the forced angle was so beautiful against the symmetry of the rest of him. If he'd stayed, would he look the same? More gray hair? Or less?

"I'm not here for forgiveness." His voice was huskier. Older, without questions in every vowel.

"I'm glad you didn't waste a trip."

"I never expected this to be easy."

"So why did you come back?"

"I heard about Jonathan. I knew you'd need me."

I leaned back, relaxing my posture enough to show him I was paying attention but I wasn't open to bullshit.

"When I went home to New York that Christmas," he continued, "I didn't intend to disappear."

The memory of the empty apartment with his clothes gone was a shot of adrenaline to the chest.

"When I got back to New York," I said, "the apartment was empty. You saying you didn't intend that?"

It was hard to keep that from sounding like an accusation.

"I went to the old house in Nashville. I thought I'd come back, but I didn't."

"No, you didn't."

"You chose this, Margie. As much as I did. I told you what I needed, and you couldn't give it to me. You chose your family. So what was I supposed to do? Keep you from them? Chase you? I respected your wishes. I stayed away because you wanted me to. Stop making it sound like I left you in a ditch."

If my face didn't flinch, it was only with extreme effort. He'd hit me in a place I hadn't looked at in a long time. I hadn't given a single thought to my culpability.

I'd left him in a ditch.

A part of me that I considered strong got sick and withered away.

"Shifted blame and handsome faces," I said and continued before he could interrupt. "Things that improve over time. I blamed you, and you stayed guilty. It got easier over time. And your face. I didn't think it could improve, but here we are."

He ran his hand over his scruffy cheek as if he wanted to hide it from the compliment. What else about him had improved with age?

"You've changed," I said.

"We all change, and we're all the same."

"Did you come early to take an inventory?"

He rubbed his hands together with a dry *hshh*. "Sixteen years. I've been drifting for more than a decade and a half. I've had seven different names."

"What was your favorite?"

"Indy McCaffrey." He smiled with the pain of regret. "Most days, I wish I could go back. Protect you. Protect us both."

"You know what I wished for?"

"Tell me."

"The exact same thing."

"I was…" He considered what he was going to say before he continued. "I was with this woman for a while." He took in my reaction, and seeing that I wasn't shocked or hurt, he continued. "She owned a little dress shop outside Tucson. Didn't have a serious bone in her body. It was like a vacation."

"Sounds nice."

"I wanted to come home to you. Every day. I didn't even realize it. But no woman compares to you. We had something, Cinnamon. We had something great."

Youth was insidious. Taken for granted. Dismissed. It was scorned by those who had it, and those fortunate enough to live through it craved its return.

"Did you ever think of me?" he asked.

I slid off the counter and went up to him. If he told me to sit down, I wouldn't this time. "Can I see your hands?"

He tilted his head with an unspoken question.

"Come on," I said, waving my fingers over my outstretched palms. "Show me."

He held out his hands. I laid mine underneath, raising and turning them so I could see what I needed to in the stripes of light. Dark, rough spots at the tips of three fingers from pressing guitar strings against wood.

"Your callouses haven't softened." I ran my thumb along them. I had fond memories of that spot where it was rough on my clit and hard on my tongue when I sucked his fingers.

"Neither have yours."

"You're still playing," I said, letting his perception hang unanswered.

"I play for myself. And I write songs under another name. I have a few about you that are still making royalties."

"They about a woman who changed while you were gone?"

"They're about a girl." I let his hands go, but he grasped me gently. "A beautiful young girl I ruined."

"You misstate the case," I said. "I ruined you."

"That goes without saying."

Slipping my hands out of his, I went back to the safety of my counter.

"You know I loved you," he said.

"It's the one thing I never doubted."

He nodded, looking away. I was mad at him. Mad at myself. So angry with our self-inflicted wounds I couldn't even think.

And yet, the rage was drowned out by tears of relief. I tried not to blink, but I had to, and they fell down my cheeks. I couldn't wipe them away before he saw me.

"I'm sorry, Margie."

"Shut up."

"I'm so sorry."

If I didn't get ahold of myself, he was going to keep apologizing and his regret would make me mad again.

"What did you do after Nashville?" I asked.

"Drank. A lot. Thought about you when I sobered up and then drank again."

"You could have called."

"I drank instead. I was…" He squeezed his eyes shut and pinched the bridge of his nose. "I've been sober two years and not a day goes by I don't have to choose between thinking about you or draining a bottle of NyQuil."

I laughed. "That's…"

"It's disgusting. Trust me." He was laughing a little too. "But when there's nothing else in the house?"

"You drink the whole thing?"

"No. I just think of you."

I wiped my eyes again. "Stupid man."

The hardest thing I ever did was not hold him. I fought the urge with words of comfort carefully disguised as an insult. Like the man he was and always had been, he understood the intention.

"I was a coward. I should have come back to LA and fought for you. I let you dump me on an answering machine."

I remembered how the outgoing message had changed between calls. "Did you get the message where I begged you to come?"

He laughed sharply. "Of course not. I got pissed and took off. You did that?"

"Not that it matters. I should have fought for you."

"You have every right to be mad," he said.

"I chose my family. You have just as much right. Maybe we should both just get over it."

He looked at me as if he hadn't seen me yet. "Are you over it?"

"No."

"I want another chance."

My laugh was more derisive than I intended. My insides were taking control of my outsides. That hadn't been a problem in a long time because my insides had been in a coma.

"Drew," I said. "Come on."

"I mean it. And you want it too. You sent someone to find me."

"Hang on there…"

"And I spent the next year trying to find a way to earn you back. I haven't come empty-handed." He slid off the counter and came closer, stopping in the middle of the room when I stiffened. I wasn't ready to be in the same room with him, much less be seduced by the return of the happiest days of my life.

"Look at you," he said, giving me the look he wanted me to turn on myself. "You're still everything. Line up a million perfect women and I'd still choose you. Do you see what you do to a room when you walk into it? No, of course you don't. Now even more than when we met the first two times, you bend the space around you. Look at you." He repeated the phrase with his eyes locked on mine. "You own yourself and everything around you. You were a princess. Now you're a queen."

"Are we back to flattery?" I whispered.

"I wasn't worthy of you. Now I am. I'm sorry I took so long, but I had a long way to go."

I looked away, watching my thumbnail worry the edge of the bottle's label. I never would have allowed someone on the other side of the negotiating table see me fidget.

"This is not a good time," I said finally.

"What are you afraid of?"

"Right now?"

"Right now." He sat back on the counter, giving me room to breathe.

"Right now, I'm afraid that my brother is going to bleed into his chest faster than they can give him transfusions. I'm afraid there's no heart out there for him. I'm afraid that he's going to die because I didn't tell the doctors his father had a heart condition. That it'll be my fault and I'll live the rest of my life crushed between grief and guilt. And now... right now, I'm afraid I'll believe you."

He bent his body at the waist, putting his forearms on his knees, loosely holding his bottle between his fingertips. For the first time, as if it just occurred to me that a lifetime had passed, I looked for a wedding ring. None. Neither a gold band nor a tan line where one used to be.

"You don't have to believe me. Not yet. But I'm here to set you free. Then you can believe me."

"Free?"

He nodded slightly, watching my reaction. "You're a prisoner. Can't you see that?"

What was freedom like?

It looked like the Palihood house and it smelled like cigarettes and cinnamon. It was our apartment in New York and a job where no one knew my name.

"I still can't leave my family. That hasn't changed."

Nodding, he let the silence get heavy. It was as if the birds stopped chirping so they could hear him and the wind waited for him to speak.

"In Nashville," he said, "I was given a warning. Stay away from Margaret Drazen or she'd be cut off. I got three broken ribs and a bruised kidney."

"Who did that to you?"

He shook his head slowly.

"Tell me. Was it Franco? Franco Junior? How old was he? What did he look like?"

It didn't matter who'd landed the blows. We both knew who'd paid the fists.

"I didn't care if they killed me," he said. "But they threatened you.

And even if the guys who fucked me up thought it was all about money, I knew better. If I went back to you, you'd never see your son again. It would kill you."

My mouth opened to apologize for something I hadn't done, or express a feeling of gratitude tainted with regret that was too complex to define. But nothing came out.

"It's not an excuse," he continued. "But I left you alone out of love. And now, I'm coming back for the same reason. You don't have to give me another chance." He slid off the counter. "But I'm free. I want you to be free with me."

His resoluteness wasn't completely new. It came from the same place as the clarity he brought to negotiations when he saw an injustice being done. But it was a change in balance. He'd made it a part of his identity.

I'd been left by a man who couldn't handle my family. A man with a hole in his life that could only be filled with music. Whose manhood had been stunted by an abusive father before my own father had scared him into the self-immolation of addiction.

He wasn't Drew or Indy. He was a third, powerful, unpredictable thing.

"You're going to set me free?" I said. "How?"

"Not yet. Let me get you back to Jonathan first. He needs you."

"He does." When I went for the door, he moved like a cat, blocking the way enough to make a point but not enough to trap me. "It was always about you, Cin."

Without thinking, I put my hand on his chest. I shouldn't have been able to feel his heartbeat, but as if the muscle wanted me to know it was there, it beat hard enough to feel. "That's Margie to you."

When he moved, a band of light streaked across his rueful smile. "You still love me. You can refuse me, but you still love me."

"I have no idea what I feel."

With a little push, I cleared the way and walked out.

In the dark kitchen, I barely slowed to grab my bag, then I opened the back door. The door, and the stale air of the room, was overcome with palm and smog.

"You wasted lot of time, McCaffrey," I said with my hand on the knob and one foot out the door.

"And I won't waste another minute."

I left, closing the door, and rushed out the driveway gate.

How dare he. My pumps clopped on the neighbor's paving in patterns of three.

How. Dare. He. How. Dare. He.

I'm Margie Drazen.

How. Dare. He.

The car was waiting. I got in. "Thanks for waiting."

"My pleasure. Where to?"

"Wilshire and Cañon."

He tapped the glass on his phone to call in the ride. He was going to take too long. I had to get away from that house.

"Please start driving."

"Okay, okay." He shot a glance back. I didn't know what he saw, but he stopped fucking with his phone and drove.

I relaxed as soon as we made it past the corner.

Not really.

I didn't relax. I didn't Zen. What I did wasn't rainbows and unicorn farts. It was much more sinister. I stopped worrying that he'd catch up and I'd have to continue the fucking conversation. I was trapped in a car on the way back to my life, but everything had changed.

Indy was back.

Drew.

Neither.

Both.

Not the dipshit I'd played strip poker with. Not the musician I'd watched mature into an artist. Not the competent lawyer I'd watched devolve into an overwhelmed drunk.

None of it. All of it.

And how had I changed?

What had I become?

I couldn't stop cataloguing what I'd done in the years between us.

I was a fixer. I fixed problems. Moved money. Leveraged knowledge. Brought justice and vengeance. I made life bearable for the people I loved. I'd kept my hands clean, but washing them so often had made the knuckles cracked and bloody.

That was a metaphor, but I looked at my hands anyway. They were shaking.

I didn't know if I loved him anymore, but I sure as hell couldn't say I didn't. I'd locked it all away. Hadn't even peeked in to see if it was still there.

And now?

That love was wearing jeans and black boots. It hadn't aged. Hadn't seen what I'd seen. Didn't know what I knew. It threatened my life and my work but didn't even speak my language.

My phone rang. I could barely still my hand enough to answer Will's call, but I needed him. He knew everything that needed knowing.

"Yeah," I said as the car hit the 405. "What's up?"

"Possibly relevant," he said. "I'm not a doctor."

"Is he—"

"Jon's the same. But Patalano."

The gangster with the head wound.

"We unearthed some info," Will continued. "He's brain dead."

I wasn't a stranger to the organized crime families in Los Angeles. Paulie was a camorra operative in the same cell as Theresa's current problem, Antonio Spinelli. The web of malfeasance was too tangled for a single conversation, but Will didn't expect me to cry for Patalano.

"Good," I said.

"What happened at the meeting with the doctors?" he asked. "Your mother's been medicated."

What happened? Was it only a few hours ago that I almost blurted out the truth? That the secret had stayed locked up because it didn't know how to be free?

"Nothing," I said.

Everything.

"Sheila's trying to sue the hospital."

You should have let Sheila be the fixer.

"Sheila hasn't practiced law in a decade."

"My question is, why aren't you trying to sue them?"

"Delta," I said, "we make threats from a position of power. Got it?"

"You're a tiger, you know that? A four-star general."

You're a prisoner.

"Your faith in me is inspiring."

I hung up and took a deep breath. I was trapped in the back seat of a car navigating traffic on the 405. A captive of circumstance.

I could be free.

What would a free woman do?

"Change of plans," I said to the driver while dialing the next problem on my list. "I need to go to Sequoia Hospital."

TWELVE

It took more than a deep breath to get my head on straight, but not much more. The orderly patterns of thought that drove my existence were a habit. Emotions had never been strong enough to move the levers. They tried, but they'd been overruled so many times that love was a motion denied and fear had already been led out the side door in ankle cuffs.

Drew was back. I'd been in a room with him. A room in the Palihood studio. Now. Not 1982. Now. After everything.

The only thing stranger than the coexistence of Drew and the date was the bubbling stew of feelings rattling the lid I kept on them. I'd assumed they were sealed away and whatever warmth I had left was worthless sentiment.

Maybe I was wrong.

Maybe I'd misunderstood everything.

Or maybe sentiment was no more than a lie wrapped around something too real to handle.

As the cab was getting onto Olympic, I got a text from Will. It was a thumbs-up, and I knew exactly what it meant. Paulie Patalano was a match for Jonathan Drazen. The internet told the rest of the story. The mobster was brain-dead. The shooter had been killed in an explosion. My son's life was in another man's chest, two floors above him.

I went to the hotel room first. The curtains were pulled back so we could look at the landing pad on the hospital roof behind the darkening eastern sky.

Sheila was on the couch, feet tucked under her, flipping through a magazine. "Nice for you to show up."

"How's Mom?" I asked, pointing toward the master bedroom.

"Sleeping." She tossed aside the magazine. "They gave her a shot so she'd be too thick to testify in our lawsuit later."

"Paranoia suits you."

"If you weren't so naïve, I wouldn't have to be so paranoid."

She reached under the stack of newspapers on the coffee table and came out with a red folder. She handed it to me.

"What's this?"

"The UNOS organ candidate list."

I opened it. Gibberish. Well-defined, organized, anonymized gibberish. I closed the folder. "Where did you get this?"

"You're not the only one with people."

"Look at you," I said, dropping the folder back on the table. "With the confidential, top secret list. Impressive."

"Not so much. They determine who gets the organ based on immediate need and proximity to the donor. I can't tell if it's bad. I don't know if he's first or last."

"Still. Nice work."

"Thank you." She slid the envelope under her magazine. "Wouldn't hurt to pull the plug on the mobster on six."

"Margie!" Mom's voice came from the bedroom. "Is that you?"

"Joking," Sheila said.

"I know."

But she hadn't been joking. Not really.

"Coming, Mom!" I bent over my sister so I could speak softly. "I know your filters get thin under stress. But letting them see you angry isn't a strength. It's a vulnerability." I headed for the bedroom door.

"Who's *them*?" she hissed.

"Everyone who isn't named Drazen."

I pushed into the bedroom and closed the door. The curtains were drawn, and my mother was on the edge of the bed with half her hair out of a bun.

"Hey, Mom," I said. "How are you doing?"

"What time is it?"

There was a digital clock right in her line of sight.

"Five thirty," I said.

"In the morning?"

"Afternoon."

"I feel like I've been asleep all night."

There wasn't much light left in the day, but I opened the curtains as if I had a point to prove. "I was going to call down for dinner. Did you want something?"

"Any news about Jonathan? Did they find a heart for him?"

Maybe?

"No." I swung a chair to sit across from her. "Mom. At the meeting with the doctors."

"They said some scary things." She ignored what I'd said.

"I never meant to imply you were anything but a good wife."

"I know."

"I was out of my head."

"Do you think he's going to die?" She swung to a lateral subject. Was she trying to save me from the shame of my delusions? Or trying to save herself from the truth?

No, no, I didn't. He was too real to me. Jonathan was the weight of my past and the albatross around the neck of my future. That fucker was hope and light and every rainbow I'd turned away from because I had other things on my mind. Life without him would be carefree and joyless at the same time, so he was going to live. Period.

Dad said I was having a hysterical delusion. Maybe he was right. The prognosis was shit. I could spray-paint it twenty-four-karat gold, but it was still a pile of shit.

"We have to hope a heart shows up," I said. "That's all there is to it."

My mother had been married to my father nearly fifty years. She'd raised eight children, but from some angles, she looked younger than me. Not in years. She carried her extra decade and a half in the lines on her forehead, but her guileless expression made a trick of her experience. It lied to me as ardently as my mother lied to herself.

"When I had him," she said, looking at her hands, "he looked so blue. And he was quiet as a ghost. I never had a baby who didn't cry when it was born. Deck told me not to worry when the nurses took him away. Two days he was gone. I thought he must be dead. I begged your father to tell me I'd lost him, but he swore the doctors were working and the nuns were praying." When she brought her gaze up, tears lined her eyes with evening-lit glass. "And when he came back, he was so perfect and pink... and he was crying so hard until he was in my arms. It was a miracle. *He's* a miracle." She squeezed my hand, a new hope in her face. "I know you're worried. We're all worried, but you? You take on so much for us. So I want you to believe me when I say he'll make it through this, even if it takes a hundred miracles."

I squeezed her hand back for the life of her fucking stolen miracle baby. We wanted the same thing, after all.

"Is it too early for a drink?" I said.

Mom laughed. "You said it was afternoon."

THIRTEEN

AFTER A DRINK AND THE LITTLE FOOD WE COULD HOLD DOWN, MOM, Sheila, and I entered the waiting room. Monica was already there with her eyes wide open, seeing nothing, tapping her finger on her knee as if writing a silent song.

"That girl," Mom whispered.

"What?" I replied.

"Mom thinks Jon's going to marry her without a prenup," Sheila said.

"Her showing up now is convenient, that's all." My mother tossed off the accusation like a true child of privilege.

Monica loved Jonathan, and fuck anyone who said otherwise. I wished I could do something for her, but when she looked at me across the room as if I was the one lawyer willing to fight for clemency when the death penalty seemed like a lock, I knew I was doing exactly what she needed.

"Jesus, Mom," I said. "Stuck in the hospital for days. Dealing with our bullshit. I couldn't imagine a worse circumstance."

Monica stood when I approached, and she hugged me. Mom, still unconvinced that the girl was there to do anything more than cause trouble, went right into Jon's room.

"You need to take a nap," I said. "You're purple under the eyes. Isn't she?"

"Sure is," Sheila said, craning her neck to look at Mom, who was sitting at Jonathan's bed.

Deirdre was asleep in a waiting room chair. Fiona was walking around with her arms folded. Theresa was on her way. Leanne was on a plane. Carrie was excommunicated. The Drazens were accounted for, planets circling the son.

"I'm fine," Monica said.

"We have a hotel room across the street. Go take a nap. If anything happens, you know I have your number."

"I can't... I... he keeps making the machines beep and they keep running in to defib-defib-de—" She put her hand over her mouth, descending into sobs. I held her as if she was a seventh little sister until she pulled away. "I'm fine. Tell him I'm fine."

"I'll tell him you were dancing a jig."

"Good, good," she said absently as if a jig would do just fine.

"Here." I took the cash-filled envelope from my pocket and laid it in her lap.

She looked in and closed it quickly. "I can't take this."

"You can and you will. As long as you're sitting here all day for him. Once this is over, pay him back. And if you need a lift, you use his driver. You're one of us."

She nodded. "Thank you. You should go see him."

Mom and I went in. No amount of scotch could prepare me for Jonathan's deterioration. My dinner wanted nothing to do with me, threatening to leave the way it came.

Bags of blood hung over him. His skin was gray and flaccid on the chiseled bone structure of his face. His eyes were deep in purple hollows, staring at the ceiling, moving slowly as if changing direction hurt. He didn't look like an old man living as much as he looked like a young man dying.

When he swallowed, I saw the organs of his throat move.

Mom was at his side with her hand over his, mid-conversation.

"I'll try," she said.

"For me," he said with a voice like an engine that didn't want to start. "Forgive him. It's been too long."

"Dad?" I said. "You're fighting for Dad? You can't stand Dad."

"Don't stress him, Margaret. Be nice."

"I'd be worried if she was nice," he said, turning his head a fraction of an inch toward me. "How's Monica?"

"Hanging in there. She's pretty tough."

He smiled wider than I thought possible under the circumstances, then—as if they were on a timer—the machines howled and whined. His eyes closed.

Mom and I backed away as the doctors rushed in.

FOURTEEN

Hearing the doctors shout and the machines cry while they sent electrical shocks through Jonathan's chest made me shake so hard I could barely hold my mother's hand. They gave her another sedative, and Deirdre took Mom back to the hotel. I went to the hallway to breathe, and leaning against the wall with my eyes closed, I wished Paulie Patalano dead.

It was late by then. After visiting hours. Rubber shoes squeaked at the other end of the hall. I didn't open my eyes as they got closer. Not until I heard "Taste of Cinnamon" from passing earbuds did I open my eyes.

The orderly nodded to me. He wasn't listening to thirty-year-old rock. Not at all. Drew was just in my mind, changing the way my brain processed what it heard.

I went downstairs.

The cafeteria was mostly empty. The counter was unmanned. Muzak played for no one and everyone. The buffed steel chafing dishes were wiped clean. The vending machines flashed smugly as if they knew they had a monopoly. A table of people in scrubs laughed over coffee. An old man in an out-of-season scarf stared at a granola bar.

In the corner, my father sat across from Drew.

"Shit," I muttered.

Drew leaned on his forearms on the edge of the table like a man at full attention.

You can be free.

When we were together, Drew had had a casual insolence toward my father I hadn't wanted to correct. You didn't get casual with my father. You never let him think you didn't care. Not until you had the upper hand. But I hadn't wanted to pit them as adversaries. I'd thought there was no reason to. I was wrong.

Declan looked at me as I approached, and Drew followed his gaze. I kept my face implacable so my father wouldn't see my alarm and Drew wouldn't see my questions.

"How does my son look?" Dad asked as I sat at the head of the table.

Did he just emphasize "my son" as if he knew I couldn't refute it? Was he testing me? Or Drew? We were the only three people who knew.

"Like he needs a new heart."

"Paulie Patalano doesn't need his heart," Dad said, creasing the edge of a napkin. "Never has, if the past is any indication."

"This is a fascinatingly ghoulish conversation," I said. "And more relevant than I'm comfortable with."

"You've met this gentleman?" Dad held his hand in his guest's direction.

"A few times." I turned to Drew. He smirked, and I tried to extinguish a desperate anxiety that wouldn't be quelled. "Been a while."

"I heard about Jonathan, so I came."

"We were just reliving old times," Dad said. "When he and his friend came past the gate looking for you. What was his name again?"

"Stratford. Gilliam." Drew's tone was an accusation.

"Ah, right." My father acted as though he was having polite conversation before he swung with the blade. "The animal who couldn't stop himself from fucking underage girls."

His gaze went to Drew as if he knew the man across from him was guilty of the same crime. For once, the man I'd loved didn't flinch or look remorseful when my father attacked. He didn't look as if he wanted to run away. He looked as though he wanted to fight.

And he looked like a man who knew something he wasn't going to talk about until he was good and ready.

Was that what Drew had been unearthing for a year? My father's sick proclivities were known to all of us, but he'd only been caught with Theresa's friend.

"God rest his soul," I said, hoping a subtle reprimand about speaking ill of the dead would shut him up.

"God rest the addict's soul," Dad replied, standing. "I'm sure you two have a lot of catching up to do. I'll leave you to it." He buttoned his jacket and headed for the exit.

"What the—" I hissed to Drew.

"I told you I wasn't fucking around."

"Fuck." I shot up and caught my father by the door. "Dad."

"Margaret."

"Leave him alone."

He glanced over the room. The table of scrubs was empty but for a few napkins. The guy with the scarf sat over the empty granola bar wrapper.

"He doesn't want to be left alone. Maybe you should let him face the consequences of his own life."

My guts went cold. In all the years Drew was gone, I knew he was all right as long as he stayed gone. And here we were, back at square one. Same choices.

"I'm warning you," I said but didn't complete the threat.

"I made the mistake of trying to save you from the consequences of your choices and look where that's gotten us. Delusional ranting in front of your mother."

He was sticking to his story and scolding me for nearly speaking the truth at the same time. I wouldn't be scolded or controlled. I wasn't fifteen anymore.

"I know everything and I'll burn it all down."

He smirked, nodding a little. "When you talk like that, Margaret Drazen, I couldn't be more proud of you. You're formidable. It's awe-inspiring. But you're also the most misguided woman I've ever met. You sold your life to this family because you didn't know what to do with it. I gave you a purpose. But that's not good enough. Your brother's in trouble and you're looking for meaning. You forget... you have meaning. This family. If it wasn't for us, you'd be six feet under with your precious Stratford." He stepped toward the door. "You're welcome."

"You're the delusional one."

Even as I said it, I knew it wasn't true. My father was a lot of things. Delusional wasn't one of them.

"Your mother's going to be back where she should be. With me in her bed and her life. Do not use your lack of purpose to interfere."

He left before I could argue that I'd always had a purpose, even if it was changing.

"He looks happy," Drew said, handing me the bag I'd left on the back of the chair.

"Don't let him fool you. He feels absolutely nothing."

"I can walk you upstairs."

The idea of that waiting room made me claustrophobic. I had to get out of the hospital, but across the street, a hotel room full of Drazens waited with their brokenness and their poisoned history.

"Not a word in all these years," I said. "And twice in a day You're like a litigious client with a list of grievances."

"Once I decided, it was easy." He put his hand on my lower back as we turned a corner. He was stronger and steadier than I remembered. Unflappable in the most driving winds.

"I'm going to stop upstairs to make sure everything's okay," I said, hitting the up button. "Then I'm going home."

"Meet me in P2." He hit the down button. "I'll take you."

Refusing was an option. Probably the best option. But the lines in his face emphasized his concern, and the gray hair at his temples gave that concern a gravity that I didn't realize I needed.

"It's just a ride," I said, drawing my boundaries.

"It will be."

FIFTEEN

Monica was with Jonathan, staring at him as if he was the last man on earth. To her, he was. Everything wasn't fine, but there wasn't anything I could do but intrude. I left her alone with him and went to P2.

He was waiting for me with a black motorcycle helmet under his arm and a white one in his hand.

"You're joking," I said, not taking it.

"You crack your head open and you're going to be the heart donor you're wishing for."

I took the helmet.

He guided me to a BMW motorcycle with shiny chrome touches and a bright blue gas tank. Drew had been a cocksure lawyer and a chaotic boyfriend. Indy had been a purposeful artist. The man who handed me a white helmet was more Indiana than Andrew, and I kept thinking of him as Indy.

"Can't we take a car?" I said. "I'm too old for this."

He swung his leg over the bike and flipped the kickstand with a *clack*.

"Live a little, Margaret."

"It's been a long day. I've been hysterical, deluded, tranquilized, lied to, and hit broadside by a guy I haven't seen in years."

"And tomorrow will come whether you like it or not." He pushed the helmet into my chest.

"Not if I die on that thing."

"Fear will keep you awake, then."

I took the clip out of my hair and let it fall over my shoulders. "Call me Cin."

He revved the engine. I got on behind him and put my arms around his waist. I didn't want to hold him like that. The warmth and firmness of his body was too tangible, too distracting. It reminded me of years of blissful, ignorant happiness.

Before I was the fixer. Before I was the problem solver. Before I managed my relationships like chess pieces, I'd been rebellious, happy, and free.

Once past the gate, he went north and west, turning onto PCH. I knocked on his helmet.

"You all right back there?" I heard the sound of his voice in my ear. The helmets had radios.

"This isn't the way to my house."

"I know."

"Indy, I'm tired."

"It won't be long." He stopped at a light and held the bike still and straight with his legs. "If you want to go home right away, I'll take you. I thought you could decompress a little. Up to you."

I wanted to go home to that big, empty house with the big, empty bed and listen to the vents whoosh and the clocks tick. Collapse into bed so I could fall asleep and wake up in the same house with the same empty sounds.

"Okay," I said. "Decompress me."

"Atta girl."

The light changed and we lurched forward. He sped up on a turn, pressing our bodies together. I didn't slide away. I held him tighter. With the bike rumbling under me and this man in my arms, on the way to nowhere, I couldn't think about Jonathan, or Theresa, or my parents. The contract came unknotted, clauses disengaged from sentences and promises not to breach. I had to lean into his turns, forward into his acceleration, and brace myself against slowdowns.

We turned off the road and onto a service road that ran alongside the beach. I held him tight to keep from falling backward, the bottoms of my feet numb from vibration and a gray wall of sound stuffed in my ears. My senses were so stimulated and my concentration so honed on where I was leaning that my mind had nowhere to look but inward. Nothing to think about but all the things I'd spent years avoiding.

Who was I? What did I want?

The service road turned into a narrow parking lot. It was crowded with twenty-somethings. The smell of beer swirled with the salty sea. The music that came through the gurgle of the ocean sounded like a live band.

Was I happy?

I was burdened and busy. But was I unhappy?

Drew parked the bike in an empty corner and let me dismount. We took off our helmets. He brushed back his hair. A woman squealed with laughter. A man in the opposite direction shouted. The music changed to a different song. The scene was like the night we met on the beach. A blank sheet of possibilities. At least for an hour or two, before exhaustion and the thought of Jonathan's destroyed heart took over.

"Are you going to invite me upstairs for a game of strip poker?" I asked.

"We don't have all night." He put his arm around my shoulder, looking at me. "I have one thing to do. Then I'll take you home if you want."

My arm slid around his waist.

I'd been single so long. So very long. Yet it was so easy to navigate the crowd with him. He guided me along a row of sawhorses to a makeshift staging area with busy staff running between equipment trucks.

"Where are we going?" I asked as we approached an entrance.

A burly black man with a long beard and a radio waited there, next to a similarly-outfitted white woman with close-cropped pink hair.

"Going to hear some music," Drew said as he pulled a tag and lanyard out of his pocket. He looped it over his head with his free hand.

"Evening," Burly said.

"Evening." Drew held up his nametag. "I'm on the list."

Burly ran a laser reader over the tag's QR code. It beeped.

The woman checked it on an iPad. "Indiana McCaffrey. *The* Indy McCaffrey?"

People who worked with artists didn't get star struck. But in the light of the iPad, the pink-haired woman's eyebrows went up a good half an inch.

"I'm sorry," she said. "It's been a long time."

Drew smiled. "Reports of my death have been exaggerated."

The guy was less impressed. "You have a guest? What's your name, miss?"

My name could raise as many eyebrows as Drew's, but that wasn't why I answered the way I did. "Cinnamon, and ma'am is fine."

Drew squeezed my shoulder. Pink Hair tapped the screen.

"You're here," she said, putting the iPad away before opening the rope. "Get a tag from the table to your left. And welcome back, Indy."

We went to the table. Drew checked his watch as I got my tag and earplugs.

"You have a hot date?" I asked.

"Yeah." His arm tightened around my shoulder. "Kinda."

"What's her name?"

"Life."

He took me closer to the stage. I could see the net of lights above. We were jostled by roadies and blocked by two men in sports jackets and conservative haircuts. When we went around them, Drew faced the other direction.

"Do you not want them to see you?" I asked.

"Not yet."

We walked through the makeshift backstage area in the beach parking lot. The concert was a band I'd never heard of, but thousands had gathered on the sand to see them. The stage faced the ocean and a beach dotted with campfires.

"Hey!" A pale guy with long brown hair approached Drew. They shook hands. "You're all set."

"What's going on?" I asked when he left.

Drew didn't have a chance to answer me. People approached him, one after the other, with questions and clipboards, guiding us closer to the stage, then up the steps. His arm slid from around my shoulders and landed on my hand. I let him lace his fingers in mine, feeling the thrum of excitement that something was going to happen. Something great and fun. Something that wouldn't make everything all right, but it would make all life's aches and pains worth it.

We were on the boundary between the backstage and the front, where the band blasted the last of a song and the lights dropped. The crowd cheered and the lights went back on.

"One song," he said.

"Wait…"

"Then I'll take you home."

"You're playing? Publicly?"

"I'm not hiding any more."

I hadn't watched him play from backstage since I was a teenager. The years between dropped away and I was a girl again, learning that my idols were human men. My life faced front. Everything was possible.

"Just one song?" I asked.

"I want to kiss you so bad right now."

I would have let him kiss me, but he turned back to the stage and the lights blinded me for a moment.

The singer leaned into his mic. "We have a surprise for you assholes. Who remembers Bullets and Blood?"

When the audience screamed, I squeezed Drew's hand and looked at him. He was looking in the middle distance with a serious expression. My smile was so wide it hurt.

The singer turned to face us as he spoke into the mic. "Back from who the fuck even knows where." He pointed at Drew.

I let his hand go in the heavy pause and watched him go on stage. Drew turned to me, taking a step backward, and blew me a kiss. In full light, his age was more apparent. It suited him. The fading tattoos on his arms were not a map of regret, but evidence of a life in the process of being lived.

A roadie handed him a guitar, and he went up to a microphone.

"Hello, Santa Monica." He hit a chord that couldn't be mistaken for anything but Bullets and Blood, cutting it off mid-squeal. "I'm Indy McCaffrey."

The crowd went wild, and when he hit his first notes, Drew—once and for all—was Indy again.

SIXTEEN

ONE SONG, AND IT WASN'T BULLETS AND BLOOD.

I'd heard the song on the radio in another artist's voice, with a string quartet, a timpani drum, and gentle guitar riffs. Everyone had heard it. In coffee shops and in cars for five years running, this song was the generation's anthem to loss and grief.

Indy played it as he'd conceived it, with a growl of rage over what he'd lost and a long, purposeful howl of despair at the end, crumbling into the last words of the refrain.

When I lost you

I lost myself

I'd heard that song a hundred times, but before that night, I hadn't heard it at all. It was ours. It was our loss. Our loneliness. It was a love song to our choices.

Margie Drazen was never reduced to tears. She was never reduced to anything. Period.

Cinnamon, however, was a silly, soft girl and she cried when she heard truth.

I was blind with tears when he reached me. His hands clutched my arms, and when he leaned down, he blocked the light again, becoming the only thing in my tear-streaked world.

"Margie," he said. Behind him, the band started another song. "Cin."

I couldn't answer to either name. I was shaking and hitching like a fucking baby.

Why did I always break in front of him? I'd kept myself in check for a decade and a half, and there I was, crumbling the day after he showed up again. I was humiliated but I couldn't stop the gush of raw emotion.

My feet went from under me. I wrapped my arms around his neck and sobbed like a teenager. The hoots and cries dimmed as the sound of the ocean took over. He set me down on the bike.

"I'm sorry," I said.

He handed me a folded plaid hankie. "If I thought you'd be so upset, I wouldn't have played it."

I laughed to myself and wiped my face. "Thank you for playing it. You have a way of being the valve on the shit I hold in."

"I've always admired your self-control."

"It's a shitty way to live." I folded the hankie with a last sniff.

He took it then laid his hand on my cheek. I let him. I shouldn't have, but I let him. I needed the touch of a man I trusted.

"You're also exhausted and worried." He took his hand away to grab the helmets. "Let me get you home. You need to rest."

We mounted the bike, and I leaned my weight against him the whole way home.

I GUIDED him to the side of the house, and he parked his bike by the back deck. From there, we could see the pool and the garden overlooking the pattern of night lights in the city.

"Nice place," he said, pulling off his helmet.

When he ran his fingers through his hair to put it back in place, I recognized the gesture as a habit. It didn't take long for new patterns to lay themselves on top of expectations.

Looking out over the glowing turquoise rectangle of the pool, I shrugged. "I hate it." I handed him my helmet. "It's a mausoleum to good taste. That pool? No one's been in it for over a year."

"That pool?"

"That pool." I turned away and took the first step onto the deck. "It's a nice pool, and every day it gets more depressing."

I was really letting loose on this poor guy. I should have been paying him three hundred for a fifty-minute hour. At the top of the deck, I realized he wasn't behind me. A split second later, I heard a splash and the perfect glass surface of the water was shattered. It had to be fifty degrees.

He swam to the surface as I ran down to the pool.

"You keep it heated?" he asked as he swam toward me.

"It's winter."

He put his arms over the edge. His hair was spiked and uneven. He looked as if he'd just pulled off his helmet and forgotten to run his fingers through it. "But you said no one swims in it."

I crouched by him. "I like everything to be in order. Just in case."

"It's nice. You should come in." He grabbed my arm as if to pull me down.

"I can't."

He let go of my arm. "Why not?"

"Because I'm already fighting guilt for not sitting by Jonathan. If I get in this pool and enjoy it, I'm going to feel worse." A drop fell from his hairline and down his cheeks. "Are you still wearing your boots?"

"Unfortunately."

I laughed. "Jesus, Indy. Do you need me to help you out?"

"I got it."

I gave him room as he got his elbows under him and pulled himself onto land. His boots gushed from the tops and his shirt stuck to his chest. He was that lawyer in the rain I'd kissed so long ago. I didn't have long to wonder if he'd made the same connection.

When he came toward me, I laid my hand on his chest. I felt his heart through his jacket. I wanted that heart to beat for me, but I couldn't demand that. Not when I wasn't sure what mine beat for anymore.

"Do you want to come in and dry off?"

"I have a warm hotel room," he said. "Besides, I don't want the temptation. I'm not going to kiss you. Not until I set you free."

"That's a tall order, Indy."

"You're worth it, and I'm a liar."

"No, I—"

I was going to tell him that no one was worth the kind of trouble he'd get himself into, but my denial was smothered in a kiss.

Shit. This was trouble.

Not the kiss. The kiss was perfect. It listened. It responded. It wasn't stolen in a moment of passion, but an equal exchange of affection that turned rejection into acceptance and transformed a calculated debate into a heated exchange.

I loved him and I had no reason to. If I knew why, I could argue against it and win. But without a cause, I couldn't shoo it away. I couldn't pat it on the head, tell it I understood, and open the exits. Reason was love's egress, but love didn't have the sense to leave when logic opened the door. It bumped around the walls like a blind child in a silent room. Uncomfortable. Unhappy. Unable to get out.

He was made of concentrated heat. He was a vector. A direction without coordinates. I reacted by emptying like a tipped water glass. Every thought shut down. Every feeling hushed. I was a place, a still thing, yielding to his force.

In the empty moment, the blind child in the silent room banged against the walls of my heart.

Emotions were habitually mispackaged, mispronounced, misnamed.

But not this. I knew what it was.

The kiss was trouble because I loved him and I didn't know how to save him.

SEVENTEEN

I'D AGAIN INVITED INDY INSIDE TO DRY OFF, BUT HE'D THANKED ME, KISSED my cheek, and taken off with wet boots and hair. The last of my energy left with him. I brushed my teeth and fell asleep with my clothes on, waking with all the anxiety he'd helped release the night before squeezing my chest anew.

Another day gone by.

Another day with Jonathan bleeding into his chest.

Another day carrying the dead weight of a secret.

And yet, Indy made it all different. Not better. Different.

He'd overlaid hope over the bleak landscape of my situation. The hope was uncomfortable. It jabbed me in the soft underbelly of my guilt. I had no business feeling good about him when my son's life hung by tubes and wires.

Let it go.

As the weight of the hospital elevator floor pressed against my feet, I tried to get my mind back on my responsibilities.

The skill I had in compartmentalizing only worked with crises. Optimism didn't quite fit inside any of the boxes I was used to creating. The lid wouldn't close over Indy's song or the way he said his old name.

Let it go.

I had *feelings,* and on the rare occasions I let them in the door, they overstayed their welcome.

Define the feelings. Call them by their name.

"Let me go," I whispered to myself as the elevator stopped.

Set me free.

The doors opened.

Will Santon was there.

"Delta," I said in my snappiest tone, "your timing's impeccable."

"I have to talk to you," he replied as I brushed by him.

We fell into step down the hall, and I ran down his assignments.

"You're sorting out my brother's ex-wife?"

"Sorted."

"Theresa?"

"She's fine."

"My mother keeping it together?"

"Yes."

As we turned a corner, he ran around me, blocking the way. Will and I always had plenty to discuss, and if there wasn't enough business, he told me about Hannah, which I could listen to for hours. But this was different.

"What is it?" I said.

"I got dumped last night. I'm a conflict of interest."

What had he called me at the restaurant? A friend? She either didn't believe him or she knew better.

"Was that all she said?" I asked.

"Did she need to say more?"

"I'd like to know how many things I have to juggle."

"What happened in 1999?"

"Nothing. Everything."

"I can't help you if you don't trust me enough to talk to me."

"Will. You know what you need to know."

He put up two index fingers as if one wouldn't make the point. "Listen to me. I've covered your tracks without a single question because you told me flat out what I was doing and why. What changed?"

"You're dating a Fed."

"Not anymore, I'm not. You think I'm looking for more exposure than I already have?"

"You weren't involved. Warren Chilton raped my sister and promised to do it again. He was found hanging from a tree on the Westonwood grounds. Not by his neck. No, no. In a web of knots he couldn't undo because he was paralyzed and full of Nortyl."

"The despair drug?"

"I hear it makes you happy until you take too much, which he did. He tried to hang himself, screwed up, and damaged his spinal cord. That's what happened. The end. I thought it was poetic justice, myself."

Will scanned my face for the truth. I wanted to tell him everything, but I couldn't. I wasn't the only person who had to worry about the statute of limitations.

Dr. Thorensen appeared over Will's shoulder, spotting me. "Ms. Drazen. I'm sorry to interrupt."

"It's fine. How is he?"

"Can we talk for a moment?"

I swallowed, put the panic inside its panic-sized box, closed the lid, and followed the doctor down the hall.

DR. BRAD THORENSEN had a small office. I stood in the middle of it when he closed the door and he still had to excuse himself to get past me.

"Sit." He indicated the chair across his desk.

I sat with my hands in my lap.

"You're, ah, concerned about the size of the office?"

Had to give him credit for being intuitive.

"I thought you ran thoracic."

"Cardiac."

"I mean you no offense, but we can afford the best."

After the imbalance of the morning, being straightforward felt good.

"Yeah." He leaned back in his squeaky chair. "I could have a small office near my patients or a big office on the eighth floor."

"A wise choice. How is he?"

"I'll get to that." He sat up straight with the change of subject. "Yesterday at our meeting, you mentioned the possibility that there might be some uncertainty surrounding your brother's paternity."

Shit.

This was what emotions did. They fucked you up. They made you say things you shouldn't. They took a normal brain and rewired it like a drunk electrician.

There was no use denying it, but there was also no use elaborating. "I did."

"It's too late, in a sense, to do anything about the fact that we didn't already know. The damage is done. But if you were right, in order to head off any potential future problems, I looked up Stratford Gilliam."

My throat closed at the sound of his name on strange lips.

"Luckily, an old *Rolling Stone* had the information I needed to locate his death and medical records."

If you'd asked me if there was any sound in the room, I would have said no, it was quiet. But my heart stopped beating, and the wind stopped rattling the window, and the birds outside flew instead of sang. The vents shut down and the squeaky gurneys and burping phones all went mute.

"What I can tell you, from page one, is Mr. Gilliam's blood type was O. Your brother is AB. He can't be the father. It doesn't work that way."

My swallow made the loud *guck* of a clogged sink opening.

"Also, aortic valve stenosis is genetic, but so recessive it can pass ten generations without showing up. So you can rest easy."

I could rest easy.

Why again?

"Strat's not Jonathan's father."

"He is not."

"I'm…"

His mother?

"Glad."

His sister?

What else was I wrong about?

I had to get out of that room. It was too small to fit everything I'd misunderstood.

"I'm sorry I got agitated in the meeting," I said, standing.

"It's fine. You're all stressed. I understand. We just have to make him comfortable until a heart comes down the pike."

I put my hand on the desk to feel something solid. "How long does he have if there's no heart?"

"Hard to say."

"How long, in your opinion?"

He didn't want to tell me, and I didn't blame him. Not that it mattered what he wanted. I needed to know.

"The condition of the muscle is getting worse. His organs aren't getting enough oxygen."

"How long?" I didn't waver. I sounded as strong and decisive as I intended. "Doctor. My mother is breaking down every hour that goes by. We're going to need to make plans for her in the event that he dies. Something besides pumping her full of sedatives."

With his hands folded in front of him, he regarded my face and expression and decided to believe me. I steeled myself for the answer.

"Days."

The steel rattled but held. It wouldn't for long.

"What about that mobster who got shot? " I asked. "Isn't he upstairs?"

Doctors had a way of hiding their reactions to crazy suggestions, and Thorensen was no different. I couldn't scrape hope or disappointment from the bottom of that barrel.

"It's up to the family, and we have a lot of people on the list waiting for a heart." He waved as if swatting away the bad line of inquiry. "It's best not to get attached to any one donor. Okay?"

"Yes. Of course you're right."

He stood. Meeting over. Good. I had things to do.

I'D PRAYED for freedom and I got it.

I was free of guilt. Strat wasn't Jonathan's father, nor was the heart condition an issue. The secret my life revolved around was irrelevant to the proceedings.

That is, if the secret was even a secret and not a wild fantasy cooked up in the Drazen wine cellar by a couple of lawyers with nothing better to do.

What if it was all fake?

My mouth went dry. My veins went brittle. All the moisture in my body turned to steam and floated away, taking my entire self-image with it.

What if I'd let Drew go to protect a boy who wasn't mine? What if I'd made every life decision based on a lie?

What if my father had done the same?

Taking the stairs down to the first floor, where I could find water, I called Will on our secure line. He picked up in a crowded place with echoes.

"I hate to do this to you," I said, looking over the worn metal banister to see if anyone else was avoiding the elevators. "I need something and I can't explain why."

"I don't know if I should," he replied. "Someone gave me the stink-eye on the pick-up line at preschool last night."

"I'm sorry I ruined that for you. She seemed nice for a second."

He sighed and the background noise quieted. "She said to me, at the restaurant, 'Is that Declan Drazen's daughter?' and I said you were. I should have lied and I didn't. So maybe you shouldn't explain why."

Pushing the bar lock, I went into the hospital lobby and strode outside where I was one of a dozen people no one was listening to.

"So you'll do it?" I asked.

"Depends what it is."

"It's all about 1983."

JONATHAN WAS UNCONSCIOUS.

I didn't think I'd ever be grateful for that, but I could inspect his face from all angles.

He wasn't Strat's. Despite all the times I'd seen him in Jonathan's face, Strat wasn't his father.

Was Jonathan mine?

Had I gone through all these years on a faulty assumption? Had the nurses taken a silent blue baby out of my mother, nursed him for two days until he was pink and wailing, and put the same baby in her arms?

Chin, nose, forehead, hands. An intubated chest draining blood and putting it back. Six-foot-two with a ginger tint to his hair.

Had I reshaped him to match a set of bad ideas? A string of false hopes?

How many decisions had I made out of those assumptions?

I sat next to him. "I love you the same, but who are you?"

Did it matter?

Maybe not for Jonathan, but it mattered.

Footsteps behind me stopped in the doorway. Not medical staff. They didn't pause before they came in.

"Will?" I said, not looking around.

"Unfortunately for you"—the sound of my father's voice was accompanied by footsteps as he entered—"it's just me."

He sat next to me, all six-four of him folding into a chair made for someone shorter. I had no recollection of Strat's height. Was he tall enough to be Jonathan's father? I was five-six and change. Was I tall enough to be his mother?

"I was just leaving."

"Please stay," he said. "I want to talk about this man being back in your life."

"Jesus, Dad. You can't send me away anymore."

"He was part of an insane period for you, and I want to make sure you keep your wits."

"My wits are fine."

Were they?

Yesterday, I would have said that of everyone in the family, I was the sole bearer of truth. In that quiet hospital room, with the machines chirping like horny crickets, I wasn't so sure.

"You wouldn't let an insane person manage what I manage," I added.

"You can be perfectly reasonable about business and delusional about other things. And when your boyfriend told me about your little fantasy, we needed you to fill a role that came naturally to you."

"Drazen fixer."

"You were stuck. You couldn't hold a job because you were better than any job they'd give you. Your life up to then was a string of bad decisions. Your man wasn't worthy of you and you knew it. You refused help. You insisted on the hard way. You were empty. Without us, you'd still be empty."

"Maybe I was, and maybe I'm not anymore. Maybe it's time to move on."

"This boy? This man lying here? He filled a space for you. He gave you something to protect. And now, with him dying, you're going to think of leaving the fold."

I looked at him finally. Motherfucker. I'd never threatened to leave, and he didn't look shaken or taken aback. Not even a little.

He continued without the slightest waver in his voice. "You always thought your brother was the only thing holding you to this family. That's ridiculous, Margaret. You're one of us. You always will be. A daughter to me, and a sister to Jonathan."

No. I wasn't ready to let go. Jon was mine. The only thing I'd ever had.

"You're wrong," I said. "I know the truth."

"I thought with that man gone, you'd stop with this. I should have made sure he'd stay away from you for good."

"How, Dad? Same way as Strat?"

He leaned over the arm of the chair to get close enough to whisper. "If you keep talking like this, they're going to put you away before you hurt yourself. Do you understand me?"

That was a direct threat, and it wasn't an idle one. He'd find a way to put me in a mental institution.

But he'd forgotten who he was dealing with. Who he'd molded in his own image. He'd made me recklessly impervious to intimidation, even from a master like him. Even when the extortion was real and the stakes were high.

"I suggest, *Daddy*, that you take your new relationship with Mom and you thank God for it. Wake up in praise. Because she's all you ever had. She's the only person who ever loved you without being afraid of you. Even when she hated you, she loved you. So you light a hundred candles in thanks, because I'll tell her about this 'delusion' and I'll bring her the DNA records to prove I didn't make it up."

That got him. The DNA threat was complete bullshit, but fear flickered across his face like a half-screwed lightbulb.

The flicker was gone. J. Declan Drazen was never afraid for long.

"You won't win against me, Margie."

"Maybe not, but it's my choice to play."

I stood and kissed my son on the forehead. It was cold and dry, and through the forward motion of my game with my father, sorrow slipped through.

ON THE WAY HOME, the air got dense, as if the space between molecules had tightened ten percent and exerted pressure on my body. Cracking the windows only added velocity to the density.

Nothing had changed. San Vicente met Bronson, which kissed Wilshire all the way to Santa Monica.

Nothing but reality. The streets existed in a world I didn't live in anymore. I existed in a thick, crushing parallel universe where I was unmoored from the reality I'd known and crushed by the reality no one could see.

It was all the same. Whether he was mine or not, he was dying.

It still mattered. I'd still give him my heart if I could. But I was completely, utterly alone, holding down a fabricated secret.

That night, I dreamed of wings.

I often dreamed I had wings. Sometimes they were feathery and white. Sometimes they were the slick black of patent leather. But in the dream, which had recurred frequently as a child and less so as I got

older, they were mine, they'd always been mine, and they were always
a part of me. Some nights I flew. Some nights I was grounded. During
one especially vivid dream, the wings were tiny fish fins and one was
broken.

My dream-self despaired but didn't lose faith in who belonged to
those fucking wings.

That night, the wings didn't fit.

Every time I opened my eyes to a flightless life, I spent the first few
minutes of the morning feeling as if I'd lost something. It was enough
to make a girl stay up all night just so the sun would come up without
the accompaniment of grief.

Stupid grief, of course, because I'd never had wings and my jackets
wouldn't have fit over them. I'd lost nothing. I hadn't lost wings any
more than I'd lost a son. You can't lose what you never had.

But I'd had him in my heart. My secret. My unacknowledged baby.

I kept thinking of him as my son. Years after I told myself I didn't
think of it every time I spoke to him, I knew I'd lied. I'd always
thought of him that way. He was never a brother.

He wasn't Strat's, and if he wasn't Strat's, was he even mine?

And if he was still mine, there was only one other possible father.

And that couldn't be.

I SPENT the day managing Theresa. If my life was fucked up, hers was
a close second. So I did what I always did. Made arrangements. Kept
her safe. Fixed what I could, and what I couldn't, I let fate handle.

If Indy hadn't returned, if Jonathan wasn't dying, if my father
wasn't making threats, Theresa's problems with her capo would have
occupied my complete attention. But I was simply pissing on whatever
fires I could reach.

Whenever I thought about contacting Indy to tell him what
Thorensen had told me, another little fire went up, and I was grateful
for it. I wasn't ready to tell him. It would break a bond we'd had even
when he was far away.

Avoidance was like a secret. It could be kept up as long as all parties agreed on it. Drew never got the memo, and texted me as I was on my way home.

—I KEEP LOOKING FOR YOU—

A week before, a text from him stating that he was looking for me would have knocked me back three feet. Instead, it washed away the distractions and made avoidance unmanageable.

He texted again.

—HOW ARE YOU HOLDING UP?—

I couldn't answer without telling him. Not without lying. Nor could I see him without breaking the bond that held us.

—Meet me at my place. And bring a bathing suit if you want to swim—

Maybe I had to break that bond.

Maybe if it was the only thing that had been holding us together, it was time to untie it so we could both be free.

EIGHTEEN

WILL SHOWED UP IN HIS SUBURBAN SOON AFTER I GOT HOME. BETWEEN Dr. Thorensen's revelation, Indy's presence, my father's threats, and Jonathan's illness, I didn't want to see Will. I didn't want to see anyone. I didn't want to see the inside of my eyelids either.

So I let him in. He slapped a banker's box of documents on the kitchen counter. I'd asked him to go to the Drazen Enterprises record storage warehouse downtown. I'd given him two days.

Obviously, he hadn't needed them.

"Highlights from 1983." He took off the lid and unpacked folders. "As requested. Atypical business transactions and/or transactions involving members of the Carloni crime family and/or any investments in pharmaceuticals. Amphetamine makers in particular."

"I sure can overwhelm a guy." I took out the last folder.

"It's ninty-nine percent garbage." He handed me a folder. "But this is interesting."

I laid it open.

"Drazen Enterprises bought a coffee shop in Brooklyn," he said as I scanned a page.

"In Bensonhurst, no less."

He picked up the paper under it.. "And you sold it back to Franco Carloni the next business year."

"Junior. We sold it back to Franco's sixteen-year-old son for ten percent of the price. Two hundred grand, laundered right through." I put down the papers. "Okay, honestly, we know how my family works. This is normal Tuesday business. Is there anything else?"

"Related." He held up a finger and pushed another page to me. "As the owners of the coffee shop, Drazen Enterprises bought ten thousand in traveler's checks."

"Hello, 1983." I put down the paper. "So what are we thinking? Franco took a two hundred fee, and we sent through another ten that disappeared? Where did it go?"

"Can't trace traveler's checks, so they probably went to someone who couldn't launder it. But the point is, Carloni Senior had just gotten out of prison for racketeering. His three sons had started a side business while he was gone. The oldest went to prison six months after his father got out."

The last page in the folder was a microfiche of a newspaper article. Alessandro Carloni was tried and convicted for...

"Illegal manufacture of prescription drugs," Will said. "In particular—"

"Amphetamine."

He closed the folder.

"Did Junior do it? Or his father?" I asked absently.

"Do what?"

Before answering, I checked the dates on the documents. The transactions occurred while I was in Ireland. The traveler's checks were purchased right before Strat was murdered. Alessandro hadn't been put away until after I returned.

"Arrange an overdose. Pay the Carloni family swap too much speed into a bag of heroin and sell it to someone my father wanted to get rid of. The Carlonis took the money from the sale of the coffee shop and the dealer got the traveler's checks."

"This is flimsy as hell."

"I know, but it's a start."

"Who was your father trying to get rid of?"

"There are things…" I tapped my nails on the counter. "There are things I haven't told anyone. Two other people know, and we don't talk about it. Thirty-one years, I've kept this secret, and today I found out it may not even be true."

Will bent his head down to see my face. Out of either exhaustion or because Dr. Thorensen's revelation had reduced the value of my suppression, my unbreachable wall had gotten thinner, or lower, or a break in the rose vines had formed.

I trusted him. He was my friend. I needed to tell someone with no skin in the game.

"Hey," he said, putting his hand over my wrist. "You don't have to tell me."

"I know. But I'm failing here. There are too many fires to put out. The hose is losing pressure. I need your help, and you can't help if you don't know."

With a final squeeze, he took his hand away. "Do you want me to make you a pot of coffee?"

"No." I launched from there. "Here's what I can say. I was a young girl. I liked exciting things. I liked trouble. I liked getting out of it. But there's some trouble… smart and rich as you are, there's some trouble you can't get out of."

Never having told the story or even considered speaking the words aloud, I hadn't figured out what was necessary and what could be left out.

What did he need to know?

What did I need to say?

Why was I so unsure? I always knew what to say. Why was this any different?

There was the story you told to litigate a case before a judge, and a story you told to a jury. There was a story you told the client and a story for opposing counsel.

Which was I talking to?

I sat straight and looked at Will with his elbows on the table and his head thrust forward, waiting. He wasn't in a listening posture as much as a posture of partnership. Give him the facts and he'd work on the problem.

He was neither judge nor jury. Neither client not opposing counsel. He was Will, and that informed how to reveal the secret, but it didn't make the secret any smaller. It was too big for my mouth. Like a rock bouncing across an empty sieve, it wouldn't get through.

I stood. "I have an exquisite bottle of Japanese scotch."

"I can't imagine it."

Pulling it from the cabinet, I set up two glasses and began. "I was shockingly young. Don't get your knickers in a twist over it. But it was 1982. I was out a lot. Parties. Clubs. Concerts."

I handed him his glass, and he held it out.

"To the eighties," he said.

"To the fucking eighties." I clinked with him and we drank.

"This isn't bad," he said.

"Fuck you, it's amazing." I took another sip. "So you know I had a relationship with Indy McCaffrey. Drew. But it didn't start in 1994. It started in 1982."

He nearly choked on his exquisite Japanese scotch.

"Yeah," I said with a smile. "So you can do math. I was friends with Drew and the singer Stratford Gilliam. Strat to his fans. And by friends, I mean I was in love with both of them and they were both in love with me."

He snapped up the bottle and refilled me. My mouth was already hot and dry from the alcohol. A shame to waste such a good bottle on a burning tongue.

"On one hand," he said, "I can't blame them. You were probably adorable. On the other…" He swirled his drink as if the right words would rise to the top. He drank them instead, leaving his glass half-full.

"It was consensual." I held up my hand to cut off his objections. "I know the law, okay? So stop. I never felt used or traumatized. I have nothing but fond memories from that whole episode. Don't come shitting on my parade. It was what happened after that fucked me up."

"Can you drink please?"

I kicked back what I had left and he filled my glass.

"You don't like it?" I asked, pointing at the drink he was nursing.

"I'm driving."

"I thought this would be so disturbing to hear you'd drink the bottle and call a cab."

"I'm not disturbed."

Believing him was a choice. An unexamined choice. A half-drunken choice. But a choice nonetheless.

"I got pregnant." When he didn't seem surprised, I plowed on, because of course that was how the story went. "My father found out early. Actually, it was the night my mother announced she was pregnant with her eighth child. And thus, my father whisked me away to Ireland to give birth in a convent."

"Jesus."

"I know it's a cliché, but clichés come from truth. He arranged an adoptive family there. Handily, my mother was also giving birth in the mother country. My guess is that my father wanted access to both of us. Which turned out well for him, because my mother's baby was stillborn and my baby was right there. The adoptive couple was told my baby didn't make it."

Head down, hand up, Will stopped me. "Wait."

"Yes. You know how this goes."

"No." He rubbed his eyes with one hand, knuckles digging deep as if he wanted to punch his brain.

"Yes." I swallowed.

The scotch and the company had made my throat a little wider and the secret a little smaller. I was going to say the words. I had to. He knew already. I'd marked the path with tiny colored stones of information. He could only go in one direction. He knew and I hadn't even said the words.

"Jonathan…" A lump of gunk rose in my throat to block the words.

Will's eyes were red where he'd rubbed. He wasn't shocked, dismissive, or disgusted. He wasn't angry, though there was a shade of that to his face.

Once the words were out, they were out. I wouldn't have plausible deniability. I wouldn't be able to claim the colored rocks led somewhere else. There would only be the secret, spoken out loud.

Will didn't tell me I didn't have to say it. I did, and I'd have to deal with it. The secret was a living thing I'd lose control over like an adolescent with a driver's license, but he had me. I wasn't alone.

Fuck it. I tossed it the keys.

"Jonathan is my son."

The kind thing to do for Will would be to pause so he could digest and ask questions, but this wasn't about him. Today had been painful in a way I hadn't appreciated until I needed to continue. Everything had been upended.

"Or I thought he was." I swirled my scotch. "Drew and I assumed he was Strat's. He looks just like him. But today I found out the blood types aren't a match, so now I'm not so sure. It was a crazy few months, but the timing... Jonathan should be his. And if he's not Strat's, is he even mine? Did I make up the whole thing?"

"Because you're fickle and imaginative?"

His response was so quick and conclusive that I laughed and kept on laughing. My eyes watered. In five words, he'd validated me and taken the burden off me. When my vision cleared, I had a full glass.

I held it up. "To... fuck if I know."

"To that." We toasted and drank. He put down his glass and tapped his ring on the edge. "You know the Irish couple's baby was stillborn?"

"Drew had the records."

"And your mother's baby? Proof?"

"Rumor."

"And your baby was alive?"

"He was beautiful. And alive."

"Natural birth?"

"I was wide awake."

He nodded once, sharply, and gave the glass one final tap with his wife's ring. Will cut the air with a flat hand, putting an end to doubt. "He's Drew's and yours. Indy... whichever."

"He had on a condom."

The argument was fake. The relief of knowing Jonathan was mine gave me a high that couldn't be explained by scotch. I was dotting Is and crossing Ts. He was mine again. Those hours without him should have been a parting of the clouds, but they were the darkest I could remember. I'd felt as if he'd been stolen a second time.

"Condoms in 1982?" Will said. "It broke. Slipped off. Had a hole in it. I'm not judging when I ask if there was a third guy in there somewhere?"

I didn't feel judged. He was a thorough PI. He was touching all the bases before running home.

"No third." My hand went to my chest to make sure my heart was still beating. "God, why am I relieved?"

"Margaret Drazen." Will picked up the bottle and put it down again. "You are the most gentle and sensitive woman I have ever met. You are complex as fuck. Hard to get through. Demanding. Bossy as a five-star fucking general. But inside? You're just a human. I could have really fallen for you."

"I wouldn't have let you."

"I know."

A bell rang through the house. The front gate.

Drew.

No.

Indy. He wasn't Drew anymore.

I drained my glass. "I'll walk you out."

Will stopped me as I reached for the doorknob. "You think your father killed Strat?"

I opened it. "I do. I have a ton of circumstantial evidence on my counter."

He walked to his car as Indy parked his bike. When he got his helmet off, Indy stared at Will then me.

"Indiana McCaffrey, you've met Will Santon."

They shook hands.

"How's the music blog?" Indy asked. His hackles had no business being up after so many years, but men were men.

"Ineffective." Will waved to me and got in the car.

We watched him drive away—me from the top of the stairs, Indy at the bottom.

"Should I ask if anything's going on with that guy?"

"Sure."

He looked at me. "Is anything going on with that guy?"

"No. Did you bring a bathing suit?"

"Bathing suits are for pussies." He came up the steps.

"New boots?" I asked, looking at his face, not his feet.

"You like them?" he replied, looking back down at my eyes.

"I told you the others would be ruined."

"They're drying out. I don't throw things away just because they see a little wear."

"Nothing time can't fix?"

"I love those boots. They'll get all the time they need."

He'd forced a smile out of me. I put my hand on his arm. "Come on into my big, empty house."

I led him into the kitchen where two glasses and a third-empty bottle of Japanese scotch waited.

"Can I get you a glass?" I asked.

He leaned on a stool by the kitchen island. "Water, please."

Of course. Two years sober and I'd offered him a drink the minute he came in the house. I grabbed the scotch by the neck and closed it.

"What's this?" Indy picked up a page.

"A money trail from my father to a dead man." Leaning on the bottle, I nodded to him slowly, giving the moment the weight it deserved.

"Strat?" he said.

I flipped to the last sale. "His life was worth three hundred thousand minus closing costs."

He laid his hand on the last, damning paper. "I want a drink so bad I can taste it."

"Then you don't need it." I put the bottle back in the cabinet.

"Cin," he said, still looking down, "do you think your father's capable of murder?"

Did I?

I knew a lot. Did I know everything?

"He is. No doubt he is." I tapped the counter, staring at the webbed patterns in the marble. "What would you do if you were me?"

"If I believed he'd killed someone I loved?"

"Not if you believed it," I said, crossing my arms. "If you knew it."

"In that case, you know what I'd do."

"Do I? The guy I knew, the lawyer Drew would have done one

thing. But I don't see that guy in you anymore. You're different. Part Indy. Part something else. So seeing what you see and knowing me…"

"Knowing how you've changed too?" he said.

"Knowing that. Yes. If you were me, what would you do?"

He stated a fact with no more urgency than a shrug. "I'd destroy him."

"And if you were you?"

"Same. And I intend to." My eyes deceived me. In the soft lights over the counter, he looked approachable and sexy, but the sound of his voice was comfortable with its own menace. "I don't know if your PI told you this, or if he even knows. I said I was two years sober. If you count my time in prison, it's three and a half years."

I nodded.

"You knew," he said.

"I did."

"I killed a woman while I was driving drunk. She wasn't doing anything but coming home from a party. She didn't drink because she was responsible, and I came along and killed her." He turned back to the counter as if he couldn't stand to look at me. As if he had to pretend he was the only one in the room. "I was up for parole after six months, but I said nah. I couldn't face the world. That was the bottom. Once a person hits bottom, Margie, nothing's scary. Not death. Not prison. Nothing."

He looked like the only man in the world. I couldn't let him stand there alone.

I went to him, putting my hands on his shoulders. "I'm sorry."

"Don't feel sorry for me. Feel sorry for what I've done and what I'm about to do."

"Indy." I leaned onto the counter next to him until we faced each other. "You're not going to premeditate a murder."

He laughed a little. "God, no. Even a man who's hit bottom has limits." He tented his fingers over the folder. "But I can hold him accountable, and I'm sorry. It's going to be hard for you."

"I can't help you." I closed the folder and pushed it away. "I don't know if you can do this without taking everyone else down with him. And it's… it's disloyal."

"After everything he's done to you?"

"He's done nothing that hasn't been what he thought was best for his family. He's misguided, unevolved, conniving, and controlling, but it was all for us. And I know he's done more harm than good, but he's my father. I can't pull him out of us as if he's a discrete object. The whole thing could come down."

He laid his thumb on my chin. I could feel the callous.

"I didn't come back to hurt you, Cinnamon."

"What if I asked you not to?"

"Why? Because he's your father?"

"Because..."

He's your son's grandfather.

I didn't think anything could make it worse.

I took his hand away. "Once I tell you what I'm about to tell you, you might change your mind."

Or make it worse.

No going back now. He stood up straight, attention redirected from the countertop to me. We'd switched postures. I put my hands far apart, leaning into the center of the triangle as if it was the only way to hold myself up.

"What is it?" he said.

Like a child, I wanted to make him promise to be calm, but like an adult, I knew he couldn't modulate his reactions with assurances.

I wasn't afraid of his anger. I was afraid of hurting him. But between lying to him to keep a fragile peace or telling the truth to no purpose at all, I only had one choice.

"Jonathan can't be Strat's."

"What?" The color drained from his face.

"The blood types." I spoke quickly, as if I needed to get all the information in before his body decided on a final reaction. "Something with the blood types I don't understand completely... but Strat was O and Jonathan's AB. Os don't make ABs. Only a couple with As and Bs can." I swallowed. My throat was bone-dry.

Indy was frozen in place with his brow in a knot and his lips parted.

"I'm B. I don't know yours."

"AB," he said.

I scanned his face for any knowledge of what that meant. Found none. "We can look it up, or we can accept what we already know is true."

"No," he whispered.

"Maybe not."

"He looks just like him."

"We saw what we wanted to see."

"That's *not true*. No." He slapped his hand on the counter. "Don't tell me I didn't want him. I wanted us. I fantasized about it every god damn night."

"I know, but—"

"No but. I would have made a hundred different choices if I'd known."

I let him pace as he processed the information as if I'd completely digested it.

"No," he said. "The heart problem..."

"Can skip a bunch of generations before it shows up again."

He rubbed his face. "I came here to fuck you."

Unable to control myself, I laughed and took his wrists, pulling down until his bloodshot eyes were visible. "And I let you in to fuck you up. I'm sorry."

"I'm going to destroy him. He took you from me. He took my... my son. Jesus." He pulled his wrists away. "I can't believe I'm saying that."

I reached for him again, but he stepped away as if I was one thing too many.

"I told you I came back with something," he said. "I knew a guy in prison, up in San Luis Obispo. He used to move money for your father, and he wanted to tell me so many things, but I didn't know what to ask." He pointed at the papers on the counter. "Now I do."

"We need to talk about this."

"No. I need to think. I have to go. Right now. I have to go."

He walked out so quickly, I couldn't catch up to him. He was on his bike before I was at the front door, and his lights were shrinking dots in the night before I realized he'd left his helmet on the porch.

I HAD A PIANO. The house was too big to not have one. The maids dusted it and sometimes I had it tuned. I didn't look at it or touch it on the way to bed, but I felt it there as I remembered one Christmas in Malibu.

Jonathan had been thirteen. One recital away from never having to touch a piano again. Two years after we realized he was mine.

Drew sat next to him on the piano bench. My brother was slouched and sullen. He wanted to be outside with his cousins, but Daddy had said he needed an hour of practice and Drew had slipped in next to him when no one was looking but me.

"This is a hard piece," Drew said, running his fingers over Chopin. "Do you like it?"

"Yeah, I do." Jon sat on his hands. "I hate playing it."

"Why?" Drew ran his fingers over the keys as he read the notes, fucking up, doing it again.

"See?" Jonathan's eyes were wide. "When you play, it sounds good."

"I'm messing it up."

"Even your mess-ups sound good. Do it again."

"You do it."

Jonathan took an exasperated breath and played. I never knew much about music, but I knew enough to hear that even though the notes were there, it sounded like shit.

We were back in New York by the time Jon had his recital. Good chance that—even after Drew sat with him for ninety minutes—Chopin still sounded like an arrhythmic cacophony under my baby brother's fingers.

Once the recital was over, Jonathan never played again.

But after that, whenever Drew was around, Jonathan asked him to play. Drew would put his drink on a coaster and pluck at the keys. They'd tell stories while my boyfriend added music to the narration, laughing like family.

NINETEEN

"A HEART," SHEILA SAID. "THERE'S A HEART."

It was three in the morning and I'd been playacting at sleep when the phone rang. I stopped pretending when she said the word "heart."

"How do you know?" I turned on the light.

"You keep asking that and I keep saying I have people."

"Is it for Jonathan?" Grabbing whatever clothes were handy, I got dressed. "Are they prepping him for surgery?"

"I don't know."

"You need better people."

THE 10. The parking lot. The elevator. The hallways. The private waiting room.

My sisters. My mother. The shared news. The love. The hope.

A familiar pattern with a familiar next stage.

"We haven't been called," the night nurse said from the other side of Jonathan's bed. She was in her twenties. Peach complexion. Black glasses. From the minute she rolled in her little diagnostic cart, she'd had the disposition of a phone tree that—after twenty minutes on hold —says your call is important to her.

"Is it possible there's a heart somewhere?" I demanded.

"It's possible." She checked tubes then typed with two fingers.

"Is it possible anyone could need it more?" Sheila growled.

"Yes." *Tip tap tap.* "Did the doctors explain the list to you?"

That list. Everything revolved around it.

"You fucking—" Sheila had her finger out, ready to point threats at a nurse who had no power, no knowledge, nothing to offer but a call to security.

"Thank you," I said over my sister, grabbing her wrist. "We'll take it from here."

MORNING.

No heart.

Three defibrillations.

Dr. Emerson.

Another day.

It was getting worse.

Hours. His time was measured in hours.

It was so bad, I called Carrie.

Six fourteen in the morning.

I didn't call Carrie for life or death.

Another defibrillation.

I called for death.

The list was a dead weight. The stakes of Jonathan's life in code.

I had my own list. I juggled it like a clown at a birthday party.

A heart. The papers. Strat. Drew. The list. Will. Indy. The list. A donor. The proof. Declan. Will. Indy. The list. A donor. Jonathan. The proof. Will. The FBI. The list.

I couldn't think. I weighed the phone in my hand, trying to put together the pieces of an impossible puzzle. There had to be a way. There was always a way.

But the list was locked down. It couldn't be changed. I talked to a state senator and an assistant to the Surgeon General, hoping to call in favors.

There was no way to affect the list. It was locked down, just like me.

Jonathan was going to die. His father—his real father—deserved a chance to see him.

"Indy?" I said when he picked up the phone. I was in the stairwell, huddled in the corner behind a fire extinguisher.

"I'm sorry about last night," he said.

"Where are you?"

"I'm here. Where are you?"

———

BREATHLESS, I arrived at the waiting room. Indy's shirt was stretched over his back and I realized it was because he was hugging my mother.

"It's so good to see you," she said into his shoulder. "So good."

My sisters encircled them. Fiona had a hand on Mom's back. Deirdre's hands were folded in prayer. Sheila approached and put her arms around both of them.

"It's good to see you too."

"He always shows up in a crisis," Dad said from a few paces away. He may have been invited into the room, but he was left outside the embrace.

"I'm so sorry," Indy said, pulling back to look my mother in the face. "Truly."

"Will you stay?"

Indy looked at me, then back at my mother. He held out his hand to me, and I took it in both of mine.

"Yes," he said. "I'll stay."

———

NO ONE ATE LUNCH. Our stomachs were twisted. When he was strong enough, we took turns seeing Jonathan. I brought Indy in.

"How are you doing?" I asked.

"Ask me something else," he croaked. "Anything else."

"How's your Chopin?" Indy asked.

Jonathan turned his head just enough to see him. "You! Fucking hell!" A smile spread across his face. "Get me out of here, would you? I feel like the god damned Mona Lisa. You line up for a viewing."

"She's prettier," Indy answered.

"Where have you been?"

"Around."

Jonathan may have been too sick to notice the reverence in Indy's gaze. How he inspected every inch of Jonathan's face, trying to see himself.

"I was going to kill you. When I found out you left my sister—"

"I chased him away," I said.

"You're lucky I was locked up," Jonathan added. "She was hurt. She didn't cry or complain, but she was hurt."

"Don't get yourself excited," I said, "or the machines will go off."

I was being ignored. Jonathan only had enough energy to pay attention to one person, and Indy was talking to him as his father for the first time.

"If you get better, you can punch me."

"I'm not an adolescent behind the gym," Jonathan said, then swallowed and looked at me. "You happy to see him?"

"Yes. Very."

"Good. Very good. I'll let him live. I always liked him."

"You liked him because Daddy didn't."

"He felt more like family anyway."

The nurse came in. Our time was up. I walked to the door, but Indy didn't move.

"I'm sorry," he said to Jon. "This shouldn't be happening to you."

But he was already unconscious and the machines were wailing.

Indy hustled out behind me with his hand on the back of my neck. We went right through the waiting room and into the hallway, stopping by a water fountain.

"The fuck. What the fuck?" His eyes were frantic with energy he couldn't direct.

"Take it easy," I said. "Breathe."

"He's a man. A full-grown man, and he's mine. I don't know how to feel about that and I'm never going to find out."

"Don't break, Indiana." I held his face in my hands. "Not yet. Breathe."

Hands on my arms, he looked at the floor between us, chest rising and falling. "How can it be too late already?"

"There's nothing we can do. Trust me. I worked all the angles. The donor list? It's a government thing and I tapped—" I stopped myself mid sentence.

"What?" he asked, looking at me with an expectation I hoped I could meet.

If I uttered another word, I'd be committed to destroying my family. Even if I tried to back out, this man would push forward, and he'd be right.

"I have an idea," I said.

"I'm listening."

"I need you," I said. "If you're not with me, I won't do it."

"Margie, don't you get it?" His gaze went from panicked to tender as he cupped my face the way I'd cupped his. "I'm not going anywhere."

WILL MET me by the elevator. We spoke in the corner in hushed, urgent tones.

"You want me to what?" he asked as if he hadn't heard me, which he had. Loud and clear.

"Get Angela here with whomever else she needs for a proffer." The first time I said it, he looked shocked. Now he looked furious.

"They have to come here," I continued. "I'm not leaving."

"No fucking way."

"If you're too humiliated after getting dumped—"

"Please, Margaret. You're better than that."

"Give me her number and I'll take care of it."

"What are you proffering?"

"I am not, right now, in a place where I can explain myself." I spoke through my teeth, growling with impatience and frustration. "My brother's dying. I need you to manage his ex-wife, and I need you to make a single fucking phone call."

He put his weight on his back foot, moving just enough for me to see I was getting my way and to realize his objections were legitimate.

"When this is over," I said, "I'll explain over a bottle of scotch."

"Or from a jail cell."

"Please, Will."

He nodded, but he didn't like it.

I'd make it up to him somehow. Even if it was from a jail cell.

NO ONE WOULD CALL the air in Los Angeles fresh, but the rooms and halls of the hospital were getting claustrophobic and stale. I met Indy on a bench in the concrete courtyard behind the parking lot. The unforgiving sunlight made him even more handsome, as if full light validated the hardship of his years away. I could see every bit of gray, every line on his face, every crevice where he'd been cruel to himself.

"I need you," I said.

"Feeling's mutual."

"To be my lawyer."

He laughed. "Cin, I haven't practiced law in a decade and a half."

"You're also a felon, but they overlook it if you're nice and you pay your dues."

"I'm not and I haven't."

"You just have to sit there and know what you're talking about."

He twisted in his seat to face me, draping his arm over the back of the bench. "But I don't."

"Not yet." I planted my hands on my lap. "I'm going to tell you what I need and why. I'm not going to leave anything out."

His gaze landed on the place where my neck met my jacket as if that was the seam where my need met my request, then back to my face. "I've never met a woman who could make legal representation so sexy."

"Will you represent me or not?"

"Whatever you need. I'm here."

I took a breath and organized my thoughts again. "I'm meeting with the FBI to make a proffer."

He looked away, then back.

"Don't tell me you practiced copyright law," I said. "I know full well. But I trust you, and no other lawyer would let me do what I need to do."

"Okay," he said as his thumb touched my shoulder. "Go on. What are you proffering?"

"In 1999, when you came to LA with me, a lot was going on. A lot. And I was new at this. But Fiona, my sister..." I waved away the words. He knew Fiona was my sister. "When she was in Westonwood, she was attacked by Warren Chilton. Charlie Chilton's son. A sociopathic little prick if ever there was one. He was going to get away with it and it was going to break her. So I arranged for justice."

His expression changed from openness to a kind of wary surprise. "Did you have him killed?"

"No."

A tide of relief crossed his face. "Did she know?"

"At the time, no. And I haven't discussed it with her, but some of the people involved are close to her still. So she knows now. The Feds also know. They're tracking that down and who knows what else."

"And you want to proffer before they get a warrant?"

I shook my head. "I don't believe they'll ever have what they need for a warrant. Too many people did things that aren't necessarily illegal. It was only a crime in sum. And I was the only one who knows every piece of the puzzle."

"I'm not sure why you're doing this, Margie."

"I'm going to offer myself in exchange for immunity for the people involved."

"What?" He sat up straighter, the hand over the back of the bench gripping the wood as if he wanted to squeeze it to splinters.

"I'll get a criminal lawyer for the plea. Eighteen months. Tops."

"You think they're going to stop at that? They're going to dig deep. The charges won't stop with an assault in 1999."

"No. But they'll find corporate crimes. The Drazen operation as we know it will be over, but the people in the family… they'll be fine."

He swung straight and put his hands on his knees, shaking his head slowly. "This is crazy."

"It's just business." I put a hand on his, digging my fingertips into the space between his palm and his leg. He tightened his fist around mine.

"What could be worth trading everything for?" he asked.

"Jonathan's life."

He took a deep breath and looked out over the parking lot. A car alarm went off in the distance and stopped. The birds called back in the same rhythm as the alarm.

"I don't like this," he said.

"Me neither. But it's all I have. If I have one last card and he dies because I was afraid to play it, it's going to be a long and bitter life."

A police car flew down La Cienega. Soft then loud then soft in the distance again.

"I don't have a suit," he said.

"I don't want a lawyer in a suit. I want someone who understands what I need."

He tapped our clasped hands against his knee and pressed his lips together. "When I came back, I promised myself I'd be here for whatever you needed. I didn't imagine it would be this." He looked at me, and I met his eyes. "I wish you needed something, anything, besides me standing by you while you sell yourself out. But you have me now. Whatever you ask, it's yours."

We unlatched our hands and put our arms around each other. I laid my head on his shoulder. Relaxed, secure, with the world as I knew it ending—he was there with me.

"Stand beside me," I said.

"I will."

TWENTY

W‍ILL, BLESS HIM, ARRANGED FOR THE HOSPITAL CHAPEL TO BE CLOSED FOR
a few thousand in donations. He was unhappy at being out of the loop,
but more than that, he was worried about his part in a play with a
tragic ending.

Just outside the chapel, I fixed Indy's lapel. He was in the jacket
and button-front shirt we'd bought. His jeans and boots would have to
do. When he turned to walk to through the door, Will stood in his way.

Indy was maybe an inch and a half shorter, but when he stared at
Will, they might as well have been the same height. They held each
other in stasis.

"Judges came back with a ruling," I said. "You both pissed the exact
same distance. Contest over."

Will moved a little, and Indy made up the rest, going to the pews
where we'd sell a piece of my life for all of Jonathan's.

"Did he put you up to this?" Will asked, closing the doors. Behind
him was a shelf of flowers that had been moved from patients' rooms.

"You don't even know what it is."

"I know I don't like it."

"It's not your fault."

He smiled in spite of himself. "But it is. I introduced you to Angela. I made the call."

"You act like I couldn't get the Feds in the room without you. It would just have taken an extra day." I patted his arm tenderly. "Don't worry. It's for the best."

A soft rap at the door interrupted us. Indy nodded to me and I nodded back as Will opened the doors, revealing Angela and two men in dark suits. She glanced at Will, then sharply away.

"Hello, Angela," I said.

"Ms. Drazen," she said, then held up her ID. "You can call me Agent Shaw. This is my partner, Special Agent Gonzales."

The stocky man with the thick, wavy black hair nodded.

"And Director David Park."

The taller Asian man smiled when he offered his hand. I shook it. He had an immediately friendly manner that was disarming. It must have been quite an arrow in his quiver.

"This is my counsel—" I stopped myself. After seeing him on stage again, he was Indy to me, but we hadn't discussed who he was to be in the jacket. "Andrew McCaffrey."

Will, staying outside, closed the doors, and we sat in the pews, Feds in front, Indy and I behind. Angela and Gonzales turned to face us, and their boss stood between the altar and pews with his arms crossed and his legs wide. I wished for a table to hide behind. That hadn't been the plan. I had to present as if I was hiding nothing.

"So," Gonzales said.

"My client understands you have some information about an assault on Warren Chilton in 1999," Drew said.

"Attempted murder," Angela cut in.

"No," Drew said. "The evidence doesn't support an attempt on Chilton's life."

"We only have to prove intent."

"I'm aware," I said. "And so are you. If there had been intent to kill, he'd be dead."

The silence was as thick as a brick of plastic explosive.

"I will sign a confession to my part in the assault. I'll explain how it happened and why. You'll have me."

"Why?" Agent Shaw asked.

She did not like me at all. I didn't know if it was because I'd come between her and Will or because she needed to have negative feelings about someone to prosecute them.

"My client is willing to proffer the confession," Drew said, "in exchange for first... immunity for all the other parties involved."

"Come on," David Park said as if Drew had told a silly joke. "That's like giving us the candles on the birthday cake. It's not even a slice."

He was already rejecting the offer and he didn't even know what else I wanted.

Nice move.

"It's a solid proffer," Drew said.

"I'm greedy," Park said. "Evil villain greedy. I want more."

"I want all my family members immune to criminal prosecution in anything you turn up during questioning," I said. "And things will come up."

"We have enough," Angela said.

Knowing the rules they had to adhere to, it was easy to underestimate the FBI. It was easy to get lazy and careless about the little things. Taxes, for one. It was too tempting to leave the business wide open to fraud charges and a subpoena for the love of a few million dollars.

It was also easy to trust them when they told you they had something.

But this wasn't my first rodeo. I knew the game.

Yet I could still make mistakes. It was also easy to overestimate them.

"Then what are you waiting for?" I asked. "Testimony maybe? Maybe you have a bunch of paperwork, but nothing wins cases like testimony. And who knows? Once you get me in a room, you might be able to twist my words into all kinds of admissions."

They waited, giving no sign of the value of my offer.

"Not Declan Drazen," Park said. "No immunity for him. Period."

His sociable demeanor had disappeared, revealing its real usefulness. A friendly face turned antagonistic was more valuable than sustained hostility. I wanted to look at my lawyer. Let his face assure me that this was the right time.

I reached into my bag and pulled out Sheila's red folder.

"No immunity for my father." I handed it to Park.

"What's this?" He opened it.

"It's the UNOS organ recipient list. My brother goes to the top of the list. Any heart. Anywhere. He gets it first."

"How the fuck did you get that?" Gonzales asked.

Angela gave him a wide-eyed look, indicating the altar. No cursing in church. Cute.

Park didn't glance at his agents or give any outward sign that my demand was even on the table. "We have no jurisdiction over this."

"The justice department has ways of making things happen," I said. "If they want someone badly enough."

"I know you're concerned about your brother." Park handed the folder back to me. "But this is not on the same planet as reality."

Both his fake friendliness and his sharp antagonism were gone. His face was eased in sympathy, and his voice held nothing but compassion.

He was telling the truth. It wasn't a game or a ploy. A human heart wasn't in their arsenal.

It had been a long shot. I felt foolish for asking.

I couldn't show them that, nor could I put another deal on the table. I'd flashed a pair of deuces as if it were a winning hand. There was no taking it back now. I'd gambled away my leverage for nothing.

"There's no proffer without it," Drew said.

"We have enough for a warrant already," Park said. "Honestly, I'd rather have you come in willingly. But we'll be able to make an arrest in twenty-four hours. Maybe less if the judge gets up early Monday morning."

Angela and her partner looked at him with concern.

Their boss shrugged. "She's not going anywhere."

He was right. I wasn't a flight risk as long as my son was on his deathbed. I'd be in that same chapel, kneeling for the repose of his soul, when they came to get me.

"I'll consider," I said, putting away the folder. "Have you ever cared about something besides yourself, Agent Shaw?"

They all thought they did. I didn't want the answer as much as I wanted the picture of that thing to take up space in their heads.

"Cared so much you gave your life to it? Ever had it threatened from all sides by people who didn't understand what you'd sacrificed or what you'd continue to sacrifice? If my brother's dead before we come to an agreement, you can take your offer and shove it. Jail doesn't scare me."

"It should," Angela said, standing. "It really should. Because it's not just you. Your brother's implicated. Your sister's husband. Your father."

"What if we gave you Declan Drazen?" Drew interjected.

"What?" I exclaimed.

"For?" David asked.

"The murder of Stratford Gilliam in 1983."

"Drew…" We hadn't discussed this. I wasn't ready. My evidence was flimsy at best.

Park leaned forward, bending at the waist until his arms were on the back of the pew and he was right in my face. "What do you have?"

"Sworn testimony," Drew said. "In exchange for immunity for my client in the matter of Warren Chilton."

David shot his gaze over to my lawyer. "Testimony from whom?"

"The middleman. We won't say who until you accept our proffer."

"We need more than the promise of testimony." Park said. "What else?"

My lips tightened. Past Jonathan walking out of Sequoia Hospital, I couldn't see much of the future, but in the present, Drew was working for my best interests and I decided to trust him.

"A money trail," I said.

David stood straight with a smile.

"Immunity," he said with his palms up as if he was accepting a gift from the heavens. "For your client and the family in the 1999 case *if* they weren't involved in the murder. But the heart? I'm sorry. Even if you brought me Judas Iscariot and a receipt for thirty pieces of silver, I couldn't deliver that."

A heart was the one thing I would have brought him Judas Iscariot for.

"No." I stood and gathered my bag. "Do your own legwork. No proffer."

The room didn't have an echo until my heels clacked against the hardwood floor as I made my way out. I felt Indy behind me, catching up to put his hand on the door latch.

"Don't leave town," David called. "I always love saying that. It's like the movies, don't you think? It's got such tension. Especially when the audience knows the cop just has to get a warrant before nabbing the criminal the next day."

"Thanks for the warning," I said.

"Bring me that middleman, Ms. Drazen, and you'll be a free woman."

Without acknowledging his promise, I walked out.

I BLEW past Will without looking back. People everywhere. Ears and eyes. Well-tread halls and rooms. I had no place to go, but I walked there fast with Indy at my side. He pulled me into a stairwell, down one flight, backing into the metal bar of the door at the bottom with a *clack*.

I went through into the cavern of underground parking lot. Grime everywhere. Tires screeching around turns. Bars of light in the concrete ceiling. He led me to a corner by a steel box marked DANGER and held me.

"Breathe," he said.

Everything. Everything at once. Like a slow-moving tsunami, I was swimming one minute and pulled under the next. The currents moved in all directions, making it impossible to surrender or fight. I was made of alabaster. Heavy. Worthless. Cut into a shape that didn't fit the life I was in.

I could fall apart. Crack down the middle before shattering. In a moment of weakness, I could explode into a hot blossom of shards and dust.

All I had to do was let it happen.

No one would blame me.

I backed away with my hand on his chest as if it could steady me.

"I feel like an idiot." I continued without letting him reassure me. "Who does that? Thinks about what they want most and offers a trade with the first person who wants something from them? I could have asked to be an inch taller or ten years younger. Would have made the same difference."

"You did what you had to."

I tightened my fist around the fabric of his shirt. "I thought I was making decisions, but I was only making choices."

"Give up your father," he said.

"For what?"

"For yourself. Do it for your own well-being or I will."

"The middleman? The guy from San Luis Obispo? You sure he'll testify?"

"Now that I know what to ask, maybe." He held my arms and my stare. "Look. We can't help Jonathan."

"Don't say that."

"We can't. You can't. But I can save you, and I can do it before they come for you."

They were coming for me. Finally. I loosened my grip on his shirt.

"Maybe it's time I took my medicine," I said. "It's been a long time coming."

"Margie," he replied, bending so our eyes were level, "there're a lot of years between who we were and who we are. But I know you. Have you ever done anything out of greed? Or for power? Or was it all for love?"

"Does it matter?"

"To me, it does. It's the only thing that matters."

"I can't feel anything, Indy. I want to hear you and be relieved that you believe in me. I want to care about what's happening to my life, but I can't feel anything but pain about Jonathan."

"I know." He put his arms around me and held me. "I'm going to feel it for you. I'm going to decide for you. I'm going to go talk to the guy in San Luis."

"You need to be here. You just found out he's yours."

"I wasn't there for you or him all these years. Let me be what I was always supposed to be."

I pressed my cheek against his chest where I could hear his heart beat. I listened with a kind of awe that it worked day in, day out, keeping him alive where others failed. Every beating heart was a miracle, but the human race was one miracle short.

TWENTY-ONE

INDIANA MCCAFFREY WENT NORTH TO THE CALIFORNIA MEN'S COLONY IN San Luis Obispo to obtain a guarantee of sworn testimony, saving me from arrest, burying my father, breaking my promises so I could be free. Jonathan was unconscious most of the time. Sheila was ready to sue the entire medical establishment. Deirdre was inconsolable. Fiona was on her way. Leanne too. Carrie couldn't get on a plane without ruining her life. My mother was sedated, emotionally flat, pointlessly holding on to hope.

Paulie Patalano was two floors above us—stable, with a Catholic family that would keep him hooked up to every machine known to man while my son died. My hands were ice cold thinking about how close he was, and how far away.

"Where's Drew?" Fiona asked. Entropy had taken hold of her perfect coif, pulling loose strands out of her braids and leaving a flat greasiness at the roots. Cameras followed her everywhere, so she rarely looked less than perfect.

"He had to run an errand."

"We missed him. He was one of the family for a long time."

"He was." I put a cup under the urn and poured a cup of coffee I didn't want to drink as much as I wanted to hold.

"Who knows? Maybe we'll gain a brother." She dumped three packets of sugar in a cup of hot water that had four lemon wedges floating in it. "Even Dad seemed happy to see him."

Dad had looked neutral to me, but we see what we want to see and Fiona had wanted to see happiness. I couldn't blame her.

"Where is he anyway?" The cup warmed my hands.

The last time I saw my father, he'd been striding past me in a hallway, talking on the phone as if he was managing important business.

She shrugged and blew on her hot lemonade. "He missed his shift."

Monica and my mother were in Jonathan's room. In ten minutes, we'd switch the bedside vigil, and I'd sit by him and catalog all the ways I'd failed him. Without a donor, this would go on for hours or days, but not longer. Not a moment longer.

What business did my father have? What could possibly be important this late at night? I checked my phone. No word from Indy. There was nothing to worry about. He was only going to secure testimony that my father had murdered my ex-lover. Nothing to see here.

Except... had Dad found out about my proffer?

He knew a number of judges in the city, and they weren't above a payoff in either favors or cash. Had one of them signed my warrant? Had they contacted him?

I looked for him, hoping to see him talking to someone who would fill in the blanks. Standing in the lobby, I watched people come in and out, wondering if there was some kind of precautionary measure I should have taken after the meeting with the FBI. Worry made standing still seem like betrayal. Worry was a sense of responsibility for outcomes we're not responsible for. Worry also made intelligent decisions impossible. It made prayer seem like action.

"Margaret?"

I started at the sound of my father's voice as he came up behind me. "Dad."

"Did I startle you?" He put his phone in his pocket.

"I'm just tired." My coffee was cold. I threw it away. "I was on my way back up."

"It's going to be a long night," he said as we walked to the bank of elevators. "You should get some rest."

"It's almost my turn with Jonathan. Mom will be out." I pushed the button. "She'll need you."

"It seems strange to hear you say that." A pleased smile curled his mouth. "After all those years, it took this to bring her back."

"You can thank Jonathan if he's around to hear it."

"Brought your old flame back too," Dad said, ignoring me. "Everyone was glad to see him."

"Except you."

"No," he *tsk*ed. "I am glad. I always liked him."

"You despised him. He didn't control me, and he didn't take orders from you. If he'd done at least one of those things, you would have tolerated him."

The elevator doors opened. When it was empty, we got in.

"You misread me." He pressed the button with his thumb.

"I've watched you try to marry off my sisters, so please spare me the myopic hindsight."

The doors closed. We were alone.

"You hated him because he knew what you'd done."

"Actually," he said, "I liked him very much. He loved you. He was good to you. I know he was impulsive and a little immature, but he had a good heart."

Everything he said after "I liked him" was true, but immaterial. Indy's love and respect for me were as irrelevant as his flaws. The only things that mattered to my father were loyalty and power. Like an old world king, he'd marry us off to make alliances. Sometimes it worked. Sometimes it was a disaster.

I watched the numbers light up. "We're together for good this time."

"That's wonderful! I'm very happy for you both."

I looked at his profile. I couldn't read him. If he was being truthful, he wouldn't get excited or show delight, but he'd be generally pleased. His voice made him sound happy, but not gushing. The half of his face I could see seemed exactly calm and gratified enough. His lack of resistance to my reunion with Indy was either a perfectly modulated act or the truth.

"I should tell you now though," I said. "So you can prepare."

He turned toward me. I stepped back as the elevator slowed so I wouldn't have to crane my neck to observe his expression.

"Prepare?" Eyebrow up. Listening with caution. So guarded.

The elevator stopped.

"This time, I'm leaving with him."

"Leaving what?"

The doors opened.

"I won't be working with this family anymore."

Before I could read him, he walked out. I followed then stopped.

"Dad," I said. "Did you hear me?"

He stopped a few feet in front of me.

"And you're not going to draw me back," I said.

Finally, he turned with a smile as unreadable as the Mona Lisa.

I continued. "They're adults. They can fix their own problems."

"I agree," he said, holding his hand out for me. "It's about time you found your own happiness."

I went closer, half-believing that maybe I'd misjudged him or maybe he believed it was too late for me otherwise. Might as well give up and let his oldest do what she wanted... right? Let Sheila or a hired hand run things. Maybe even Jonathan if he made it.

Then my father spoke again, shattering his well-crafted illusion. "Drew coming back was the best thing for everyone."

I didn't have an answer for that. My mind went completely clear for a moment while what he said sank into the empty space.

He knew. As sure as the sun rose for New York before California was even awake, he knew.

"Are you coming?" Dad asked.

I went with him to meet our family, but neither of us said a word.

"WHO ARE YOU CALLING?" Jonathan asked as I walked in and sat by him.

"Nobody," I said, hanging up when my call to Indy went to voicemail.

"How—" Sheila started.

"Don't ask me how I'm feeling," he said.

"You look like a towel that's been bleached and wrung out," I said.

"Margie!"

"She's honest," he said. "It's fucking refreshing."

Silence fell over the room. Outside Jonathan's heart, there wasn't much polite conversation to choose from.

Fuck polite conversation.

"I have a question," I said, straightening my back and putting my hands in my lap. "For both of you. But first…" I held up my right hand. "Pledge."

Sheila rolled her eyes and raised her hand. "Open."

"Open," Jonathan said, picking his hand up half an inch and letting it drop. "I can't salute."

"It's fine," I said. "I trust you."

"Mistake," Sheila joked.

"Hypothetical question."

"We opened pledge for a hypothetical question?" Sheila leaned back, crossed her legs, and laced her fingers across her torso as if, despite her words, she was ready for a juicy hypothetical.

"If one of us ever tried to hurt our father, what would he do?"

"Hurt?" Sheila asked. "Like how? Like Carrie?"

Carrie had nearly killed him, but that wasn't what I meant.

"Like in business."

"Like steal?"

"Sure." I didn't want to get any more specific. What I was doing was close enough to stealing. "And I mean, really hurt him."

"Like make him broke?"

"Sure."

"He'd…" Sheila shrugged. "Make your life miserable, but without money, he wouldn't have the power to really do that. I don't know. Not nothing, that's for sure."

"Impossible," Jonathan said. "Can't make him broke. There's too much."

"Just pretend," I said.

"You're funneling all his cash into your pocket?"

"It's just a hypothetical."

He shook his head slowly. He was getting weak from this conversation alone. "Then why open pledge?"

Sheila leaned forward, putting her elbows on his bedrail.

"Carrie left," Jonathan said. "He takes that personally. Still. Now. Take all his money and he'll respect you. Separate him from his kids and he'll send Franco after your husband." He turned slightly toward me. "You never married. That gave you power. Nothing to take."

Drew coming back was the best thing for everyone.

"That's why he kept you close," Sheila added. "I was always convinced of that."

It's about time you found your own happiness.

I held up my hand. "Close pledge."

TWENTY-TWO

"WILL?" THE BATHROOM WALLS ECHOED HIS NAME. I HUDDLED IN A STALL on the closed toilet lid.

"Margie?" he whispered in half-sleep. "Is everything all right?"

"I need you. Can you do something?"

"Now?"

"Now. Right now."

"Yeah." He sounded more awake already. "Nanette can take Hannah to school. I can do without the drop-off line."

I hated doing this to him. He had a life.

"Franco Carloni," I said. "His son, Franco Junior, works with him. Do you have someone who can find Junior?"

"I hope you don't need contact."

If Will consorted with known felons, he could lose his license.

"No. I wouldn't do that to you. Find out if Junior's out on a job. That's all."

"What's going on, Margie?"

Drew coming back was the best thing for everyone.

"My father said he's happy Indy's back."

"And? That's a problem?"

"It is when it's a lie. When it's said to soothe me into looking the other way. Indy knows things my father doesn't want known, which is as good as a target on your back. Dad threatened him years ago, before he went underground. Now he's back and if my father's happy it's because he's easier for Franco to find."

He was silent long enough for me to know that he saw the pieces I'd put together. "I don't know what I can get you, but we'll try."

"Thank you."

"Roger."

I cut the connection and dialed Indy.

Got the same message.

Hung up.

It was like 1999 all over again, but this time was different.

This time I wouldn't let him go so easily.

TWENTY-THREE

"HE WAS BETTER THAN ALL OF US," SHEILA SAID, CROUCHED INTO HERSELF. Behind her, the lights of Los Angeles dotted the night horizon under the line of the mountains.

"Stop talking about him in the past tense," I replied. It was dark, and the world still moved under us as if I'd have a son in the morning.

"Remember that time he gave that kid the ball?" Deirdre said, absently paging through a magazine for the hundredth time. "At Dodger Stadium?"

Jonathan had been twelve when Drew and I took him to a Dodger game in the bleachers. Before that, he'd only been up in the boxes where the cushions were leather and waitresses brought gourmet food. Drew had insisted Jon had never really experienced a baseball game the way they were meant to be experienced.

"But the six-dollar seats?" I'd said. "Can't we get something in the mezzanine?"

"It was all over the news," Sheila said.

"That he was in the cheap seats," Deirdre replied. "With the masses."

Jonathan had brought his glove. His coach had worn it in with shaving cream and rubber bands. He sat between Drew and me, explaining the strike zone, how it moved, which pitches did what. Behind us, a family chattered in Spanish, and in front of us, a line of guys from San Pedro drank too much beer.

"This is the perfect view for a slider," Jonathan said. "And Urias has got a mean one. It's one and two. He can afford to be out of the zone, so watch this…"

I didn't know what Urias threw, but it was smacked down the center of the field so hard the outfielders didn't bother running for it. The sound got to us the same time as it reached us. Guys in front stood with their arms out. One fell. Jonathan stood, reached, leaned back far, farther, and caught it with the *smack* of leather.

Drew and I cheered, and when Jonathan straightened, we could see behind him.

A kid of about seven had his glove up. It was Dodger blue. Plastic. Peeling in the pocket. His big brown eyes were wide with surprise and his lip quivered with disappointment.

"Fair catch, kid," one of the guys in front had said.

His mother comforted him in Spanish, and he nodded, shrugging as if he was a big boy.

"Good catch," he said to Jonathan, who was about to sit down.

Then something had happened between Jon and Drew. A communication without words or gestures. Just a look. An exchange of ideas where righteousness came up against what was right.

I hadn't known Jonathan spoke Spanish, but he nodded to Drew and turned to the kid, saying something more than *gracias*. He held out the ball. The mother tried to refuse it, but the kid held out his cheap glove. Jonathan tossed the ball up and a little to the left so it was just hard enough. The kid caught it and held it up.

The San Pedro row gave up a little round of applause, as did the rest of the stadium. Jon chatted with the family in Spanish and we sat down. The whole thing had taken no more than a few seconds.

"He always knew what to do," Deirdre said in the waiting room.

Past tense again. I didn't correct her.

Drew had told him what was right, and Jonathan had listened.

I was proud of both of them.

TWENTY-FOUR

THE SISTERS HUDDLED, WEPT, SOOTHED EACH OTHER. THEIR HUSBANDS brought little comfort. Tactical grief was women's work. My father wasn't sitting still. I found him talking to random people in the hospital halls and huddling over the phone multiple times. His preoccupation could only be attributed to one of two things.

One, getting Jonathan a heart, which had to be far outside his purview. But there was no law against him trying.

Two, shutting Indy up, which not only was within his power but well inside his bailiwick.

Drew coming back was the best thing for everyone.

He'd never accepted the man I chose. Why now?

Because Jonathan was dying?

Because he'd made peace with my mother?

Because I was a grown damn woman?

It's about time you found your own happiness.

Let him love you.

He'd tried to get me to look at Will as more than a contractor.

I liked Will. I cared deeply for him and his family, but could I trust him?

When Will strode out of the elevator, I was waiting.

"What do you have?" I asked.

"Franco Junior's not at the club. Not at home. Gareth checked the liquor store he works out of. Not there."

I crossed my arms and planted my feet apart as if I needed to steady myself against gravity.

"He could be anywhere, Margie. Can you just tell me what you're thinking?"

"Why?"

"Do you want me to do my job or not?"

I did. I needed him to do his job, but maybe I wasn't so sure who he was working for.

"Can I see your phone?" I held out my hand.

"For what?"

"Recent calls."

He turned his head slightly, giving me side-eye. "I don't owe you my life."

"You don't. And I'll never ask again." I held my hand higher. "But these are mitigating circumstances. I don't know who I can trust."

"You can trust me."

"I hope so. You have no idea how much. I'm getting it from all sides. The only person who knows the difference between the rock and the hard place is you."

"Which side do you think I'm playing?"

"Did my father send you to find Drew? He pay you to pretend you were a music blogger?"

Nothing enrages a reliable man like questioning his loyalty.

He snapped, "That was one hundred percent my stupid idea."

"Because you care about me?"

"Hard for you to believe, Margie, but you're worth caring about."

He took me aback for a second. He'd disarmed me. I felt my walls drop. Felt my vulnerability. I was exposed and I didn't like it. Exposure was dangerous.

"This is business," I hissed, but it was too late. My defenses were down.

"And the suddenly reappearing boyfriend? Did you ask for his phone?" He took out his phone but didn't hand it over. "Maybe you should be treating that like business."

"No," I growled, putting my finger to his chest. "I didn't. Because he took off up the 101 hours ago and I haven't heard from him since. He's risking his life and he doesn't even know it. My father's making threats disguised as compliments, so I need to know that you're an ally, Delta. I need to know you're not the one he's been on the phone with."

He put up his hands, pressing his thumb to the home button of his phone until it flashed to life. The elevator doors opened.

Will had two recent calls at nine at night. HANNAH.

Three after. GARETH

No blocked numbers. No dad. No FBI.

From the corner of my eye, Monica got out of the elevator. She looked terrible. I felt the pull of her need.

"Thank you," I said to Will before going after Monica.

SOMETHING ABOUT MONICA shone with hope where none existed. Even hungry with preemptive grief, she was my son's future. She was the way he heard music from Indy's fingers when his own failed. Her connection to him was a connection to me.

I held her so tightly, I thought I'd break her ribs.

"I envy you," I said. "You know that?"

She didn't ask me what I envied, and I didn't have time to list the ways.

"If something goes bad," she said, "like if I do something wrong, would you represent me? No matter what?"

I pushed her away, holding her by the shoulders. "What are you talking about?"

"Stuff. Life. Say yes."

"Fine."

Will was waiting. We hadn't finished.

"Go see him," I told Monica. "I'll be there in a minute."

She left, and I met my trustworthy, loyal friend in the middle.

"Did he really make a threat?" he asked.

"Yes, he did."

"What were the words?"

"'Drew coming back was the best thing for everyone.' And 'It's about time you found your own happiness.' More than a threat. He was positioning himself—"

"I know what he was doing. How can I help?"

Do the impossible. Find Franco and every one of his goons.

Do what he'd already promised. Manage Theresa and Jon's ex-wife.

Do the unexpected. Produce Indy.

As if he'd pulled the last request from my mind and executed it, my phone rang.

Indiana Andrew McCaffrey was calling. Will saw the name.

"I have things to do." After squeezing my arm for comfort, he walked away.

I picked up to hear a rumble. "Indy?"

"Hey, Cin." He sounded as if he was trapped in a tin can.

"Where are you?"

"Riding the 101. Just getting into Ojai."

"How are you calling?"

"Phone's in the helmet. How are you doing?"

His voice was an anchor dropped in a storm. He was far away, but he was with me. Right here.

"You left the helmet at my house."

"I have a spare. I like my head the way it is. Fits like shit, but it's better than nothing. You didn't tell me how you were doing."

"Fine. Terrible. When you get back to the hotel…"

"What?" There was a delay. Half a second on his side of the headset. Enough to feel like an hour. "Sorry. Shit, this guy's an asshole."

"I want you to…" Do what? How was I supposed to keep him safe?

"I'm coming back to the hospital to meet you."

No. He was expected. He had to go somewhere until I could figure it out.

He wouldn't go where I told him. His son was here.

What a fucking idiot I was.

"Indy..."

"I got him, Cin. I got a statement for proffer." His tone jerked as if he was talking to someone else. "What the fuck? Dude. The Camaro's not for fucking with people."

"What's going on?"

"He'll testify. The money was for the Carloni brothers to sell stuff to Strat."

He thought I was asking about the murder. I wasn't.

"Indy. The Camaro. Who—?"

"He had a physical description. It's going to work, Cin baby. We're going to set you free, and you're going to be mine again. I'm happier about this than I've ever been about anything."

"Pull over!"

"I just need to know if you'll have me. Will you? Fuck!"

A screech came over the headset, followed by a crack that sounded like thunder right after lightning. And another crack, then a scrape.

"Indy!" I shouted in the silent hall. "Yes! Yes, please... yes!"

The phone hissed in my ear, then... nothing.

CALLING Indy back got me nowhere. He'd been in an accident. I knew what I'd heard. And either the phone was busted or the helmet was.

Please, God. Let it be the phone.

Let.

It.

Be.

The.

Phone.

My mind was confused, but my body had habits. It was habit that walked me to the elevator and habit that sent me up to the floor where my family waited.

If Indy was dead or even hurt, I was going to lose my shit. Even as my body sent me upstairs because that was where I always went, I calculated odds and distances. Ojai was an hour away without traffic. I could go. Shit, how long did it take to clean up an accident? How long did they wait before they sprayed blood and brain off the asphalt?

Indy could be dead.

Jonathan would be dead.

My father should be dead.

Getting arrested tomorrow would be a relief.

I went to my family even though I wanted to be alone with my impotence. I didn't trust myself to make a decision or open my mouth. I wasn't thinking. I couldn't think. Couldn't come up with a decision or a tactic. I didn't even know what I wanted except for everyone I loved to be all right.

When I got to our waiting room, the pristine box that held us like pigs in a pen, everyone looked at me. Waiting.

I had the answers. I fixed everything. I was the rock the Drazens were built on and I was crumbling.

My feelings had picked the lock. Stormed into the room and overturned the tables, wrote on the walls, marred the floor.

Let them.

I could have fought the emotions having a brawl in my head.

Let them come.

But I didn't. Because anger and sorrow wrecked the joint along with love. I couldn't pick through them. They all had to come.

"Don't look at me," I said, moving my attention between my sisters and mother. "I can't fix this. I can't fix anything. I'm done. Mom? You take Dad back, you live with the consequences. It's not on me."

"Margaret?" my father said from the shadows.

I'd known he was there. He always was.

"Fiona," I said, looking at her in her designer shoes and unkempt coif, "I'm going to jail for you. That's the last thing I'm doing. For anyone. Leanne." I turned to her. "I'm not moving any more money. Bribing factory owners and laundering kickbacks isn't my job anymore. Deirdre—"

"Margie." Mom came up to me, almost within reach, but she stayed back as if she was afraid to be within striking distance. "What—?"

"Deirdre," I said.

Her magazine had gotten soft at the corners and her eyes went big and empty.

"If you go into rehab again, I'm not standing between you and the gossip columns. If they eat you alive, so be it." I glanced at each of them. "Theresa can deal with her own decisions. I'm out." I landed on the sister closest to me in age. "Sheila, it's all yours if you want it."

"You're under stress," my father said with a dog whistle of condescension.

An hour before, I would have collected vague answers like bright stones and chosen the vaguest and most distracting. But it wasn't an hour before, when my thoughts were driving the bus. This was now, and my emotions steered me toward a cliff with their full weight on the gas pedal.

"And you." I pointed at him.

My father didn't have an immediate reaction or surprise. He didn't go on defense. I didn't expect him to blink—and he didn't.

Until the lights went out.

AT FIRST I thought I was fainting, but the emergency lights went on. When an alarm went off, everything was forgotten and we rushed to the hallway. It looked different floodlit. The generators went on. A nurse hustled us out a set of swinging doors to follow the throng of people headed to the stairwell. We had no information. No news. Just instructions.

I wanted Indy. I wanted Will to go up to Ojai and find him. I wanted Jonathan to be okay so I could go myself.

None of it was going to happen.

Sheila had me by the arm. "We have you. I don't know what's going on, but you're going to be all right."

"You have no idea what's even going on."

"So?"

We turned at a landing and headed down the next flight, and in the turn, I had the chance to see the tenderness in her eyes. She meant it.

Her ability to execute her promise was in question, but her intentions weren't.

"I'm not quitting to spite you," I said.

"I know," she said. "Even if you were, we'd help you."

"I'm not going to ask anything of any of you."

"We'll be there anyway." We walked abreast down a short hall to a set of open emergency doors. "We're not abandoning you."

She looped her arm through mine and held up her chin. In the hard light and thick shadows, she looked like a warrior stepping into battle. I glanced over my shoulder. Fiona and Leanne's faces were lit by the outside light coming through the doors. Deirdre and Mom were behind them, striding forward. I hadn't asked any of my sisters what they thought of me quitting. I hadn't even wondered. I'd assumed they'd fight it because they needed me.

I was wrong. I needed them, and I was glad.

"Thank you."

We stepped into the parking lot where we were guided away from the path of the fire engines. There were so many flashing lights, I could barely see. So many sirens I could barely think. A helicopter circled overhead.

Patients were being wheeled out on gurneys, their IV bags swinging like balloons. It didn't look safe for those people to be out under the stars.

"Jonathan," I said, going toward them so I could find my brother.

My son.

Indy's son.

Dr. Brad Thorensen was leaning over a patient and talking to a nurse when he answered his phone. I picked up the pace to a near-run. I had to find out where Jonathan was. Tell him about Indy before he died. Look at him and see the man's face in the face of his adult son.

My arm was still while the rest of me ran, and I nearly fell. A cop had taken me by the bicep to keep me from getting near the patient staging area.

"Hold on there, lady."

He was huge, but I was deadly.

"I'm looking for someone." My voice was loud and growling

because my emotions assured me that I had the full right to break
the line.

"I'm sure they're fine."

"Get off me."

"Lady—"

"Whoa, there." It was Thorensen, holding his phone as if it were an
extension of his arm. "She's all right. I have her."

The cop let me go.

"Where is he?" I asked between gasping breaths.

"He's fine."

How could he smile?

The motherfucker.

If he didn't answer my next question correctly, anger was going to
travel from my brain stem, down my arm, and to my hand, which
would feel the satisfying sting of that smile being slapped right the
fuck off.

"Where is he?"

"Not just fine," he said. "We have a heart."

"You…" My brain stem cranked the rage back so I could think. The
emotional fog cleared enough for me to make sense of the details. "You
have a heart? For him?"

"It's his if it's a match, and we need another test, but it looks like
a match."

"Is it near?"

"It's about an hour away," Brad said.

"Okay, that's… that's good, right?" I looked back at the building.
"If the hospital's not on fire."

"It's probably not, but even if it is, we can do the procedure at
UCLA." He put his hand on my arm. "He's going to be all right."

"I'll tell…" I indicated the area I thought my family was, but they
were right behind me.

Fiona took my hand. Sheila squeezed my shoulder. Mom was near
tears. A sense of relief wove through all of us.

"Them," I said when I turned back to the doctor.

"Dr. Emerson's on his way. You all should rest. It's a long
procedure." He stepped back.

The thought of his absence made me feel as if something wasn't quite finished. As if I had one more question.

"Doctor!"

"Yeah?"

"I don't know if you can tell me this."

"I will if I can."

"Where's the heart coming from? Geographically?"

He thought for a second, then must have decided he wasn't breaking any rules by revealing the location.

"Ojai."

TWENTY-FIVE

I DIDN'T KNOW WHETHER TO GRIEVE OR REJOICE. COMMITTING TO EITHER was a betrayal.

Jonathan was going to live.

His father's heart was going to save his life.

That's why it was a match.

Margie.

All bad. I knew what happened without being told.

Indy had died in an accident on the 101 because someone in a Camaro was fucking with him.

Snapped neck.

Or his ill-fitting helmet flew off and his skull was crushed.

Margie.

But his heart was undamaged.

It was getting cut out of him and brought to Los Angeles.

To save his son.

"Margie."

The word cut through the choice between grief and glory.

Will looked at me with concern. "Are you all right?"

Was I?

"Indy. Send someone for Indy's body." I held back tears. I had to finish. "He had a motorcycle accident in Ojai."

"Margie," he said, "I'm sorry."

His sympathies could wait. I scanned the parking lot for the Drazen clan and found them a few yards away, watching me with the same concern as Will.

I pointed at my father. "I'm not done with you. I'm going to finish you off like a bottle of scotch I've left in the cabinet too long. And when you're empty, I'm going to break you."

"Margaret!" my mother scolded.

To hell with her. I was a grown woman. I walked right up to Declan Drazen's smug, implacable face. I felt more than saw my family follow me. A hand lay on my back. Another took my hand. My sisters came to me, silently passing their power to me.

They were on my side. All of them. They'd all been hurt and they were all tough in their own way.

"Those are very strong words," my father crooned as if relishing the challenge.

"Indy was the last straw. If he's dead, kiss your life goodbye. If he's alive, I'll destroy you for everything else. For stealing my baby. For Strat. For every shitty thing you've done. I'm going to make your life into a misery. You're going to wish I was never born."

They were all shaken into silence. Even my father, who I thought couldn't be shocked by anything.

His brows knotted and he spoke with the conviction of a man who knew only a few truths. "No, Margie." He came toward me. "You're the only worthwhile thing I've ever made. You are the pride of my life. No matter what you do, you are and always will be my chosen one."

So surprised by his words, and so convinced of their truth, it was my turn to be stunned into silence. For a moment, I felt the normal satisfactions of a father's approval. It was replaced by regret. Things would have gone much differently if I'd known.

My hand was squeezed tightly. It was Sheila. The unchosen. The dismissed. She was with me.

Dad took a slight bow of farewell, regarding each of my sisters then my mother, and walked away. A hand slid from my shoulder, and Mom rushed to his side. A grudge long held was a grudge completely shed.

Good.

He'd need her.

TWENTY-SIX

PRETENDING TO HEED DR. THORENSEN'S ADVICE TO REST WHILE JONATHAN was in surgery, I went home. As much as I needed my sisters, I also needed to be alone. My bulwark against emotional discomfort was action. Plans. Strategies. I didn't have the middleman's name. But I could get it even after the FBI came with an arrest warrant. The satisfaction of ruining Declan Drazen would taste just as sweet from prison.

But first, that bottle of fine Japanese scotch wasn't going to finish itself.

"To Jonathan." I raised my glass to an empty kitchen. "If anyone deserves Indy's heart, it's you."

I drained the glass and refilled it. Joy over Jonathan's life was drowned out by grief for the life lost. I didn't know how to shift from one to the other or give my attention to the positive.

I raised the glass again. "To Indiana Andrew McCaffrey." I choked on the name, but powered through. "You gave your son everything you had."

I put it to my lips, and as I did, his song—the one he'd sold when we were separated—came to my mind.

When I lost you

I lost myself

I poured it in the sink for him.

"You don't feel gone," I said to the drain. "And feelings are for children. Sons and daughters. All their lives."

The buzzer rang. It didn't surprise me. I'd known it was going to go off a split second before it did.

"Jesus. I'm caught talking to the plumbing."

I put down the empty glass and buzzed in Will's Suburban. He was here to tell me what he'd found in Ojai. I went to the front yard to hear it.

The car wasn't even at a complete stop when the passenger door opened and Indiana Andrew McCaffrey jumped out.

His arm was in a cast, but he was alive. Gloriously, viscerally, fully alive—and so was I.

My elation was so complete, I screamed.

In his arms, surrounded by his scent and the solidness of his body, I kissed him. He tried to talk, but I didn't want to hear it. I wanted to feel it. Feel him. Taste him. Let his tongue search out mine because he was more than a heart. He was whole.

"I'm... uhh..." Will said.

I waved goodbye without opening my eyes or ending the kiss. I heard Will chuckle and drive away. He'd be home before I let Indy's lips go. He'd be at Hannah's college graduation. I'd die connected to this man.

Eventually, he pulled away with a smile. "I need to breathe."

"Yes! Please do. And this." I pressed my ear to his chest to hear the healthy, strong beat of his heart. "God, that's the best sound in the world."

"You thought Jonathan was getting my heart."

"I didn't know whether to cheer for him or wail for you."

"You can wail for Franco Carloni the second."

"It's his heart?"

"A word of advice." He touched my nose. "Wear a seat belt."

"And a helmet." I dug my fingers in his hair, grateful for the wholeness of his head. I couldn't stop looking at his lips moving because of the signals from his mind. Nothing was more alive than that mouth.

"The paperwork from San Luis Obispo's a little shredded, but I have it."

"I don't care."

"When's Jonathan out of surgery?"

"A few hours."

"Will you take me back, Cinnamon?"

"I'll never let you go again. Ever again."

We kissed as if we'd spent a decade and a half waiting for it.

WE KISSED our way up the steps. Groped past the threshold of the house. I kicked the door closed. His good hand went up my shirt, unhooking the front latch of my bra, touching me with the confidence of a man who knew my body and the excitement of a boy feeling a woman for the first time.

He pulled my shirt over my head with one hand and dropped it. "A few hours."

"A lifetime."

He gave me his tongue with heat and urgency. Pushing me against the wall so hard the hall table rattled. I unbuttoned his shirt as if the fastening was offensive. He worked on his pants. When I reached between his legs, he took my wrist and pinned it to the wall. A picture fell and broke. He kissed my nipples, sucking them as if they gave life to more than the pulse of my own pleasure.

I opened my pants, and he kissed to the edge of the zipper, pulling them down as he kneeled before me. He slid the fabric down my legs, along with my underwear, and helped me step out of them.

"The moment I saw you in Palihood a few days ago," he said, putting my knee over the shoulder with the broken arm, "I've wanted this."

His mouth explored inside my thigh, then the crook where my leg met my hip, then waited a beat for me to want it before kissing right between my legs. I cried out when his tongue touched my clit. He held me against the wall and sucked me, studied me, remembered me.

Time folded into itself. The years became a moment. My skin was electric with the current between us, as if I were a charged battery that had sat unused all this time. He was here and I'd never chosen otherwise.

Breathless, I pushed into him. "Indy. Drew." I moaned both of his names. "I'm close."

He groaned and flicked my clit with his tongue just the way I liked.

I came so hard I thought I was going to unfold.

Gasping, I took my leg off his shoulder and put it on the floor. He stood and kissed me. I tasted the tang of sex on him. Felt the warmth from the friction of my body.

I pulled off his shirt.

He was as magnificent as ever. The tattoos were beautifully faded with time and experience. I ran my hand over them and to his waistband. I tugged it down, freeing his erection from his briefs.

When he saw me looking at it, he took my hand and laid it on him. "It's been hard for you for years."

"Let's make up for lost time."

I started to lead him upstairs, but our hands and lips wouldn't let us make it to the bedroom. We fell onto the stair landing, naked except for a cast on his arm that wasn't much of an impediment, rolling against the walls in the small space. I was on my back when he lifted my legs and pushed my knees apart, exposing my entire body to his eyes and lips.

"Ms. Drazen," he whispered, worshiping me with his hands. "You're beautiful."

He drew his tongue from nipple to hard nipple, sucking each enough to make the invisible line between my breasts and my clitoris hum. I didn't feel the hard floor under me. I was floating over it.

"Don't make me wait anymore." I wrapped a hand around his shaft and put it to my entrance, but he wouldn't thrust forward.

"You have somewhere to go?" he asked, hovering there.

"No. Nowhere."

"I want to savor this moment." He put a little pressure forward, kissing my face and neck.

My body tried to pull him in. I felt the heat of it against me as I looked at him, hands on his scratched shoulders. "You're killing me."

"You're not dead yet."

"I'm practically a doornail."

He had a look on his face that I'd seen on men before. It was a proud vulnerability. It was a dare. It was an ambitious intimacy that usually made me run away as if my clit was on fire.

I'd had sex with a lot of men, and I'd inadvertently made a few of them get that look.

This wasn't inadvertent, nor was it frightening. It was an emotion and it was right.

"I love you," I said, touching his face. "I've always loved you."

"Good." He slid into me as if I'd been built for him, all the way to the root in a single stroke. "Fuck." He whispered the profanity like a prayer, closing his eyes.

"Good idea."

He smiled, opening his eyes to lay his lips on my cheek. He thrust inside me, slow and steady, before picking up the pace, listening to my body as I listened to his. My breaths turned into gasps.

My fingernails dug into him. I went rigid with pleasure, clenching his cock inside me, coming harder with each stroke. I couldn't take it. I was going to break under it, but he kept driving into me. I called his name. Both of them, because he was the sensible and warm Drew and the wild and talented Indy. Both. All. Neither. One man I'd let go and one who had come back to me. I came for him, making an offering of my body.

Opening my eyes, I saw him watching me with his jaw clenched. A second later, he released with a grunt, emptying himself inside me.

"Yes," I said, studying his pleasure. "All of it."

He jerked with a last spasm while I kissed the scratches on his shoulder. We panted and sweated together until my back ached and I had to shift. He got up on his knees between my legs.

"I say this without sarcasm," I said. His cock was at half mast, wet with sex, the most desirable thing in the world. "You're as good as ever."

"I'm not finished yet."

"I need a minute."

He picked up my hand, looked at my wristwatch, and tapped it. "I want you again and we have things to do before we get back to the hospital." He let go of my wrist and stood over me with his hand out. Magnificent. I'd forgotten how glorious he was. "Unless you want to do a perp walk, you don't have a minute."

I could have used a glass of water and a nap, but sometimes no choice was the best choice. I took his hand, and he helped me up. We went to the bedroom and fucked as if we hadn't seen each other in sixteen years.

TWENTY-SEVEN

JONATHAN'S SKIN HAD LOST ITS GRAY CAST. AFTER THREE DAYS IN A
medically-induced coma and a week in recovery, he was flush and full.
Not ready to get back on the pitcher's mound, but I could see his path
forward.

So could Monica. She was unable to contain herself. She chattered
about nothing and laughed at his every joke.

"They won't say when I can go," Jonathan said, holding her hand
over the bedrail.

"Soon," she said. "I can't wait."

The way he looked at her spoke volumes about what he couldn't
wait for.

"We have tickets to opening day at Dodger Stadium," I said.
"Monica, do you like baseball?"

"Does she?" He laughed. "Don't get her started on Harrington's
on-base percentage."

"Please," I said, "don't get started. Also, Indy insisted on the
bleachers. I hope you don't mind."

"They're twelve dollars now," she said, still looking at Jonathan as
if he were a hero home from a long war.

"You two really make me ill." I smiled when I said it. "But can you excuse us? I need a word with my brother."

"I have to go anyway." She leapt up. "I'll see you after my shift."

After a kiss that went on too long, she left.

"You're letting her work?"

"Did anyone ever stop you from working?"

"I guess not." I sat in Monica's seat. "You're antsy."

"I'm done with this bed. I'm done with people coming in and out like I'm a shrine at the end of a pilgrimage."

"We're all pretty done. I'm not trying to make you feel guilty, but it's been a nightmare."

"Don't worry. I don't feel guilty." He circled his finger in the general area of my face. "You're looking pretty good for a woman coming out of a nightmare. Is it because of Drew... sorry, Indy now?"

"He answers to both. I like Indy. It's sexier."

"That'll be enough of that."

"When did you become such a prude?"

"It's like hearing about my mother's sex life."

It was exactly like hearing about his mother's sex life, but I wasn't going to tell him that. Ever, if it could be avoided.

"Sheila told me something you said in the parking lot during that drill."

"It wasn't a drill."

"Wasn't a fire either. But you accused Dad of stealing your baby?"

Of course that came back to bite me in the ass. I had no quick answer, because I didn't know which lie I needed to tell. Some secrets were better left kept.

"I did say that," I said.

"What did it mean?"

"It meant I was pretty fucking pissed off."

"You're avoiding." His arm started going up.

He was going to call pledge, and that wasn't going to work. I put my hand over his and pressed it down.

"Do you remember when we signed you into Westonwood?" I asked. "You and I were alone for a minute while Mom and Dad signed papers?"

"Barely. I think you were wearing a lavender pantsuit."

"I have no idea what I was wearing." I leaned toward him. "But I know what I said. I know what I promised you."

His eyes narrowed as if squinting would bring the memory into focus.

"I promised you I'd stay by you. I promised you I'd make our father pay for the things he did."

The squint relaxed. The upward pressure of his arm stopped. "I remember."

"He removed someone very important to me from the world. You'll be hearing all about it. You're stuck in bed, so you won't be there when they arrest him. I'm sorry for that, but not sorry enough to delay what's coming."

"You got him? I thought you'd never turn." His chin thrust forward as if he wanted the answer half a millisecond earlier.

"I did. Finally. We're going to be free, Jonathan. Free."

I COULD HAVE STAYED AWAY. I could have watched it all on television or read about it in the news, but I had to be sure he didn't know and I had to make him available to arrest. The only way to do that was to use his trust to have him in a public place at an exact time.

Jungco's was Indy's idea. Declan looked relaxed and happy. Mom's influence, I was sure. Love did the best things for the worst of us. I told her Indy was asking Dad for my hand in marriage so she'd stay home.

"She's my everything," Indy said. "And I know how important her family is to her. So I'd like your blessing."

"You hardly have to ask me," Dad said to Indy as the salads came. "She's a grown woman. Her hand in marriage is hers to give."

Declan had been surprised to see Indy, but over the past week, he had offered him a grudging respect for his ability to survive a run-in with Franco Junior's Camaro.

"Thank you," Indy said, holding up his water glass. "I promise I'll make her happy."

Dad and I toasted Indy's water with our wine. The doorway was behind Dad. I had to force myself not to check it every time it opened.

"Now," my father said to Indy, "if you could promise to make her see sense."

"Sense is her middle name."

Six silhouettes came through the front door. They walked with a purpose more driving than an expensive lunch. One spoke briefly to the manager. My lungs stopped working. My toes tingled.

It was here. It was now.

"Her middle name is Erin," Dad said. "And she needs to come back to work. She doesn't have a single problem a vacation won't fix."

"You're talking about me like I'm not here."

They walked toward us, out of the back lighting. David Park. Angela Shaw. Agent Gonzales. Indy reached into my lap and took my hand.

"You, daughter"—Dad leaned on his elbows—"don't have a single problem a vacation won't fix. Stay at the house in Nice. Run on the sand. When you come back, you'll be refreshed. Somewhat less cranky."

"I'm not coming back to work for you," I said. "I'll take care of my brother and sisters for the rest of my life. But I'm not the kind of lawyer you need anymore."

"Really—?"

"Declan Drazen?"

David Park had said his name. They surrounded him in their dark suits, guns bulging at their waists.

My father looked up, seemingly unperturbed. "If you have to ask, you might need to find another line of work."

"You're under arrest," Park said. "I've waited a long time to say that."

My father looked at me, then Indy, then me again.

"I told you," I said. "The night of Jonathan's transplant. I warned you."

"I thought you were being emotional."

"Please stand up," Angela said, "and put your hands behind your back."

"I was emotional," I said. "And dead serious."

As he stood, he nodded to me once, slowly. A sign of respect to the winner. He wasn't getting how serious this was. He didn't know Indy's witness had corroborating dates, names, and receipts. Not yet.

"Declan Drazen," David Park recited with no little joy in his voice, "you're under arrest for the murder of Stratford Gilliam."

It wasn't until he heard Strat's name that my father showed any kind of surprise. These weren't complex financial crimes. A long-forgotten chicken had come home to roost. And that one moment, accompanied by Indy squeezing my hand, was satisfying beyond words.

"Don't worry, Daddy," I said. "We'll get the check."

I squeezed Indy's hand and hid my smile behind my glass as my father was read his rights. All I heard was Indy's whisper in my ear.

"You're free."

I was.

Winged like a hawk, with him by my side, I was free.

EPILOGUE

Carrie was coming home for my wedding on one condition. We couldn't talk about why she'd left or where she was. Not a word about her ex-husband or what had happened with the man after him.

"How am I not supposed to bring it up?" Will asked, tugging at his shirt collar. In the back room of the church, which had been outfitted with a light buffet and a makeup table. He made a handsome, if uncomfortable, groomsman.

"Like an adult with a respectfully low curiosity level."

"Where's she flying in from?"

"See? This is why I had Indy go and get her. Keep your head in the game."

"My head would be in the game if you'd let me run the security," he growled. So serious. So worried. Poor Will.

"Tell me how gorgeous I look."

I held out my arms to show off my dress. It was skin-tight white satin with a hem that skimmed the floor and a side slit halfway to home. My hair was up, undyed so, if you looked closely, you could see the gray streaks in the copper.

"Instruments to measure how gorgeous you look haven't been invented," he said.

"Well done."

Squealing and laughter bounced off the marble walls of the outer hall.

"What's that?" Will asked, leaning out the doorway carefully, as if he was going to stop a bullet with his head.

"Those would be grown women," I said, grabbing my bouquet,

With Will, I strode to the narthex in the highest heels I'd ever strapped on. Under the stained glass windows, boys in robes held candles on sticks and Fathers Harris and Acton waited at the front with their hands folded on their albs. They were all lined up as they should be. As expected, my sisters were in a scrum.

"You're waking dead saints," I said.

They parted like a redheaded sea to reveal the center of the huddle.

Carrie had always been the most beautiful of all of us. Her eyes were the clearest blue and her hair was the prettiest shade of red. Her skin was radiant. Her proportions were mathematically perfect.

Sometimes I wondered if she went through what she did as payment for her loveliness.

"You look so beautiful." Carrie's eyes filled up. No makeup would run. She'd never needed it. "I'm so happy for you."

I took both her hands. "You look like a gray dishrag."

"Margie!" Sheila cried.

"Really?" Carrie smiled as if she didn't find the idea insulting at all.

"No." I touched her face. "Not at all. Is this a wrinkle?" I ran my thumb over her smooth cheek. "Nope. You need to get yourself some laugh lines."

"I know."

"We're going to give you some this week."

"I can't wait."

The organ laid down the first few notes of the procession Indy had written for the occasion. Carrie went stiff.

"Go sit," I said, pointing at the side door. "Indy saved you a space on his side. Look for the guy in the Bullets and Blood jacket."

She took off, hair fanning out as she twirled and trotted away.

The priests and altar boys filed down the aisle.

"Psst!" Only Sheila could shout a hiss. She jerked her thumb to get

me in the back of the line, where I was supposed to be. I was the
attended. The serviced. It was my day. But these people were my
world and I couldn't just let them walk.

"Get back there!" Sheila said as she and Indy's friend and
bandmate, Jacob came to the doorway. I hugged her.

"Thank you," I said. "For being my maid of honor. For everything."

"What*ever*. Get in line."

She and Jacob stepped out. I watched them and caught sight of
Indy at the altar. I put my hand to my chest.

"You are not swooning," Leanne said as she approached with Will.

"She's swooning," he said. "It's making me nervous."

"It's fine." I hugged Will. "Thank you thought. For always looking
out for me."

I held Leanne, thanking her for years of favors big and small.

Jonathan and Monica were next. He was healthy and hale. Every
day was a miracle.

"Thank you, brother," my lips said while my heart sang *my beautiful
boy*.

He took me by the back of the neck and planted a kiss in
my cheek.

"You look too happy," he said. "I could get used to it."

I hugged him and each sister as they passed expressing gratitude
for letting me help them, for making me the person I was, for the
smallest and biggest thing they'd ever done for me.

Hannah was so darling in her white dress and Mary Janes and she
looked so nervous I had to crouch by her.

"You ready?" I asked.

She picked a handful of rose petals out of her basket.

"I throw on the floor."

"Exactly."

"I'm allowed."

The head usher patted her on the back. Her turn.

"Go make a mess, kid."

The church exploded in *aws* when she threw her first handful.

As I watched her go, I heard the squawk of a police radio.

The last person in line was thinner than he'd ben the last time I'd seen him, but no less powerful, even surrounded by guards or with the bulge of an ankle bracelet ruining the break of his cuffs.

"Dad."

"Margaret. I appreciate being allowed this."

"Mom's a convincing lady."

"Yes. She's the one who demanded I thank you for speaking for me to be out of prison when you were the one who put me in prison in the first place."

"I'm doing the thanking today. So. Dad. Thank you for making me strong."

"It's the job." He gave me his arm. We stood in the doorway, waiting for our turn. "I did it too well."

"You don't have to forgive me."

"I don't."

Couldn't beat the honesty.

"How's prison?"

"Boring. That's the worst thing about it. The boredom."

The last pair split at the altar. Indy and I made eye contact across the church. Will had been right. I was swooning.

"You can make a shank and shiv someone," I said. The music changed and we stepped onto the rose petals. "Make life interesting."

"You have it wrong," my father said. "Shiv is a noun. Shank is a verb. One might use a shiv to shank, but one cannot sensibly use a shank to shiv."

Indy watched me intently through the thick air of the church.

"Thank you," I said, tearing my eyes away from Indy long enough to look at my father. "I appreciate the grammar lesson. I changed my mind. Don't shank anyone."

"It's more interesting to have someone else do the shanking. More of a challenge, don't you think?"

He stopped and gave me to Indy without flourish. Then he turned to me and winked with an evil little smirk.

Indy took my hand and stood beside me.

"What are you smiling about?" he whispered as the priest opened the ceremony.

What I was smiling about wasn't funny unless you knew my father. Then the complete predictability of our conversation was hilarious.

"Declan fucking Drazen will never change."

My husband didn't seem to react. He let the service continue while my smile spread wider and my shoulders bounced. I covered my mouth with my free hand.

"Are you all right?" Indy asked.

Tears flowed as my laughter got deeper and louder. My manner needed to match the sobriety of the occasion, but I couldn't help it. I'd utterly lost control of my emotions.

"What's so funny?" the groom asked through a half-laugh. Having caught the contagion, he was near an outburst himself but had no idea why.

"He said a shiv..." My voice squeaked too loudly.

Father Acton turned around.

"I'm sorry..." I waved in front of my face, but I was laughing so hard that Indy was bellowing.

Father Acton smiled. The guests were either murmuring or chuckling.

"And shank. And..." I lost the ability to speak. My eyes were cloudy with tears and my body heaved with laughter.

I threw my arms around Indy and buried my face in his neck, as I calmed and the congregation laughed with me. They only cared that I was happy. They didn't care why.

"Breathe," he whispered in my ear.

With my love's arms around me, I breathed deeply, letting my chest fill with peace.

"Thank you," I said. "Thank you for coming back to me."

"Ahem," an amplified voice echoed. It was Father Acton looking as if he had a wedding to preside over.

"One second," Indy said.

Then he held me and kissed me long and hard, while the entire church and my beautiful, glorious, crazy family consecrated my marriage in laughter and love.

THE END

READY FOR ANOTHER kinky KU read?

READ THE SUBMISSION SERIES FREE

Monica doesn't think she's submissive. Jonathan Drazen's going to prove her wrong... if he doesn't fall in love with her first.
Now FREE in Kindle Unlimited.
Get Complete Submission!

YOU CAN FIND me on FACEBOOK.
I have fan groups on GOODREADS and FACEBOOK.
I'm on TWITTER, INSTAGRAM and TUMBLR with varying degrees of frequency.

THERESA'S STORY is told in **COMPLETE CORRUPTION**
If you haven't met Fiona, download **FORBIDDEN!**

ALSO BY CD REISS

The *New York Times* bestselling Games Duet

Adam Steinbeck will give his wife a divorce on one condition. She join him in a remote cabin for 30 days, submitting to his sexual dominance.

HIS DARK GAME

Monica insists she's not submissive. Jonathan Drazen is going to prove otherwise, but he might fall in love doing it.

COMPLETE SUBMISSION

Fiona Drazen has 72 hours to prove she isn't insane, just submissive. Her therapist has to get through three days without falling for her.

FORBIDDEN

Margie Drazen has a story and it's going to blow your mind.

THE SIN DUET

Her husband came back from the war with a Dominant streak she didn't know he had.

The complete Edge series
EDGE OF DARKNESS

Contemporary Romances

Hollywood and sports romances for the sweet and sexy romantic.

Shuttergirl | Hardball | Bombshell | Bodyguard | Only Ever You